LEAVING BLYTHE RIVER

Also by Catherine Ryan Hyde

Ask Him Why
Worthy
The Language of Hoofbeats
Pay It Forward: Young Readers' Edition
Take Me With You
Paw It Forward
365 Days of Gratitude: Photos from a Beautiful World
Where We Belong
Subway Dancer and Other Stories
Walk Me Home
Always Chloe and Other Stories
The Long, Steep Path: Everyday Inspiration from the Author of Pay It Forward
How to Be a Writer in the E-Age: A Self-Help Guide
When You Were Older
Don't Let Me Go
Jumpstart the World
Second Hand Heart
When I Found You
Diary of a Witness
The Day I Killed James
Chasing Windmills
The Year of My Miraculous Reappearance
Love in the Present Tense
Becoming Chloe
Walter's Purple Heart
Electric God/The Hardest Part of Love
Pay It Forward
Earthquake Weather and Other Stories
Funerals for Horses

LEAVING BLYTHE RIVER

CATHERINE RYAN HYDE

LAKE UNION
PUBLISHING

This is a work of fiction. Names, characters, organizations, places, events, and incidents are either products of the author's imagination or are used fictitiously.

Published by Lake Union Publishing, Seattle

www.apub.com

ISBN-13: 9781503934467
ISBN-10: 1503934462

Cover design by Shasti O'Leary-Soudant / SOS CREATIVE LLC

Printed in the United States of America

Late in the Worst Night of Ethan's Life

Chapter One: Tremble

Three months before his father disappeared

Ethan remembers the shaking most clearly. Probably because it was the first moment of the shaking. That most familiar of things making an initial appearance.

When he thinks back on that night, it's that bone-deep trembling—the out-of-control shivering, the chattering teeth—that still feels vivid. He tried to stop it, to calm it. But he was powerless. In more ways than one.

Ethan tries not to look back on that night. At least, as much as human nature allows. But it's a funny thing about your darkest moments. They have a life of their own. They come around because they've got you pinned. Because they can. The harder you try to push them back into the shadows, the stronger they grow. They draw power from your resistance.

If it had been cold in that police station the trembling wouldn't have been so humiliating. But an ancient furnace bellowed heat right onto Ethan's side. He hunched over himself on that hard wooden bench and felt sweat break out on his forehead, run down his back. It was overheated in that place.

But still Ethan trembled.

He looked up to see a uniformed officer looming over his bench. He jumped, startled, enough that he knew the officer could see, would know. The cop was obviously no threat to him, which made his reaction humiliating. But when you're already swimming in a sea of humiliation deep enough to drown you, it doesn't matter much if somebody throws in another bucketful. It's not worth it to stop and pay attention to that when you need to keep paddling.

"Ethan Underwood?"

Ethan tried to answer. A simple yes would have sufficed. But his voice failed him. It seemed he no longer owned one. A strange feeling, to reach for something so basic and find it missing.

He nodded.

"You want to come with me, please?"

Ethan followed him into a tiny cubicle with one tiny window. The officer sat behind the desk. Behind his head, the blackness of the city night threatened. Even though it was out there and Ethan was in here, still it threatened. Ethan perched on the edge of a chair in front of the desk and held his own arms against his sides to try to ease the trembling. It did no good.

"You cold?" the cop asked.

Ethan shook his head.

"Didn't think so. It's like an oven in here. You okay?"

Ethan only shrugged. It wasn't the easiest question in the world to answer.

"You talk?"

So that was it. He would have to reach inside and find his voice again. He would have to force it out of hiding.

"Yes, sir," he said. But it didn't sound anything like the voice he'd lost. It was a whisper that seemed to creak, as if it had rusted and needed a good oiling—another bucket of humiliation that Ethan barely had time to process.

"I get it that you've been through a scary experience," the cop said. He had greasy hair and a long chin. Ethan couldn't stop looking at that chin, even though nothing could have mattered less. "But most people've usually stopped shaking by this time."

A sarcastic response ran through Ethan's head. *Gosh, I'm sorry if I'm not doing this right.* It didn't make it out of his mouth.

He knew then why his voice had abandoned him. Because it takes courage to talk to people. A cop you've never met before, on the worst night of your life. Even your own family. Hell, especially your own family, sometimes. He'd always had that much courage before. He'd never been anything like courageous, not even close, but he'd owned enough strength to work his own voice.

Now even that tiny measure of bravery was gone.

The cop was still staring at him. Not particularly coldly. Not particularly helpfully. Just staring.

"I'd stop if I could," Ethan said, with barely enough volume to travel across the desk.

"It wasn't exactly a criticism. I was just wondering if you needed some kind of help."

The word surrounded Ethan like a salve. Pressed against him like a hot-water bottle. *Help.* It even stopped his trembling, but only for a split second. One tremble was skipped, the way one heartbeat had seemed to drop out of the pattern earlier that night. Then the trembling returned, stronger if anything. Because it was only *the word* help. It was not as though any meaningful help had actually arrived.

"Like what?" he croaked.

"Now that's a very good question. Some kind of counseling, I guess. There are counselors for trauma. But I guess that's more something to talk about later, when your parents get here."

My mother, he thought. *When my mother gets here.* They sure as hell weren't going to come together. Not tonight of all nights. And the idea that his father might come to get him, well . . . he'd be just as happy to see his mugger walk through that door to pick him up.

And there was no way Ethan was getting any kind of therapy. Unless his parents split, moved apart, which seemed likely now. If he went with his mother, there might be a slim chance. But his father didn't believe in therapy. Not the mental kind, anyway. He was an athlete, Ethan's father. An ultramarathon runner, a triathlete, no stranger to sports injuries. Physical therapy was well within his comfort zone. But what's on the inside . . . his father believed you take care of that on your own.

The officer picked up a clipboard and began scanning what Ethan could only assume was the form Ethan and another cop had completed earlier. A moment later he looked up and narrowed his eyes.

"What?" Ethan managed.

"Looking at what you put down for your date of birth."

"I'm seventeen."

"Right . . ."

"I know I don't look it. I get that. But it's the truth."

"Got some ID? Oh, wait. That would have been in your wallet. And that got stolen, right?"

"No. I never had it with me. It's in my carry-on bag. Long story. It's at home."

"Okay, well, your parents can bring it later."

"Am I the suspect here?"

Before asking that question, Ethan had been pleased by the gradual return of his voice. It had made him feel a tiny bit more optimistic, as though lost belongings could be relocated. But now it had gotten him in over his head.

The cop sat back in his chair. "No. Of course not. And I didn't mean to make you feel that way. Just . . . sometimes it's a little bit of a red flag when somebody lies on the reports."

"I didn't lie. I'm seventeen."

"Okay. Well. We'll just put a pin in that for now. I've read the report of the incident. And I just have one question. What were you doing out on the street by yourself at two thirty in the morning?"

Ethan looked down at his own jeans and said nothing.

"I mean, it's not illegal or anything. Maybe I wouldn't even ask if you looked seventeen. But however old you are, you must know you look like a kid. I would have made you for twelve or thirteen. It just seems strange that you'd be wandering around all alone at night in the city. You know? I just thought there might be a story around that."

Ethan said nothing for what felt like a long time. He just sat and trembled, and hoped this unexpected line of questioning would go away.

When it seemed clear it wouldn't, he asked, "Do I have to answer that?"

"Was it a drug thing?"

"No! It wasn't anything like that. It was just some stuff in my family. There was just this stuff going on. That I had to get away from."

"This 'stuff' . . . is it anything you need to report?"

"No, sir."

"You getting hit at home?"

"No, sir."

"Anybody getting hit at your house?"

"No, sir."

"Because, you know. It was enough to drive you out onto the street at two thirty in the morning. And you don't seem like the bravest little guy on the planet. No offense. Just, you have to have some confidence to walk around Manhattan at that hour. I'd just want you to tell me if you feel like your safety is in danger at home."

Ethan sat trembling for a moment, not knowing what to say. Not knowing how to say, "It's the kind of stuff where you're getting hurt on the inside. And people don't get arrested for that. Even though maybe they should."

"It's not that kind of stuff," he said.

"Okay, fine." The officer seemed to wrap up his concerns just that easily. He could just finish up and move on. Ethan wished he knew how such a thing was done. "You got a good look at the guy, right?"

The room swam again, too brightly, as the man's image came clearly into Ethan's head, his unshaven face just inches away.

Bye. Bye. The words kept playing on a loop in Ethan's brain.

"Yes, sir," he said in a trembly whisper.

"Okay, then. We're going to have you look at some mug shots."

—

It was five thirty in the morning when Ethan looked up to see his father standing over his chair. He squeezed his eyes shut and looked away.

They were in a very bright room with mug books on the table. Ethan had seen many horrible faces over the last couple of hours—and a few pleasant-enough ones, and others that just looked sad—but he had not seen the horrible face that had loomed so close to his own.

Bye. Bye.

"I know I'm the last person you want to see," his father's familiar voice said. "I know you were hoping for your mom. But I don't exactly know where she is. She left right after you did. So you got me."

Ethan looked up. Just to see if he looked as familiar as he sounded.

Ethan's father was tall. Over six feet. Which seemed flat-out unfair when Ethan was so tiny. Well, he knew why. He took after his mother is all. But it still seemed unfair. His father, Noah, was lanky and athletic, too. And notably handsome, with a long, chiseled face and a strong jawline. And a terrific head of thick sandy hair that apparently had no plans ever to thin.

His dad looked the way he always had. Recent events hadn't changed him. At least, not on the outside. Then again, Ethan thought, maybe that was the problem. Maybe Noah Underwood hadn't changed at all. Maybe he was what he had always been.

Noah opened his mouth to say more. Ethan held up one hand, a stop sign, to say, Don't. Just don't.

A movement caught his eye. It was a uniformed cop, a different one, who moved into the room behind his father.

Ethan wanted to ask, "Why did it take you so long to get here?" But his voice had run out on him again.

As if he could read minds, his father said, "I got here just a few minutes after they called. I've been waiting to get in to see you." He turned his head toward the cop. "Is he done here? Can I take him home?"

"Yeah," the cop said. "I think that's enough for one night."

"He's looked at all your pictures?"

"No. He couldn't very well do that. They're sort of . . . infinite. But sometimes enough for one session is enough."

"Does that mean he'll have to come back?"

"If we bring in a suspect, we'll want him to come in for a lineup."

The words hit Ethan like a bat. And the trembling set up again. Ethan realized he hadn't noticed it had ever stopped.

The cop apparently saw his alarm. Because he said, directly to Ethan, "Don't worry. We almost never catch 'em."

"Lovely," Ethan's father said. "That's very encouraging. Come on, Ethan. We're going home."

Ethan followed him out of the room.

Through the bright, hot police station.

Out the doors into the cold, still-dark morning, where a cab waited. Ethan's brain got stuck on what it would cost to keep a cab waiting so long.

His father held the door open, and Ethan got in. Sank onto the vinyl upholstery of the cab's backseat. His brain plunged so suddenly into whether his mother would still be there when they got home that he forgot to look at the meter to answer his own question about costs.

His father dropped heavily onto the seat next to him, slammed the door, and gave the cabdriver their address.

Then they were moving. And then the experience of that night was over, except to the extent that it never would be.

Ethan was afraid his father would talk to him on the way home. Try to explain. Want to pull it out onto the table for examination. Or maybe he would light into Ethan for being stupid enough to run out into the city night.

He made up his mind that whatever he was asked, or told, or no matter how he was chastised, he would remain silent. He owed his father nothing. And he had no intention of paying the man more than he was owed.

Ethan had worried for no reason. They rode home in silence. Utter, crushing silence.

Still, Ethan trembled.

Five Days Before That Worst Night

Chapter Two: Catch

Three months and five days before his father disappeared

Ethan dragged Glen down the hall to his room by the sleeve of his friend's hoodie.

"Seriously, dude," Glen said, for the second time, "what's in the bag? You're starting to freak me out. Is this like a drug thing?"

Ethan only snorted at the joke. Glen knew it was not a drug thing because he'd gotten Ethan high a grand total of once. And Ethan had hated every minute of it. Vocally, insistently hated it.

He pulled Glen into his bedroom and closed the door behind them.

"Please tell me it's not a sex thing," Glen said.

"Not with *you* it isn't."

"Thank you. That's what I needed to hear." He flopped onto the end of Ethan's bed. "I'm totally curious now."

Glen had been Ethan's friend since grade school. In other words, since long before Glen had grown five inches taller than Ethan, found a hidden talent for athletics, and sprouted fairly serious facial hair. But Glen had never lorded any of those developments over Ethan, so the friendship continued in spite of a measure of inevitable jealousy on Ethan's part. Ethan had grown into a straight-A student without even trying hard, while Glen only managed Cs with a lot of study and Ethan's tutelage. But that didn't help much, because girls don't ask to see your report card.

"It won't live up to the hype in your head," Ethan said.

Ethan set the small brown paper bag on his dresser and unrolled its top. He reached in and pulled out one of the three lollipops he had bought at the drugstore. The ball-shaped kind with the caramel fudge in the middle and the wrapper that twisted at the base of the stick.

"Unless that's laced with something," Glen said, "you're right."

"Here," Ethan said. "Catch."

He tossed it in Glen's direction by its stick. Glen reached up and snagged it out of the air. Effortlessly, it seemed.

"How do you make that look so easy? How does everybody make that look so easy?"

"Because . . . ," Glen began unsurely, ". . . it *is*?"

"Throw it to me."

"I don't get it."

"I need the practice. Please. Throw it."

Glen flipped the lollipop through the air in Ethan's direction. It flew end over end toward Ethan's hand. Then it hit the tips of his fingers, bounced off, and landed on his bedroom carpet.

"Unless you're Ethan, it's easy," Glen said.

Ethan picked it up off the floor and tossed it back. Glen caught it this time, too.

"Throw it again," Ethan said.

"Somehow I'm missing the point of this game."

"It's not a game. I need to learn to do this."

"Because . . . ? If your goal is to try out for softball, I suggest we practice with a real ball. Seriously, dude. What's this about?"

"Every time I go into my dad's office . . . Jennifer has these in her desk drawer. And she always says, 'Ethan. Think fast.' And then she throws me one. And I always miss it."

"Oh. Jennifer."

"Yeah. Jennifer."

"How many of these has she thrown you?"

"I don't know. Let's see. Three times a week, maybe. For almost a year. So maybe a hundred and fifty."

"And you haven't caught a single one?"

"No, I have. I wasn't being serious when I said never. I catch maybe one in four or five. It's getting humiliating. She's nice about it, but now my dad's been teasing me right in front of her. She says, 'Ethan. Think fast,' and he says, 'Don't you know by now that Ethan's a slow thinker?' It's starting to piss me off."

"Yeah, especially since thinking is what you do best. So, let me get this straight. You seriously brought me up to your room so you can practice catching a fudgy pop?"

"If you're my friend, you'll just shut up and do it."

"If this is the kind of stuff I have to do to be your friend, you should've warned me when we met."

They tossed the candy back and forth about two dozen more times. Ethan caught it twice.

Then Glen caught it, held it, and did not appear inclined to throw it back. He cleared his throat. "Listen. Dude. You honestly think Jennifer's going to change her whole opinion of you because you can catch?"

"No. Of course not. I'm just tired of being embarrassed. Wait. Wait a minute. What do you mean, 'change her whole opinion' of me? Why would you even say a thing like that? Her opinion of me is not bad, you know."

"Didn't mean it was."

"Well, what *did* you mean, then?"

Ethan consciously tried to calm himself. He could feel a heat building up behind his ears. He tried to will it away. All he wanted was to sound casual. And, as usual, it wasn't working.

"I just think she doesn't see you the way you want her to."

"She likes me."

"Yeah. I'm sure she does. But I think she likes you like a kid. You're her boss's kid. I'm not trying to be mean, I just—"

"I'm not a kid!"

"I know. I know that, buddy. I didn't think you were. We're the same damn age. I just think . . . you know . . . since you don't look it . . . I just think maybe sometimes people think of you more as the age you look. You know. Instead of the age you really are."

"She knows I'm seventeen. She sees me as seventeen."

"She gives you candy."

"She gives everybody candy!"

It came out as something like a full-throated shout. Glen winced. Ethan was startled by a light rap on his bedroom door.

"Everything okay in there, honey?" His mother's voice.

"Yeah, Mom. We're fine."

He held very still until her footsteps faded down the apartment's hall.

"Look, I'm sorry, man," Glen said. "I'm not trying to hurt your feelings or anything."

"I know."

"Here. Catch."

Glen flipped the lollipop in Ethan's direction. A good, arcing throw. Ethan missed it again.

—

When Ethan arrived at his father's office, Jennifer was in her usual spot, seated at her desk in the reception area. Ethan's dad was nowhere around. Nearly one whole wall was a window into Noah's office, and it wasn't hard to see that his father's desk was empty. Ethan couldn't help being pleased and relieved, but tried to do so in a way that wouldn't be plainly visible.

"Ethan!" Jennifer said, and her voice sounded delighted. Elated, almost. "Here. Think fast."

She pulled her desk drawer open, and then the fudgy pop was flying through the air, arcing, flipping end over end in Ethan's direction. In that strangely compressed moment Ethan thought if he missed it or dropped it—after all that practice—it would just be too depressing for him to live through.

He reached out, and the candy landed in his palm. He closed his fingers around it, fast, and smiled.

"Hey, you got one!" she said.

The phone rang.

"Underwood Financial," she said in her professional voice, which was strangely different. "This is Jennifer."

A pause, during which Ethan stared at her. Her perfectly straight hair was so long she had to move it aside to sit down. And her hair and eyes were exactly the same color—the exact color of the buckwheat honey his mother put on the kitchen table every morning at breakfast. Ethan found it hard not to stare at the honey on the breakfast table, too, his mind far away and more drifting than thinking. Once, Ethan's dad had apparently watched him for a time without Ethan's knowledge and then asked, "Something going on in that jar that only you can see?"

"No, I'm sorry," Jennifer said, knocking him back into the moment, "he's having lunch with a client. Can I take a message?"

He watched her scribble on her pad, occasionally punctuating the silence with "Uh-huh."

"Okay, thank you," she said, "I'll tell him. Right. Bye."

She hung up the phone and leveled Ethan like a demolition ball by looking directly into his face. His ability to breathe dried up in his lungs, and his skin felt hot.

"Don't tell me, let me guess. You came by hoping to have lunch with your dad."

Ethan nodded silently. Now that it was clear he couldn't have lunch with his dad, having lunch with his dad formed a great excuse for dropping by. And it was hard coming up with excuses. The more the drop-ins stacked up, the harder it became.

"Here's a thought," she said. "You and me."

Ethan tried to swallow and failed. His brain raced like a trapped wild animal, wondering what he had missed.

"Um," he said, and then feared he might not be able to continue. He put force behind the words. "You and me?"

"Yeah. You and me. Giovanni's. I have the corporate credit card."

She held it by its edges and tilted it back and forth as if it were a priceless object on display, itching to be sold. It was silver and shiny, and reflected light from the window into Ethan's eyes.

"Sure," Ethan said. "Yeah. You and me."

—

"I've been wanting to do this for a long time," she said as the waiter held out her chair. "You know, just get to know you more. But right now . . ." She looked over her shoulder at the waiter. "Thank you, Charley, but I'm not even sitting quite yet. I'm going to use the little girls' room before I do anything else. Ethan, will you excuse me?"

"Of course," Ethan said, half rising again, bumping his thighs on the edge of the table.

She smiled once, and then Ethan was able to watch her walk away, his single-pointed attention blessedly unobserved. He watched the long, honey-colored curtain of her hair swish back and forth as she walked.

The minute she disappeared from sight, Ethan pulled his phone out of his pocket.

He texted to Glen: `Big news.`

Then he waited, chewing slightly at his lip, willing Glen to be there to talk to him.

`Yeah what?`

`Having lunch with her`

How'd you manage that?

Her idea

Right

I mean it. She's acting all weird like she's dying to get to know me

A long pause, during which Ethan had no idea what Glen was thinking. And he really wanted to know. In fact, he needed to know.

She say why?

No just that she's been wanting to for a long time

Look dude

Another painfully long moment of no new messages appearing.

What? Just say it

Don't get your hopes up too high. I mean I hope it's a good thing but now I'm worried. I know you. You'll crash hard if you're wrong. Maybe it's just because you're the boss's son

Ethan glanced up to see Jennifer walking down the long restaurant hallway in his direction. She smiled at him, and something inside him melted. And he thought, *Right, Glen. Sure. Don't get my hopes up too high. I notice that advice doesn't come with a manual of step-by-step instructions.*

Ethan had yet to understand how anyone exerted authority over his own hopes. They seemed to chart a course all their own. If anything, it seemed Ethan's hopes steered him rather than the other way around.

He slipped the phone down into his lap and texted: `Gotta go.`

Jennifer sat across the table from him and smiled warmly into his face. Ethan looked away. It was the wrong thing to do, but he couldn't help it. Her eyes and her smile felt like fire. Like the sun, burning his eyes if he tried to look directly.

"You need to tell me all about this big trip you have coming up," she said.

She plunked her elbows onto the table, laced her fingers together, and set her chin on her hands. And just waited, staring into Ethan's face.

"Oh, you heard about that."

"Oh, yes. We're all looking forward to it. Only five days left to wait!"

"But only my mom and I are going."

"Oh," she said, and seemed to stumble briefly. "Right. Of course. But I just meant your dad and I are so happy for you guys. How long have you wanted to see Machu Picchu?"

"Just about forever. My mom got me this picture book about it when I was a kid. I was, like, maybe four. She always said we'd go there someday. She said we'd hike the Inca Trail and sleep in these camps that're over thirteen thousand feet up in the Andes, and wake up to see the sun glinting off the glaciers. It was just one of those big dream things that get stuck in your mind, you know? But I'm not hiking. Which is hard for my mom to accept. She's disappointed in me."

"Oh, I don't think that's true," Jennifer said.

But it doesn't really matter what anybody thinks about it, Ethan thought. *She's disappointed in me and I know it.*

"I think when I was four she just assumed I'd grow up to be an athlete like everybody else in my family. But I'm so not. It's kind of embarrassing."

"I don't see why," she said, her voice oddly light. As if she was trying too hard. But trying to do what, Ethan wasn't sure. "I'm sure you have other good qualities."

Ethan snorted. He wanted to look up at her face, but he was afraid of being burned again.

"Yeah, maybe. Maybe someday I'll figure out what they are."

"You're smart. Your dad's always telling me how smart you are."

"He says that?"

"Of course he does. So your mom's hiking but you're not? How's that work?"

"Well, first we're going to spend a few days in Cusco. Getting used to the altitude. And, you know. Sightseeing. And then she's going to hit the trail, and I'm going to take the train up to Machu Picchu Pueblo, which is right at the foot of the monument. And I'll get a couple or three days all to myself up there, which should be kind of fun."

"What about school?"

"That's one of the best parts. My mom convinced the principal that it would be educational. Like a history and social studies lesson all in one. We wanted to wait and go at spring break, but she couldn't get off work then. So we're going now. I'll regret it when I get back. I'll have catching up to do. But it'll be worth it."

"Of course it'll be worth it!" she said. "That's an understatement. Gosh, I envy you."

Just then something strange happened. Something Ethan would go over untold times in his head in a fruitless search for significance.

Ethan looked up—way up—to see his father smiling down at their table. Literally at the table. Not so much at either one of them.

"Dad? What are you doing here? I thought you had a client lunch."

"It ended early," Noah said. "He got called away."

"Join us!" Jennifer said, too cheerily, too enthusiastically. Ethan thought he heard her voice squeak slightly, the way his own voice used to when it was changing. "Sit down!"

Ethan's heart fell. Not in a purely figurative sense, either. At least, not by the feel of it. It felt as though his heart had been resting just below his Adam's apple, and then sank to a place sickeningly deep in his gut.

His dad sat down. And reached both arms out, resting one hand on Ethan's shoulder, one on Jennifer's.

"This is so great," he said. "My two favorite people."

There was something wrong with Noah's energy. It was tight, and too artificially cheerful. And there was something wrong with the statement. Because . . . Ethan almost didn't know where to begin. Wouldn't his father's two favorite people be Ethan and his mom?

"We're your two favorite people?" he asked, mostly without thinking. He almost added, "That's weird," but stopped himself in time. Still, it was clear by his tone that he found it weird. Unfortunately clear.

"*Two of* my favorite people, I meant."

Ethan stared for a moment into his father's face. The tight facial muscles. The artificial smile. Noah quickly looked away.

"Why are you being . . . ," Ethan began. But then he decided not to go any further in that direction.

"Why am I being what, Ethan? How am I being?"

"You seem kind of wound up."

"This is my high-energy time of the day," Noah said.

Which Ethan realized made no sense at all. His father didn't have a high-energy time of the day. Ethan had known the man for seventeen years. He would have noticed. Besides, it wasn't energy. It was something else. More like nervousness. But he didn't have it sorted out in his head, so he didn't say any more about it.

"Ethan was just telling me about his big trip," Jennifer said. "About how he's going to take the train up to Machu Picchu Pueblo while his mom hikes."

"Aguas Calientes," Noah said. "That's the name of the town. Aguas Calientes."

"No," Ethan said. "It's Machu Picchu Pueblo now."

"I was there, Ethan. I think I know the name of the town."

"Yeah, you were there. Then, Dad. You were there *then*. But this is *now*. And now it's called Machu Picchu Pueblo. They changed the name of it."

But Noah's attention had flitted elsewhere. He looked around the room as if he'd lost somebody or something important. A moment later he caught the eye of Charley the waiter, who veered over to their table.

"A menu," Noah said. "I could use a menu. I'm going to order something, too."

"Very good, sir," Charley said, and veered away again.

"I thought you just ate with a client, Dad."

"Hungry today," Noah said. "What can I tell you?"

Ethan had a lot more questions in his head, but none that wanted to form into words, and nothing he thought it would help to ask.

He decided to stop asking.

He slipped his phone out of his pocket again and held it down in his lap. The message app was still open, so he typed in: `I'm in the twilight zone.`

`What? Tell me`

But Ethan never did.

Earlier in the Worst Night of Ethan's Life

Chapter Three: This is Embarrassing

Three months before his father disappeared

Ethan stood at the check-in line at the airport, shoulder to shoulder with his mom. When the line moved—which was not nearly often enough for Ethan's tastes—he pushed their bags forward with his foot, sliding them across the linoleum floor.

"At first I thought the late flight was a good idea," he said to his mom. "Now I'm not so sure."

"You tired, honey?"

She brushed the hair off his forehead and held her palm there as if feeling for a fever. But probably she was only trying to be comforting.

"Yeah. I'm getting kind of sleepy is all."

"Oh, it'll be so worth it, though. It's such a long flight. Just think how happy you'll be when you wake up in the morning and we're about to land in Lima."

"I guess," Ethan said. "If this line would ever move."

And then, just like that—as if the universe had been listening to Ethan's wishes—the line moved. Significantly moved. Four groups of travelers peeled away from the airline counter nearly at once, and Ethan and his mom found themselves at the head of the line.

"Won't be long now, honey," she said. "You can even nap at the gate."

"I'm not so good at sleeping sitting up."

"If you're tired enough, you'll manage. Oh. That's us. We're up."

Ethan trudged behind her, pulling two bags by their shoulder straps and pushing another with his foot. By the time he made it to the open station—which was a discouragingly long way from the head of the line—Ethan was audibly out of breath. In his defense, they were unusually heavy bags.

"Good thing I'm not hiking at high altitude," he told his mom.

"Get your passport," she said. "And don't you dare tell me you don't have it, because I reminded you three times."

"I have it."

He pulled it out of his jacket pocket and handed it to her. She handed both passports to the airline employee, a tall woman who scrutinized them closely before setting them on her keyboard and beginning to type.

"Destination?"

"Cusco," his mother said. "With a stopover in Lima."

"I just need to see your tickets."

Silence. Ethan watched his mother's face, startled at the blankness he saw there. He couldn't shake the feeling that the earth was holding still.

"Tickets?" his mother asked. It was more than just a question. It was a criticism of the request, an accusation of its foolishness. As if the woman had asked to see their sailplanes or their giraffes.

"Yes, ma'am," the woman said, either ignoring the subtext or too tired and burned out to recognize it.

"They're e-tickets. Everything is e-tickets these days."

"No, ma'am. Not everything. Some smaller non-U.S. airlines still use paper tickets on certain flights."

"But we weren't given paper tickets!"

Ethan could read the panic in his mother's tone now. This was not a simple misunderstanding. They were missing something they really would need to board this flight. It dawned on Ethan that they might not be going to Peru that night. It was a nearly impossible chasm for his brain to jump.

"Well, you should have been issued paper tickets, ma'am. Did you book the flight through a travel agency?"

"My husband did."

"You might want to call him. If you wouldn't mind moving over enough that I can help the next person while you call . . ."

Swallowing what felt like his heart, Ethan leaned on the counter and watched his mom call home on her cell phone. For too long. With every beat that passed, he could see the irritation and fear grow in her eyes. If his dad was ever going to pick up, Ethan was sickeningly sure he would have by then.

"Damn!" his mother shouted suddenly. She raised the phone as if to smash it on the counter, then stopped herself. "I'll try the landline," she said.

More waiting. More of that sense of growing panic.

Ethan made up his mind to let the trip go. To simply release that beautiful dream. It was better than being tense and afraid. Anything was. And if everything somehow worked out, and the dream was handed back to him, so much the better.

"I'm going to kill him," she said under her breath.

"Not picking up?"

"No. I swear he has the worst timing."

His mother waved at the airline employee. Tried to talk to the woman. All she got for her trouble was a signal that Ethan and his mother would have to wait until she was finished with the traveler currently being helped.

—

"Okay," the tall woman said. "There's another flight to Lima leaving at ten forty tomorrow morning. You can go home, see if your husband has the tickets. If not, he can contact the travel agency, and you can try to get them in time. I can switch your reservations to that flight right now if you want. We have seats available."

Ethan's mom looked into his eyes. Her panic seemed to be fading. Well, not so much fading. Not going away on its own. She seemed to be forcing it into some kind of submission. Breathing it down, one lungful of air at a time.

"That's not so bad, right, Ethan? It's less than twelve hours' difference."

"Yeah," Ethan said, still thinking it felt like a big deal. "We'll manage. Besides. What choice do we have?"

—

Ethan had no intention of sleeping in the cab, and no memory of drifting off. But the next thing he knew, his mom was shaking him by the shoulder. He looked out the window to see the front of their apartment building.

He stumbled onto the cold street as she paid and tipped the driver. Their doorman came out to help with the luggage, and the cabdriver popped the trunk lid.

Ethan felt strangely vulnerable to the cold, and as though he were walking in a dream.

"Thought you were off to Peru," the doorman said, apparently to Ethan. "Something go wrong?"

"You might say that. Turns out we were supposed to have paper tickets."

"Paper tickets? I didn't think they even had those anymore!"

"Neither did we. But I guess we were all wrong."

"And the travel agent didn't tell you that?"

"We're not sure. My dad made the arrangements. We couldn't get him on the phone. He's not picking up."

Ethan felt his mom move close to his side. It was a comforting feeling.

"Sorry about your trip, Mrs. Underwood," the doorman said.

"Thanks. I'm going to go upstairs and kill my husband now. He's still home, isn't he? He was home when we left. Did he go out that you know of?"

"Sorry, Mrs. Underwood," he said, lifting the last of their bags. He had one over each shoulder, hung by their long leather straps, and now one in each hand. "I just came on shift at midnight."

They followed him through the door and across the lobby to the elevator.

"You can just leave the bags here, Robert. Ethan and I can carry them up."

He nodded and tipped his cap to them, and as he walked away the elevator dinged. They dragged their luggage inside.

Ethan's mom looked over at him as the doors closed. Pityingly, as though only Ethan were having a bad night.

"You okay, sweetie?"

"Yeah. Just sleepy."

"I know you're disappointed."

"We'll still go, though. I mean, if you can get those tickets in time."

"You let that be my worry."

She stroked his hair back off his forehead, and then the elevator stopped. It made his stomach tip slightly. The elevator always made his stomach tip slightly. It stopped and started too suddenly.

The doors opened. They hauled their bags a few yards down the hallway to their apartment door.

"If he's in there and just vegging out by the TV with his phone turned off, I swear I'll kill him."

She turned the key in the lock and swung the door wide.

"Oh, good God," she said. Breathed, really. Just a bare whisper.

Ethan couldn't see around her. Couldn't see what she saw. Without thinking the action through, he put one hand on his mother's shoulder and pushed her out of the way.

On the couch he saw his father. And Jennifer. His father was wearing only a short purple silk robe, a robe Ethan was fairly sure belonged to his mother. Jennifer was only wearing one of his father's big shirts, her long bare legs draped one over the other. They were half sitting, half lying on the couch, Jennifer resting her upper body on Noah's chest. They were eating something together, something from a bowl. Ice cream, maybe, or yogurt. Noah's arms wrapped around Jennifer, offering her a spoonful, and she had to take his hand in both of hers to direct the spoon to her mouth.

They looked up.

Jennifer jumped to her feet, using her hands to keep the long tails of the shirt in place.

"Oh my God, oh my God," she said. "I'm so sorry."

It was a strange, disjointed thought, but it struck Ethan that if he and his mother had not walked in, Jennifer would be happy. She would be having fun. Having a great night. She would not be sorry. Not at all.

"I'll get dressed," she said, and ran out of the living room, purposely avoiding Ethan's eyes.

Ethan felt his mother brush by his shoulder. Watched her stomp down the hallway. He heard a door slam. Hard enough to make him jump. And wince.

He looked at his father. His father looked at him.

First there was only silence.

Then Noah said, simply, "This is embarrassing."

But there was a different truth hiding in plain sight in that moment. It was a truth that Ethan would go over time and time again, just underneath the level of his consciousness. Anytime it reached a level of conscious thinking, he would push it down again. Still it played down there without pause, like a film clip set to run on an endless loop.

It was the look in his father's eyes. Noah wasn't embarrassed. Not even a little bit. He looked pleased with himself.

He looked like he'd won.

Ethan couldn't bring himself to put a name to it beyond that, or to look at it for a moment longer. He turned and ran out of the apartment, slamming the door behind him. He expected his father to try to follow him. Try to apologize. Try to keep him home.

Noah never did.

—

It's hard to account for everything that happens while a brain is switched to the off position. Maybe Ethan was too stunned to use his brain in a normal way. Maybe he was in a mild state of shock. Or maybe all the thoughts available to him in that moment were thoughts he didn't want, and refused to allow.

Even a sense of how much time he'd been walking seemed beyond him.

He didn't know exactly where he was—not because he didn't know the area, or wasn't capable of finding his way around in Manhattan, but because he didn't bother to look. At anything. Street signs, familiar businesses. Nothing got in.

He remembered traffic noise. And cold. Not much else.

Now and then a thought would force its way through. For a minute or so he found himself unable to prevent replaying his lunch with Jennifer in this new light. Everything looked different. Everything felt reframed. Her enthusiasm at getting to know him seemed so obvious now, its meaning revealed. More the interest of a woman who hoped to be his stepmother. Or maybe she'd been told she could be at some point.

And that comment she'd made about how they were all looking forward to Ethan and his mother's trip . . .

He forced the thoughts away again. Forced his brain to shutter itself, lock the door. Put out the lights. Admit nothing and no one.

It could have been two minutes later when he noticed the man across the street. It could have been two hours. Time had become a yardstick with no lines and no numbers. Something you could only stare at while feeling perplexed.

Two things about the man broke through. First, he was looking at Ethan. Not glancing. Looking. Second, Ethan thought this was not the first time he'd seen this guy. Ethan hadn't been paying attention the first time, or the second time if there had been one. But in that slightly jolting moment, Ethan played back the tape in his brain and realized he had made eye contact with this man before.

Ethan stopped. He looked behind and around himself, searching for the assurance of others. Of someone else on this block with him. There was no one else.

The man didn't stop walking, but neither did he take his eyes off Ethan. He veered diagonally in Ethan's direction and began to cross the street.

Ethan broke into a run. He didn't look around, but he could hear footsteps.

Ethan found himself level with an alley, and made a sudden right-hand turn into it. The minute he did, he knew he'd made a mistake. The man would see which way he'd gone. In theory it worked, to make a turn to throw someone off the trail. But the footsteps told him the man wasn't far enough behind for it to work now.

Ethan couldn't see if this new route was a dead end. He saw a delivery truck parked in the alley. It was impossible to see around it. Maybe he could run around the truck and keep going. Maybe he would be trapped there. Irreparably trapped.

Ethan could feel his heart pounding in his ears. He'd been afraid in his life—many times, in fact. He'd been afraid of being hit or taunted. Afraid of getting in trouble at home or at school. Afraid of humiliation, or losing something that mattered. But he had never thought he might be about to die. Until that moment.

The thought of a dead end was just too terrible, so Ethan made another huge mistake. He turned and tried to sprint back to the street.

Something big and dark blocked the light from the streetlamps, creating shadow, and then a hand grasped his throat. Ethan felt himself slammed up against the brick of a building, hard enough to knock the wind out of him.

He held very still, in a state of complete surrender. He could think of no other survival plan but to hope to survive.

The hand disappeared from his throat and Ethan swallowed desperately, still trying to restart his breathing. He felt the sharp tip of what could only be a knife pressed high on his throat, just firmly enough that Ethan could feel the sensation of its presence underneath the base of his tongue.

Ethan looked at the man's face. It was reflexive. He didn't really want to see it, but still his eyes went there. Flickered up for a second.

The man's eyes looked dark and cold. Dead. Like no one lived behind them. Like nothing mattered. He wore a stubble of beard that he'd probably been growing for several days.

"What're you looking at?" The man growled the words more than spoke them.

Ethan could smell the man's rancid breath. He quickly averted his eyes.

The man's other hand, the one that wasn't holding a knife to Ethan's throat, began exploring. Ethan was relieved to feel that his pockets were the target. Giving the man all the money he had was nothing. Easy. That was the least of his fears.

He felt his small wad of bills extracted. The man held the money close up under his face and peered at it in the dark.

"You better have more than just this."

That's when Ethan knew he was going to die. Because he didn't. He didn't have more. He had maybe twenty dollars. Maybe thirty. He had his passport in his jacket pocket. And nothing else. His mother had been holding everything else they would need.

Ethan desperately needed to swallow, but he couldn't. Because he didn't dare increase the pressure of his neck against the tip of the knife. The more he knew he couldn't swallow, the more he needed to, and it was a panicky feeling, as if he were drowning. For a flash he wished it could be over. If he was going to die, better to die in that moment. Not have to endure the terror of waiting.

He felt his watch roughly pulled off his wrist. The expensive watch his father had given him as a gift when he turned sixteen.

"You better have more than just this," the man said again, crushing Ethan's hope that the watch would be enough.

He wanted to say that it was, that it should be. That it was worth a lot. But he couldn't speak. Even if the knife had been withdrawn from that frighteningly vulnerable soft spot, Ethan could not have made so much as a squeak.

The man patted Ethan's back jeans' pockets for a wallet. He rummaged in Ethan's jacket pockets. Pulled out the passport. Glanced at it. Threw it away on the filthy concrete.

The horrible face leaned in until its nose was just an inch from Ethan's nose. Ethan felt a small trickle of blood, just a drop or two, as the knife nicked him. He pressed his eyes tightly shut.

"Bye . . . bye," the man said.

Then the knife was gone. But Ethan fully expected it back. He was going to cut Ethan's throat—that's what Ethan thought. That's how it felt. Ethan felt strangely sure it was his last moment on earth. He waited for it. Just for a split second he thought he knew what it felt like to be dead.

Still the moment dragged on.

He heard a light shuffling noise at the end of the alley, and instinctively opened his eyes.

He was alone.

His bones seemed to dissolve, and he slid down the rough brick and landed on his butt in the alley. He wrapped his arms around himself.

It took Ethan a minute or more to realize he was trembling. And that he was alive.

Chapter Four: Far

Seven weeks before his father disappeared

The phone woke him with a start. Ethan lay in bed feeling his heart pound.

His mother had picked it up on the first ring. But Ethan still couldn't get back to sleep. Because the shock of the sudden sound had been replaced with a different, more concrete fear. It was dark outside his windows. His alarm clock said it was barely five.

Nobody calls at five in the morning with good news.

He could hear his mother talking from her bedroom on the other side of the wall, but faintly. Just a trace of voice. He couldn't make out words.

He slid out of bed and padded quietly to their common wall. Pressed his ear there. But her voice was still nothing but a buzzy, garbled series of sounds. He slipped back into bed and waited. Waited to hear her hang up the phone. Or even to hear her voice go silent. Then he would go in and ask her what was wrong.

—

Ethan opened his eyes to see that it was after seven. He had fallen back asleep in spite of himself. In spite of everything.

He found his mom sitting at the kitchen table, her face in her hands.

"What happened?" he asked her. "What was that call?"

"Oh," she said. Sudden and unbalanced, as if he'd wakened her. "Ethan. You're up. It's your grandmother."

Ethan just stood a moment in his pajamas and bare feet, waiting for the jolt of her simple statement to settle. Ethan had assumed it would be about his dad. That all bad news tracked back to Dad.

"Did she die?"

"No. But it's a bad situation. She had a stroke. A serious one."

Ethan slumped into a chair without even meaning to.

"A stroke *on top of* the cancer? Does that mean she won't even live as long as the doctors thought?"

"Not necessarily. But it does mean that she won't be able to take care of herself in the meantime. And that means nobody to look after Grandpa, either. She was the only thing keeping him from leaving the stove on all day or wandering off."

"I didn't know he'd gotten that bad."

Ethan waited for her to say more. To get to the part about what this really meant. What would have to happen now. She didn't speak for a long time, and he didn't ask her any questions. Because these were her parents. And he knew she was upset. So was he, but in that moment it seemed right to let it be more about her.

"When it rains, it pours," she said at last. On a long sigh.

"I never did know what that meant."

"It means everything happens at once. So, you know I have to go to Albany and stay with her, right?"

"Guess so," he said. "When?"

"As soon as I can. She's in the hospital but your grandpa's alone."

"So . . . do I go with you? Or do I stay here and keep going to school?"

"I'm thinking neither," she said. She lifted her head away from her hands. Looked Ethan in the eye for the first time that morning. He winced inwardly at what he saw there. Something was coming. And he wasn't going to like it. "I really can't have you there, kiddo. I'm sorry. This is going to be so hard for me. I'll be sleeping on the couch, and there's no room for you, and I won't have an ounce of energy left over to take care of anybody else. You know how I am when I'm under stress like this."

He did.

"Fine. I'll stay here."

"I don't think so."

"I'm seventeen. I can stay alone."

"I would have said so. Before what happened. But think about it, Ethan. On your own in Manhattan. Every time you have to go to school or go out for food . . . The way you've been since the mugging, it just doesn't seem right."

In the pause that followed, Ethan mulled the flavor of her words. "The way you've been . . ." She probably hadn't meant to let on that it was a problem for her, the way he'd been. That she thought it was time he pulled himself together. But those sentiments had a way of bleeding through.

"So where do I go?"

"I think you should go stay with your dad until . . . you know. Until things are resolved with my parents. I'll probably have to find some kind of home for Grandpa. I'll stay with Grandma for as long as she's got."

Ethan opened his mouth to speak, but she stopped him with a raised hand. Like a stern crossing guard. Someone whose authority you don't question.

"Please don't, Ethan. I'm begging you. I know you don't like the idea. I know this is hard for you. But it's hard for me, too. So please, please . . . just do this. Just accept it. I'll make it up to you ten times over when all this is past. You don't have to forgive him. You don't even have to speak to him. Please just go, so I can know you're okay. And then I can give my energy to Mom and Dad."

Ethan closed his mouth again.

He got up from the table. Found the cereal he liked best. Took it down from the counter. Pulled out a bowl and a spoon.

It didn't seem right, not even letting him argue his side of the thing. Then again, she was right that he hadn't been about to tell her anything that could be considered breaking news.

He sat down at the table again. Realized he hadn't gotten milk out of the fridge. But it was too much trouble and he didn't care. He wasn't hungry anyway. Just going through a bunch of empty, shocked motions.

"Can I at least go see Grandma one more time before I go to Dad's?"

Her eyes came up, and softened. "Of course. Of course you can."

"I don't even know where Dad's living now," he said. "He hasn't even tried to call. Does he know I'm coming?"

"I called him."

"And he doesn't mind?"

"Mind? Are you kidding? He'd give his right arm for the chance to redeem himself with you."

Ethan only shook his head. And kept shaking it for a long time. Too long. But he still never managed to process what she'd just said.

"So where is he living? Is he in a hotel in Midtown or something?"

"No. He needed to get farther away than that. He's on a sort of . . . sabbatical."

"Please don't tell me he's living way the hell far out of the city, like Yonkers or Flushing or upstate or something."

He watched his mom's face, but couldn't quite interpret her expression. Something like a cross between dread and some dark amusement.

"It's way outside the city all right," she said. "But Yonkers or Flushing it's not."

Chapter Five: Blythe River

Six weeks before his father disappeared

"None of this makes a damn bit of sense," Ethan said.

"Oh, Ethan," his mom said with a sigh. "We talked this to death on the plane."

They were in a rental car, traveling along a narrow two-lane highway through what Ethan would have described as exactly nothing. They hadn't seen a man-made structure in more miles than he could remember. If you didn't count split-rail fences.

"Look," she said. "Those are the mountains up ahead. The Blythe River Range. Aren't they beautiful?"

Ethan had been looking at them already, before she pointed them out. He supposed they were beautiful. If you liked mountains. They were unusually shaped. Pointy, like photos he had seen of the Tetons, but with more high peaks, narrower, and more closely wedged together. Their tops were packed with heavy snow, the sky a deep navy behind them.

"I guess," he said.

He reached into the backseat and stroked his dog's ears. Rufus was still whacked out on tranquilizers from the plane trip in the baggage hold, and barely noticed. An awkward mix of pit bull and bloodhound, Rufus had loose brown skin that flapped whenever he ran, and massive ears currently trailing onto the seat.

Then, after hoping she'd say something for another mile or so, he added, "*Please* let me go to Grandma and Grandpa's with you."

She sighed again.

She had always been a beautiful woman, Ethan's mother, but it had been an inside-out beauty. It shone out through her eyes, and in her smile. But that was missing now. Had been for weeks. Now she just looked older. And all too tired.

"I feel for your situation," she said. "But it's getting tedious, having the same conversation over and over. Besides, this place might be just the thing for you. It'll be good for you to get out of the city. The air is clear out here. It's safer. Might be great for your confidence."

Which was yet another way of saying that Ethan's constant fear since the incident was a problem for her. Another disappointment. She hadn't said so out loud. She hadn't needed to. Ethan knew her well enough to know.

A long silence. Ethan thought maybe the conversation had ended.

Then, finally, he said, "Do we ever get to go to Peru now? Or is that whole thing just over?"

"We'll go. Sure we'll go. I just need to tend to my mom. And everybody just needs time to settle."

—

"See, this is where you'll be going to school."

They'd pulled into the tiny town of Avery. Not much more than a cluster of homes and businesses, turning the slightly wide spot on the highway into a Main Street of sorts. High-clearance pickups sat parked at an angle, something like perpendicular to the sidewalks. There were two churches. A school. A grocery. A tavern. A tack and feed store.

Ethan thought it looked like the set of a Western movie, except with trucks instead of horses.

"So we're pretty much there, then," he said.

"No." A hint of apology in her voice. "It's another twenty-seven miles."

He felt his jaw drop.

"How the hell do I get to school? I don't want to sit that long in a car with Dad every day."

"You won't have to. There's a bus. A school bus comes around and gets all the kids from the outlying areas."

Just that fast they were back on an empty highway again, the town in their rearview mirror. *Welcome to Avery. Don't blink.*

They drove toward the snowy mountains in silence for a time.

"I swear, Ethan," she said. "I really did arrange this because I thought it would be the best thing for you."

—

"Look," she said. "There it is."

Ethan looked out the window to see his dad walk out of a house a few hundred feet down the plowed road, swinging on a heavy winter parka. It was tiny, that house. An A-frame, its roof weighted with snow, framed by the snowy mountains behind it. It made Ethan feel as though he were in a commercial for hot cocoa mix. The house couldn't have been much more than five hundred square feet.

"It's so tiny," he said as she swung the rental car into the freshly shoveled driveway.

"Why do you care about the size of the place, Ethan? You have the great outdoors for a backyard. Besides, it's only for a while."

"Yeah, but a while with *Dad*. Would you want to be pushed into a place that small with Dad?"

He thought he saw her jaw tighten.

"The answer to your question," she said, "is no. I wouldn't. But then again, it was me he betrayed. Not you."

Ethan knew that wasn't true. In fact, he was surprised by how thoughtless it was of her to think so. And he wanted to point that out. But he never got the chance. His father walked right up to the driver's side window, and his mother powered it down, letting a blast of biting cold air into the car.

"Noah," she said flatly.

Ethan couldn't hear what his father said in return. It might have been her name, which was Emma. It might only have been a grunt. In any case, it ended Ethan's chance to protest the statement that he had not been betrayed.

Though, truthfully, it was possible that he wouldn't have said it out loud anyway.

Ethan held his phone in his lap, and, as inconspicuously as possible, texted to Glen: `This sucks`. But he couldn't send it, because he had no reception.

—

Ethan walked his mom out to her rented car, Rufus wagging at their heels.

"I wish you'd stay," he said.

"Stay?" she asked. As if Ethan had suggested she throw herself off a bridge. "Ethan. You know I'm not comfortable with him."

"Oh, and I am?"

"Look. Honey." She moved closer to him. Brushed his shaggy hair back behind his ear on one side. She was only five feet tall. And she didn't have to reach up very far. Not for Ethan. "I could've just put you on a plane. You know that. You're not a child. You're seventeen. I could have driven you to JFK and said good-bye to you at security. Made your dad haul into Casper to meet your plane. I came this far with you for moral support. But now I have to go back. I know the thing with your dad is hard. I know this is hard for you in lots of ways. And I know this is not exactly your kind of place. But I only have one mother, and I'm about to not have her anymore. So please . . . this is not going to be a happy time for me, either. Please just get through this for me."

"But I don't know what to do out in the middle of the freaking *wilderness*."

She kissed him on the forehead, her lips pressed against him for an extra beat or two. They felt warm. They were the only thing that had, for as long as he could remember. He didn't want them to go away.

They went away.

"This is your chance to find out," she said.

She gave the same forehead kiss to Rufus, except more briefly. Then she climbed into the rental car and drove away.

Ethan stood and watched until her car disappeared down the snowy road. Then he stood a bit longer. Only when he got too cold to stay outside did he go back inside with his father.

"Hey," his father said, without even looking up from the kitchen counter. There was something too airy in the word, as though he thought he could make everything lighter with just the tone of his voice. "You hungry?"

Ethan stared at his three duffel bags. They sat in a triangle on the floor, right where he and his mother had dumped them.

"No."

"Long plane ride."

"I ate on the plane."

"Since when is there food on planes these days?"

"We got something to go at the airport. We brought our own food onto the flight."

"Oh," his father said. There was a definite disappointment now to his tone. As if the offering of food was the only card he had to play.

Ethan still did not walk closer to him. Or sit. Or move.

Ethan looked around, hoping to see something that reminded him of home, but the furniture was all unfamiliar. The house must have been a furnished rental. The only thing Ethan recognized was the gun rack near his father's bedroom door, a vestige of bragging rights that seemed to carry no purpose.

"Why do you even keep those?" he asked, indicating the rifle and shotgun with his chin. "Why did you even bring them up here? You planning to go out in the wilderness and kill a moose and drag it home?"

"They don't have moose around here," his father said. "So, look . . . we haven't had much of a chance to talk."

That was true enough. His father had gone to a hotel the day after the great disaster. Stayed respectfully away after that.

"Good," Ethan said.

"Don't be like that."

"You could have called. If you'd wanted to talk."

"I want to talk now."

"Well, *I don't*," Ethan said.

"Sooner or later we're going to have to. Ethan, listen. I know how you felt about her. Everybody did."

Ethan's eyes snapped shut. If only he could have done the same with his ears. He said nothing in reply.

"But it's not like anything was going to happen with that. I mean, you didn't think it would, did you?"

"No," Ethan said, but it wasn't an answer to the question. "No, no, no, I won't listen to this."

He turned abruptly back to the door. Reached it in two long strides. Threw the door open and stepped out into the cold afternoon, holding it open briefly for Rufus.

"Wait!" his father called. "Before you start walking around out here you need to—"

Ethan slammed the door.

He and his dog set off up the road together in the direction of the mountains.

The road turned to dirt in no time. Not graded dirt, either. Four-wheel-drive territory. Apparently they now lived as close to this national wilderness as it was possible to get without a 4x4 vehicle or a good pair of hiking boots.

He knew why his father would want to live in a place like this. Noah used to be a backpacker. He used to be a through-hiker. He had done the entire Appalachian Trail by the time he was twenty-one, and all at one time. The entire Pacific Crest Trail by twenty-three. At twenty-four he'd climbed Mount Everest, one of the typical moneyed Westerners who paid guides and Sherpas tens of thousands of dollars to get them to the top, sucking bottled oxygen all the way. Sure, this place was a magnet for Noah. But it meant nothing to Ethan.

The sun felt strong and warm, but the wind carried an icy chill. Ethan had a heavy winter coat on, but no gloves. And nothing like the good boots he would need to go much farther. The road had begun a steady uphill grade, making him puff as he walked. He knew he couldn't keep going for long. It was a strangely desperate feeling. He needed to be anywhere in the world except the inside of that house, yet he could feel himself forced back toward the safety of shelter.

He stopped and looked down at Rufus, who looked back at him. Then he sat. Right in the middle of the road. It's not like any cars were about to come by. Rufus sat beside him. Ethan scratched behind the dog's impossibly huge, floppy ears, and they stared down at the house in silence, breathing clouds of steam.

—

In time, a car actually did come up the road. Well, not a car exactly. A big white SUV. It turned into the driveway of his father's new house. Ethan couldn't see much from the distance, but he was ninety percent sure it had a light bar on the top, like some kind of rugged police vehicle.

He watched somebody get out. Maybe a man, or maybe just dressed enough like one that Ethan couldn't tell the difference from so far away. He knocked on the door of the A-frame, whoever he was. Talked to Ethan's father for a minute or two.

Then he started up the SUV again, turned it around in the driveway, turned up the road in Ethan's direction, and began to drive toward him.

Ethan felt his heart hammer. He tried to swallow but seemed to have forgotten how.

His father had called the cops on him? That seemed to be what was going on. It was the only thing Ethan could figure. And for what? Running away? Is it really running away if you're sitting in the middle of the road close enough to see your own house?

Still the vehicle kept coming, bouncing and rocking over the rutted, frozen dirt road.

Just for a moment, Ethan almost ran. But to where? He stood his ground—actually, sat his ground—and tried to calm his own shaking.

When the SUV got closer, Ethan was able to read the words on the side of it, painted within a green strip that ran the length of the vehicle. "Park Ranger." With that National Park Service insignia that looked like an arrowhead.

The SUV pulled up right beside him in the road. The man driving wore one of those classic wide-brimmed ranger's hats Ethan remembered from the bear cartoons he'd watched as a child.

The ranger powered down his window.

Ethan figured him to be maybe thirty, if that.

"Ethan Underwood?"

"Yes, sir," he said, trying and failing to keep the words from trembling.

"You weren't exactly what I was expecting. Your father said you were seventeen."

"I *am* seventeen."

"I'll take your word for it. Your father asked me to come talk to you."

"Because I ran out of the house? That's a little . . ."

"Oh. Is that what you thought? No. Nothing like that. I didn't drive out here to punish you for anything. He told me you were coming three days ago. He said you've lived in the city all your life. We thought it would be good if I showed you some basic moves to stay safe out here."

He stepped out of the car and stood. And did not tower over Ethan the way most adults did. It was hard to tell from his sitting position, but Ethan guessed the man was only two or three inches taller than Ethan's five-foot-two. Rufus stood and wagged enthusiastically at the ranger, who didn't seem to notice.

The man reached a hand down for Ethan to shake.

Ethan took it. And shook it. He was embarrassed that his hand was still shaking, but it always took hours to calm the trembling once it had started.

Besides. You can get accustomed to embarrassment. You can get to the point where you don't expect better.

Ethan pulled to his feet. Dusted off the seat of his jeans. He'd been right—he was nearly as tall as the ranger.

"Dave Finley," the man said. "But you can call me Ranger Dave. That's what most people call me."

"Ranger Dave?" he asked, not realizing it would sound rude until he asked it, and it did.

"That's right. Problem?"

"No. Not at all." *Except it makes me feel like I'm in a bad after-school special, is all,* he thought but of course did not say. "I thought the whole point of this place was that it was safe."

"The point of the place?"

"Well. I mean the point of sending me to this place."

"Every area has its own special dangers," Ranger Dave said. "We thought it would be a good idea to teach you the proper use of bear spray."

"There are *bears* out here?"

"Oh, yes. Quite a number of them."

"What kind of bears?"

"Black bears. And a growing population of grizzlies."

"Grizzly bears," Ethan repeated. "My mom wanted me to feel safe, so she sent me to a place that has grizzly bears."

"With the proper use of bear spray—"

"Aren't grizzly bears the ones that come after you even if you're minding your own business?"

"Not always. But they certainly can."

"And maul people to death?"

"By using smart—"

"And they weigh, like, hundreds of pounds?"

"Yes, about four to seven hundred is the average for an adult male around here."

Ethan realized his mouth was gaping open. He processed the information briefly and decided the bears might be a good thing. Because they might be his ticket out of here. He could just call his mom and tell her there were grizzly bears here. Which she must not know if she'd agreed to send him. Any fool could see he'd be better off on the streets with the muggers and the murderers. At least they didn't weigh seven hundred pounds.

He could learn the proper use of bear spray and bring a can home to Manhattan with him.

"Couldn't I just stay out of those mountains? I mean, I know I live less than a mile from this national wilderness place. But couldn't I just not go in there?"

"The sign marking the boundary of the Blythe River National Wilderness is about a quarter of a mile up the road from where we're standing," Ranger Dave said. Sounding official. "You're welcome to be on either side of it you want. But the bears can't read. So I wouldn't count on their staying inside the boundaries. My advice would be to carry the spray anytime you're outside the house."

"Like, I open the door and step outside so my dog can pee . . . I'm supposed to have bear spray on me?"

"A lot of people don't. But it's what we advise. I'd be especially careful taking out the trash. An awful lot of people run into bears at their trash cans."

Ethan stood, mouth still open, wondering if Ranger Dave had brought some of the stuff. Because he realized he shouldn't even have gone this far from the house without it. He had already made a potentially fatal mistake. He had no idea what he was doing out here. It wasn't his fault, he thought. He'd tried to tell his mother he didn't know what he needed to know to live in the wild.

Meanwhile Ranger Dave was unclipping his can of bear spray from his belt and beginning the demonstration.

It was a big can to have on you everywhere you go, Ethan thought. At least twice the size of a can of soda. It reminded him of a miniature fire extinguisher. He pictured going through the next year of his life doing everything with only one hand, because he had that big can in the other. Except he wouldn't be here a year, he realized. Because the bears would be his ticket home. Who sends a traumatized teen out to live with a bunch of grizzly bears?

"Now, if you're out on a longer hike," Ranger Dave said, interrupting Ethan's thoughts, "and you're carrying a pack, you never want to put the bear spray in your pack. Big mistake. You want to put it on your belt, right where you can get to it. If you need it, you're going to need it fast."

Ethan's head felt a little swimmy, so he sat down in the rutted road again and said nothing.

"Now. The first thing you want to do is check the expiration date on the bottom of the can. Make sure it's not expired, or close to expired. Make sure it's made specially for use on bears. You want to get one that says bear repellent or deterrent. But it's not a repellent like mosquito repellent. You don't spray it on your clothes. That'll actually attract the bear. Now, most bear attacks happen when a bear is surprised at close range. So it's a good idea to make some noise as you move along. Some people like to sing while they hike. Or give a shout now and again." Ranger Dave cupped his hands around his mouth. "Hey, bear! Hey, bear!"

"You sure they won't think you're calling them?"

Ranger Dave laughed. But Ethan hadn't meant it as a joke.

"The bears around here don't come when you call them, so don't worry about that. Okay. Let's say a bear is approaching you. And he's close. Make sure the wind is in the right direction. You don't want to spray this into a strong wind. You won't like having it come back into your face."

"Wait," Ethan said.

"Okay. What?"

"How do you choose your direction? You have to spray it in the direction of the bear, right?"

"Well . . . yes."

"So what if the wind is coming from behind him? I'm supposed to turn my back to the bear and spray it the other way?"

"No. You have to spray it in the direction of the bear, like you said."

"So I have no control over whether I spray it into the wind or not."

"You just do the best you can with that," Ranger Dave said. Ethan gathered from his tone that he was running out of patience with Ethan as a student.

"That doesn't really explain much. Let's say I have to spray that stuff right into the wind, because that's where the bear is. Then what? What would you call doing the best I can?"

"I'd say turn your head and shield your eyes as much as possible. It's going to hurt. But probably not as much as a grizzly."

Ethan pulled to his feet again.

"I've heard enough of this," he said, and began to walk down the road toward the house.

"But the demonstration isn't over."

"Oh, yes, it is," Ethan said over his shoulder. Then he stopped. Turned back to Ranger Dave. "Does my father know the proper use of bear spray?"

"He does. Yeah."

"Then why didn't *he* give me the lesson?"

Ranger Dave seemed to chew that over for a minute. Then he said, simply, "Guess you'd have to ask him about that."

—

Ethan banged back into the house, throwing the door open so hard it hit the wall. His father jumped. He was standing in the kitchen. Still. Or again. Still looking a bit aimless.

It felt good to show his anger in front of his father. He'd been waiting to do that for a long time.

"Are. You. Freaking. Kidding me," Ethan said. None of the one- or two-word sentences came out as a question.

"What? Are we still talking about what we were talking about when you stomped out? It's hard to keep track with you."

"No, now we're talking about eight-hundred-pound grizzly bears who hide near your trash cans and maul you to death."

"That's why I had the ranger—"

"Right. Thanks so much for Ranger Dave. He was a treat. How could Mom bring me to this place by telling me it would be good for me because it's so damned safe?"

"Ninety percent of bear attacks are shut down immediately when they get the spray in their faces."

"Ninety percent."

Ethan's father seemed to realize his misstep. His face took on a sheepish look, one Ethan wasn't used to seeing. Ethan tried to remember the last time he'd seen the slightest crack in his father's confidence.

Noah opened his mouth but no words came out.

"So one in ten people who use the stuff get mauled anyway. Those aren't the best odds, are they, *Dad*?" Ethan threw the word almost tauntingly. A clear insult. "I want to go home. Give me a can of that bear stuff and let me go home. I'll stay alone if I have to. I'll carry that crap around in Manhattan. I bet it'd stop more than nine out of ten muggers. Look. This is stupid. I don't want to be here. Mom arranged this because she thought it would be safe, so it would be good for me. I'm just going to call her and tell her about the bears."

"She knows there are grizzlies up here. Everybody knows that, Ethan. We're less than a hundred miles from Yellowstone. Even you would have known if you'd thought about it."

Ethan shook his head and locked himself in his bedroom.

—

A few minutes later his father called through the door.

"Ethan? I'm going for a run."

"Fine. Go."

"I'm taking the bear spray with the holster. But there's a spare can in the pantry."

"Whatever. I'm not going out there."

"It'll be hours. I might do about eighteen miles today. So don't get worried. Just figure I'll be back before sundown."

"The longer, the better."

Ethan heard no reply come through the door. He might have heard a sigh.

When he heard the front door slam, he ventured out to use the phone. To call his mother.

He had to leave a message. Well, three messages. Ethan was glad his father would be gone for a long time, for a number of reasons.

When she finally called back, Ethan didn't hear the phone ring. He just heard her voice on the machine from his bedroom. The ringer must have been turned off on the phone. He ran to pick it up, but the first thing she said stopped him.

"Honey, I know," she said. "But you have to know no place is completely safe. I was thinking it was a place that would improve your opinion of *people*. Just carry your bear spray and learn as you go. I really think it could be good for your confidence. I know you're upset, but . . . please give it a chance. That's all I ask. Just try it. Love you, sweetie."

Then she hung up.

Ethan just stood, staring at the phone and wishing he had stayed for the rest of Ranger Dave's lesson.

Chapter Six: Horses

Three weeks before his father disappeared

It was a Saturday, and Ethan had been counting on his father going out for a much-of-the-day run. He usually did on the weekends. But on this Saturday his father was nursing a slightly pulled hamstring, and stayed home.

So Ethan had to be the one to leave.

It was just after dawn, and still quite cold at the high altitude that had unfortunately become Ethan's life.

He strapped on the bear spray with the holster, the one his father usually carried when running. He pulled on his winter parka and boots and stuffed gloves into his pocket.

"Where are you going?" his father asked as Ethan opened the front door.

Ethan stood a moment, light, dry snow swirling into his face.

"What do you care?"

"It's always smart to tell somebody where you're going."

"Why?"

"In case you get lost."

"I'm not going to get lost. I'm just going to walk down the road. If the road doesn't get lost, neither will I."

"Which way?"

"What?"

It felt cold now, with the wind sweeping past him into the house, and Rufus had bounded out of his line of vision.

"Which direction are you planning to walk down the road?"

"Oh. Well. Let's see. Which direction has the most grizzly bears? Figure that out and then figure I went the other way."

Ethan stepped out and slammed the door behind him. Hard.

He set off down the road, glancing nervously over his shoulder every third or fourth step.

—

He'd been trudging cautiously along behind the bounding Rufus for ten or fifteen minutes when he was startled by movement at the corner of his eye. It made his heart race instantly and caused him to miss a step.

He'd just reached the first house. The closest house to the A-frame. It had whitewashed board fences along the road in two sections, breaking in the middle to line both sides of a long, rutted dirt driveway.

It was along this driveway, outside the confines of the fence, that Ethan caught the movement. Two large animals barreled in his direction. But when he turned his head to face the danger, shocked into blankness, he saw they were not grizzly bears. Only horses. Two young-looking horses, chestnuts, their winter coats shaggy and thick. They looked almost like twins, except the white blazes on their long faces didn't match. They wore leather halters. Ethan could hear and even feel the drumming of their hoofbeats on the hard ground.

"Stop 'em!" a voice bellowed out.

But Ethan didn't see anybody, and couldn't locate the pleading disembodied voice. So he just stood still at the head of the driveway, watching the horses gallop closer. Just as it struck him that he'd best get out of the way so as not to be trampled, he heard the voice again.

"You there! Head 'em off! Please!"

"How?" he shouted, still not knowing whom he was talking to.

Then he saw the man. He was behind the fence, near a rough barn that looked like a good wind could take it down. He was maybe fifty, with a gray beard and a ring of gray hair over his ears. His bare scalp glowed strangely red from either sun- or windburn. He had a potbelly. A little bit like Santa Claus might look, Ethan thought, before you got him cleaned up for the holidays.

The man held his hands wide at his sides and waved them upward in a pantomime of how you stop a horse. He seemed to honestly suggest that Ethan stand in front of the runaway pair and risk being trampled.

Just as Ethan prepared to walk on, he heard the last desperate word.

"Please!"

Deciding he could always jump away at the last minute, and assuming he would, Ethan positioned himself at the head of the driveway and raised his hands. To his amazement, the spooked pair of animals stopped, tossing their heads and snorting their opinions. Time stretched out, the moment frozen. Then Mr. Grungy Santa had them by their halters.

"Holy cow, did you ever just save my ass," he said to Ethan. "Gate didn't latch proper. You look cold. You want some coffee or hot cocoa or something? What're you doing out in the middle of nowhere all by yourself?"

It sent a jolt through Ethan's gut, because it reminded him of the cop. That dreadful night. The way the cop asked him what he'd been doing out in the city alone. Was it too dangerous, just walking down the road as he'd been doing? Should he not be out here?

The man led the two young horses back down the driveway toward the gate. Ethan followed. Partly because a conversation had been started, and was clearly not finished. Mostly because it seemed safer to be with someone else. Anyone.

"I'm staying just right up the road," Ethan said.

He watched the horses' flanks shift under their shaggy coats. Watched their tails swish nervously.

"Oh. Up in that A-frame? The rental?"

"Yes, sir."

"Please don't call me sir. Makes me feel old."

"Okay," Ethan said. But he didn't know the man's name, so he didn't know anything else to call him. He waited, but more information didn't arrive.

He looked down the road toward town and saw Rufus standing alone, looking to see which way Ethan had gone. Ethan cupped his hands around his mouth and called the dog's name as loudly as he could manage.

Rufus's head came up, and he bounded in Ethan's direction. The horses spooked and jumped, dancing and throwing their heads.

"Sorry," Ethan said.

He followed the man and the horses through the gate.

"Get that shut behind us, okay?" the man asked him. "Make sure it really latches. In other words, be smart. Not like me."

Ethan had to take off his gloves to secure the board gate, the metal of the latch cold against his fingers. The man let go of the twin halters, and the chestnut horses cantered away, disappearing behind the barn.

Rufus ducked through the boards of the fence and joined up with Ethan.

"Yearlings," the man said. "Not much training yet. You have no idea how much trouble you just saved me. No idea. I would've had to go out searching. On a horse. With a rope. Only it's not easy to rope two colts more or less at once. I likely would've had to pay somebody to go out with me and track 'em down. Might've taken days. I owe you one. So, look. Hold tight to that dog. Some of the mules are none too friendly. I got one who'll trample a dog if he gets half a chance. And don't you get near him, either. He bites and he kicks."

"Maybe I should be going," Ethan said, his voice trembling just slightly.

"Don't worry, they're in that big corral. Let me get you some coffee to warm you up. That A-frame, you say? I saw there was a guy living there now but I didn't see any kid. I mean, until this. Wait. You're too young to drink coffee, aren't you? I'll make some cocoa."

"I drink coffee," Ethan said, holding tightly to Rufus's collar.

"Still and all, I don't want to be the one corrupting a kid."

"I'm seventeen."

The man leveled him with a stare that made Ethan's face feel hot. "Really?"

"I know I don't look it."

"I didn't say that."

"You didn't have to."

"I take people at their word. Besides. Not everybody looks their age. Now you take Jone. Our neighbor in one of those houses downhill. She's seventy. Got children and grandchildren and great-grandchildren over on the Blythe River Reservation on the other side of the foothills. And she's beautiful. Doesn't look a day over fifty. You know Jone?"

"No, sir. I haven't met any of the neighbors. Except you. Just now."

"Well, there aren't many to meet. At least, not until July or so when we thaw out for real. In the winter, and in spring like it is now, it's just me and Marcus and Jone. If you ever meet her, put in a good word for me. With Jone. Not Marcus. I don't care so much about him."

"A good word?"

"What do you take in your coffee?"

"Oh. Um. Cream and sugar?" It came out as a genuine question. As if he wasn't sure how he took his coffee and was counting on this man to say if he was right.

The man disappeared into his run-down house. Ethan wandered over and leaned on the top rail of the big corral, watching horses mill and crowd each other away from a feeder full of hay, teeth bared as necessary. But when one of the mules came trotting in his direction, long ears laid back against his neck, Ethan jumped away fast, pulling Rufus back with him.

"That's the one you gotta watch out for." The man's voice startled him from behind. "That's Rebar. That's the one that'll bite you or kick you quick as look at you. Usually a bad-tempered horse or a mule, they'll bite or kick if you give 'em cause. But not this guy. He'll seek you out for it." He handed Ethan a steaming cup of coffee in a chipped, ancient mug. "Never met a creature on God's green earth with a snarkier disposition. Unless it was Jone." But still he got a dreamy look in his eyes on that last sentence.

"So why do you want me to put in a good word for you?"

"Did I not mention she's beautiful?"

"Oh. Right. But you also said she's seventy."

"And that she doesn't look a day over fifty?"

"Right."

The biting, kicking mule retreated to the hay feeder again, so Ethan leaned on the fence rail beside the man and sipped his steaming coffee. It was so strong he felt for a moment that the kick of it might take off the back of his head.

"Whoa," Ethan said. "Strong."

"Yeah. Kicks like Rebar, huh? The only way to go. Man does not live by wimpy coffee. I'm Sam, by the way."

"Oh. Ethan."

"Well, you really saved my ass this morning, Ethan. I feel like I can't say thank you enough times."

"How would I put in a good word for you?"

"You mean with Jone?"

"Yeah. If I ever met her."

"Oh, I don't know. Just say what you feel. Like 'Gosh, that Sam is one hell of a fella. Nice guy.'"

"I barely know you. Why don't *you* tell her you're a nice guy?"

"Don't think I haven't tried. But what good does that do? Every guy'll tell you he's a great guy."

Ethan wondered briefly if his father thought of himself as a great guy. And would still tell you he was. Probably.

"So what do you use all these horses and mules for?"

"Pack."

The single word meant nothing to Ethan in that context. He waited, thinking Sam would say more.

"Pack?"

"Yeah. You know."

"I don't think I do."

"I'm a pack guide. It's how I make ends meet. People want to go up into those mountains. Want the full-on wilderness experience. But it's hard hiking. Over thirteen thousand feet of elevation on some of those passes. Takes your breath away, literally. Lot of steep uphill. And not many people want to carry forty, fifty pounds of tents and sleeping bags and supplies up those steep passes, enough to live on out in the wilderness for days. And most don't know what they're doing enough to get into the mountains so deep. So I take 'em in on horseback with ponies and mules carrying the supplies. Hey, maybe that's what I can do to repay the favor. I know it doesn't seem like much, just standing in the way of those yearlings and waving your arms to stop 'em, but think about it. What were the chances you'd be there at just the right moment? I could go a month sometimes with nobody walking down the road across my driveway. And even that's in the summer. And there you were. Like my own little miracle to start my day. Not so little, really. Ever been up on that Blythe River Range?"

"No, sir. Sam."

"Prettiest place on God's earth, and I'm not just saying that. I've seen a lot of places. I could take you up there. No charge, but you have to tell your friends about Friendly Sam's Pack Service."

"I don't have any friends," Ethan said, effectively stopping the conversation.

They leaned and sipped in silence, the clouds of steam they blew looking thicker and more dense after gulps of the hot liquid. The sun was up over the mountain now, so it would warm up soon. Might even get up into the fifties as the day wore on.

"Now why would that be?" Sam asked at last.

"I have friends back home," he said. "Just not around here."

"How long you been here?"

"About three weeks."

"You go to school in Avery?"

"Yes, sir. Sam."

"I guess three weeks isn't much time to make new friends."

Ethan snorted out a great cloud of steam. "You could give me three years and I couldn't turn any of those guys into friends."

He waited. But Sam said nothing. So Ethan took a great gulp of the dreadful coffee and jumped back into talking, still holding the dog's collar so Rufus couldn't duck through the rails of the corral and be trampled to death by a bad-tempered mule named Rebar.

"They think I'm a joke," Ethan said. Another silence. "They laugh at me because I'm skinny and pale. Because I've lived in the city all my life. Not right to my face. They laugh behind my back, but it's not like I don't know. These kids . . . they drive tractors. They break horses. Even the girls. They ride in the roundups and help castrate calves and brand them. They drive their parents' pickup trucks and mend fences and sling hay around. And they look at me like I'm absolutely useless. And like it's really funny. You know. That anybody should be so useless. Even just the concept that there are people like me who don't do all that cowboy stuff is hilarious to them."

Ethan ran out of steam and waited again, in case Sam wanted to jump in. Sam didn't jump in. It struck Ethan that he'd been wanting to talk about this. To someone. He couldn't talk to anybody at school, because they were the problem. Even the teachers seemed to find him amusing. He couldn't talk to his father because he couldn't talk to his father about anything. He couldn't call his mother and tell her because he would only risk disappointing her again by not being too tough to care.

He'd told Rufus, but it hadn't helped enough.

Ethan briefly wondered if that was the real reason he'd followed this strange Santa-man with the runaway horses onto his property. Just to know somebody. Somebody who wasn't back in New York. And who wasn't his father.

"Sounds like a trip into those mountains would be just the thing for you," Sam said. But he sounded unsure. As though Ethan had more problems than Sam could trust himself to fix.

"Maybe," Ethan said, but it was a lie. He knew he wouldn't go. "Thanks for the offer, anyway."

He drained the rest of the dreadful coffee and handed the mug back to Sam.

"Stop by anytime," Sam called as he was leaving.

"I will," Ethan said. But he didn't figure he would.

He was careful to latch the gate well behind him and his dog.

—

On the way home a gigantic long-haired orange tabby cat began to walk along with them as if he were a dog just aching for a good outing.

Rufus tried to sniff the cat, then tried to get him to play, and was rewarded for his efforts by a claw to the soft black tissue of his nose. The dog yelped pathetically, probably more hurt on the inside, and walked ten paces behind the cat from that point on.

When Ethan arrived home, the cat was still following. So Ethan figured the stray must be hungry. He slipped inside and snuck out with a slice of the meat loaf his father had made for the previous night's dinner.

The cat seemed happy to scarf it down. Which was fine with Ethan, who figured that just meant less of the awful leftover stuff he would have to eat himself.

Chapter Seven: Snark

Two weeks before his father disappeared

Ethan arrived home from school to find that big stray cat mewing around on the porch steps of the A-frame. Again. For the sixth or seventh time in as many days. He could see the cat pacing near the door before he'd even stepped down off the big yellow bus.

The cat was huge, maybe twenty pounds. Or probably close enough to it, anyway. His long coat looked a bit matted here and there. He seemed fat, but Ethan worried that was just the cat's coat—that maybe his ribs would show if he were wet, or shaved. Because he always meowed so plaintively for food. Why would he do that if not really in need?

Ethan opened the door of the A-frame with his key, and the cat wound around his legs all the way through the door. Rufus ran to greet Ethan, but retreated to a spot behind the coffee table when he saw the cat.

"Dad?" Ethan called out.

No answer. He breathed a sigh of relief.

"Come on into the kitchen," he said to the cat. "I'll try to find you something."

Ethan was wondering in a disconnected way if his father would tolerate Ethan's taking the cat in permanently when he saw the note on the table.

GONE RUNNING

That was all it said. Just those two words in big block letters.

"'It's very important to tell someone where you've gone,'" Ethan said, more or less in the cat's direction. He tried to imitate his father's voice. "'Because you could get lost.' Great. I can see it all now. Dad gets lost. And Ranger Dave asks, 'Do you know where he was going?' And I say, 'Yeah. Running.' Way to practice what you preach, Dad."

He stared into the fridge until his eyes fixed on the half-and-half his father used in his coffee. He pulled it out, took a shallow soup bowl down from the cupboard, and poured. There wasn't much in the carton, and he all but used it up serving the stray. Ethan didn't care. His father could drink his coffee black, or drive into town, giving Ethan more alone time. Nobody here had serious problems with food supplies except the poor cat.

Ethan warmed the half-and-half in the microwave for thirty seconds or so, then set it down on the floor. The cat started in on it immediately. Rufus wagged in the direction of the kitchen, obviously jealous and hurt, but did not dare come in.

"You don't miss too many meals," Ethan told him.

A knock on the door nearly stopped his heart. Because it was a huge knock.

Actually more of an insistent pounding, like someone was standing on the porch using the back of his fist, and swinging his arm full force.

Like somebody was already mad.

Ethan's heart began to hammer, and the trembling began in a spot behind his belt buckle.

"Who's there?" he called, without moving even one step closer to the door.

"Why are you trying to steal my cat?" It was a woman's voice. Big and deep. And unafraid.

Ethan took a long, steadying breath and walked to the door. He stood a moment with his shaking hand on the knob.

Then, because he could think of no way out of doing so, he opened the door.

The woman on the porch had snow-white hair, long and thick and done in a braid that trailed over her left shoulder. Her dark eyes narrowed at him. She wore overalls with a flannel shirt underneath. Cowboy boots. She looked about the same age as Sam. She looked like someone Ethan wouldn't want to cross. Halfway to grizzly bear territory.

"I'm sorry," he said. "Is that your cat?"

"It is," she said, all lumber and steel in her voice. Sure, and right. "And I don't appreciate your trying to win her away."

"I wasn't. Really. I thought he was a stray."

"She. Her name is Mirabelle, and she's a she."

"Oh. Sorry."

"You thought that overweight cat was a stray? How do you figure a cat with no home gets to be that size?"

"I thought maybe it was all matted fur."

"Don't know much about cats, do you?"

"No, ma'am."

They stood awkwardly for a moment, each on his and her own side of the open door. Ethan knew he should invite her in. But he didn't want her in. That was the problem.

"So you're my neighbor?" he asked, as though the answer might be dangerous. Deadly, even. Then, before she could even answer, it hit him. "Oh. You must be Jone."

It was an easy deduction. The neighbors were Sam, Marcus, and Jone. And she was neither Sam nor Marcus.

Ethan took her in all over again, trying to imagine someone calling her beautiful. It didn't quite work. Then again, maybe if he were fifty . . . He tried again, as if through Sam's eyes, but still didn't quite see it. But maybe thirty-plus years of growth was simply impossible to imagine.

She narrowed her eyes further. "How'd you know that?"

"Sam the pack service guy told me about you."

"What'd he tell you?"

"Oh. Nothing."

The woman sighed. Then she marched past Ethan uninvited. He had to jump out of the way. It struck him that two young, untrained horses had stopped in their tracks when he stood in front of them. But not Jone.

She stopped in the middle of his living room, looking into the kitchen where Mirabelle lapped at the half-and-half. Then she burned her gaze back onto Ethan, who still felt a mild tremor in his hands and throat.

"That's a good trick," she said. "He told you about me but he told you nothing. How's that work exactly?"

"He just asked if I'd met you. That's all." He squirmed under her gaze for a brief moment of silence. "He seems like a nice man."

Jone snorted. "He tell you to say that?"

"No! Not at all. Why would he tell me to say that?"

"Because he tells everybody else to say that." She unmoored her feet suddenly and marched into the kitchen. Picked up the carton of half-and-half and held it up like an accusation. "Half-and-half? And you still mean to tell me you're not trying to steal my cat?"

"No! Not at all. I just thought he was hungry."

"She."

"Right. Sorry. She." Silence. Ethan swallowed hard. "It was all I had."

"I knew she'd been going somewhere. Coming back fatter than ever. Today I decided to follow her. See who had the gall to be feeding her."

"I just thought . . ."

"You thought what?"

"I thought if he said he needed food, he needed food."

"Wow, you *really* don't know cats."

"No, ma'am."

"What *do* you know? Anything?"

Ethan felt his mouth drop open. He didn't—couldn't—respond.

"Oh . . . I'm sorry," she said. "That was over the line, I suppose. I just get a little ticky regarding my animals. Don't like anybody to get between me and what's mine. But, hell. You're just a kid."

"I'm seventeen," he said.

"You don't look anything like seventeen."

"And you don't look anything like seventy."

It had been intended as a defiant comment. A way of standing up to her. And that was exactly how it came across. But the moment it came out of Ethan's mouth he wanted to grab hold of it and drag it back in.

Don't poke the bear.

He waited, watching her face and shaking.

A huge sound burst out of her, and it startled Ethan. It took him a second or two to realize she was laughing.

"So I been told," she said. "So here's the best I can say to make you feel better: When you get to be as old as I am, looking younger than your age is not such a raw deal."

She strode three steps through the tiny kitchen and picked up Mirabelle, who strained to get down again and finish her treat. Rufus bolted in to clean the bowl.

"If my cat comes around here again," Jone said, leveling him with that withering gaze, "you tell her she's too fat as it is, that she eats fine at home, and to get her butt back where it belongs. And next time you talk to our neighbor who you think is so very nice, you tell him the answer is still no."

She stomped out of the house, slamming the door behind her.

Ethan looked at Rufus, who looked back. The dog was licking stray half-and-half off his nose.

"Whoa," Ethan said. "Sam was right. She's worse than Rebar. I wonder why he thinks she's so beautiful and wonderful, then?"

Still, if anybody understood how love could do strange things to a poor guy, it was Ethan.

Chapter Eight: Alone

The day his father disappeared

Ethan's eyes flickered open.

There had been a moment—an all-too-brief moment—every morning upon waking for the last three months. This was one of those moments. Ethan had been studying the art of making it last, but it was a lost cause. As soon as you acknowledge you're in the moment, you're out of it.

When in it, his heart was not shattered, nor were his nerves. There was nothing haunting him from behind, nothing dark and shadowy down the road. No betrayals in the past or grizzly bear possibilities in the future. If not for the fact that it lasted less than a second, there would be nothing to be said against that moment. It was perfect. Except it was too short.

Then it passed, and the truth of his life settled into his stomach like a clamp. It always felt like something had grabbed his stomach and was holding it too tightly. Painfully tightly. He pictured the sensation as one of those claw-foot traps people use to catch bears. But maybe he just had bears on the brain.

Because it wasn't really a trap holding his belly, because it was him doing the holding, it always made him feel tired.

It was the first day of summer vacation. He allowed that thought to come in and join all the others.

Ethan sat up and looked out the window. There were no shades or curtains on the window, because none were needed. There was no one out behind the house. Ever. Unless you think it's important to maintain your privacy from coyotes, elk, and the occasional black bear or grizzly.

A fresh fall of light, powdery snow had fallen in the night. Yes, still. In early June. Where Ethan came from, such a thing would not happen. Where he found himself now, it did. Snow still clung to the rocky towers of the mountain range outside his window. It was beautiful, Ethan thought, but in the abstract. Really no different from a painting on the wall.

So he had actually elevated his opinion of the mountains in the time he'd lived here. But they still didn't mean much.

Rufus was up on the bed with him, thumping his tail on the quilt.

Ethan scratched behind the dog's droopy ears.

"Let's see if there's time to catch him. Talk him into taking you with him on his run."

He threw the covers back and stepped out of the bedroom, Rufus bounding ahead into the A-frame's more or less one big room. No Dad. He looked to his father's bedroom. Its door stood wide open, making it clear that the bedroom was empty. The house was empty.

"Damn it," Ethan said. "He ditched you again."

Meanwhile he was half aware of the message machine beeping. Someone must have called without waking him up.

He stumbled to the machine and hit "Play."

"Dude."

Glen.

"Wish I'd gotten to talk to you before I go. Let's trade places. I'll sit in that tiny house with your dad all summer, and you go out and probably drown on a sailboat with my dad for three weeks."

A pause.

"Oh, well. Wish me luck."

Ethan felt a pang of regret at having missed the call.

He stumbled into the kitchen area, divided from the rest of the house only by a tile counter, and looked, blinking, into the cupboards. Maybe for cereal. Maybe for kibble. He wasn't even sure which.

"It's such a dirty trick," he told Rufus. "Who likes to go running more than a dog?"

Then again, Ethan thought, not all dogs are suited to a run over twenty miles long, which was a possibility on any given day.

Giving up on looking for anything, and half asleep, Ethan sat down at the table with a surprising thump.

"I'll have to take you out," he said.

Without that holster of bear spray it was not a happy thought. Except to Rufus, who swung his tail with renewed vigor.

"No. I can't take you till he gets back. He has the bear spray. Unless I can find the spare can. He keeps saying there's a spare can. But I haven't seen it."

He stared at the mountains for a moment in an unfocused way. His eyes were focused, but his brain was not. So when the thought came into his head, it surprised him. He hadn't seen any thoughts coming.

"What the hell am I supposed to *do* all summer?" he asked the dog. "I mean, if I'm here all summer?"

It seemed to disturb Rufus to be asked a question. He seemed to feel he should attempt to answer, or otherwise help, but ended up just wiggling uncomfortably.

"At least at school I dared to go outside. At least I was in town. But out here in the middle of nothing and nowhere? With the wolves and the bears?"

He realized he'd been so focused on getting away from the young cowboys and cowgirls who found him so funny that he hadn't really thought about the downside. All that time to kill. Right in the foothills of the wilderness.

He looked around the one big room they now called home.

"We should get this over with."

He began to rummage around the house for the spare can of bear spray. He found it fairly quickly in the kitchen pantry. Because his father had the holster, Ethan would just have to carry it in his hand. That was okay. That was not the problem. The problem was, when he checked the expiration date on the bottom as he'd been taught to do, it had passed.

"It's expired," he told the dog.

For a moment Ethan wondered how a product that's made to last for a year and a half had expired in less than three months. It must have been old when his father bought it. He must not have looked at the date when he chose it. That sounded about right for his father.

"Sure," he said out loud. "It's only life or death."

Rufus slithered over to the door and wagged desperately, and Ethan realized his father probably hadn't even let him out to pee before running. The poor dog had probably been holding it since bedtime the night before.

Ethan sighed, and opened the door for him.

"Don't go far!" he shouted as the dog bolted past him.

His worst fear was always that Rufus would disappear, led astray by some wonderful scent. And then Ethan would have to go out there alone to find him.

"Great," Ethan said. "Great place to be all summer. Let's get Ethan out of the city. It'll be good for him. Nothing to be scared of out here. No thieves or muggers or murderers. Just eight- or nine-hundred-pound grizzly bears. Who murder people. But we'll give you this nice can of expired bear spray. See? Nothing to worry about."

To his relief, Rufus came wagging back.

"Okay," he said, closing them back into the safety of the house. "We'll go for a real walk when he gets home."

—

Ethan's father never got home.

For most of the day Ethan felt dissatisfied and angry at the inconsideration of it all. It wasn't until the sun began to set that he realized it might be time to be afraid.

Of something new for a change.

—

Ethan tried to call Ranger Dave after dark, using a general number for the Blythe River Ranger District. He got only a recording stating the office hours, and suggesting 911 for an emergency.

But it didn't feel like an emergency. Well, that's not entirely true. It *felt* like one. But Ethan didn't figure it would seem like one to anybody else. He couldn't imagine convincing a 911 dispatcher that a father out late was an emergency, especially when a person had to be gone for something like forty-eight hours before being reported as a missing person.

But gone into the wilderness . . . didn't that make a difference?

What if he told the dispatcher that his father had been out running in a wilderness area full of wild animals, a place freezing cold at night, and better not faced in the dark?

Still, Ethan couldn't imagine a search party going out to look for anybody in the pitch blackness. He would have to wait and call the rangers in the morning. Assuming his father wasn't back in the morning. Which he still might be.

And what if Noah wasn't even out in the wilderness? Lately he'd been making vague excuses, like "Ethan, I'm going into town to buy groceries," before disappearing for eight hours or more. Ethan had been so happy to have the house to himself that he'd asked no questions. Even the couple of times he'd come back close to dark. Maybe Noah had finished his run hours ago and had gone into town for a drink. Or a few drinks.

Maybe he was seeing somebody in town.

Ethan went to bed and tried to sleep. He failed miserably.

—

Shortly before midnight he got up and let himself into his father's room, where he had never trespassed before. He began plowing through Noah's things. Dresser drawers. Desk drawers. Closet.

If someone had asked him why—if his father had walked in and demanded an explanation—Ethan would have been hard-pressed to justify his actions. But somewhere in the back of his head he felt there must be something to find. Some *reason* for this sudden abandonment.

Maybe there was something Ethan didn't know. God knows there had been in the past.

And now he felt it was his right to know. So much so that he didn't even try to cover over the fact that he'd been in each drawer, each cubby. Quite the opposite. He pulled clothes out onto the Persian rug and left them there. Pulled socks and briefs out onto the dresser and didn't put them back. Other than a box of condoms, which did seem to indicate something Ethan hadn't been told, he found nothing to help explain the situation.

In fact, he did not find anything related to the disappearance.

But he did find something.

He opened a wooden box on his father's dresser. He'd expected it to contain some kind of male jewelry. Watches and rings, maybe. In it was one single lollipop. The kind with the wrapper that twisted around the white paper stick, and the caramel fudge in the middle of the hard candy sphere.

It hit him hard. It was sudden and unexpected. If he had walked into the living room and found Jennifer sitting on the couch as if she lived there he would only have been marginally more shocked.

He stared at it for a long time, a kind of buzzy static setting up in his chest. Trying to think of nothing. Trying not to remember.

Then he picked it up from its box and carried it to the front door, Rufus wagging behind. He opened the door, holding the dog's collar so he wouldn't dash out into the night, and threw the candy as far and as hard as he could. Which wasn't far. He vaguely pictured all the kids from school smirking at his latest inability. He could almost hear them adding "throws like a girl" to their ever-growing list.

Ethan slammed the door and went back to bed.

—

Twenty sleepless minutes later he got up, left Rufus closed into the bedroom, and found the big flashlight in the pantry. He let himself out into the cold night, searching a grid in the A-frame's front yard.

A minute or two into his search he realized he didn't have bear spray, and almost ran back inside. But just then the beam of his flashlight landed on the lollipop, its red wrapper bright and obvious against a thin dusting of snow.

He scooped it up and carried it back to his room, where he hid it in a balled-up pair of socks in his own dresser drawer.

He wished he could tell Glen about it.

He still never got to sleep.

Chapter Nine: Search

The day after his father disappeared

It wasn't until Ethan was standing in front of Sam's whitewashed board gate, wondering if it was too early to yell out to his neighbor, that he realized the weather felt strangely warm.

That nasty mule, Rebar, caught sight of Ethan and his dog from the far corral and laid his ears back. Ethan grabbed his dog's collar. Just in case.

Right around the time Ethan was thinking he should wake Sam up if necessary, that his own situation was dire enough to warrant it, he saw the older man emerge from the tumbledown barn.

Ethan waved desperately, windmilling with both arms.

A smile broke onto old Sam's face, and he approached the gate.

"Ethan," he said, as though this were merely a pleasant visit. Then, when he got close enough to see Ethan's face, "Uh-oh. You look pretty upset. Everything okay?"

"My father went out for a run yesterday morning and he's still not back."

"Damn. That's not good, is it? You call anybody?"

"I tried to call Ranger Dave. But I only got a recording."

"Where does your dad run?"

"He goes up into the mountains. Into the Blythe River Wilderness."

"How far?"

"Farther than you'd think. He does twenty miles sometimes. Sometimes even more."

"Damn. He training for a marathon or something?"

"Not exactly. He just does his own personal marathons as often as he can. The older he gets the harder he pushes."

"That's pretty extreme. Running on those steep mountain passes in the snow?"

"Well, that's my dad for you."

Sam shook his head and appeared to lose himself in thought for a moment.

"You sure he's up there, though? You sure he didn't go somewhere else *after* the run?"

"I can't really be positive about much of anything," Ethan said, feeling the panic buzz again. Feeling his utter lack of sleep. "But his truck is sitting right by the side of the house. Last time he tried to go into town it wouldn't start. He was supposed to call for a tow into the repair shop in town when he got back from his run. So he couldn't have just gone off to do errands or something. I really think something might've happened to him out there."

"Yeah. That's a worry," Sam said, scratching one cheek through his rough, untrimmed beard. "Tell you what. You go back home. In case he calls or shows up. I'll go get the rangers on this."

"It's only seven, though," Ethan said. He glanced at his cheap plastic watch. It always hurt his stomach to look at that watch. He'd bought it quietly out of his allowance after the good one was stolen. His subconscious mind had never stopped associating one watch with the other. "Will their office even be open?"

"No, but you leave this to me. Dave's an early riser. I know where he goes for coffee and breakfast in town."

Then Sam turned and walked away, disappearing into the house, and Ethan didn't know why. And he didn't know if he was supposed to wait there at the gate. He stood frozen, wishing somebody would give him better directions. Or that he could be the kind of person who handles things correctly on his own. In moments of panic, frozen always seemed to be Ethan's go-to status.

A moment later Sam reappeared, a ring of keys jingling in his hand.

"Well, go," he called to Ethan as he headed for his battered pickup truck. It was one of those trucks with the huge, knobby tires, like tractor tires, and a suspension so high above the ground that Ethan would practically have needed a stepladder to get in. "I'll take care of getting a search going."

"Thanks!" Ethan called, feeling an easing in his belly. A moment of warmth, like the reaction to the word "help" on that awful night. Sam was going to help. Ethan was not in this moment alone.

He walked back up the steep road with Rufus, panting with his exertion. He actually felt a few beads of sweat break out on his forehead with the effort. Which was weird. It must have been nearly sixty already.

His neighbor's huge cat tried to follow, but Ethan gave his dog permission to chase the cat away. He had enough problems without another run-in with Jone.

Halfway back to the A-frame, the feeling of inner warmth abandoned him. Partly because he realized he'd gone out without bear spray. But there was more. Sure, he had Sam to contact the rangers for him. To help launch a search party. But his father was lost. And the fact that somebody was about to search for him didn't alleviate all the fear. In some ways it made it worse. Something could have happened to Noah out there. Now Ethan was in danger of finding out what it was.

—

When he got home, Ethan went through his father's closet and took a quick inventory of his shoes. His father had brought five pairs with him to Blythe River. Which for a clotheshorse like Noah was quite a sacrifice.

The only ones missing were the trail runners.

—

Ethan called his mother in New York, where it was later. Still, even if he had been about to wake her up with the call, this felt plenty serious enough.

"Hi, honey," she said when she picked up the phone. She'd obviously seen Ethan come up on the caller ID. "Early out there. Why not sleep in since it's summer vacation? Everything okay?"

"No," he said flatly.

"What's up, Ethan?"

"Dad went out for a run yesterday morning and he's still not back."

Long silence.

"Did you call somebody?"

"My neighbor down the road is off finding the ranger. They're going to get a search going, I guess."

Another silence.

"Are you freaking out, Ethan?"

"Not exactly."

"Good. Good boy. Because if you were all alone out there and freaking out, I'm not sure what I'd do. I'd be pretty desperate, being so far from you and all. I'm really glad you're holding it together."

"I did want to ask you a question, though. My neighbor asked if maybe he might've finished his run and then gone somewhere. You know. Maybe gone into town or something. I said he would've called me if he was going to be out all night."

Another long silence, which Ethan hoped his mother would fill. She didn't.

"He would. Right?"

“I would think so. Yeah. Yeah! Of course he would. He’s not *that* bad.” A brief pause that felt weighted to Ethan. “Then again, he does surprise you sometimes. You know. In the badness department.”

“So you’re not sure?”

“I don’t know how you can ever be a hundred percent sure about things like that. Things like . . . what people will do.”

Ethan pulled a deep breath. Brought out the big guns. The important information.

“You know that secondhand truck he bought? Well, the starter went out, or the battery died or something. So it’s stuck right here beside the house. So how would he have gotten into town? And the only shoes that are missing are his trail runners. So if he went into town some other way—and I have no idea how he could have done that—it means he didn’t even come home to change into better clothes. Into nice shoes.”

“Oh, God,” she said.

She didn’t go on to say more. But she didn’t really need to. Now she knew, too. She knew that Noah really was out there in the wilderness alone. And that Ethan was alone in the foothills. Waiting.

—

Ranger Dave showed up a few minutes later. How many minutes, Ethan found it impossible to judge.

The ranger took off his wide-brimmed hat at the door, as if feeling conciliatory for some unknown reason, and asked if he could come in. Ethan swung the door wide, his heart pounding.

They sat together at the tiny house’s only table.

“I have a lot of questions I need to ask,” Ranger Dave said.

“I hope I know the answers, but I’m not sure. I just know I woke up yesterday morning and he wasn’t here. He left a note on the table saying he'd gone running. He always does that. Leaves a note. That's really all I know."

"And you didn't get concerned until after the sun went down?"

"No, sir."

"Didn't that strike you as a long run?"

"Not really. I mean, yes. I guess. When you think about it. But you have no idea how far he runs. Sometimes he does this combination of walking and running. And it can be more than twenty miles. It takes hours. So, yeah. It seemed long. He's not usually gone literally all day. But he always says he'll be hours and not to worry until the sun goes down."

"Could he have gone somewhere else instead of the run? Or after the run?"

"I don't think so. He's really proud about clothes. He wears his trail running shoes out on a run, but he wouldn't be caught dead in town with them. Besides. His truck won't start. It's broken down."

Ranger Dave's face warped into a frown.

"Oh," he said. "Sorry to hear that."

"He can afford to get it fixed."

"That's not what I mean. What I mean is, the truck is the most compelling reason to mount a search. The fact that it's parked close to the trailhead. As opposed to someplace else. That usually indicates where a person started out on foot. But if it doesn't start up and run . . ."

"If it doesn't start up and run, how could he have gotten someplace else?"

"People get places without their own cars all the time."

Ethan's head felt a little swimmy. He groped around inside a sensation he couldn't quite describe. There was some subtext in the conversation that he wasn't properly decoding yet.

"Let me ask you a really important question," Ranger Dave said. "Can you search this house right now and find me his wallet?"

Ethan's heart fell. Because he already knew the answer. "No, sir. I can't."

"You know it isn't here?"

"I know I can't find it."

"That doesn't bode well for launching a search," he said. Then, as if backing up in his head and listening to Ethan's words again, he added, "What's the difference? Why would you think not being able to find it is any different from its not being here?"

Ethan sighed, and said nothing for an embarrassing length of time. But the question wouldn't go away. And the silence got too crushing.

"I heard him promise my mom on the phone that he would either hide his credit cards or take them with him every time he left me in the house alone. They think if they give me a moment's chance I'll try to jump on a plane and go home."

Ranger Dave scowled, an exaggerated gesture. "That really doesn't help us. The location of a person's car is supposed to be a clue. The location of their wallet is supposed to be a clue. Everything's in doubt here. I just don't know what to make of this one."

"Are you saying you won't go out there and search for him?"

"No. Not at all. He could be out in the wilderness. So we'll search there. He could also be somewhere else. So we'll search everywhere else. Not because he needs to be found if he's in civilization. So we can stop searching the Blythes if he's not out there. It's a big deal, mounting a wilderness search. It costs a lot of money. We'll need to bring in search-and-rescue people, and dogs. We'll need a plane or a helicopter. If the weather conditions turn bad, searchers' lives are at risk. Then again, the weather is taking a turn all right, but it's turning unseasonably warm."

"That's good, though," Ethan said. "Right?"

"It is and it isn't. If he's lost or hurt out there, sure. It's not even forecast to go down to freezing tonight, and that could save his life. But the snow is melting fast up there, and it's only going to get warmer. So if he left tracks in the snow . . . if he left a scent trail in the snow . . .

and the snow melts and runs down the mountain, and more snow melts above the trail and pours down like a river and washes the trail clean . . . I think you get the picture."

"The dogs won't be able to follow him."

"And neither will we."

"So what do we do?" Ethan asked, feeling a slight tremble in the words. Then he realized his use of the word "we" wasn't quite right. Ethan would not be any part of the search-and-rescue team. "I mean, what will you guys do?"

"We'll just have to do our best," Ranger Dave said.

It struck Ethan that this was perhaps no more meaningful a statement than the pronouncement that Ethan should do his best not to release bear spray into the wind and so into his own face. In both cases it seemed to mean "We're screwed and there's nothing much we can do but make vague statements."

Ranger Dave startled him by speaking again. "We have to balance our plans, though. He might be out there, which is a big priority. Or he might just be gone, which is a big waste of our efforts. Somehow we have to walk a line with that."

"How?" Ethan asked, more trembly now. But then he knew. "No, never mind. I get it. You'll just have to do your best."

Ranger Dave stood, swung on his wide-brimmed hat, and promised to keep Ethan posted.

And that was that.

—

Much later in the morning a loud pounding on the door made Ethan jump. Because it must have meant they knew something. Somebody had come to tell him what had happened. It meant his father wasn't still missing—he was either okay or he was hurt. Or dead.

"How come you never bark?" he asked Rufus on their way to the door. Ethan was surprised by how unsteady his own voice sounded, even for him.

It really hadn't been a lighthearted question. He was alone now except for the dog, which made him wish the dog could be a better protector.

He opened the door.

On his porch stood Jone, holding a covered casserole dish, her orange cat blinking on the porch behind her feet.

"Oh," Ethan said. "I thought you were a ranger." He felt a great rush of relief, because he didn't have to hear the news yet. Sure, Jone was scary. But not scary like that.

"I brought you some chicken stew," she said. Her words sounded flat and dense, as if she found the subject of chicken stew uninteresting.

"Oh," he said. Stupidly, he thought.

"With dumplings."

"Thank you."

"It's homemade."

"That was nice of you."

"I heard you were up here by yourself, and I didn't know if you had plenty of food in the house. You know. While they're searching."

"Do these searches take a long time usually?"

"Depends," she said.

"On what?"

"On when they find the person. What do you think? Usually a couple days at least."

Ethan felt around inside himself for a reaction, but apparently the inside of him had gone numb. Head and body both. Numb.

"You should come in," he said, stepping back from the door.

"Maybe just for a minute. I'll just put this in the fridge."

"Let me put it in a different dish, so you can have yours back."

"Don't worry about that. You can bring me back the dish anytime."

But Ethan didn't like the feeling of a visit to his scary neighbor hanging over his head. He wanted nothing to think about except what was right ahead of him, which was already too much to think about.

"It'll only take a minute," he said.

She came in. The cat did not.

She stood by the table, her big tanned hands on the back of a chair, watching him take down a mixing bowl. He couldn't find anything better to hold stew. Not on this kind of notice, and with his head so swimmy and his hands shaking.

"I saw your cat one more time," he said. "I didn't let her follow me home."

"I knew you wouldn't," she said in that deep, throaty voice of hers.

"How did you know that?"

"I can tell when I've scared somebody good. I scare most everybody. Even people who don't scare so easy. You, though, you looked like you'd be scared of just about anybody or anything. No offense. So I didn't figure you'd chance another run-in with me. Most people don't. Only person outside my own kin ever tried to get closer to me on purpose is that fool Sam. But you know that, I guess. Because he told you all about me."

"He didn't tell me much of anything," Ethan said. He was spooning stew with a serving spoon from one dish to another. But that was taking too long, he realized. So he began to pour it instead. "He just asked me if I'd met you."

"And he told you how old I am."

"Oh. Yeah. Right. I guess he did."

"And he told you to say nice things about him if you ever did."

"Well . . . yeah."

"Ha!" she shouted, startling Ethan, and causing him to spill some stew onto the counter. "I knew it. That fool."

"I don't know if liking you and thinking you're pretty makes him a fool."

"He told you I was pretty?"

"Beautiful, I think he said."

"And you still don't think he's a fool?"

Ethan didn't answer. He'd gotten too tangled up in the conversation. And he had too deep a feeling that he could never get anywhere in a conversation with Jone. Never win.

Instead he just rinsed out her serving dish in the sink, and dried it with a clean dish towel, all the time feeling her gaze burn onto him from behind.

"It was very nice of you to come by and bring me something to eat," he said.

"You got food here?"

"Yes, ma'am. But nothing that looks as good as this."

"You don't have to call me ma'am. Jone is fine. It's my name. J-o-n-e. Not the usual spelling. Not that it matters when you're calling me by it. But sooner or later somebody writes it out, and then I realize they had it wrong in their head the whole time."

"Why do you spell it like that?" Ethan asked, surprised at how different the name felt in his head now that he knew.

"Because that's how it is on my birth certificate, that's why."

"I just wondered why—"

"I didn't ask," she said, cutting him off. "Maybe my mom didn't know how to spell the name. Maybe she was still woozy from the drugs when the nurses handed her those forms. Or maybe that's how she wanted it spelled. I don't know. I just know it's my name. What's the point of asking questions?"

Ethan didn't answer. He just handed her the dish and shrugged.

"You okay up here by yourself for now?"

"Yes, ma'am. Jone."

She stared at him for a long time. It made his face burn, and forced his gaze down to the rug.

"I hope this turns out okay for you," she said at last.

"Thanks," he said. "Me, too."

Then he walked her to the door, and she stepped out. And Ethan closed the door behind her and breathed out his relief.

He stood at the window and watched her walk away down the road, empty dish trailing from one big hand, Mirabelle the cat trotting along behind.

He found himself wondering. What would "turn out okay" mean in this situation? What would be the best way for this to turn out? It seemed like an obvious question. But it wasn't. It was a complex one. He just hadn't realized it yet.

Would it be best if his father came walking through the door right now? And they struggled on together like this all summer without the benefit of school to separate them? And Ethan had to stay in the land of the giant killer bears? Wouldn't it be a tremendous relief to be sent home to crowd his poor mother and grandparents or stay alone in New York?

But he felt too guilty even entertaining that thought. Noah was well short of father of the year, but he was the only father Ethan had.

He tried to let go of any thoughts about the outcome. It's not like there was a damn thing he could do about any of it anyway.

—

It was fully dark by the time Ranger Dave pulled up in front of Ethan's house again, so Ethan didn't assume the ranger knew anything, and his heart didn't pound to see the SUV. He figured Dave had just come to say they were giving up for the day.

He opened the door.

The ranger pulled off his hat and held it in front of himself as he came up onto the porch. "No luck today," he said.

"Oh."

"Didn't want you having to wonder all night."

"Thanks."

"One question."

Ethan knew he wouldn't like it. He could tell by the ranger's tone. He said nothing.

"Did you know your father was seeing a young woman in town?"

"*Was* seeing? Past tense?"

"Yeah. Past tense. She broke it off with him the day before he disappeared. Because he had a seventeen-year-old son. She's not so much older than that herself, just a handful of years, and she wasn't exactly in the market for a readymade family."

"Oh," Ethan said.

It filled him with a horribly familiar feeling. It was that ugly moment when you had to back up through time inside your head, and reframe everything you thought you knew about somebody. You had to revise reality after the fact. At least the reality you thought you knew.

Again.

"You still didn't answer the question," Ranger Dave said.

"Question?"

"Did you know about that?"

"Does it really matter whether I knew it?"

"Yes," the ranger said, and his voice sounded hard. It made Ethan want to back up a step. "Yes, it matters quite a bit or I wouldn't be asking. Because the fact that he just went through a breakup, along with the details of that breakup, seem to add up to his going away somewhere. You know. Purposely as opposed to accidentally. But you think he wouldn't do that without telling you. So I'm curious as to how much he tells you. I think you can follow my line of reasoning here."

Ethan held on to the door frame with both hands, leaning his chest against it.

"He would tell me he was going into town," he said, his voice heavy with shame. "I didn't ask for any details."

"Got it," the ranger said. As if that was the end of the mystery. As if that was the last bit of information he needed.

“Does this mean you won’t look for him anymore?”

“No,” Ranger Dave said. “It means I really don’t think he’s out there. But I don’t know for a fact that he’s not. And it’s life or death if he is. So we’ll search again tomorrow. But frankly I think we’re wasting our time. I’m sorry to say all this to you, because he’s your dad, and I know it must be hard to hear. But it’s the truth. We’ll look until there’s no place else to look, but I’ve got to be honest and say we think he took off and left you. You might want to get your stuff together, because we’ll probably make an arrangement for your mom to fly you home. She says it’s okay for you to stay alone here in the meantime. We’ll put the plane up tomorrow and look for him all the same. Because that’s what we do.”

Then he set his hat back on his head and turned away. Walked to his big ranger’s vehicle.

It struck Ethan that the ranger was angry with his father, and some of that anger had just spilled off onto him.

He thought about flying home to his mother. It should have been a comforting thought. It always had been before. This time it wasn’t.

Chapter Ten: Help

Two days after his father disappeared

The following evening, just as the sun hit a long slant on its way to going down, Ethan heard a rhythmic sound out front on the dirt driveway. Then it stopped, and he couldn't decide if he should ignore it or go find out who—or what—was there.

He walked to the window and pulled back the curtain.

His neighbor Sam was sitting on the back of a saddled mule in Ethan's driveway. It wasn't Rebar he was riding. It was a shorter, stockier mule. Sam's cowboy boots didn't seem to hang far enough above the ground in their stirrups, and the mule's front end took up a bizarre amount of space between those jean-clad legs.

Sam must not have seen Ethan pull back the curtain, because he just sat his mule, a few yards from the front porch, staring off into space. Actually, they both looked off in the same direction, man and mule, as if thinking the same deep thoughts.

Sam wore an old cowboy hat, which he took off and hooked over the saddle horn. Then he scratched his bare scalp as he stared.

It seemed strange to Ethan that Sam had chosen to ride down his driveway before turning into a statue. Behind his neighbor, Ethan could see the sun nearly touch the horizon, off to the west where the land was flat and there was a proper horizon for the sun to touch.

He walked to the front door and opened it.

Sam looked over at him, but nothing more. He didn't dismount his mule. He didn't squeeze its sides and ride closer. Ethan thought the older man looked hurt somehow. Not on the outside. Not injured. He looked as though he might be nursing an insult or a slight, or just couldn't reconcile himself to the world in that moment.

Ethan walked closer.

"Is it okay to get near this mule?"

"This one, yeah," Sam said. "Dora's like a kitten."

"What brings you up here?"

"Down here, actually," Sam said. "I been up riding the Blythe Range all day. Thought I could help with this search thing. Not sure if I did any good or not. Probably not."

It was dawning on Ethan, gradually, that Sam had not come here for no reason. Also that whatever was weighing the man down was about to be delivered to Ethan, who likely would have the same look on his face afterwards.

"Still wondering why—" Ethan began.

"Dave didn't want to come."

"Why not?"

"He didn't want to be the one to tell you."

Ethan felt as though something struck his chest, something sharp. As though an arrow pierced him there.

"He's dead? My dad?"

"No. Not as we know of. But . . . I guess . . . compared to *that*, what I got to say might not seem like such bad news. The search is called off."

"Because . . ."

"They just don't think he's out there. They were never sure that damn wilderness was the last place he'd gone anyway. Now that they've combed it for two days, they don't believe they're doing anybody any good. They think he just ran off without you, guy."

"I know that."

"You do?"

"Yeah. The ranger told me so. More or less. But he said they'd keep looking. Because it's life or death if he *is* out there."

"Well, there's one more piece of the puzzle, Ethan. Something about a recent cash withdrawal your dad made from the bank. More than just normal walking-around money. I think they said it was five hundred bucks. That was the last straw, I think. Now they figure they did their due diligence. Dave said to tell you to get your stuff together. He's gonna ask your mom to make some arrangements to fly you home."

So that's it for this place, Ethan thought. He shielded his eyes against the setting sun, which glared into his pupils when he tried to look up at Sam. He touched the mule's neck without really thinking or knowing why. It felt sweaty and damp.

So I get out of here. And that's good.

Except it made his throat tighten to think of going back to the city. And something else stole his joy over going home: What if his dad was out there? Out in the wilderness alone? There was a recurring thread of doubt in Ethan's mind as to whether Noah was indeed out there. But in a deeper sense he truly believed it. The bigger question was whether he was out there alive.

Was he really going to get on a plane and just leave him there?

"Thanks for coming by to tell me," Ethan said.

"Hated like hell to be the one," Sam said. "Sitting here thinking and I'm still not quite sure how they roped me into that."

—

Ethan jolted out of sleep, coming to consciousness sitting up in bed in the pitch-dark. His face felt cold, and his chest was so tight he had to work to draw breath.

It was nothing new or unusual. Every few nights since that awful night in New York, Ethan had been blasted out of sleep by what he could only assume was a fearful dream. But he never knew what he'd dreamed. He could never remember.

He turned on the weak little lamp by his bed. It was eleven thirty.

With one hand on his heart to concentrate on slowing its beating, Ethan thought what he always thought in such moments. He thought about the word "help." The way it had struck him in the police station that night. The way it had soothed him. It continued to soothe him—the idea that there was help somewhere. That somebody would help him. Even in the middle of the night, halfway into a wild wilderness, with his father gone and not a soul around to provide the help in question, the word still carried comfort.

That's when it hit him.

It was a mental image more than it was a thought. Suddenly he could imagine himself inside the mind of Noah Underwood. It really didn't matter how fit you were, Ethan now knew, or what a take-charge kind of guy you'd always been. Ethan's father was scared out there. He was human, so he was scared. If he was alive.

He needed help.

Ethan pushed the dog off his legs and swung out of bed, hopping on the cold wooden boards of his floor. He hadn't bothered to make a fire or run the heater because it was only getting down into the forties overnight the past couple of nights. He threaded his way into the kitchen in the dark, grabbed the cordless phone by feel, and took it back to bed with him.

He dialed his home number by heart, then turned off the light.

The moon was big and bright, maybe three or four days before full, and he could see it through his bedroom window—see the spooky moon shadows of the fence posts. He thought he saw a shape move in the dark, off in the distance, but it was much smaller than a bear. A coyote, maybe, or somebody's dog too far from home.

He heard the first few rings on the line.

It was late there. The middle of the night. He would wake her, there was no doubt about that. But the thought caused him no hesitation. This simply needed to be done.

She picked up.

"Ethan? What is it?" Her voice was tinged with panic, yet dulled by sleep. It was a strange combination. "Did they find him? Is he—"

"No," Ethan said. Surprisingly calm. "No, they still didn't find him. He's still just gone. And I knew what you'd think when I called so late, and that it would scare you, and I'm sorry. I just had to talk to you. I had to call."

A medium-length silence. Ethan pictured her sitting up, trying to shake cobwebs out of her brain. He decided to picture her as confident and radiant and pretty—the way she always had been. Not the way he'd last seen her.

"Okay," she said. "Talk away."

"It's not why I called, but how's Grandma?"

"Not good."

"Oh. I'm sorry. I can't fly home yet. That's why I called. To tell you that."

"Why can't you?"

"Because he's all alone out there. He needs help."

"That's what the rangers are for. That's what search and rescue is for. They're pros. They can do their work just as well with you in New York."

"Oh," Ethan said. "They didn't tell you?"

"Tell me what?"

"They called off the search. Last night."

"Why?"

Her voice teetered just on the edge of screechiness, and it struck Ethan that she was scared, too. What if everybody was scared, most of the time? What if it wasn't only Ethan? Maybe everybody else just handled it better. Or were better liars in that department.

"They just don't think he's out there. They think he took off and left me."

Then he wondered why he hadn't told her about the cash withdrawal. Maybe because it made it sound like he should give up and fly home.

"But they don't know that for a fact. They can't prove that."

"Which is why they brought in search teams and dogs and planes and combed that wilderness every minute the sun was up for two solid days. Even though they didn't really think he was out there. But now they figure they did enough to prove their point."

Another long silence. Ethan's eyes had adjusted to the dim of the moonlit night, and he could see the edges of the mountain peaks through his window. He imagined again how it would feel to be lost out there. It made him shiver briefly.

"I could make some phone calls," she said at last. "I don't know if it would do any good. But I could try."

"Thanks."

"But I still don't see why you shouldn't come home."

"Because . . . if they're not going to look in the wilderness, then I think *I* need to."

"Honey. That's really sweet. Especially after everything that happened this year with your dad. But it's not a very realistic thought."

"I know," Ethan said. "I just need to do it anyway."

"Do what, though? What exactly would you do? Wander around out there and get lost yourself?"

"No, I've got a better plan than that. We have this neighbor. Sam. He runs a pack service. He has riding horses and mules that can carry packs or people. He takes people up into those mountains all the time, so he knows the place like the back of his hand. I did him a little favor, so he said he owed me one. He said he'd take me up there."

"You're right," she said, "that's a better plan. But I still don't know how you think the two of you are going to find him if the professional search teams can't."

"I actually don't," he said. He felt sure, and it felt good to feel sure. He hadn't felt sure of himself, even of his words, in as long as he could remember. "I *don't* think we'll work some magic and find him. I just think I have to try. I can't leave here without knowing I tried. When we've been looking for him longer than anybody could survive out there anyway, *then* I'll be able to live with myself if I give up and fly home."

Another long silence.

"It feels good to hear you talk like this," she said.

"I know," Ethan said. He didn't say more about that, or need to.

"I guess it's not a bad thing to take a trip into the wilderness if you do it the right way like that. And for such a good reason. But be careful."

"Right. Because I'm such a wild risk taker."

She laughed, but it was a bitter, subdued sound. "Tell me the name of this person you're going with. I want to check him out."

"Friendly Sam's Pack Service."

"Okay, good. I'll call the ranger and tell him not to scoop you up and ship you home just yet. Call me and tell me when you're going. Call me the minute you get back. Keep me posted, okay? Relentlessly posted."

"Okay," he said.

And it was settled, just like that. And with it, Ethan's life felt reasonably settled, too.

He hung up the phone and actually got back to sleep.

Chapter Eleven: Huff

Three days after his father disappeared

Ethan forced down the last bite of his cereal. It didn't taste like anything. None of the other bites had, either. Probably nothing would have.

He set his bowl in the sink without even bothering to rinse it.

"Oh, crap," he said out loud, in the general direction of Rufus. "We have to walk all the way down to Sam's house with no bear spray again. Or with expired bear spray. I wonder which is worse. Maybe the expired stuff isn't totally useless . . ."

Then his eyes landed on his father's gun case. It sat in the living room, near Noah's bedroom door. It held a deer rifle and a twelve-gauge shotgun. And his dad never kept it locked, because he knew Ethan wanted nothing to do with it.

Ethan's father had tried to take him hunting. Once. When Ethan was thirteen. Upstate, in the woods. Ethan had not only hated every moment they spent camped in that dense, spooky forest, but had resolutely refused to point a gun at anything—animal, vegetable, or mineral. Noah had been smart enough not to try such a thing again.

Ethan settled on the shotgun, because it held five rounds. He didn't trust himself to hit anything with a single-shot weapon. Also because it sprayed shot in a wide pattern. If something was close enough, hitting it would almost be the default outcome. And if it wasn't, he would have no reason to pull the trigger.

Still it felt radical to walk out of the house with a loaded weapon. But not as radical as walking through grizzly country with nothing. No form of defense.

"Come on," he said to Rufus, who was all too happy to hear the words. "Let's go see Sam."

—

Ethan sat on Sam's front porch steps, leaning back against a railing post and feeling the sun bake down on him. It felt good. Comforting.

It was the only thing that did.

"Why did I think he'd be home?" he asked Rufus, who looked into his face and wagged nervously. "I just assumed he would be home. I guess I figured, when you live out here . . . where else would you be? I mean, he's not at the movies. He didn't go to a comedy club. Or the mall."

He leaned forward and peered around into his neighbor's driveway, surprised that he hadn't thought to do it sooner.

"His truck is here. So he must have gone out on foot or on horseback. Or muleback."

Ethan stood and trotted down the steps. He made his way through the yard to the stock corral, bending over to hold on to his dog's collar so Rufus wouldn't get himself kicked or stomped. He still held the shotgun tightly in his other hand.

He leaned on the rail, Rufus clutched between his knees, and tried to decide if one of the horses or mules was missing. Which was probably pointless, he realized, because he didn't know how many there were, and he didn't know most of them on sight. He knew the chestnut yearlings and two of the mules, Rebar and Dora.

It seemed Dora was missing.

"You think he went out looking for Dad again?" Ethan asked his dog. "Even though the rangers won't look anymore?"

That would be awfully nice if he did, Ethan thought. *But probably not.*

Ethan hated to get his hopes up too high about that. Probably Sam just had a customer. Went up into the mountains with somebody who wanted to do a pack trip. Ethan again wished he knew how many horses and mules there were. Then he'd know if some were missing. But he didn't. And besides, Sam might have just taken one person up there. Ethan would never figure out if *one* horse or mule was gone.

A bad thought came up from Ethan's subconscious and lodged firmly in his brain. So bad he couldn't bring himself to say it out loud. Not even to his dog.

If Sam was off on a pack trip, he'd likely be gone for days.

Ethan sat down hard in the dirt.

"I think we might be screwed," he told Rufus.

He sat a minute or two, the sun baking through his hair and onto his scalp. He should have worn a hat. He should have brought a bottle of water.

"Come on," he said to his dog after a time. "I guess we'll just have to go home."

He let himself and Rufus out through the gate, latching it carefully behind them. Then he walked down Sam's driveway in utter defeat.

When they reached the road again, Ethan almost made a right and walked downhill to Jone's house. Even though he wasn't sure which house was hers. But he could knock on a few doors. If the doors weren't hers they would likely belong to Marcus, whom it wouldn't hurt him to meet, or to somebody who was gone until later in the summer anyway. He wouldn't be bothering anybody.

But the idea of her coming to the door gave Ethan heartburn. Just that—just her answering his knock and seeing who it was, and then standing there, arms crossed over her chest, waiting to see what he'd come to say. At least, he figured her arms would be crossed over her chest. It seemed like a Jone way to wait.

And then he would have to ask her a favor. Not a little favor, either. Not "May I please borrow some sugar?" A massive favor. "Will you please drop what you're doing and form a search team with me? Go out into the wilderness, maybe for days? With the grizzly bears? To find a guy the professional searchers can't find, and who I can't prove is even up there at all?"

Ethan sighed and turned toward home.

—

A few yards short of his own driveway, Ethan found himself filled with a radical thought. It was terrifying and exhilarating, all at the same time. It made him feel bigger inside, as if his lungs held more air than they ever had before.

He looked down at Rufus, who looked up into his face.

"We could just go up there," he said. "Just walk up there ourselves."

He stopped in the road to think the idea through.

He could go into the house and get a hat and a jacket. Just in case they were still out when the sun began to set. He had a backpack. It was more of a school backpack than a wilderness pack. Still, it would hold the jacket and some snacks and a few bottles of water.

"I have a shotgun," he said out loud. But not really to the dog. Actually, he didn't know whom he was addressing. "I'm not sure why I'm so afraid of wild animals if I'm holding a loaded twelve-gauge shotgun."

He would have to be extremely careful not to get lost. He had no way of telling anyone where he'd gone, so he had no safety net against taking a wrong turn and losing the trail. But he could memorize his surroundings. He could even bring his smartphone. It wouldn't get reception up there—hell, he couldn't even get reception at the house—but he could take pictures of landmarks and use them to find his way back. If the trail became hard to follow, he could always turn around and head home.

Rufus wagged by his side, anxiously waiting for Ethan to make some kind of move. It seemed to worry the dog to simply stand in the road doing nothing.

"Now for the big question," Ethan asked out loud. Rufus wagged harder. "Will it do a damn bit of good?"

Probably not, he knew immediately. If his dad had been in plain sight within a few miles of the trailhead, he would have been found days ago. But Ethan could call for him. Maybe he was lying hurt somewhere, and would recognize Ethan's voice.

It was longer than a long shot, he knew. Ethan figured the chances of anything good coming of this plan were next to nonexistent. But at least he'd be moving forward with some kind of plan instead of standing still.

And there was something else, something more pressing. A better reason. Ethan would know he'd been brave enough at least to try. Everyone would know he'd been brave enough at least to try.

His mother would be proud of him.

He pictured himself telling her, *Mom. I went up there. Alone.* And in that moment of imagining, he was the son she'd always wanted him to be. And if he ever saw his dad again, maybe even Noah would have to admit to some pride in Ethan.

No one would ever dare think he was a coward again.

He looked back down at Rufus.

"You want to go for a *real* walk?"

The dog exploded into happy motion.

"Wait. Not yet. Let me just go in the house and get a few things."

He thought briefly of leaving a note. Then he realized there was no one to leave it for. No one would read it if he failed to come home.

—

Less than a mile up the hill from his house the rutted dirt road curved around behind a hill and widened out, ending in an unpaved parking area. It was big enough to accommodate maybe ten cars.

No cars were parked there.

Ethan stopped dead in the road, and Rufus bounded ahead without noticing.

Maybe this is a terrible mistake, Ethan thought.

As he looked at that empty trailhead parking lot he was struck with a frightening truth: He was about to be utterly alone in a mountain wilderness. And nobody would know he was there.

"Rufus!" he called, and the dog stopped and bounded back.

He almost told the dog they were going to turn around and go home. But he could see the trailhead from where he stood. It was clearly marked by a wooden sign with letters burned in—a list of distances to intersections with other trails, and to camps and mountain peaks. And the trail was wide and obvious and looked easy to follow.

"Maybe we'll just go in a little way," Ethan told his dog.

—

The trail led them sharply uphill, and Ethan had to stop frequently to drink bottled water and catch his breath. At the top of the first pass, he looked down into a compact valley. He could see and hear water flowing through it. The snow was melting fast in the higher elevations and rushing downhill. The streams seemed to cross right over the trail, which wound underneath the flows of water and then rose to a much higher, rockier pass on the other side.

"Not sure how we're supposed to get across those," Ethan said to his dog.

But he moved forward all the same.

He thought briefly about bears. Holding the shotgun between his knees, he cupped his hands around his mouth.

"Dad!" he shouted with as much volume as he could muster.

He didn't expect his dad to hear him. But if there was a bear nearby, it could consider itself forewarned. No point startling any wildlife at close range.

—

When he reached the first of the creek crossings, Ethan nearly turned back. The water was fast flowing, and probably deeper than his knees. It flowed over smooth stones that Ethan imagined would be slippery and treacherous. And he couldn't imagine walking on along the trail with his boots full of water.

Rufus bounded across, splashing Ethan as he ran, and Ethan sank into a squat and contemplated his options. Then he plunked into a sit and set the shotgun on the dirt. He untied his bootlaces, pulling off his boots and socks. He rolled up his jeans legs as best he could, but they were snug and wouldn't roll past his calves.

He stood—holding the boots and the shotgun up higher than necessary—stepped into the flowing water, and shouted out his alarm.

"Ah! Man! Holy crap, that's cold!"

On a lovely warm day like this one he'd expected to step into lovely warm water. Instead he found himself up past his knees in water that felt as cold as the snow it had so recently been. It soaked the rolled legs of his jeans.

He slipped once on a smooth stone and almost went down, but he managed to right himself in time.

He stepped out onto the dry trail again, leaving wet barefoot prints in the dirt. The trail had a scattering of small stones that bit into his tender feet.

Rufus looked back to see what was taking so long.

Ethan looked down at his bare feet, then up at the trail ahead. It was probably only a hundred feet to the next stream crossing. So he tied the laces of his boots together and draped them over his shoulder. He moved slowly and carefully along the trail, hopping and cursing as sharp stones bruised the soles of his still-freezing feet.

—

By the time Ethan had inched his way almost to the crest of the second pass he was sweaty, out of breath, and thoroughly exhausted. He turned and looked back the way he had come and realized he'd hiked over a mile into the wilderness. Maybe closer to two miles.

The trail up to the pass was more a collection of rock shards than it was dirt, so of course Ethan had snugged his socks and boots back on before attempting it.

Ethan stopped to breathe again, looking up at the narrow keyhole between mountains, gauging the distance until he could stop climbing. Maybe then he would see what lay ahead of them. Maybe he could even cruise downhill for a change.

There was something bleak about this part of the wilderness. Nothing grew here. No water flowed. There seemed to be nothing living at this elevation, and nothing about it seemed conducive to life. Just a place where two sheer, uncaring mountains came together at their bases, giving a person half a chance to scramble over and on to the next section of nothingness.

A chill ran through Ethan's gut as it struck him again that he did not belong here. At least not alone.

He stopped and called for his dad again, more for the sake of bear safety than from any notion that it would help in his search.

Then he walked on.

A few minutes later he crested the pass. He stopped, leaned on his knees, and panted. Only when he had more air in his lungs did he look up at what lay ahead and beneath him.

"Wow," he breathed aloud. The word came out long and modulated.

Below him the trail descended sharply to a miles-long, narrow valley dotted with twenty or more mountain lakes. The sun gleamed off their perfectly still water, which was so clear Ethan could see the rocky linings of the lake bottoms at their shallow edges. The flat land between lakes was a fresh light green from two or three days' growth of new grass. Beyond the valley Ethan saw the towers of mountains he had never glimpsed before, peaks that could not be seen from home. They sat up, jagged and narrow, looking like pictures Ethan had seen of the Alps, or Patagonia, their tops still white with snow. The sky behind them was a perfect midday cloudless blue, a color of blue Ethan didn't know a sky could achieve.

A huge bird with an amazing wingspan soared over the valley without once flapping its wings. Just riding effortlessly on a current of air. Ethan could see its long, separate, drooping wing tips silhouetted against the sky. They looked like fingers. As the bird coasted in Ethan's direction, Ethan could just barely see that its head was white, which he figured made it an eagle. He just wasn't sure enough.

In that brief moment Ethan thought he knew why people bothered to climb up to such remote places. But he didn't think it in his head exactly. It was more like a knowing in a place between his throat and his belt. It was just there, something that had existed all along, but which Ethan had never noticed: an appreciation for something that could take his breath away.

"That's so beautiful," he said to Rufus.

He looked down at the dog.

Rufus stood with his head lowered, his hackles up. Ethan heard him growl deep in his throat, a strange rumbling that had never come out of his dog before.

"Rufus, what—"

Before he could even finish the question, Rufus charged. He took off down the trail. Then, once out of the narrow pass, he veered left and downhill, quickly disappearing over the side.

Ethan ran after him, desperately calling the dog's name. He didn't dare plunge down the edge of the steep and rocky slope, and he couldn't see where the dog had gone. But he could hear Rufus, and it made his heart pound. Because these were noises he had never heard before. Somewhere between a bark and a bellowing of sheer canine fear.

If it's so terrifying, run away from it, Ethan thought. *Don't run toward it!*

Just as that thought finished its route through Ethan's head, he saw his dog again, head low, running fast up the slope in his direction. Behind him, running much faster and closing the distance between them, was the very stuff of Ethan's worst nightmares.

A bear.

A full-grown, full-size bear.

A bear with a long snout and honey-colored, ragged fur, which probably made it a grizzly.

Ethan felt himself vacate his own body. He only vaguely felt himself stumble backward. It seemed as though he was watching the scene more from above, and less through his own eyes. His heel hit a rock and he fell onto his back on the trail, hurting himself on the bulk of his pack and dropping the shotgun.

He unclipped the strap of the pack and left it on the ground, stumbling to his feet. He did grab the shotgun, of course. Because he was about to need it.

He turned to see Rufus scramble back up onto the trail, not twenty feet away, moving fast in Ethan's direction. That was the moment when the full weight of the situation came to rest on Ethan, though he was far too panicked to register the details consciously. But the pattern was apparent. Rufus had smelled a bear. Charged the bear. Challenged the bear. Riled up the bear. Now the bear was charging in return, and Rufus was running to Ethan for protection. And bringing the angry beast along behind.

Ethan stumbled backward a few more steps and hit vertical stone, hard. There was no more room to stumble. He was back at the top of the narrow pass, hemmed in by sheer walls on both sides. He would have to run back down the trail into the smaller valley, back the way he had come. He looked in that direction. Willed his body to turn that way. Then he looked up to see it was already too late.

Rufus ran, panting, behind Ethan's legs, wedging himself between Ethan and the sheer stone wall of mountain. He stuck his head out from between Ethan's knees and bayed wildly at the bear, who was only a handful of loping paces away. It would be a matter of seconds before the monster caught them, and running didn't seem like the answer. Ethan instinctively knew he couldn't outrun the bear, not now. Not when it was this close. His only chance was to shoot.

He quickly wrapped one hand around the dog's muzzle to silence him. It helped, but not enough. The strange, strangled noises in Rufus's chest and throat continued.

And Ethan now had fewer seconds. Two or three seconds, maybe. If that. He shouldn't have wasted time trying to silence the dog. He should have fired the gun while he still had time.

In what felt like the last two or three seconds of his life, Ethan's head leaped farther away from the scene, from reality. His hands did not move as they should have, as he instructed them to do.

He had a trace of a disconnected thought: He'd just recently been complaining that Rufus never barked. Never protected him. *And this is the moment he chooses.*

Then it was too late. Too late even to raise the gun.

Ethan looked up and waited for his life to be over.

The bear stopped a few feet away, and reared up onto its hind legs. Ethan looked up, the sun glaring into his eyes over the beast's shoulder. He actually had to crane his neck to look up that high. Stretched up on its hind legs, the grizzly probably stood eight feet or higher.

Ethan felt the gun in his right hand. His finger was not on the trigger, but it needed to be. Fast.

The bear rocked from side to side and made a terrible noise. It wasn't a huge noise, at least not for a bear. It wasn't a full-on roar. More of a huffing. It seemed to come from deep in its chest and resonate through the massive expanse of its sinuses. Ethan could smell its fur. It smelled rank and musty, like a carpet that's been left dirty and damp for months. He could smell the stench of the bear's breath on each huff. There was something agitated and threatening about the way it rocked from side to side, blocking out the sun, then blinding Ethan as it unblocked the sun and allowed it to blast into Ethan's eyes again.

For the second time in his life, Ethan thought he was already dead. That he knew how it felt to be on the other side of that ending.

The bear was getting higher. Taller. Ethan had to crane his neck farther and farther to look up at the vast silhouette of its head. Then he realized the bear was not getting higher, but rather Ethan was getting lower. His knees were liquefying, giving way, allowing him to sink until he was more or less sitting on his dog.

Still another second ticked by, and it was not the end.

Shoot the gun, a voice in Ethan's head shouted.

But shoot it where? At the rocky trail in front of the bear, hoping to scare it away? Or directly into the living fur and flesh of the grizzly? And what if a shot at its feet did not scare it away? What if a shot into the bear did not kill it? Ethan had no idea what size pellets were loaded into each shotgun shell. It might only have been heavy enough shot to kill a rabbit or a bird.

What if firing the gun only made the bear madder?

Ethan saw and heard one huff that was greater than all the huffs that had come before it. The bear leaned in toward Ethan, who could feel the breath of the huff like a wind against his cheeks. It opened its mouth, pulling its lips away from those horrible teeth. One long fang was missing, or broken off.

Ethan's finger found the trigger, and he knew he had nothing to lose. He could try this and then die, or he could die without trying.

He aimed at the rocky trail in front of the bear's hind paws and squeezed the trigger.

The trigger didn't move. Didn't give at all.

Ethan looked down at the gun, wildly searching for the lever of the safety. He found it despite his panic, and flipped it off.

When he looked up again, the bear had dropped to all fours and turned its shoulder away. It looked around at Ethan—who was now sprawled on, and half crushing, his dog—and gave one final huff.

Then it turned its head away and took three unimaginably long strides toward the valley. It stopped. Looked over its shoulder again. Rose up onto its hind legs.

Ethan's finger found its way back to the trigger.

The bear dropped onto all fours and turned away a second time, loping down the trail toward the lakes. Every ten paces or so it stopped and looked back at Ethan and his dog. Then it rose. Rocked. Fell to all fours and loped farther away.

He felt Rufus wiggle out from under him, dropping Ethan's butt hard onto the rocky trail.

Ethan dissolved into trembling. Or maybe he'd been trembling all along but just hadn't had time to notice.

—

Ethan stumbled along, looking more at the sky and less at the place where his feet touched the trail. At times the stumbling became quite literal. Still, each time he managed to right himself and move on.

There was something robotic in his movements. Ethan could feel that, but didn't know how to change it, and was in no way motivated to try. He felt as though his true spirit, whatever essence of Ethan had animated his body in the past, was gone now. What moved him down the trail in its stead felt jerky, automated, and unemotional.

And there was a recurring noise. Something he kept hearing. As it got steadily closer, it began to sound like his name. Like someone calling his name over and over. But he couldn't seem to connect with any sense of what the word meant, or how he should respond to it. It reminded him of that moment when the phone is ringing in your sleep, and it's half waking you but you're half still dreaming, and you can hear it perfectly well but you can't remember what it means or what it wants you to do.

A hand touched his shoulder, and he shouted out a big sound, something from deep in his throat. It startled him so much that he fell over, part backward and part sideways. He landed on one hip, rolled over onto his butt, and looked up into the face of Sam. Sam was standing over Ethan, holding the reins of his mule Dora, who waited patiently behind him.

"Ethan?" Sam asked.

"Um," Ethan said. "Yeah."

"Where are you going?"

"Home," he said, pleased with how it sounded. As if he were right there inside his body and knew exactly what he was doing.

Sam helped him to his feet.

"What's wrong with you, buddy?" Sam asked, peering into his face.

"Wrong?"

"You look like you're drunk or something."

"Drunk?"

Sam sighed, and picked Ethan up. Just swung a big, beefy arm around Ethan's waist and lifted his feet off the ground. The next thing Ethan knew, he was perched on the bulky western saddle on top of Sam's mule. Sam let go and took one step back, as if to see how well Ethan would stay in place without help. But Ethan wasn't balanced, and he swung dangerously to the right. Dora had to take a wild step to one side and square her stance to compensate. Ethan shouted out that strange grunting noise again and grabbed the saddle horn.

Sam steadied Ethan with one hand. Then, when he seemed sure it was safe to let go, he began to rummage around in one of Dora's saddlebags. The bags were secured to the saddle behind where Ethan sat, and Ethan didn't dare turn around to look, afraid of unbalancing himself again.

A moment later he felt a canvas strap wrapped twice around his waist. When Sam tied it to the saddle horn it jerked Ethan's body forward uncomfortably.

Then they were moving. The mule had a rocking walk, jarring on each footfall, and Ethan could feel himself shifting slightly back and forth within the confines of the snug strap.

Sam walked ahead, and he didn't have hold of his mule in any way. She simply followed.

Ethan looked around to see if Rufus was still with them. He was. He trotted placidly behind, looking tired but not especially upset. Some very distant part of Ethan's brain marveled at that. Imagine being a dog and being able to leave an experience like that behind. Just come back to the moment. But it was a disconnected thought. Almost as if someone else were having it.

It was interrupted by Sam's voice. "Where were you going?"

"Home," Ethan said, wondering if it was only his imagination telling him he had established that already.

"I meant in the first place."

"Oh."

Ethan didn't answer the question, because he didn't understand it. He knew in a distant way that he *should* understand it. That it was simple enough. But he could make no sense of it. He furrowed his brow and decided the rocking of the mule's gait felt comforting. Then he tried to drag his mind back to the question, but he'd forgotten what it was.

"Why were you even out here?" Sam asked.

"Now that's a good question," Ethan said.

He didn't say it sardonically. It was an honest answer. He knew there had been a reason, some kind of thinking involved in his being out on the wilderness trails by himself. It wasn't even so much that he couldn't remember what he'd been thinking. More that he could no longer imagine why he'd found the collection of thoughts convincing. He wasn't sure why he'd ever listened to them in the first place, not to mention obeyed their directives.

In other words, he knew only that it had seemed like a good idea at the time. Which wasn't much to know.

—

Just as they crested the first pass—now the last pass between them and home—Sam attempted to talk to him again.

"Good thing you didn't go in any deeper than you did. There was a big grizzly sow down in that second valley. Twenty Lakes Valley, we call it. And not in a very good mood, either. The sow, I mean. Not the valley. She had some kind of thorn in her butt. Figuratively speaking. I thought she was going to charge me and Dora when we rode back through. She did, really, but it was only a false charge. She never got very close. She was big enough I thought she was a full-grown male. But it was a sow all right."

"What's a sow?" Ethan asked. Or heard himself ask, anyway.

He could feel his brain coming back slightly. Coming around. But he still felt half asleep.

"Female."

"I thought a sow was a female pig."

"That, too," Sam said. "Anyway, I'm glad I was the one to run into that lady, not you."

"Actually," Ethan said, "we met."

Sam stopped. Dora stopped. Ethan rocked forward in the saddle. He looked down to see Sam staring up into his face—as if deciding whether to trust Ethan's information.

"What happened? You come up on her and surprise her?"

Ethan shook his head. It still felt wobbly.

"The dog went after her," he said. "And vice versa."

"Oh, crap. You're lucky to be alive."

"Well, I had this shotgun," Ethan said.

But he held up both hands, and he did not have the shotgun. He had no idea where it had gone.

"How close she get to you?"

"She had one fang broken off. And really bad breath. And her fur stank like mold. That close."

"Damn."

Then no one said anything for a long time.

"Well, that explains a lot about your condition," Sam said, and started to walk again.

Dora followed.

As Ethan attempted to lean back in his tight lashings—because they were headed so steeply downhill—Sam shot one last sentence over his shoulder.

"Anything else about the experience you care to share?"

"Maybe later," Ethan replied.

Sam walked the rest of the way to the rented A-frame in a respectful silence. Dora followed like a faithful old dog.

—

Ethan sat on the couch, his knees pulled up to his chest, his arms wrapped around them and drawing them even closer. He kept his eyes on Sam, who was rummaging around in the cupboards of the A-frame's tiny kitchen.

"What are you looking for?" Ethan asked at last.

"Looking to see if your dad has any booze around the house."

Ethan snorted. It was a sound vaguely related to laughter. "I would think *I* was the one who needed a drink."

"Who do you think I want it for?"

That brought its own moment of silence.

Sam broke it.

"I know what you're thinking. You're underage. But whatever age you are, if you're out in the freezing weather or you're in shock, one or the other, I've found a good snort is useful. Think of it as medicinal. If nothing else, it might help stop the shaking."

Ethan looked down at himself, surprised to hear that he was shaking. Sam had been right about that. Ethan wondered how he could have been so unaware of something happening so close to home, so directly in the core of what should have been his being. Right in the spot where he was meant to live, but so often couldn't.

Meanwhile Sam was still talking.

"Hell, I was a lot younger than seventeen when I had my first snort. My daddy gave it to me. For snakebite."

"What does liquor do for snakebite?"

Sam stopped rummaging briefly. Looked up above his own head, as if considering the question for the first time. As if the answer must be on the ceiling. "Ah, hell. I don't know. Not much, I guess. Keeps the patient calm."

"Under the sink," Ethan told him.

What felt like thirty seconds later, a short, squat glass appeared in front of his face. In the bottom of it sat about two fingers of a thick-looking brownish liquid.

"Slug it down all at once if you can bring yourself to do it."

Ethan took the glass, watching it quake in his grip. Watching the liquid slosh up the sides of the glass and then coat it brown for an instant longer than he might have expected. He counted to three, tipped it back, and drained its contents all in one big swallow.

It exploded in his throat like fire and made his eyes water, but Ethan staunchly resisted the urge to cough. He wanted to drink like a grown-up. Like a man, not a little boy. Even if it *was* only one snort given as medicine for shock.

When the burn subsided, Ethan held as still as possible and felt the warmth of it move through his belly, and down the muscles at the core of his arms and legs.

"Now," Sam said. "What were you doing out there?"

"Oh," Ethan said. "Didn't you ask me that already?"

"Yeah. But I never got much in the way of an answer."

Silence.

"It would sound incredibly stupid," Ethan said.

"You were looking for your dad."

"Yeah."

Sam sighed and plunked down on the couch next to Ethan.

"That doesn't sound stupid," he said. "It sounds like a plan without much chance of success. But I figured that must be it. I can understand why you would want to do that. I mean, he's your dad. You love him."

"I hate him," Ethan said, marveling at how the shaking really was beginning to subside.

"Then why go look for him?"

Ethan kept his gaze firmly trained down to the rug. "Maybe I love him *and* hate him. Both. Is that possible?"

"Oh, yeah," Sam said, laughing something rueful out with the words. "It's more than possible. It happens all the time. Trust me. I've got two ex-wives. I know."

He rose to his feet, took the empty glass from Ethan, and carried it to the sink.

"I went by your house first," Ethan said. "I wanted to ask you to take me up there. But you were gone. I thought you had a paid customer. I thought you might be gone for days."

"No," Sam said.

Ethan waited for him to say more, but he never did. He felt the liquor warm him up inside. Sand off the rough edges. It made it easier to talk. It made it feel possible to exist.

"So why were *you* up there with Dora, then?"

"Same reason you were," Sam said, washing the glass under steaming water and carefully avoiding Ethan's eyes.

"I want to form our own search party," Ethan said.

"You're kidding."

"No. Why would I kid about a thing like that?"

"After the experience you just had?"

Ethan felt himself internally retreat again at the mention of the bear encounter. Even though the word "bear" was never uttered. For a moment he thought he was watching the scene more from the ceiling and less from his own body.

"If he's out there," Ethan said with the alcohol as fuel, "he's going to die really soon. I mean . . ." He stalled for a long time. "I guess I really mean if he's out there, there's like a ninety-something percent chance he's already . . . But if he's not . . ."

"Yeah, I get it," Sam said. "You're right about that. Time's running out for him. But . . ."

But then he never said but what.

"You don't think he is, either."

"Hard to know," Sam said.

"Part of you must have thought he was. You rode up there today."

"Yeah. Well. You kind of have to make your mistakes on the side of a person dying in the wilderness."

"Here's the thing," Ethan said, and it felt interesting to hear himself say it, because he was sure he didn't know what the thing was, and was curious to listen to himself and find out. "Nobody around here knows my dad. Except me. He's not the world's greatest guy. He's done a lot of really crappy things. He's hurt my mom and he's hurt me. But all the things he's done . . . they all kind of fit into one category. He does them to feel better about himself. To make himself feel more . . . well, I guess . . . like he's winning. To keep thinking he has the world on a string. But to take money out of the bank and walk out of the house without saying a word to me and just leave me here to wonder where he is and if he's ever coming back . . . there's no sense to that. There's nothing in it for him. All he had to do was call my mom and tell her to arrange my transportation back to New York. All he had to do was leave a note. There's nothing for him to gain by not leaving a note."

Sam came back and sat on the couch near Ethan, looking worried and more than a little bit sad. Ethan hated it when people were sad on his behalf. Even though that was most of the time these days.

"So what you're saying is . . ." But then Sam couldn't seem to finish the sentence.

"He's out there. I just know it. And if I'm wrong . . ." Then it was Ethan who couldn't wrap up a thought.

"If you're wrong," Sam interjected, "at least you get the most incredible experience of your life. You get to go out into that mind-blowing wilderness. You get a full tour of the Blythe River Range. That's no small thing, you know. That's kind of its own reward."

Ethan wasn't at all sure he agreed, but he forced such thoughts away again.

"The thing is . . . ," he said, and then he paused for a long time. Wondering if he even knew. ". . . I don't think I'm wrong."

—

"You sure you're going to be okay here on your own?" Sam asked. He was lingering by the door but not looking much inclined to use it.

"So long as I don't have to go outside."

"Got food?"

"Yeah, I still have some of that chicken stew with dumplings that Jone brought me. It's good."

The mention of Jone's name seemed to knock something loose in Sam. Before the older man even spoke, Ethan knew Sam had been sitting on something for a while, something he'd wanted to say but wasn't saying. In fact, Ethan realized he'd known it all along.

"Now that you mention Jone . . ."

"Yeah?"

"A big search party is better than a small one. Bigger is better."

"You want to ask Jone if she'll come with us?"

"I was thinking it might be better if *you* did. You know. Given our history. Or lack of it. Given the fact that she knows I wish we had a history. Or a current . . . Let me start over. She'd probably think I was just making an excuse to get to know her better."

"Are you?" Ethan asked, surprised to hear himself ask a brave question. Especially at a time like this, when he felt even smaller and less confrontational than usual.

"No," Sam said firmly. "Not *just*. More really is better in a search party. I'm not making that up."

"What can an extra person do?"

"All kinds of things. Stay with the horses if a couple of us go off on foot. Hold a rope if we need to go up or down a cliff."

Ethan's stomach tipped sickeningly at the first descriptions of what they might be required to do out there. Sam seemed to notice that, or sense it.

"And she's not afraid of bears," he said.

"How can anybody not be afraid of bears?"

"Don't know what to tell you, buddy. She's not afraid of anything. I'd almost go so far as to say bears are afraid of her. If there was a showdown between Jone and a bear, I'd put my money on Jone. In fact, I'd feel sorry for the bear. I'd try to call the fight because the poor bear was overmatched."

"Are you exaggerating?" Ethan asked. "It sounds like you're exaggerating. She can't exactly beat them in a fight with her bare hands."

"No. Not with her hands. With a rifle. She's good with a rifle. Like, legendary good. One day a couple years ago she was over on the reservation on the other side of the foothills. Seeing her great-grandchildren. She was walking in the woods with them, picking mushrooms. This big grizzly charged them. They charge fast when they charge. You don't get much time. She had probably something like five or six seconds to fix it, or somebody was going to get hurt, if not worse. Just right in those few seconds she fired a shot into the dirt in front of the bear, and when it kept coming she chambered another round and dropped it in its tracks. Most people hesitate at that moment because they'd rather get out without killing the bear. But she didn't have time for any hesitation. She knew what she had to do and she did it."

"Okay," Ethan said, finding comfort in the thought of such a person as an ally. He didn't want a bear to die, either. But if it came right down to a choice of the bear or him . . . If he'd had such a sharpshooter with him earlier that day he'd sure as hell have called for her to pull the trigger. "I'll ask her. When do we leave?"

"First light in the morning."

"What do I bring?"

"Not as much as you'd think. Just your personal items. Toothbrush. Change of underwear and socks. A hat. Sunscreen. Good sturdy boots or shoes. I've got dehydrated meals and water filters. Tents, sleeping bags, rain gear, you leave all that to me. You just bring what you'd pack to go away for a couple or three days, only less. You know. Just the bare bones. Just what you can't live without."

He swung the door open. Ethan got up off the couch and walked to the door as if to politely see him out. The late afternoon sun blasted into Ethan's eyes. In the glare he saw Dora waiting patiently, head down, tied to nothing. Her reins were simply lying in the dirt a foot in front of her nose and two feet below it.

"This's a good thing you're doing," Sam said.

"Me?"

"Yeah, you. Who else?"

"You're the one who's taking me up there just to be nice."

"Look. What I'm saying is . . . I want to say this the right way so's not to insult you. It doesn't escape my notice that you're not the most steely-nerved little guy on the planet. And getting false-charged by a grizzly can rattle the steadiest nerves ever built. I just feel like the fact that you're willing to get up and get out there again tomorrow . . . I just think it says a lot about you as a person."

Only because we're bringing someone who's legendary good with a gun and doesn't mind dropping a bear in its tracks, Ethan thought. But then he realized that wasn't entirely true, because he'd been willing to go before he knew about Jone and her rifle. Hell, that morning he'd been willing to go alone. But he didn't feel the slightest bit brave, and he didn't know what to do with the compliment, so he just looked down at the threshold.

Sam walked away across the A-frame's porch, the heels of his cowboy boots banging on the wood planks.

A moment later he stopped. Turned to face Ethan again. Ethan would have liked to see the look on the older man's face, but the late sun was still glaring into his eyes.

"Thing is," Sam said, "I wouldn't be able to live with myself if I encouraged you too much. You know. Gave you false hopes. I can take you all over that mountain range without your getting hungry or thirsty or lost. And Jone can keep you safe from bears and wolves and mountain lions. But we're not professional searchers. I don't really know what we can do that they didn't do better already."

"I know," Ethan said.

"Our chances of finding him . . . even if he's out there . . ."

"I know," Ethan said again.

"You just want to feel like you tried," Sam said. It wasn't a question.

"Exactly."

"Okay. We can do that. We can try."

Then he walked back to his mule. He gathered up Dora's reins and mounted smoothly, neck-reining her head around toward home.

A minute or two later Ethan would look back on their conversation and consider it strange that Sam's mention of bears and his own thoughts about them hadn't tipped him to what he was forgetting. But for whatever reason—probably owing to exhaustion and upset—they hadn't.

It wasn't until Sam and Dora were just a dot on the road, halfway between the A-frame and their own home, that it hit Ethan. He still had no bear spray.

"Sam!" he shouted.

No response.

He ran out into the front yard, Rufus trotting behind, and screamed the name three more times. But Sam was too far away to hear.

Ethan looked down at his dog.

"Well, that's it," he said. Rufus cocked his head, listening without comprehending. "No way I'm going down to Jone's with no bear spray. I'm just not doing it. When Sam comes by in the morning, he'll have to take me down there to ask."

They'd be less likely to get a yes in the morning, on short notice. Ethan knew that. But he couldn't imagine how to fix it. And even if she said yes, they'd get off to a late start. But all those details seemed hopelessly out of Ethan's control.

He walked back inside, calling Rufus to follow, determined to heat up some stew and leave this day behind for good. It was all he still felt able to do.

—

Just as he was putting his bowl to soak in the sink, Ethan heard a strong rapping on the door. His heart jumped, and he felt immediately panicked and unsteady, as if the grizzly sow had found her way to his front door to take up the argument just where they'd left off.

Rufus woofed once, deep in his throat, which Ethan thought was interesting. Because the dog never had before. Maybe Rufus hadn't left the events of the day behind as completely as Ethan had thought.

As he walked to answer the door, he told himself it was likely only Sam. Just Sam coming to tell him one more thing to bring along.

He swung the door wide and looked up into the face of his neighbor Jone. She was wearing a loose pullover jacket-shirt that looked to be made of some kind of thin, soft suede. Deerskin, maybe. It had fringe. She wore her hair down, framing her face and shoulders in white, like a sudden overwhelming snowfall.

"Oh," Ethan said. "That's good. That you're here. I needed to talk to you."

"Mind if I come in?"

Her voice sounded softer than usual. Less combative and urgent. Ethan briefly wondered—more on a feeling level than as thoughts in his head—if she had really dropped a bear in its tracks with a rifle, or if that was just one of those local legends. The kind that gets bigger and more dramatic every time someone retells it.

"Sure," Ethan said, even though her presence made his heart drum and his voice squeak in his throat. "Please do."

She walked into the A-frame's tiny living room and looked around as though she'd never looked around the place before. Then she sat down on the couch, emitting a cross between a grunt and a sigh.

Rufus wiggled over and set his head in her lap. A little cautiously, Ethan thought. With a dash of subservience. The way anyone in his right mind would approach Jone. Ethan expected her to roughly push the dog away again. Instead she placed her calloused hands on both sides of the dog's head and stroked back, in keeping with the direction of the fur. Rufus relaxed and half closed his eyes.

"Thanks again for the chicken stew," Ethan said. "I just had another helping. It's good."

"Why didn't you come down to my house?"

"When?"

"Just now. You said you needed to talk to me."

"Oh. Right. That. I don't have bear spray."

"Lots of people walk from one house to another without it," Jone said, as if it should go without saying.

"Maybe not if they'd been charged by a grizzly bear that very day."

A long silence. Ethan was surprised by it. He thought a charging grizzly sounded like a pretty good opening for further conversation.

Just as he became convinced she would not address his comment in any way, Jone asked, "You okay?"

"Yeah," he said. Then he added, "On the outside at least."

But Ethan didn't figure Jone would want to talk about the inside of him. And he was right.

"What did you want to talk to me about?" she asked, still stroking the dog's ridiculous ears.

"You first. You go first with what you came here to say."

Jone sighed. She looked only at the face of Rufus. Not at Ethan.

"I think their decision to call off the search was wrong," she said. "In fact . . . I think it sucks."

Ethan waited. To see if that was a complete thought. If it was all she'd come to say.

"Thank you," he said.

"I know all the details they factored in. I heard it all. Yeah, it's questionable. I get that. But let's say there's a ninety-nine percent chance he took off. That means there's a one percent chance he was out in those mountains. Then let's say there's a ninety-nine percent chance he was out there, but now he's not still alive. Sorry to be blunt, but I'm sure

I'm not telling you anything you haven't thought of on your own these past few days. So then, worst case, that adds up to a one percent of one percent chance he needs finding. In my book, given that situation, you search."

"Well . . . in fairness to them . . . they searched."

"Guess I mean given that situation you search and you don't stop."

"I don't suppose we'd ever get them to see it that way," Ethan said, his heart calming. It was strangely comforting to have this human hurricane on his side.

"No," Jone said. "I don't suppose so, either."

Then neither said anything for a strangely long time. It might even have been a full minute.

Ethan opened his mouth to ask his enormous favor. He never got the chance.

"I was thinking maybe we form our own search party," Jone said.

Ethan was surprised. By, well . . . everything. By the idea that some monumental task could be so much easier and less stressful than expected. By his inability to answer—to even know where or how to begin addressing what she'd said.

He found one tiny flaw in the fabric of his stunned confusion. One curiosity that could be addressed. For starters.

"Who's we?" he asked her.

"I'd love to say you and me. That would be my preference for a number of different reasons. But it's a lot of ground to cover on foot. So I'm thinking we have to ask Sam to take us up there on his horses, and with a pack mule or two. Save a lot of wear and tear on us, and it'll allow us to get around faster. Time being of the essence in a situation like this. But I didn't want to ask him until I talked to you. Until I asked if you were up to the task."

"You don't have to ask him," Ethan said. "You don't have to ask either one of us. Sam already agreed to take me up there. We're leaving at first light tomorrow. I was supposed to ask if you'd go." Ethan noticed, in his peripheral vision, Jone's eyes coming up to seek out his face. "Because more people are better in a search party, he says. And because you're good with bears. Legendary good."

Jone snorted. Maybe a laugh. Maybe just a derisive snort. Or some sort of hybrid.

"I expect the bears would disagree," she said. "The bears would be more inclined to say I'm bad with bears. I don't like to kill anything. Specially if I don't have to. But if I have to . . . well, let's just say I made my peace with it. Apologized to the spirit of the bear, the way the Native Americans do. Though I must say the spirit of that bear has yet to apologize to me for charging my great-grandkids."

"You're not Native American?"

"No," she said.

"I thought you were."

"Why would you think that?"

"Oh. Right. Why did I? Something Sam said. Oh. I know. He said you had family on the Blythe River Reservation, over on the other side of the foothills."

Jone's eyes narrowed, and Rufus pulled his head back from her lap and slunk away.

"Thought he didn't tell you anything about me."

"Oh. Well, that was just today he told me that," Ethan said. Even though it was only half true.

"My late husband was a member of the Blythe River Tribe. He was one hundred percent native. I'm zero percent."

"Oh," Ethan said. "I'm sorry he's gone."

"Thanks."

"How long?"

"Long time. Too long."

Then the conversation seemed to die a hard and painful death.

An awkward span of time passed.

"Well," she said, placing her hands on her knees and levering to her feet. "This's a good time to get a few belongings packed and get ourselves to bed early. Since we're leaving at first light. You know Marcus?"

"No, ma'am. Jone."

"He lives next door to me. Doesn't get out much, and when he does he heads to town. He moved here to be close to those mountains. But he must like the idea of them better than the actual reality of the thing. Because he doesn't go up there much, if he goes at all. But Sam's right about the safety in numbers. You know. With a thing like this. So I'll see if I can talk him into going. Not sure how much use he'll be, but I guess I just feel the way Sam does—ha! How often does that happen? Mark this day on your calendar. I just feel like another body is good. More is good. If I show up with Marcus at first light, it worked. If not, not so much. We'll just have to work with what we got."

She moved off in the direction of the door.

"Thank you," Ethan said.

It wasn't a tossed-off comment. It wasn't a perfunctory thank you. It was genuine. Big. Fully felt.

She turned and looked into his eyes again. His gaze quickly flickered away.

"No worries," she said. "He's your father."

"He is," Ethan said, careful to weed out any commentary, express or implied, as to whether that was good news in his mind.

"You love him," she said. Not a question.

"I do and I don't."

"What part of you doesn't?"

"The part of me that hates him, I guess."

"Right," Jone said, as if Ethan had said nothing surprising. "Parents can be like that. But if he's out there, we want him back. Anyway. Right? Right. Not that we're all that likely to work magic out there. But we can try. And if he's not out there, or we don't find him . . . or we don't find him in time . . . well, anyway, at least we tried." On that note, she opened the door. "Get some sleep," she said. "You'll need it."

Then she was gone.

—

Ethan never got any sleep. He might have dozed for half an hour sometime between two and three a.m. Or maybe he was only half asleep during that brief time.

He knew what Jone had said was true—that he would need the good night's sleep. In fact, he knew it too well. The more pressure he put on himself regarding the importance of sleep, the more that very pressure kept him awake.

And those were only the pressures that had nothing whatsoever to do with the possibility of more angry bears. And hadn't somebody mentioned mountain lions and wolves? And scaling cliffs while somebody holds you on a rope?

Every twenty minutes or so Rufus, who was up on the bed with Ethan, slipped into what appeared to be the same disturbing dream. His paws twitched, his nose twitched. He made yipping noises, muffled deep in his throat. His hackles rose, and he growled faintly.

It wasn't hard for Ethan to imagine what he was dreaming. To know that even dogs—much as they live in the present and leave the past behind—can't just turn their backs on an experience like the one Ethan and Rufus had survived earlier that day.

Chapter Twelve: Not Forgiving

Four days after his father disappeared

Sam showed up in the dark, about an hour before sunrise. Ethan knew he was coming by the sound of a small herd of hooves, and the flicker of a flashlight or a headlamp along the road. Ethan was sitting at the kitchen table eating cereal with no milk. He'd run out of milk. He put the cereal on the floor for Rufus—who had already been fed—to finish. He ran to the door.

He stepped out onto the porch to see Sam riding down his dirt driveway on a big horse he'd never seen before, or never noticed. He couldn't see the horse's color in the dark. Behind Sam and his horse he saw Dora the mule, then another horse he didn't recognize, only slightly smaller than Sam's, then the dreaded Rebar, laden with canvas packs. Ethan wasn't sure if the animals were all tied to each other like a train, but he thought they were, because all of them except Sam's big horse made the same lifting, straining movements with their heads, as though something tugged at them on every step.

Sam reined his horse to a halt in the middle of Ethan's yard, and the horse and mule train bunched up behind them and then stopped.

"You sleep?" he asked Ethan.

"Not so much, no."

"You'll regret that as the day wears on. But nothing we can do about it now. You have a good big breakfast?"

"Yes," Ethan said, though it wasn't true. He'd had maybe ten bites of cereal before feeding the rest to the dog.

"Good. You'll need it. We'll ride straight till lunch and that's a long way from now. You talk to Jone?"

"Yeah."

"She coming?"

"Yeah."

"Good."

He dismounted. Both of his hands were free, Ethan saw. The light was a headlamp protruding from just under the rim of Sam's cowboy hat. Ethan walked to him in his bare feet. Reached out to pet his horse's nose. It was velvety soft.

"Who do I ride?" he asked Sam.

"You're on Dora."

"Why am I the only one on a mule? Why can't I ride a horse?"

"I did that special for you. Dora's the calmest ride I got. You're better off on a mule on a mountain trail. They don't spook much. If something does spook 'em, they're more likely to stand their ground than run. And they're more sure-footed than a horse. What do they use to take people and supplies down to the bottom of the Grand Canyon? A horse train? Or a mule train?"

Ethan stood a moment, shifting slightly from foot to foot because the dirt was cold.

"Mules, I guess."

"Damn right mules. Because horses are more likely to spook right off the edge of a cliff."

"Uh-oh. But if we're all tied together . . ." Ethan paused, picturing Sam's horse spooking off a cliff and dragging Dora right off with him.

"We won't be. Not up there. I'll have Rebar on a breakaway. The rest of you'll have to ride for yourselves. For just that reason. You never want a situation where a whole team gets pulled over. Some two-thousand-foot drop-offs up there with a trail just about wide enough for four hooves. Trust me. Dora's a good bet."

Ethan felt a strange and unpleasant feeling in his stomach, as if he might be about to see his scant breakfast again.

"This is starting to sound . . ."

Sam tried to look him square in the face, but it caused the light of his headlamp to glare into Ethan's eyes, blinding him. Sam quickly put one hand over the light, then fumbled with the switch and turned it off. He dropped his hands to his sides again, and they stood together in the pitch-dark, predawn morning.

As his ability to see gradually returned, in his peripheral vision Ethan was aware of stars. A staggering, stunning array of stars.

The older man seemed to be taking time to gather his words carefully.

"It's the wilderness," Sam said. Sober and deep voiced. "I know the area, and Jone knows it. And that's good. That'll help keep you safe. But I'm not gonna lie to you, Ethan. It's not Disneyland up there. The ride is not on a track. Never any guarantees in the wilderness. You up for this? Think carefully and only say yes if you mean it. I need you to keep your head on straight up there. We'll be there to help you, but you need to work with us. So what do you say?"

"Let me just go put some shoes on," he said.

Then, halfway back to the porch, he stopped and looked back at Sam again.

"If mules are better than horses on a mountain trail, why do you have mostly horses and just a couple of mules? Why don't you have all mules?"

"Because everybody feels just the way you do," Sam said. "Everybody wants to ride a horse."

—

It was maybe ten minutes later when Ethan heard sharp voices outside, in the A-frame's front yard. Not yelling exactly, but a serious discussion.

He had his shoes on, and his teeth brushed, and was stuffing his baseball cap into his little bookbag-style backpack, because it felt silly to wear it in the dark.

He stepped out onto the porch to see what was going on.

He saw three figures standing near the stock train in the dark. Which must have meant Marcus had said yes, and was coming with them. Ethan figured that was a good thing. Sam seemed to have other ideas.

"You said more was better," Jone's distinctive voice said. "I think more is better. Everybody knows more is better."

"Depends on the team," Sam said, just at the edge of raising his voice. "Depends on the person. Their wilderness experience. What's another person going to add to the team if he's got no wilderness experience?"

Meanwhile the dark figure who must have been Marcus said nothing in his own defense.

"Ethan's got no wilderness experience," Jone said, raising her voice to match Sam's. "And we're taking *him*."

"Well, of course Ethan. It's his father."

A new voice spoke in the dark.

"Okay, screw this. I know when I'm not wanted. Forget it. I was doing this as a favor. You don't want me, fine. I'm better off at home."

The dark figure of Marcus tramped down the driveway.

Jone's head followed his retreat, then turned back to Sam.

"You going after him, or what?"

"Why? We're better off without him. He's an actor. And a surfer. Not exactly the skill set we need on the trail."

"You said a bigger team was better. Did you mean that? Or did you just want me to come along because it's me?"

Ethan could just barely see Sam tip his cowboy hat back and scratch his bare scalp. He couldn't see the scalp, but he knew the details from memory.

"I'd have to tack up another horse. I'd have to repack the big mule with extra food and another sleeping bag."

"So don't just stand there," she said.

Sam sighed. Then he fumbled with something near the saddle of his big horse. He came up with a loose rope and handed it to Jone.

"Here, hold this," he said. "I'll go after him." He didn't sound the least bit happy.

He swung into the saddle and rode away down the driveway, urging his horse into a trot on the hard ground.

Jone watched him leave for a few seconds. Then she led the stock train over to Ethan's porch. She stopped in a glow of light from the A-frame's front windows and tied the rope to the porch railing.

She sat next to Ethan's legs with a sigh. Ethan dropped into a sitting position nearly shoulder to shoulder with her. Except her shoulders were higher. Everybody's shoulders were higher.

"Hell of a start to get off to," she said.

"I'm not sure what Sam's upset about."

"Everybody's got an agenda," she said. "I know you're more than a little gun-shy around wild animals, but they're pretty straightforward, let me tell you that right now. Compared to us. We're the ones you got to look out for. The least predictable animal in any wilderness setting is us. People."

Ethan wasn't sure what to make of that. So he just sat. For a time neither spoke. Ethan watched one edge of the sky lighten, turning a steely color and fading the stars at the horizon.

"Oh," Ethan said. "I have to go get Rufus."

"I wouldn't," she said.

"What do you mean?"

"I wouldn't bring him on this. He's a city dog. Right? You don't want him going off hunting and getting lost. You don't want him getting under the horses' hooves. And we'll be covering a lot of miles. The horses and mules are used to it. They're in shape. They also have hard feet. How many miles can that dog walk before he gets footsore? I'd leave him home if I were you."

Ethan's face and gut tingled, and he wondered how many more of these awakenings lay in store for him. It seemed as though every time someone spoke he learned something new about this trip. Something that made him feel like a fool for ever thinking he should go.

"I have to take him, though. Who'll take care of him while I'm gone? There's nobody."

"Couldn't you just leave him a really big bowl each of food and water?"

"But he has to get out. And I can't leave him out. He'll get eaten by something. Coyotes or something."

"Hmm," Jone said. "Right. I guess I'm spoiled by having a litter box to fall back on. Well . . . I suppose we could try bringing him. Have a feeling he'll be trouble, though. Does Sam know he's coming?"

"I think so. I mean . . . I didn't say so. I thought it went without saying."

"We'll see what he says when he gets back."

Ethan made up his mind in that moment. If Rufus couldn't go, then Ethan couldn't go. And the moment he made the decision, it became a lifeline to him. If Sam said Rufus couldn't go, then Ethan was off the hook. He'd have a different reason not to go. A reason that was not fear.

He bit his thumbnail and said nothing. And Jone said nothing. They just sat on the porch together and watched dawn gather itself to make its scheduled appearance.

—

It was still predawn and not completely light when Sam and Marcus came riding back. Marcus looked about thirty, with shaggy hair that extended well into the collar of his shirt, and a pretty-boy face. He rode a horse that looked a little too small for him. He wasn't a big guy, maybe five nine or five ten and wiry thin, but the horse—a light-gray Appaloosa with spots—looked more like a big pony. He was built heavy and solid, though. Ethan figured it was okay. Ethan figured Sam wouldn't have put Marcus on the pony-horse if it wasn't okay.

Sam's horse was a big bay. Huge, really. Almost as though he had a little bit of draft horse mixed in.

The two rode into the yard several dozen feet apart, not looking at each other or speaking.

"Well, come on," Sam said. "On your feet, everybody. We're behind schedule."

Jone stood. "Don't you have to repack that mule?"

"Nah," Sam said. "I gave Marcus saddlebags with some extra stuff."

"Did you apologize to him? For not being very neighborly about accepting his offer to come along?"

Sam glanced over at Marcus but said nothing. Then he looked away. Down at his own saddle horn. Ethan took it as a "no."

Jone walked over to Sam's big bay and said a few words. Ethan couldn't hear most of them, but he thought he made out the word "dog." He trotted over to be closer to the life-altering conversation.

"I don't see what it'll hurt," Sam said. "Might hurt the dog. Won't hurt us any. He'll just have to buck up and learn as he goes. Get in shape as he goes. He's young, right?"

"I don't know," Jone said, and turned to Ethan. She seemed surprised to find him so close. "How old is your dog?"

For one shameful moment, Ethan was tempted to lie. To say Rufus was ten. Or twelve. But his mouth opened and out came the truth.

"He's two and a half."

"Aw, hell," Sam said. "He's a dog. He'll be fine. Just keep him away from Rebar when we're in camp, Ethan. On the trail Rebar'll be focused on his work. But don't let those two mix it up during the breaks. Now come on, guys. We're burning daylight."

It seemed strange to Ethan that anybody would feel as though he was burning through something that had yet to arrive.

He ran to the house to let Rufus out.

"You pack dog food?" Sam called after him.

"Oh. No. I forgot."

"Grab a bag of dry. Enough for three days at least. And more than you'd normally feed him. You can put it in Dora's saddlebags."

—

His team was mounted and halfway to the road, as if they planned to ride away without him. Dora stood near the porch, her reins in the dirt.

Ethan grabbed his backpack and began stuffing the plastic bag of kibble inside.

"No, leave the pack," Sam called. "Put everything in the saddlebags."

While he did, his team milled slowly toward the road. It made Ethan feel panicky and desperate.

The saddlebags were a sun-faded blue nylon, with zippers that had obviously been crudely replaced, and a tear that had been stitched by hand. Ethan quickly filled them with kibble, socks and underwear, toothbrush and comb. Then he straightened up to see the rest of the team sitting their horses in the road.

"Well, come on," Sam said. "What're you waiting for?"

Ethan wondered how many times that day he would find himself in this situation. Called upon, even hurried, to do something he did not know how to do.

"I have no idea how to get up on this . . . ," he shouted, ". . . mule," he said more quietly.

It was Jone who rode back into the yard. She was on a tall, lanky chestnut horse who looked like a relative of the crazy yearlings, with a white blaze on its face.

Jone stopped the chestnut horse close to Ethan.

"Gather up the reins," she said.

She didn't sound like she was in a hurry, or pressuring him, so Ethan breathed for what felt like the first time in a long time.

He picked up Dora's reins from the dirt.

"Now loop them over her head."

Ethan followed the direction.

"Now get a good hold on them with your left hand. Right in front of the saddle. And take a piece of her mane with them in that same hand. That way you won't accidentally yank on her mouth while you're swinging up."

Oh dear God, Ethan thought. *I'm really doing this. I'm really going.* Meanwhile he felt his hand grip the reins and a clump of Dora's mane.

"Now put your left foot up in the stirrup."

He did. It wasn't too hard a reach, because Dora was stocky but not tall.

"Now grab hold of the saddle horn with your right hand. And don't hesitate. Just swing up there. Commit to it and get it done. Swing your leg over in one big movement."

Ethan paused briefly for something like a tiny prayer. Even though he never prayed, and wasn't sure he believed in anything that would or could listen. It was a defining moment, and he knew it. If Jone had to get down and push up on his butt to get him up into that saddle, it would be an enormous humiliation. It would only prove to everyone, himself included, that he had no business doing this.

He closed his eyes and swung. And landed neatly, and not too hard, on the saddle on Dora's back. He pulled a muscle up through his right leg, one buttock, and his lower back. But damn it, he was up there. He opened his eyes again. The ground looked pretty far down considering she was a small mule. He fumbled to get his foot into the other stirrup by feel.

"Good," Jone said. "Now come on."

Then they were under way. Riding off toward the mountains. And it was too late to change his mind. It was all just happening, and it was too late.

—

Ethan had been worried about revisiting the pass where he'd encountered the bear. Worried what kind of reaction would be created by the fear triggered in that location.

He needn't have.

He should have worried about a whole different set of issues.

Sam steered the team to the left at a trail intersection, shortly after entering the wilderness. The trail led sharply uphill, gaining maybe two thousand feet, narrowing as it rose.

About halfway up it, Ethan could see the valleys below, but he quickly learned not to look down.

The sky was a dramatic blue now, with clouds that looked too white and dense and three-dimensional to be real. Like another set of mountains in the sky. Now and then the horses and mules had to step over—or wade through—streams of water running down onto the trail and then pitching over the cliff into the valley. The narrower the trail got, the more the water fell on them like rain as they rode through. The sound of small waterfalls seemed to follow them along.

Ethan looked up ahead to see Sam riding lead, in front of Marcus, with binoculars in one hand, scanning the rocks and trails and crannies below, tugging Rebar along behind the big bay. Ethan turned and looked back to see Jone riding behind him, also searching with binoculars.

It made Ethan feel useless. Because he wasn't even searching through binoculars. He was just along for the ride. He looked past Jone for Rufus, comforted to see the dog still following behind.

"Wouldn't the searchers have seen him if he could be seen from this trail?" he asked Jone.

"Yeah. Probably. We're grabbing at straws here, in case you didn't know. Hoping he might've dragged himself out to a more visible location since then, or that he maybe can be seen by horseback but not by plane. I don't know what else to tell you, kid. We're just doing what we can."

Ethan faced forward again, still careful not to look over the edge of the cliff. "Dad!" he called out. Big volume.

"Noah!" Sam called.

They'd developed a rhythm to it. Ethan would start, then one other member of the team would follow. Like an echo, but with one obvious difference. And not always the same team member every time. It wasn't any rotation they'd discussed in advance. It just seemed to work itself out.

Nobody figured Noah was about to call back, exactly. But there was no reason not to try. If nothing else it would serve as fair warning for the bears.

"Why did you decide to come?" he asked Marcus. Partly because he didn't know Marcus at all, and figured he would be more comfortable if he did. Partly because it was better than focusing on the drop-off.

For a time, no answer. Dora was tramping along with her nose nearly up against the tail of the Appaloosa, who didn't seem to mind or even notice.

Then Marcus turned his head.

"Who, me?"

"Yeah."

"You don't want me here, either?"

"No! I do! Definitely. I was just thinking it was nice of you. You don't know me or my dad. It was nice of you to offer to come. I was only wondering what made you decide."

"Let's see," he said over his shoulder. As if there were just so many reasons to sort through. Also as if he weren't enthusiastic about any of them. "I did move here to do stuff like this. I had this settlement. Some money from a legal settlement when I lived in L.A. I figured it was enough to keep me someplace for a couple of years. I asked myself what I really wanted to do. Where I wanted to be. I always wanted to be a serious outdoor person. A mountain man. But I've been here for seven months. And I've only been up these trails twice. Seems like a waste. That's what Jone said, anyway. That I only had just so much time I could afford to live here. And that it was a shame to waste it."

Then Marcus looked forward again.

Ethan looked up to the crest of the trail and worried briefly about what was on the other side. A flat expanse of trail would be nice. But Ethan didn't think it was realistic to expect it.

Marcus's pony-horse slowed going through a stream, and Dora didn't. She bumped the Appy in the tail with her nose, and this time he minded. This time he jumped.

"Keep that mule back," Marcus said. "Will ya?"

"Sorry," Ethan said.

They rode on in silence. Ethan felt compelled to break it.

"Was it the bears?"

He had to speak up to be heard over the waterfalls, and the distance he had been asked to keep from Marcus's Appaloosa pony.

"Was what the bears?" Marcus asked over his shoulder.

"Is that why you only came up here twice?"

"No," Marcus said. "I brought bear spray. I never saw one. I didn't think too much about bears."

Then Marcus said no more, and Ethan wasn't sure if he should press the issue. He wanted to know if Marcus had been afraid. If he was still afraid. If Ethan was not the only one on this search team who felt overwhelmed by the danger of what they were attempting. But most people didn't readily admit to being afraid, he figured, and it probably wasn't a welcome question to ask.

"Dad!" he called again.

"Noah!" This time Jone echoed it.

Just below the crest of the trail, just as Ethan was sure the conversation was over, Marcus turned his head and spoke again.

"The first time I came out here, it hailed. Big hail. Like the size of . . . well, I almost said walnuts, but that would be exaggerating. More like macadamia nuts. Doesn't sound like much, but they come down hard. And they hurt. I was in that valley with all the lakes. The sky had been solid blue when I left. Not a cloud in the sky. Then the weather just turned on a dime. There were no trees, no rock overhangs. All I could do was crouch down and cover my head. I put my pack over my head and neck, but the hail kept hitting my hands, and it really stung. Then when the hail finally stopped, it was sheeting rain and a big wind came up. The temperature dropped maybe twenty degrees. I had this jacket I thought was waterproof but I guess it was only water resistant. It soaked through to my skin, and I was shaking, and I thought I'd be hypothermic before I could get myself home.

"Second time I came out here I got up on the big pass and this dry lightning started, and it was heading right for me. I was running to get down off the pass, get someplace less exposed. I was counting the seconds between the thunder and the lightning, and it was getting shorter, and then there was nothing to count. I could feel my hair stand up. That's not a good sign."

A long silence. Sam and his bay gelding had almost reached the crest of the trail, Sam still scanning with his binoculars. Ethan could feel poor Dora puffing for breath underneath him. He wanted to stop and give her a rest, but he couldn't stop unless everybody else did.

He looked around again for Rufus, who was dutifully bringing up the rear.

"It's not that I thought it would always be rain or hail or lightning," Marcus said. "I know there are lots of nice days in the mountains. It just reminds you who's in charge. You know? Nature is not what you might call predictable. And it's not forgiving. It doesn't care about us. The lightning is gonna go where it wants to go whether you're about to get fried by it or not. The wilderness just has this way of reminding you that you're powerless. And that what you want doesn't matter. We always think we're so smart and strong, but nature always gets the last laugh."

Then Dora crested the high point of the trail, and Ethan looked ahead to see . . . not what he had hoped for. More, higher mountains. A trail that flattened out for maybe a hundred feet, if that, then rose again. Even more extreme drop-offs.

I don't feel smart and strong, he thought. He wondered if that would save him from the hard lessons. Probably not. Probably nature didn't care about your confidence level, either.

He thought of his father, running up here day after day. Thought of the look on Sam's face when Ethan had tried to describe his father's running regimen. "That's pretty extreme," Sam had said. Or words to that effect.

Now that he was seeing the place with his own eyes, Ethan understood for the first time how extreme it really was.

He wondered how much of a lesson the wilderness had taught Noah Underwood. How much of a last laugh nature had enjoyed at his father's expense.

"Dad!" he called out.

"Noah!" Marcus called after.

—

They rode around a bend, and a small mountain lake came into view. It looked green, probably because it was shallow and had grass or some other kind of vegetation on its bottom. It also looked blue and white, because it was glassy-calm on this windless morning and reflected the sky.

Sam reined his big gelding to a halt, and the horses and mules bunched up behind him and then stopped.

"Let's take a quick break here," Sam called.

Ethan was happy to dismount. Partly because he wanted to get his hat out of the saddlebag, to keep the sun out of his eyes and help with the gathering heat. Partly because he was already sore from contact with the saddle's hard seat. His stomach felt painfully empty, but he had no food in his saddlebags. Sam had told him not to worry about food. Sam had also asked if he'd had a good breakfast, and warned that they'd be riding straight through to lunch.

Ethan swung down and looked around for Rufus. When he didn't see him, he cupped his hands and called the dog's name, and Rufus came trotting to him from around the bend in the trail. Ethan grabbed the dog's collar so he couldn't get too close to Rebar.

Jone and Sam led their horses into the shallow water of the lake and took the reins over their necks, holding them loosely so the animals could drink their fill. They both wore cowboy boots with their jeans legs tucked inside. Because of the boots they could wade that far without getting their feet wet. Ethan looked down at his own athletic shoes.

He looked up to see Marcus wade in with the pony, wearing high-top hiking boots. He stayed in water too shallow to go over the tops of his boots, and encouraged the pony to go a step or two farther.

Ethan put Rufus in a sit-stay and rummaged around in the saddlebags until he found his hat, hoping someone would offer to water Dora for him when their own mount had drunk his fill.

"Let her drink some water, boy," Sam called. "That's a long march up that mountain."

"But my feet'll get wet," he said, wishing as he heard it that he hadn't sounded so pathetic.

Sam laughed a short bark. "Everybody's feet'll get wet. We'll be riding through the Blythe River in less than two hours."

Ethan tried to imagine the depth of a river that would get your feet wet while you were mounted. Not that he didn't know there were deeper rivers in the world, but . . . didn't that make it dangerous to cross?

"How deep is this river we're about to wade through?" Ethan asked, leading Dora out into the shallow edge of the lake. The water felt shockingly cold as it filled his shoes and soaked his socks and the cuffs of his jeans. The mule dropped her head and sucked water gratefully.

"We're not wading it. We're swimming it."

"Um. Maybe I should have told you I'm not that strong a swimmer."

"The mule does the swimming."

"Oh," Ethan said. And decided not to ask any more questions. Even though he had many swirling around in his head.

"Hey!"

Ethan heard a sudden shout, followed immediately by a big splash. Water sloshed high up onto his calves. He looked over to see Marcus pulling up to his knees in the shallow water, fully drenched. He'd dropped the pony's reins, but Sam ducked in and grabbed them before the mildly spooked Appy decided to go elsewhere on his own.

"You did that on purpose!" Marcus bellowed, pointing at Sam.

"Don't be ridiculous," Sam said. "I did no such thing. My horse pushed me with his nose and I just bumped into you, that's all."

"Like hell!" Marcus shouted. "What is your problem with me, man? What is your problem in general?"

"You're making a big deal out of nothing," Sam said. "It's already hot. We'll be dousing ourselves in lakes and streams a dozen times today just to stay comfortable. Look," he added, and dove forward and down until he flattened out on his stomach and disappeared in the shallow water, still holding both horses' reins. His hat floated.

He jumped up, dripping and mud covered, and grabbed up the hat.

Marcus only grunted unhappily, took the reins of his pony back, and led him to dry ground.

"Okay," Sam said. "We're burning daylight. Let's ride on. Anybody want an energy bar?"

"I do!" Ethan shot out.

He tried to walk closer to Sam, to lead Dora closer, but Rebar stood in the way. Ethan looked around for Rufus, who was standing chest deep in the lake and lapping his fill.

Sam tossed him the bar. He missed it.

"I have a question," Ethan said, leading his mule to the energy bar and snatching it up. "That trail we just came up. If my dad took that trail on his run . . . I was thinking . . . it was still snowy that day. It was just before the weather took that big turn. If there was snow and ice on that really steep, narrow section, wouldn't it be easy to slip off it? I was just wondering if we should be looking . . . you know . . . where a person would land. If they slipped off that trail."

He watched Sam and Jone exchange a look. Something solemn traveled between them, like sad news over a telephone line.

"Here's the thing," Sam said. "Slip off that trail, you land in the valley. Five hundred to two thousand feet below. Depending on how far along you were and how high the trail'd climbed. So let's say on the way back we do that. We'll come back through that valley and ride all along the far edge where a person might land. You know why I say on the way back, right?"

"'Cause we're so far past it now?"

"No," Sam said. As if he'd much rather have avoided saying it. "Because the first places we want to look are the places you might find a person alive."

"Oh," Ethan said.

He tore into his energy bar anyway, just to calm the hunger pangs.

They mounted up and rode on. With nothing more said.

Well. Nothing other than "Dad!"

And "Noah!"

—

"Ow," Ethan said, still perched on Dora's hard saddle. He'd been in the process of lifting off his baseball cap, and had accidentally touched the top of one ear.

They'd stopped for lunch on the near side of the Blythe River. It was a snaking, twisty track of fast water. Not whitewater, exactly, but it really moved along. It seemed to have no banks, probably because it was swollen with snowmelt. Ethan could peer into the clear water of its edge and see the rocks on the bottom.

He did not look forward to crossing it on a swimming mule. The longer their lunch break, the happier Ethan figured he would be.

"Ow, what?" Sam asked. "Saddle sore?"

"Maybe," Ethan said. "But I was actually talking about my ears."

He swung down off Dora, stiffly. It made him want to say "ow" again, but this time he held it in. Clenched the sound in his throat. It felt strange to stand with his feet on the ground. It felt unsteady. Ethan would have sworn he could feel the solid earth swaying like a walking mule.

Sam came close and gently grabbed onto Ethan's shirt collar, pulling Ethan even closer.

"You got yourself the beginnings of a nasty sunburn on the tops of your ears, boy. And the back of your neck."

"Oh," Ethan said, instinctively touching the back of his neck. It hurt.

"Should've worn a hat with a full brim," Sam said.

"Now you tell me."

"I told you to bring sunscreen, though," Sam said.

"Yeah, that's true. You did. But I didn't have any. Or I couldn't find it, anyway. I think my dad must've taken it."

"Did you bring a bandana?" Sam asked.

"No. You didn't tell me to bring a bandana."

"Then you might be destined to finish this adventure with a pair of underwear sticking out of the back of your hat."

"I got a spare bandana," Jone said.

She was squatting under a scrubby tree, lighting the burner on a camp stove. Marcus had gone as far away from the rest of the group as possible. He was watering the horses and mules two at a time in the river, starting with Rio, his Appaloosa pony, and Jone's chestnut horse. Rufus was also drinking his fill at the water's edge.

"Thanks," Ethan called to Jone.

Then he headed over there to get it. It seemed like a simple enough proposition. All he had to do was move his feet and walk to her. But his legs had other ideas. The muscles from his calves right up through his butt felt rubbery and weak. And the skin and muscles that covered the bones he'd been sitting on—the bones that had nearly made contact with that hard saddle—fairly screamed with pain on every step.

He could barely hobble.

Ethan heard laughter and looked up to see Sam chuckling at him. He looked at Marcus, who was watching over his shoulder and also smirking. Then he looked at Jone, who was taking everything in but not laughing.

Ethan stopped hobbling.

"What's so funny?" he asked.

"Little bit saddle sore?" Sam asked in return. He had taken the packs off Rebar's back, spread them out on the ground, and was sorting through the contents of one in the scrubby dirt.

It brought up a flare of anger in Ethan. Much to his surprise.

"And why exactly is that funny? When you see somebody in pain, that's a joke to you? Why? When I see somebody in pain, I feel sorry for them."

"You're being too sensitive," Sam called back.

"I don't think he is," Jone said. "I'm with the kid. I have no idea why somebody hurting is supposed to be funny. Like those stupid TV shows with home video of guys getting hit where it hurts. Why does that even pass for humor? It's a male thing, if you ask me. Women don't tend to laugh so much at pain. It's not in our nature."

Marcus spoke up for the first time in hours.

"So does that make Ethan female?" he called over from the edge of the river.

Jone raised her voice. Honed it into a sharp bark that startled everybody, Ethan included.

"Why don't you just shut the hell up and leave the kid alone? Both of you." She allowed a silence to radiate for a moment. Then she added, "No, it makes him the one in pain. It's never funny for the one in pain."

Sam handed her a gray plastic filter bottle of water from the river, and Jone squeezed the water through the filter into a light cooking pot. It took time. It obviously involved a lot of pressure, and the water came through in a thin stream.

As Ethan watched, he carefully covered the ground between them.

"Sit here in the shade, honey," she said without looking up. "Then before we go I'll get you that bandana. I'll show you how to put it on so your hat holds it down. It'll cover your ears and neck."

"Thanks," he said, and tried to lower himself to the ground.

It wasn't easy.

He ended up mostly falling into a sitting position, which hurt a lot. But he stifled any vocal reaction to his pain. And if Sam and Marcus had any comments, they stifled those as well.

Rufus padded over to join him, and Ethan hooked one arm around the dog's neck and looked up and around.

The radically spiked towers, the ones Ethan hadn't seen from home, were still packed white with snow. The contrast between the snow and the navy sky behind them seemed shocking to Ethan. It almost burned his eyes.

Ethan looked in the other direction to see the sky nearly black. The clouds looked dense, heavy. Threatening. Fast moving. The air felt heavy and damp, muggy with heat, and a lazy wind had begun to push them from one side. The dark side.

"We got some weather blowing in," Jone said, as if reading his mind. Or simply following his gaze.

"I hope we don't get any lightning," Ethan said, remembering the feeling that gathered in his chest as he listened to the tale of Marcus racing down the mountain. Counting.

"We're not on a peak or a ridge. I'd say our best bet is to stay down here in the valley and ride it out. Move on when things look clearer."

The idea of not climbing back into a saddle sounded good to Ethan. Even if there was lightning involved.

—

Not five minutes later all four of them were hunkered down, close together, holding one big tarp over their heads while the hail pounded. Now and then the wind whipped up and sent the hail sideways, into their faces. It flapped the edges of the tarp and threatened to uncover them and expose them and render them even more uncomfortable.

If such a thing is possible, Ethan thought.

Ethan's stomach groaned in pain again. They hadn't eaten lunch yet—or even prepared it—because they couldn't let go of the tarp.

Ethan felt Rufus leaning hard against his back, clearly afraid of the clattering noise. Hail rolled down a slight incline and joined them under the tarp, where it quickly melted against Ethan's jeans. It made him miserable to think of riding off for a long afternoon in wet clothes. Then he remembered they were about to swim their mounts through a river.

"How long does this usually keep up?" he asked, maybe of Jone, maybe of Sam. Maybe both. He had to speak up to be heard over the clatter of hail on tarp.

"Sometimes just a few minutes," Sam said.

"Sometimes hours," Jone added.

Ethan sighed and leaned out slightly to look at the horses and mules. They stood with their heads down miserably, suffering in silence. Hail bounced off his scalp, stinging.

The mountains had disappeared, replaced by black sky. Alarmingly black.

"Shouldn't we cover them, too?" Ethan asked, pulling his head back in.

At first nobody answered.

Then Sam asked, "Who's 'them'?"

"Them," Ethan said, pointing.

"Oh. The stock. With what?"

"I don't know. It just doesn't seem fair. Here we are under some kind of cover . . ."

"They got thick skin," Sam said.

Sam didn't seem like he wanted to talk much. No one did. The mood of the group had changed. On a dime, like the weather. Everyone seemed uncomfortable. Every fuse seemed suddenly short.

"They just look so miserable," Ethan said.

"Yeah, well, I got news for you," Sam shot back. "Before long you'll figure out there's enough misery to go around. It won't be confined to the stock."

Then nobody talked for a long time.

"See what I mean about this place?" Marcus asked.

It took Ethan a moment to realize the question was aimed at him. He looked over his shoulder to see Marcus staring right into his face.

"Oh. Me?"

"Yeah. Remember what I said?"

"I do. Mostly. You said it's not forgiving. Like it's hostile toward us."

"I didn't say it was hostile. I don't think it hates us," Marcus said.

"But it's not on our side."

"No. It just doesn't care about us one way or another."

A long string of words burst out of Sam. Rushed and sudden, as though they had broken through a fence.

"What the hell were you doing asking this guy about the wilderness, Ethan? What does *he* know? You want to know about this place? Ask *me*. I've been up here hundreds of times. Ask the actor-surfer guy how many times *he's* been up here."

Silence.

The tarp rose and shifted as Marcus climbed to his feet.

"I'm going out for a nice walk in the hail," he said.

And he did.

Jone threw an elbow into Sam's padded ribs, and he landed on his back with a deep grunt, dropping his edge of the tarp and causing them all to be pelted miserably with hail.

—

The hail had turned to a driving rain, soaking the ground beneath them and melting the accumulated pellets of ice. Ethan's stomach had taken to growling loudly enough that he was sure Sam and Jone could hear.

Marcus hadn't come back to enjoy their scant cover.

"This isn't showing any signs of letting up," Sam said. "We need to ride on. Tactical error. We should've crossed the river before we stopped for lunch. I was just trying to put off getting soaked. But that river could be about to get impassable. We could even be in for a flash flood. I think we'll be okay if we go fast. Since it blew in from the lower elevations. But it's up here with us now. So if we're going to get over safely, we better get to getting while we still can."

"You bring any rain gear?" Jone asked him.

"Yes and no. I got some light ponchos. But the wind'll flap them around. Drive the rain underneath them. And we're about to get soaked to our chests in the river anyway."

"It's not that cold," she said.

Ethan thought it felt cold. In the wind, and with his jeans soaked. He didn't share that thought.

"Well, it's not warm like it was," Sam said. "High fifties maybe. Leastways it's not cold enough that anybody's gonna get hypothermia."

And then, just like that, the tarp disappeared from above him. Pulled back. Ethan turned in the driving rain to see Sam flapping it to straighten it out for folding. Jone's big chestnut horse spooked slightly. The other horses and mules were too busy squinting their eyes against the downpour to react.

"What about lunch?" Ethan asked, feeling the rain soak through his hat and shirt.

"It's kind of a wash," Jone said. "Even if we hold a tarp over the camp stove, it's really hard to get it to light in all this wind. Besides, we need to cross right now, like Sam said."

"Oh," Ethan said, not wanting to show how devastating he found the news. In fact, everything felt devastating. Everything had taken a turn for the worse. The weather, the mood. The wilderness. The experience. It had gone from scary and uncomfortable to downright awful.

And now there was nothing but fear of fast water.

"You hungry?" Sam asked him, overhearing.

"Starving."

"Can you make do with a couple of energy bars?"

"Yeah. Sure. If I have to. I mean, it's better than nothing."

Sam finished folding the tarp in the pouring rain. He tucked it away in one of Rebar's big canvas packs, then rummaged around on the other side of the mule. Ethan wondered why Rebar never tried to bite or kick Sam. Maybe the disagreeable mule knew better by now.

Ethan looked down and around to see where Rufus had gone. He found the dog crouched behind his heels, head down, eyes mostly closed against the deluge.

"Well, one good thing about all this," Jone said. "If your dad's alive, he needs water. And here it is. All you can drink."

Ethan was thinking that his father had been out here for a few days now. Longer than a person can normally go without water. He wondered what his father could have done to make it to this moment. Was the early snowmelt enough? Or had his father's hydration bladder still been fairly full when . . . well, when whatever happened happened?

Ethan was opening his mouth to ask a bunch of questions Jone would never be able to answer when Sam appeared before him, dripping, holding out two energy bars.

Ethan accepted them gratefully.

"One or two?" Sam asked Jone.

"One'll do. I had a big breakfast."

"What about your friend?" Sam asked her.

And that was the end of Jone's fuse, right there.

"Damn it, Sam," she snapped. "What the hell is it with you, anyway? He's not my friend. I barely know him. He's *our* neighbor. Not *mine.*

Ours. And I don't even know where he is. For all I know he might've walked half the way home by now. I wouldn't blame him if he did."

"He's right over there," Sam said. As though it were unfortunate news to have to report. "Here. Bring him one." And he tried to push a wet bar into Jone's equally wet hands.

"The hell I will. You just damn well get over whatever this thing is you can't seem to get over. You're leading this expedition. Some leader. You go offer the man something to eat."

Sam sighed. Then he walked slowly in the direction of Marcus, who was crouched in the pouring rain near the horses.

Jone shook her head.

"Stubborn old mule," she spat, more or less in Ethan's direction. "And I don't mean Dora. And I don't mean Rebar." Then she looked over at Ethan. Her face softened. She set one large, square hand on his head. Well, on his soaking-wet baseball cap. "Let's go ahead and mount up," she said. "Get this river crossing over with."

It was Ethan's first indication that everybody had issues with swimming across a fast-moving river. Not just him.

—

They sat their horses—and Ethan's mule—at the very edge of the Blythe River in the rain. In honor of the river crossing they were a pack train again. Sam had tied each horse and mule to the next—first Ethan's mule behind the bay, then Jone's chestnut behind Ethan, then Rebar, and Marcus on his pony dead last. Much the way he'd tied them to ride them up to Ethan's A-frame earlier that morning. But in a different order.

Was there significance to the new order?

Ethan's head swam at the thought that it had been earlier that same day when Sam had come riding up to begin this expedition. That seemed impossible. So much ground had been covered since then. So much sheer time. The dawn seemed like something that must have transpired a week ago.

"Don't just hold that rope," Sam told Ethan. "Tie it real good to your saddle horn, and then hold the end anyway, just in case."

Ethan looked down at Rufus, who looked drenched and unhappy at Dora's hooves. Sam had tied the dog up into a makeshift rope harness and handed the end of the rope to Ethan. That way nobody could wash away.

Unless they all washed away.

Ethan looked at the river. It was running higher and faster than when they'd decided to push on.

He tended to the tying of the rope as a way of not looking at the water again.

"I don't know about this," Jone said.

"If this was a pleasure trip," Sam said, "I'd agree. I'd say why not be safe? Scrub the trip, or go a different way. See something else. But a man's life is at stake here."

An image exploded in Ethan's brain. He pictured his father sitting in a restaurant or a bar. Eating prime rib or drinking Scotch. Talking up a much-younger woman. Not out in the wilderness at all. That's what everybody else thought. What if everybody else was right? What if four people and six animals were about to risk their lives for a man who wasn't even out here in the first place?

Didn't that seem like just the kind of curveball Noah Underwood could be counted on to throw?

"All right," Jone said. "If we're going to do this thing it best be right now."

Then it was too late. Sam put his heels to his huge bay horse, and the rest of the train had no choice but to be pulled along. The earth dropped out sharply from under the bay's hooves, and Ethan watched the horse sink deeply into the river. Deep enough to plunge Sam into water up to his chest. Then the bay bobbed up and swam valiantly.

Suddenly Ethan was in water up to his neck, and then Dora swam just as valiantly, lifting them up so that most of Ethan's torso rose out of the river.

It was a sickening sensation, as though Ethan's heart had stopped. And he couldn't tell if it was the icy water or the fear of the current and drowning that drove his shock.

He felt the pull of the river draw them downstream. But at the same time, the bay was swimming closer to the other bank. It wasn't a wide river. No wider than the pack train was long. Maybe they could reach solid ground on the other side before they washed away.

Ethan had a panicky image of the current swallowing Dora, pushing her head under. Pushing both their heads under. But it didn't come to pass. The river pulled them off course, but it didn't sweep them uncontrollably away.

Except poor Rufus. He had been pushed to the far end of his rope, downriver. If the rope came loose, he would be gone. If he slipped out of the makeshift harness, he would be gone.

Then Sam's big bay was stumbling out onto relatively dry land, shaking himself off like a wet dog. He surged forward, urged by Sam's heels, and Dora came up onto dry land, too. Ethan pulled Rufus's rope hand over hand until the dog was able to climb up and out onto the bank.

"Dumb horse," Sam said to his bay. "Shaking water off yourself in the pouring rain."

Just then Rufus did exactly what Sam had described. Shook water off his coat in the pouring rain. But Ethan had never pegged Rufus as the smartest dog in the world.

They surged forward again, and Ethan looked around to see the Appaloosa pony desperately paw his way onto land.

They rode toward the far mountains—at least toward the spot the mountains had occupied before the black clouds enveloped them—still tied together.

"That was dicey," Jone called up to Sam.

"Yeah," Sam said. "Well. What's done is done."

—

The rain let up about an hour later. It didn't help as much as Ethan might have thought.

He rode along across the flat river valley, untied from the other horses now, thinking about how few times in his life he'd been wet with little hope of getting dry. Despite the fact that, in Manhattan, when it rained it often let go all at once. Like the sky opening up. But there had always been home to go to. And home had always been dry.

He remembered one time he'd been walking home from a museum, a place he'd visited only because Jennifer had commented on an exhibit there. He'd wanted to be able to talk to her about it. The rain had let go, coming down in buckets, splattering off the sidewalk and streets like machine-gun fire ricocheting off metal. He'd been soaked to the skin in a matter of moments.

He'd walked by a covered doorway where three men huddled to stay dry. One had an umbrella.

"Twenty dollars for the umbrella," one of the strangers had called to him.

Maybe it had been a joke. Maybe not.

Ethan had laughed out loud, loud enough for the men to hear, and asked if they didn't think their offer was coming too late. After all, it's *before* you're soaked through that you need the umbrella.

Perhaps the memory had stuck in Ethan's head because it was one of the only times in his life he had ever bantered easily with a stranger.

Ethan pulled his thoughts back to the moment. The sky was not clear, but the black of the clouds seemed to have eased away. Instead, the clouds hung all around him. All around his search party. They drifted like white cotton candy, sometimes only a few feet above where they rode. Like pea-soup fog.

Unlike that day in Manhattan, Ethan wouldn't be home in twenty minutes. There would be no hot bath waiting for him at the end of this day. Sam had told him to bring a change of underwear and socks, not a change of jeans and shirt. So he would have no chance even to change into dry clothes.

He pushed the thoughts of his own discomfort away again and rode on.

—

What might have been a minute or an hour later, Ethan woke up on the ground. He had some vague memory of hitting the wet, rocky dirt hard with his left side. But he had no memory of falling off the mule in the first place.

"Ho!" Jone shouted.

The sounds of hoofbeats stopped.

"What the hell happened, buddy?" Sam called down to him, riding closer on the big bay. "You fall asleep or something?"

"Must have," Ethan said. "Or something."

"Let's take a break," Jone said. "Talk strategy."

—

"I just don't think we dare ride up to that next pass right now," Jone said.

They had dismounted, and were watering their horses in a shallow stream that had probably been a dry gully just a few hours earlier.

"We haven't covered enough ground for one day," Sam said flatly in reply.

Ethan looked to Marcus, but the younger man had nothing to say. He looked as though he had gone home, at least in the ways that counted. Left his body, but taken his spirit someplace more hospitable.

Ethan's left hip and shoulder, and a spot on the side of his head, ached from hitting the rocky trail. His sitting bones screamed from contact with the saddle. The sunburn on his ears and neck stung fiercely. He was hungry again, and he was desperately tired and sore.

And it was only a little over halfway through day one.

"I think we pitch our tents here and wait and see if the weather clears," Jone said.

Sam jumped in to argue, but Jone cut him off.

"Look. It's not just the safety thing. We're supposed to be looking for a lost man. How're we supposed to look with no visibility? What's the point of covering more ground if we could ride right by a guy lying on the ground not fifty feet away and never see him? It makes no sense. Let the kid get dry and take a nap. With him so sleepy he's liable to fall right off the saddle, I don't think we can go up on that ridge trail right now. And another problem. For all we know it could be full-on whiteout conditions up there. Kind of whiteout where a horse can step right off a cliff. I say we plant ourselves here until we see if the low cloud cover breaks. If not, I got a bad feeling about it. It feels like what we did crossing that river. We knew it was chancy, but we did it because we figured we had to do it. But one chance like that is enough. We're not going to make things better by throwing four more fatalities on top of the one we might already have on our hands."

Ethan felt the idea of a nap drawing him like a magnet.

He waited for Sam to flare. Sam's anger was right there under the surface. Ethan could feel it. He figured everybody could. But then it disappeared somehow. Maybe just pushed back down into the older man's gut.

"Okay," Sam said. "I'll pitch the tents. You make us some hot food. We'll see which way this day wants to go."

He made no reference to Marcus, or any job Marcus might take on. It was as if Sam were making it clear—one more time—that Marcus was of no use to him at all.

Chapter Thirteen: The Peacemaker

Five days after his father disappeared

Ethan woke suddenly to a loud and terrible noise. Like the roar of a wild animal. And close. Something raged inside the tent, right next to where Ethan slept. His eyes shot open, and he half sat up, looking around desperately.

There was no wild animal in the tent.

Then he heard the dreadful sound again. It was coming from inside. From right next to him.

He leapt clumsily to his feet, half mired in his sleeping bag, and crouched, panicky, wondering how to unsheathe his legs so he could run.

Two more rounds of the terrifying roar, and Ethan realized it was coming from the sleeping Sam. Sam snored in a manner that rivaled the bellowing of an enraged grizzly bear.

Ethan sank into a sitting position, catching his breath and calming his heart. But it would be a good hour or more before he could tame the trembling, and he knew it.

He gradually shook the cobwebs out of his murky brain and assessed his situation.

It was fairly cold, maybe forty-five degrees. Ethan was wearing only clean, dry underwear that felt like his own and a huge shirt that fit him like a dress and could only have belonged to Sam. His stomach ached with emptiness. The rest of his body ached from more concrete issues and injuries.

He didn't remember changing his clothes, or climbing into a sleeping bag. Or missing dinner.

The tent seemed oddly light inside, as if someone outside had a lantern or a campfire going. In that glow Ethan saw Rufus looking up at him curiously, as if unable to imagine what could be so disturbing. Ethan decided to venture out and see if he could find some food.

He unzipped the tent flap.

There was no campfire. No lantern. Just a huge full moon casting spooky shadows. And Marcus, sitting cross-legged on a folded blanket, staring out into the night.

Ethan crawled out and sat with him, gathering the sleeping bag more tightly around his bare legs and his middle. Rufus wiggled out behind him and trotted around looking for a good spot to pee. Ethan didn't want him to go far, worried about wolves and coyotes. But he didn't want to call the dog for fear of waking Sam or Jone.

"Hey," he said to Marcus.

"Hey," Marcus said back.

Then no one spoke for a bizarre length of time.

Ethan could see the snow on the summits of the jagged mountains. It glowed in the moonlight. A half-bare tree loomed over their heads, its branches rustling in a light wind. He listened to Sam's amazing snoring, which sounded just as loud from outside the tent.

A moment later the pattern of that noise was broken up by a new sound, one that sent a chill along the nape of Ethan's neck. It was a cross between yipping and howling. Maybe six or seven animals. Maybe a couple of hundred yards away.

"Coyotes?" Ethan asked Marcus.

"Could be coyotes," Marcus said. "Could be wolves."

Rufus came scrambling back and disappeared inside the tent.

They waited, and listened. But the coyotes or wolves seemed done with their vocalizing.

"I don't remember changing into this shirt," Ethan said. "Did I even eat dinner?"

"No. You got out of your wet clothes and took a nap in the tent, and then we couldn't wake you up to eat. Sam put the shirt on you so you wouldn't get cold in the night. We saved you some stew. I could try to get that camp stove going if you want to heat it up."

"Don't even bother. I'll eat it cold. I'm starving. I don't even want to wait that long."

Marcus lifted himself to his feet. He walked a few dozen yards and came back with a medium-size round container—maybe the size of a three-gallon plastic water bottle—which Ethan couldn't understand in the dimness. He brought it back to where Ethan sat and began working on its lid.

"What is that thing?" Ethan asked.

"Bear vault. Otherwise there's no way any food would still be here in the morning. And you don't want to draw bears into your campsite."

"Do bears come out at night?"

"Oh, yeah. Mostly at night."

"Wait," Ethan said, and put a warning hand on Marcus's arm. "Don't open that."

"I thought you were starving."

"But what if it draws bears? What if I'm eating and they smell it?"

A long pause. Then Marcus shrugged. Set the bear vault in the dirt in front of Ethan, still sealed.

"Up to you," he said.

Ethan decided to starve until daylight.

"What time is it?" he asked Marcus.

Marcus peered at his watch in the dark. He reached into his pocket and pulled out a headlamp, which he clicked on. Ethan winced at the sudden light. The way it seemed to pierce his eyes.

"Three ten."

Then it was dark again, and it took time for Ethan's eyes to adjust to the light of the moon, which had seemed so strong just a moment earlier.

"It doesn't feel like the middle of the night."

"It's dark," Marcus said. "What more convincing do you need?"

"I didn't mean that. I mean I feel like I slept. Usually if I wake up in the middle of the night, my stomach is all rocky and my eyes are scratchy and sore."

"You've been asleep since four p.m. That's eleven hours."

"Oh," Ethan said. "That explains it."

Another silence.

There was something hanging in the air, but Ethan couldn't grasp it. Some subtext to Marcus sitting out in the night alone. He could feel the weight of it hanging somewhere nearby.

"What about you?" Ethan asked. "Couldn't sleep?"

Marcus snorted laughter. "Are you kidding me? Who could sleep through that?" He flipped his head back in the direction of the tent. "I used to work in a sheet-metal factory, and I swear that was quiet compared to trying to sleep in a tent with Sam."

"You were in that same tent? Why didn't you get your own tent?"

"Because he only brought two. I guess he figured it would be you and him in one, the lady in the other. Then she invited me along. Which you might've noticed he's none too happy about. The lady has to have her own tent. She's a lady. So that puts three of us in this one. I'm sure he'll use that as one more reason to be upset that I'm here."

"Why doesn't he like you?"

"I have no idea."

"You didn't have a run-in with him before this or anything?"

"I never met the man. Just waved to him a couple times from about twenty paces. Hey. Look at that."

Marcus pointed off toward the mountains. In the surprisingly strong glow of the moon, Ethan saw six animals run, loping, down the flank of a foothill. Canine animals, like big, wild dogs.

Marcus grabbed up a pair of binoculars and sighted through them for a few beats, then handed them to Ethan.

"Wolves," he said.

Ethan quickly located the loping wolves through the lenses and dialed the animals into sharper focus. It sent a shiver down his back, but it was beautiful. He could see their rounded ears and long snouts. Their mouths open and panting as they ran. They had long, rangy bodies and oddly skinny legs. They had thick fur like sled dogs. But they were not sled dogs. Even with nothing but the moon to illuminate them, Ethan could see they were not dogs. They were not tame or domestic. These were wild creatures.

Just for a moment, Ethan felt his view of life, of the world, stretched painfully. He had never realized that something so frightening could also be beautiful. That a sight could strike fear into his heart and at the same time make him feel privileged to have seen it.

It helped that the wolves were fairly far away and moving laterally. Not coming closer.

"Look," Marcus said, but clearly not referring to something that could be physically seen. Just at that moment the loping wolves disappeared behind a rise. "Don't take this the wrong way. You seem like a nice enough kid. And I hope you find your dad. I really do. Doesn't seem like the chances are that great, but I really hope you beat the odds. But the minute it gets light I'm riding out of here."

Ethan absorbed that news for a moment. Set the binoculars in the dirt.

"Why?"

"Because this is bullshit. This is just what I came up here from L.A. to get away from. People."

"People are bullshit?"

"When you can't get away from them, yeah. They usually are. I actually think I know why the old guy's being such an asshat. It's because he likes the lady. He's got a thing for her. Not that he thinks I do, too, but I think he pictured himself being the big man on this trip. The only man. But, you know what? I don't care why. It's just bullshit, and I came up here to get away from people and their bullshit. When he gets up, tell him I'll put the pony back in the pasture with his other horses."

"What if the river's even higher? And you're crossing it all alone and not tied to anyone . . ."

"That's not the only way to get back. There's a trail with a bridge. There are a bunch of ways in and out. Sam was just trying to search the best running trails first."

A long and painful silence fell. It hit Ethan that everything was unraveling. Even the search party. His life before leaving on this trip felt strangely distant. He felt unconnected to anything but the search party. And now even that was unraveling. And not twenty-four hours in.

Marcus startled him by speaking.

"If I thought it'd do any good, I'd stay. If I really thought it would improve the chances of finding your dad alive. But much as I hate to admit it, the old man was right about one thing. I'm not bringing anything to the party. I'm just along for the ride."

"More people is better, though."

"I think that's just something Sam came up with so you'd invite the lady."

"Oh," Ethan said.

They sat in silence for another minute, Ethan pulling his sleeping bag up higher around his throat to ease the cold. He thought of his father, out alone night after night in forty-something-degree weather.

Maybe in only shorts and a T-shirt. It might not be life-threateningly cold, but it sure couldn't be comfortable. That is, if his father was still capable of feeling discomfort.

"I hope you're good at being the peacemaker," Marcus said.

"Why would I need to be? Are you saying you'll stay?"

"No. I'm saying you need to be the peacemaker after I'm gone."

"Why? What am I supposed to make peace out of? What's the war after you go?"

"It's just a problem team. The old man has feelings for the lady. Like I said. And she doesn't feel anything back. Except defensive. They were already starting in on each other over dinner last night. Longer you guys are out, the more tired and worn down everybody gets, the more you're going to need to get in the middle and be the peacemaker. Got any experience in the field?"

"I don't think so."

"Your parents never fought?"

"Yeah. They did. But I didn't try to get in the middle. I just stayed out of their way."

"I tried to be the peacemaker," Marcus said. "When I was a kid. Then I got sick of it. Now if people can't get along—with me or with each other, either one—I just walk away. But you can't exactly walk away. Not unless you're willing to give up looking for your dad."

"So how do you be the peacemaker?"

"I used to do it by reminding my folks they were putting me in the middle. That they were hurting me as much as they were hurting each other. When two people have a bone to pick with each other, they're like a dog with a real bone. They just won't put it down. They feel too entitled. Too right. They won't let go. But usually they don't want any innocent third parties getting hurt. You know what? I just realized. It's going to take me a good two and a half hours to ride the long way across this valley toward home. If not three. I have enough moonlight to do that. By the time I get up on a pass it'll be dawn, or at least halfway light. I'm just going to saddle that dinky little pony the old guy picked out for me on purpose, and feed him some grain and take off."

And with that he rose to his feet and joined the hobbled stock, who stirred and shifted and snorted before realizing it was a known and trusted person. Someone they'd already met.

Rebar flattened his huge ears back against his neck and took a fast and violent shot at biting Marcus, but Marcus ducked the assault and led Rio to safety.

Ethan watched him saddle the pony in silence for a few minutes, wishing he could go over and thank him for at least trying. And for the peacemaker advice. But he felt moored. Frozen. Inoperable.

In time he wiggled back into the tent beside the trembling Rufus and the raucously snoring Sam. He curled back into position in his sleeping bag, as if he intended to go back to sleep. But he knew it wasn't likely that he would.

Even the hunger pangs were enough to keep him tossing and turning. But they were the least of what he had working against him.

He was right. He never did get back to sleep.

—

Sam emerged from the tent not long after sunrise. Ethan was standing twenty or thirty feet away, wearing his jeans again even though they were still wet in the seams and the waistband. He'd been standing there for some time, scanning the valley with binoculars, hoping to see Marcus and Rio. Because to see them would be to know they were okay. To convince himself they were safe, so he could stop worrying. Or . . . well, at least so he could stop worrying about *that*.

But there were too many dips and gullies and hills to ride around and behind, and the pair might even have crested the pass by then.

In any case, he never saw them.

"You been up long?" Sam asked.

"Since about three," Ethan said, without lowering the binoculars.

"Yeah. Well, that's the problem, I guess, with going to bed at four p.m."

Ethan looked around to see that Jone was up as well, and had begun firing up the camp stove for coffee. And hopefully breakfast.

"What are we having for breakfast?" Ethan asked. "I'm starving."

"We saved you some stew," Jone said.

"I know. Thanks. Marcus showed me where it was. But I was afraid to open the bear vault. I was afraid it might draw one into our camp. I know that probably sounds really stupid."

"It doesn't sound stupid at all," Jone said. "I always try to get my food packed up and put away bear-proof by dusk. By the way. Where *is* Marcus?"

Ethan opened his mouth to answer, but Sam cut in.

"Probably out looking for a place to relieve himself. Like I'm about to do."

"No," Ethan said. Simply. When he realized they were both staring at him, waiting for him to go on, he added, "He's gone."

"Gone where?" Sam asked, impatiently, as though he'd expected just this kind of trouble.

"Home."

"Why?" Jone asked. "Did he say why?"

"Yeah. He did. He said people who can't get along are bullshit."

"Can't get along with *him*?" Sam asked. "Or with each other?"

"Either. Both. He said he used to be the peacemaker when he was a kid, but then he got sick of it. So now when people can't get along he just walks away."

"Shoot." Sam spat the word down toward the dirt.

Then he wandered out of camp, probably for the reason he'd previously stated.

"To answer your question," Jone said, "we're having pancakes and scrambled eggs. But don't get your mouth all set for something heavenly, because these are dehydrated eggs. You know. Powdered. They look like the real thing once you get them rehydrated and scrambled, but they don't taste like fresh. But it'll get some protein in you and fill up your stomach."

"I'd eat anything at this point," Ethan said. "I'd just rather not eat another energy bar if I can help it."

Sam came stomping back into camp from behind a tree, as though something back there had angered him.

"Walked away? Or did he ride away? On my pony?"

"He rode away," Ethan said. "He told me to tell you he'd put Rio in the pasture with your other horses. Why did you give him a pony? You have big horses. Why not give him a big horse?"

"Rio's a good pony."

"I'm not saying he isn't. But you have so many bigger ones. I guess I just wondered because it seemed like you had something against the guy."

In his peripheral vision, Ethan saw Jone watching. And he thought he could feel her listening. Her attention seemed almost palpable. But she did not open her mouth. She didn't take a side this time. She let Ethan have his say.

"He tell you that?" Sam asked.

"I saw it with my own eyes. And heard it with my own ears. You were always giving him a hard time."

"He was just being too sensitive," Sam said. He said it in a strong voice, nearly shouting. But Ethan got the impression that he was shouting at Marcus, not at Ethan. Even though Marcus was gone. "I gave *you* a bad time, too, about being saddle sore. Jone had to jump in and stand up for you. And you don't think I have anything against you, right? He just had some kind of a complex or something."

"No, really," Ethan said. "Why didn't you like him?"

Jone poured about a quart of water from the big hanging gravity filter into the cooking pot, which she then placed on the camp stove burner. She pulled to her feet, looking nearly as stiff and sore as Ethan felt.

"Guess I need to follow suit and find me the ladies' room now," she said. And she wandered away.

"Damn it," Sam hissed, half under his breath, "I've been waiting a long time for a thing like this. To get to spend some real time around her. I just thought this was my one chance to impress her. You know?"

Ethan limped stiffly over to the pot and crouched down to watch the water heat. Not that it's interesting watching water heat. But he was that anxious for it to turn into coffee and rehydrated eggs.

"Why not impress her by being a patient guy who gets along with everybody?"

Sam snorted. "Yeah. Right. *That's* what she wants. Woman drops grizzly bears in their tracks without blinking, but you figure she wants a guy who plays well with others, like they teach you in kindergarten."

"You never know. She didn't want you teasing me. So she seems like a fan of fair play to me."

"Ah, I blew it now anyway," Sam said, popping the lid of the bear vault and sorting through the packets of dehydrated food.

"I don't know. Don't say that. Trip's not over yet."

"But this conversation is," Sam said.

That's when Ethan looked up to see Jone walking back into camp.

—

"You warned me," Ethan said, vaguely in the direction of Sam.

Ethan had just put away two cups of coffee, six big pancakes topped with honey from individual squeeze packets, and the equivalent of about four scrambled eggs.

The eggs had been okay, but only because Jone had cautioned him not to get his mouth set for the real thing.

Besides, it really wasn't so much about flavor. Not that morning. He'd wanted to fill his stomach. Steady his nerves with protein and that feeling of fullness. Put an end to the hunger pangs that had been his constant and unwanted companion almost as long as they'd been on the trail.

It was hard to believe that had only been a little over twenty-four hours.

But Sam had warned Ethan not to stuff himself too full.

"You'll regret it when that mule gets to rocking," Sam had said between pancake four and five.

Now Ethan found even the prospect of climbing to his feet a bit daunting. He'd slept plenty, maybe too much. But his head felt muddy and thick. He pushed such thoughts and feelings away again, because there was no place for them. No time to indulge his discomfort.

Instead, Ethan watered the horses and Dora, one by one, leading each down to the nearby creek by its halter rope, Rufus trotting faithfully—if somewhat stiffly—behind. He left Rebar for Sam to water, because he didn't dare get close to Rebar. While he performed this simple task, which seemed surprisingly challenging to Ethan, Jone washed up the camp kitchen and broke down the tents. Sam fed, saddled, and bridled each of the horses as Ethan returned them, and repacked all their equipment into Rebar's canvas packs.

Ethan thought he could feel a pall, a sort of darkness, hovering over and among the three of them. Some bad feelings left over from Marcus's desertion, and maybe fueled by a general sense of discouragement regarding their mission.

Jone walked over to get her saddled horse, and Rebar laid his ears back and lunged in her direction as if to bite her. Jone pulled herself up tall, raised one hand in a threat of her own, and looked the mule right in the eye.

"You bite me, I'll bite you right back, you swaybacked, ornery old cuss from hell. You think I won't do it? Just try me."

Rebar stopped. Froze a moment, as if considering her words. Or at least the tone of them. Then he dropped his head, shook it as if shaking off a blanket that troubled him, and turned away.

Jone led her horse back into their recently vacated camp.

"I know a mule that just met his match when I see one," Sam said. "Lemme just take Rebar down to the creek and give him a drink before we head out. Don't blame you for not wanting the job. Plus I know you're not gonna bite him. And so does he."

"Why doesn't he try to bite or kick *you*?" Ethan asked as Sam led the mule away.

"He knows better," Sam said. And left it at that.

Then Jone came back and took hold of Dora's reins, and Ethan didn't know why. Was she going to ride Dora today? He hoped not. Her chestnut horse was too tall, and a little spookier than the others. Much as he'd initially complained, Dora was just about Ethan's speed. Sam had been right on the money about that.

"Walk with me," Jone said, leading the mule into what had so recently been their camp.

Ethan did, though he didn't know why.

"I wonder why they call that mule Rebar," Ethan said, still regretting the size of his breakfast. And dreading the feel of that hard saddle on yesterday's sores.

"I asked that same question last night. While you were sleeping. Sam said that used to be the only thing that could get him to go."

"Wait. What was?"

"Rebar. You know those metal rods they use when they pour concrete? To reinforce it?"

Ethan felt his eyes go wide.

"Sam hits that mule with a metal rod? No wonder he's so bad-tempered!"

"I don't think Sam did. The mule was already named when Sam bought him."

"Oh," Ethan said.

They had stopped walking now. Dora stood, quiet and with her head down, her left side close against a good-size boulder, one that came up higher than Ethan's knees.

Jone reached one hand out to Ethan, but he didn't know why.

"What are we doing?"

"I know you're sore. Take my hand and step up onto this rock."

Ethan did as he'd been told. Still not really knowing why. The hand helped a lot. More than Ethan would have wanted to admit. Everything hurt. It was hard to lift his leg that high and even harder to raise the rest of his body to join it. Ethan was sure he would have tumbled backward without the helping hand.

"Now go for that stirrup," she said.

Then Ethan understood. From his elevated position he would be swinging his leg over, not up. He really wouldn't be pulling his body upward at all.

"Oh, I get it," he said. "Thanks."

He found the stirrup and eased himself gently into the saddle, resisting the temptation to say "ow." Resisting it twice, in fact. Once as he lifted and swung his leg, and again when his weight settled onto his sitting bones, forcing them against the saddle's hard seat.

"Weather's good today," she said, before walking off to get her own horse.

Ethan looked up and around, even though he'd seen the weather. Even though he'd been watching it since three a.m. The sky had gone a rich light blue with morning. Not one single cloud dotted that perfect blue canvas.

He looked up at the trail, though not for the first time. It climbed the left flank of the mountain ahead of them, twisting up its sheer side. Ethan wondered how they would water their horses after leaving the snaking creek. Or water themselves, for that matter. He wondered if a horse or mule—or person—had ever walked off the edge of that precipitous cliff.

He noted occasional outcroppings of rock below the trail that might break a person's fall if they were unlucky enough to slip. Not in a comfortable way, from the look of it.

Jone led her chestnut horse up behind him.

"I need to use the mounting block," she said. "Such as it is."

"Oh. Sorry. I was lost in what I was thinking, I guess."

He pressed his calves to Dora's sides, and the mule stepped out of the way. Ethan reined her to a halt and turned back to watch Jone mount. Jone was sore, too. Ethan could tell. It surprised him, because he thought of her as being so experienced. Maybe halfway to indestructible. But she was older. No matter how tough you are, he realized, older has to play a role.

"What were you lost in thinking?" she asked him as she landed carefully in the saddle. "That is, if you don't mind saying."

"I was looking up at that trail. And looking at the spots where a person could go off the edge and not fall all the way down into the valley."

Jone shielded her eyes from the low sun with one hand and looked where Ethan was looking.

"I guess I see your point," she said. "But it's only a handful of places. You'd have to go off in just the right spot. There'd be some luck involved."

"Maybe," Ethan said.

Sam came riding up, towing the fully packed and freshly watered Rebar behind his solid bay.

"And I think if he was on one of those rock shelves he'd be pretty easy to see from a plane," Jone added.

Sam shielded his eyes from the sun and looked as well.

"Trouble is," he said, "you wouldn't see what's on there from below."

"But we're riding up there," Ethan said.

"And you want to walk your mule so close to the edge that you can see over?"

"Oh. Right. Maybe I should go up that trail on foot, then. Lead the mule instead of ride her. Then I could go right out to the edge. Even get down on my belly and look over the cliff if I needed to."

"Up to you," Sam said. "It's two and a half miles with twenty-three-hundred feet of elevation gain. But if you think you're up to it . . ."

"I think we're out here to find my dad," Ethan said. "If we're not willing to do stuff like that, what's the point? We can ride around out here forever, and it's pretty and all, but I just don't see what good we'll be doing if we don't look everyplace we can think of looking."

—

They rode to the edge of the valley, which Ethan figured took more than an hour. Occasionally calling for Dad/Noah. Ethan had to clamp down on a small expression of pain at the mule's every step. He found himself looking forward to walking the steep trail he could see up ahead of them, just to give his saddle-sore spots a break. Part of him knew the hike would bring its own pain. But somehow a new and unfamiliar pain felt like a worthwhile trade.

Just as they reached the junction between the edge of the valley and the climbing section of the trail, Ethan was startled by the sudden movement of a large, darting animal. He instinctively reined back on the mule and turned his head to see. Dora turned her head, too. Behind them, Ethan could hear Jone gently cooing "Ho, ho" to her spooky mount.

It was an elk, Ethan saw. Stepping out from around the flank of the mountain base and into their view. And then another elk. And then three. Two were female, with small, neat heads, necks that bulged out in front, and ears that tuned forward as if trying to bring in a radio station. The third was a huge buck with a rack of horns nearly as tall and wide as he was, bowing out from his head and then pointing skyward and halfway out along its back. Each horn sported six impressive points.

Their slightly shaggy coats looked a dusty golden brown, going to darker brown on their necks and knobby-kneed legs.

They stopped dead, apparently more surprised to see Ethan's search team than the other way around.

For what seemed like a full minute, nobody and nothing moved. The elk just stood, wide-eyed, as if holding perfectly still might prove an effective substitute for invisibility.

Then one of the females threw her head, and they darted downhill, their hooves drumming on the hard ground. And then more elk stampeded from behind the flank of the mountain. And more. And more.

A whole herd of elk galloped by, panicky and driven. Then a whole sea. Hundreds of elk. In fact, Ethan thought, they looked like a sea. Like water flowing downhill.

And they just kept coming.

At any given moment in the procession, elk filled the trail in front of the team at least a dozen animals wide.

Every tenth or twentieth elk was a baby, desperately scrambling to keep up with its mother.

The last few stragglers bolted by, and the hoofbeats grew fainter. And still the team sat their mounts and watched the herd gallop away. The elk had white on their back ends—a broad upside-down teardrop of white with a tiny flick of tail in the middle. Some of the tails twitched as they ran away.

Another movement caught Ethan's eye, and he turned to see two coyotes tracking the herd from behind. They appeared from behind the flank of the mountain and froze, heads down, staring at the horses and humans. Their eyes looked yellow and shifty, inherently dishonest, and their thin muzzles and painfully skinny legs distinguished them from the possibility of being someone's dogs. Or anything domestic or tame. Ethan instinctively looked around to locate Rufus, who sat close to Dora's back hooves.

When he looked up again, the coyotes were disappearing behind the mountain, back the way they had come.

Ethan wondered if his team had saved a weak or young elk by being in that right place at the right time. Then again, everybody and everything eats. Maybe they had starved a coyote with their bad timing.

Jone rode the few steps up beside him on her chestnut and reined the horse to a halt, looking down on Ethan from above.

"Tell the truth," she said, flipping her chin toward the retreating sea of elk, now tiny flowing dots in the green of the valley. "Totally independent of our reasons for being here. Let's pretend this was a pleasure trip. Would you rather be home right now, or here?"

Ethan took the question seriously. Mulled it over for a brief time.

"A minute ago I would've picked home," Ethan said, "and halfway up that steep trail I might pick home again. Right now I'd say it's pretty much a tie."

"That'll do," she said.

And they rode on.

—

Halfway up the steep incline, Ethan was struck by the pointlessness of the task. And not just the task of intermittently peering over the edge, either. The whole folly of being out in the wilderness, looking, overwhelmed him. It came on suddenly, knocked the figurative wind out of him, and left him feeling profoundly depressed.

How much space did a lost or fallen human occupy? A few square feet? And how many square feet did this seemingly endless wilderness contain? How many human-size spaces actually existed out here to be searched? Or, rather, how many millions of them? How long would it take a team to look in even a fraction of them? And how long could a lost or fallen person survive while they tried?

"You okay?" Jone asked, looking down at him from her horse. She'd been holding Dora's reins, ponying the mule along behind her.

"Yeah. Sure. Just winded."

Actually, it wasn't entirely true. The steep climb wasn't so much making him winded, because he was taking it so slowly, stopping above each shelf in the rock face to lie on his belly and look down. But he was wearing out nonetheless. The muscles in his thighs and calves and hamstrings had just about reached their limit. They felt both tight and trembly at the same time.

Ethan briefly thought of mounting his mule again and forgetting the idea of checking below. Maybe even forgetting the idea of being out here.

He stopped in the middle of the trail behind the team and waited for them to notice. It took a moment, and it made him feel panicky inside, as if he were being left behind. He didn't know why he didn't solve the problem by calling out to them, but he didn't. It just felt like a task that would require energy he didn't have, and couldn't find.

It was Sam who finally looked over his shoulder.

"Why'd you stop?" he called back down the trail.

Ethan walked a handful of tough, painful steps to catch up, so he wouldn't have to yell.

"How many days has my dad been gone?"

"'Bout five, I think."

"Can a person survive out here for five days?"

"Well." Sam scratched one bearded cheek. "Depends."

"On what?"

"Mostly on whether they're injured, and how, and how bad. And whether they can find water. But there's been a lot of runoff. What with the snowmelt, and then yesterday's rain. And hail. A person could gather hail for drinking water. It melts fast. They'd just have to have something to hold it in."

"He had one of those hydration bladders with the sip tubes."

"Don't count him out just yet, then," Sam said.

"You feeling discouraged?" Jone asked.

"Yeah," he said. He had planned to elaborate, but then he never did.

"Want to get back up on your mule and I'll get down and do the looking-over-the-edge part?"

"No," Ethan said. "He's my dad. I'll keep looking."

There was another reason to stay down with his feet on the trail. Another incentive to keep walking. One he didn't bother to put into words. He would have been terrified to try to mount with his stiff, shaky legs, on a trail not much wider than the mule. On the drop-off side.

He began to move his concrete muscles again, hiking up to the next spot that might have broken a person's fall. But before he even got to it, before he dutifully dropped to his belly and peered over the edge at the top of a tree that seemed to grow out of solid rock halfway up the mountain, he knew he would see nothing but a tree. The pointlessness of looking had begun to seem permanent and inevitable.

He looked back to check on Rufus, who looked to be having a worse day than Ethan. The dog limped along gingerly, continually falling behind. It was only the frequent stops to look over the edge that kept the team from riding away and leaving the dog behind completely.

"Dad!" Ethan yelled out, to disguise the fact that he saw no purpose in doing so. To disguise it even from himself.

"Noah!" Jone added in her big, deep voice.

As if they were really doing something useful.

—

By the time the trail leveled off and crossed a saddle between two mountains, Ethan's legs no longer dependably supported him. He willed them to move at each step. Forced them, almost. They only barely responded. Every fifth or sixth step, one of his knees gave way and bent without permission, threatening to pitch him forward. But he always managed to catch himself in time.

Sam got down and dropped the bay's reins in the dirt, a signal to the horse to stay put. Then he walked back to Ethan. To help him mount, Ethan figured.

Sam helped all right. He swung a big arm around Ethan's waist—the way he'd done when he'd found Ethan stumbling home from the grizzly encounter—and lifted him right up off the ground. He carried Ethan to Dora and plopped him onto her saddle.

Jone still had Dora's reins, and neither she nor Sam returned them to Ethan so he could ride for himself. Ethan grabbed the saddle horn and allowed himself to be towed.

They rode in silence for ten or fifteen minutes, picking their way through loose shale and around boulders. Ethan wondered how long it had been since they'd passed under a tree. They must have been up above the timberline.

In time they came to a tiny mountain lake, and had to ride precariously downhill through piles of loose stones to reach the water. Ethan could hear the sound of a waterfall or cascade, but he couldn't see it. He figured the sound must have been lake water overflowing and forming a stream, running down to lower elevations.

He looked up to see a tight formation of pinnacles clustered together as a backdrop to the lake, still laced with snow. Beneath them the lake bore a perfect reflection of the spires on its glassy surface.

"Don't even bother getting down," Sam said.

They rode their mules and horses into the lake to the animals' knees and let them drink. Jone handed Ethan back the reins, looping them behind Dora's neck again.

Ethan watched the mule drink and envied her. He was thirsty, too.

When Sam's bay had sucked in his fill and lifted his head, Sam rode him carefully ashore, towing Rebar behind. There he dismounted, and filled three of the filter bottles with lake water. He picked his way through the loose shale to a spot just behind Ethan and Dora.

"Think fast," he said, and a full filter bottle of water flew in Ethan's direction.

Ethan registered the irony of those two simple words as the bottle flew end over end. He told his arms to reach up. To at least try to catch it. And they might have obeyed, eventually. But they certainly didn't respond in time.

The bottle sailed by Ethan's head and landed in the lake with a splash that spooked Jone's horse. Then, thankfully, it bobbed to the surface and floated.

"I'll get it," Sam said. "I know you're tired."

He waded out into the lake after the bottle and handed it to Ethan.

"Thanks," Ethan said.

Ethan raised it to his lips to drink. And stopped.

On the other side of the lake, maybe a hundred feet away, a movement caught his eye. It was not the first time on this trip that a movement had caught his eye. And each time, his heart had missed a beat, then jumped, then hammered nearly hard enough to kill him. At least, from the feel of it. Because each time he had expected it to be a bear.

This time it was.

A dark-coated bear with a lighter brown muzzle was winding its way to the lake with two cubs in tow. Hadn't Ethan read that a mother bear with cubs was the most dangerous of all?

He opened his mouth to shout to the others, but nothing happened. No sound emerged. Ethan had lost the use of his voice again.

He reined Dora around and kicked her desperately, and she trotted ashore.

"Hey!" Sam called to him. "Hey! Where ya going in such a hurry?"

Ethan gathered himself to speak. In his panic he put enough pressure behind the words—hopefully—to break the dam.

"Bear!" he shouted.

He put his heels to Dora's sides again. But the mule only laid her comical ears back along her neck in displeasure and stood her ground. She was a herd animal, Dora, a member of a pack team. She did not care to ride away alone.

Only then did Ethan realize he was trying to ride off without his dog. And that his dog might be about to go after the bears. Was Rufus really simple enough to make a mistake like that twice?

"Sam!" he bellowed, amazed at how much voice he had just rediscovered. "Get the dog! Don't let the dog go after the bears!"

Ethan looked around desperately for Rufus. He found the dog chest-deep in the lake, drinking. Then he drummed on Dora's sides again. But the mule only kicked out with her back legs in irritation, her ears more tightly pinned along her neck.

Jone rode up beside Ethan and reached over and put a hand on his shoulder.

"Shoot it!" Ethan screamed. "Shoot the bear if you have to! You have your rifle, right? Where's your rifle? If it comes any closer you'll shoot it, right?"

He could feel himself still wildly drumming his heels against the mule's sides, trying to get her to move. She did not move. It reminded Ethan of one of those terrible dreams. The ones in which you need to run away from something horrible but your legs won't receive the signal.

"It's right here," she said, touching the stock of the rifle.

It was tucked into a leather scabbard attached to the breast collar of her horse's saddle. It made Ethan feel a tiny bit better to see that she had her hand on it. But in his panic he needed more.

"But I'm not going to shoot anything," she said. "That's just a black bear."

"So? It's still a bear!"

"Black bears don't go after humans unless they're startled. Or feel cornered. Or they're protecting their young. They're not so dangerous like a grizzly. Look."

Ethan stopped kicking his mule and looked over his shoulder.

Across the lake, the bears lowered their heads to drink, undeterred by the humans and equines on the other side. At least, now that the spooky little human had stopped shouting.

"Oh," Ethan said, wondering if he could calm his heart before it killed him. His voice sounded breathless. "I guess I overreacted."

"I guess," she said. "Still think I should shoot that nice family in the middle of their outing? Or just the mom, because she's big? And then what are the babies supposed to do without her? You don't really think it has to come down to that, now, do you?"

"Guess not," Ethan said. "But I really, really think we need to ride away now. Like, right now."

"I'll ride over the pass with you," she said. "Sam can catch up."

"Wait. We have to bring the dog."

"Sam's got him on a rope."

"But if he's going with Sam he's too close to Rebar."

"I'll go get him," she said, and reined her horse around and rode back into the lake.

Meanwhile Ethan wondered how long he could shake so hard and so deeply without falling off a mule.

—

"Something you should know about your dog," Jone said.

She was holding the end of Rufus's long rope leash, and he was limping along beside the chestnut horse. They rode together across the ridgeline between one mountain and the next, still waiting for Sam to catch up. Puffy clouds had blown in, starkly white against the navy-blue sky. Ethan thought this place they were riding might be the highest trail point in the wilderness. He could see higher, snowcapped peaks, but he was pretty sure they were suited only for technical climbing. In any direction Ethan looked he saw a wilderness of mountains and valleys and green lake-filled meadows all the way to the horizon. Like the running wolves, it was scary but beautiful.

"Uh-oh," he said. "What about him?"

"He's leaving blood on the rocks everywhere he walks."

Ethan pulled the mule to a halt. Then he just sat there in the saddle, unsure what to do. A situation needed his attention, but he had no remedy that he could think of. His head was mostly full of the truth that Jone had warned him about this. That he had been ill-advised to bring the dog, and he'd known it. And now it was coming back to bite him.

"Let's take a break and wait for Sam," she said.

She swung down off her horse and led him around close to Dora and held the mule's reins so Ethan could dismount safely.

Ethan eased his right leg out of the stirrup and tried to swing it over the mule's rump. But it barely lifted, and he ended up kicking the mule on the back behind her saddle. She surged forward, and only Jone's strong hand on the rein prevented catastrophe.

"Stiffened up a little, did you?" she asked, tugging the reins sharply to insist that Dora hold still.

"Yes, ma'am," he said.

Then he slowly and gently dragged his leg across her rump and down onto the left side of the saddle.

"Ow," he said out loud.

He leaned on the saddle and kicked out of the left stirrup, then dropped to the ground.

"Ow," he said again.

"Why are we stopping?" Sam's voice asked.

Ethan looked up to see him ride up on the big bay, towing Rebar, whose ears were laid back, and who looked as though he'd had more than enough of this adventure. Ethan knew exactly how he felt.

"The dog needs attention," Jone said. "He's leaving blood on the trail."

"Oh, dear," Sam said. He swung down. Lifted the reins over the bay's head and dropped them in the dirt. "Hey, boy," he said, approaching the dog. Sam got down on one knee and lifted Rufus's paws, one by one, and looked at the pads on the bottom of each. "Yeah. His pads are bleeding. This rough shale is hard on them. It's wearing the tough outers of them right through."

He straightened up, stretching his apparently sore back.

We all hurt, Ethan thought. *And it's only day two out here. Not even very deep into day two.*

Sam rummaged around in the canvas packs on Rebar's sides and came up with a bright-red first-aid kit in a soft nylon pouch.

"Ethan," he said, "how many pairs of clean socks you got left?"

"Just one more pair for tomorrow. After that I'll have to rinse out a pair, I guess."

"No, tonight you'll have to rinse out a pair for tomorrow. And so will I. We're both donating our last clean pair to the dog. Damn him for having four feet, right?"

He unzipped the first-aid kit and settled stiffly on a rock, pulling the dog close by his rope.

Sam pulled a full filter bottle of water out of the pocket of his light jacket. Ethan recognized it by its purple color as the one Ethan had been holding when he saw the black bears. Apparently he'd dropped it again without even realizing. Sam lifted the dog's left front paw and rinsed it in a thin stream of the filtered water. He shook it off and held it up out of the dirt while he unscrewed the cap on a tube of ointment, which he slathered thickly on the pads of the clean paw. Then he wrapped the paw loosely from a roll of gauze bandage.

Sam looked up at Ethan.

"Don't just stand there," he said. "Cough up the socks."

—

When all four of the dog's paws had been cleaned, slathered in ointment, bandaged, and covered with socks—held in place with a strong wrap of adhesive tape—Ethan asked the question he'd been dreading asking.

"Can he walk on those?"

"If he has to," Sam said. "Less he has to walk on them, the better."

"Well," Ethan said. "Maybe it'll discourage him from chasing bears."

He'd meant it to lighten the mood, but it fell flat.

Sam just smiled sadly.

"Get back up on your mule," he said. "We need to move on."

Ethan walked to Dora, still not knowing how the dog was supposed to move on with them, and afraid to ask. Jone was holding the mule's reins for him.

He grabbed hold of the saddle horn and tried to mount. And failed miserably. He couldn't even lift his left leg up to the stirrup. It felt dead. Disconnected. He let go of the horn and held his left leg with both hands, just above the knee. He physically lifted it to the stirrup. Then he grabbed the horn again and tried to swing over. He managed to lift himself a foot off the ground, if that. Then his upward motion lost power and stalled, and he landed on the ground again.

"Ow," he said.

"Here," Jone said. She moved around to the left side of the mule, one arm hooked through the reins. She laced her hands together and offered them to Ethan. "Put your knee there. A little below the knee, actually. Put your shin there."

Ethan did as he was told.

"One," Jone said, and Ethan feared the moment she got to three. "Two. Three."

He jumped as best he could, and Jone used the strength of her arms and back to launch him, and he landed in the saddle. Too heavily, and he kicked poor Dora again on the way over, hard, but he got there. And she didn't bolt. She must have expected it by then.

"Ow," he said. Then, when the mule had stopped fidgeting, he patted her dirty neck and said, "Sorry."

Ethan sat up straight again, and looked around for his dog. He still had no idea what they were going to do about his dog. He found Rufus in Sam's arms, just inches from Dora's saddle.

"Here," Sam said. "He's all yours." And he set Rufus across Ethan's legs.

Rufus scrambled for purchase and balance, but his sock-covered paws only slipped off the saddle leather again. Ethan used his arms to adjust the dog into a steadier position. But no position was quite steady enough. Rufus was uneasily perched there on the saddle at best. Ethan would have to hold him as they rode. There was no other way this could go.

"Let's make some miles," Sam said. "We haven't covered much ground so far today."

They rode on.

—

Not five minutes into the uncomfortable ride, Marcus's predictions began to take shape. Sam and Jone had a decision to make. And they couldn't see eye to eye. And they had begun bickering.

Ethan was bringing up the rear, and his mule kept falling behind, so he couldn't hear every word they said. But from what he could gather, there was a trail intersection coming up. One direction took them deeper into the wilderness. The other looped them around toward home.

Sam thought they should go deeper in.

Jone thought they'd already gone farther than a person could have gone on foot, considering he'd only planned a day trip.

Sam said she didn't know how much mileage his dad was capable of covering.

Jone said yes, she did, but it didn't matter. Because by the time they got to the intersection, they'd be halfway into a twenty-two-mile loop.

Sam said that was not necessarily true. He said it depended on the series of trails Ethan's dad had taken. And since they didn't know, they should be thorough.

Jone said the odds were greater of an accident happening closer to home.

Sam said the odds of getting lost were greater if he'd gone in deeper than usual.

Sam also said the professional searchers probably didn't believe anybody would try to cover twenty-plus miles in a day, and likely scoured the trails closer to home. And if they didn't believe the miles this guy ran, and so didn't search deep enough in the wilderness, somebody should.

Jone said maybe there was a good reason they didn't believe it. Maybe the miles you run are like fish stories. The big one that got away. She said a guy sure as hell wouldn't brag that he'd run fewer miles than he really had. She said exaggeration is predictable. It only goes one way.

The more they argued, the more they raised their voices, and the better Ethan could hear each word. Even though he and Dora and Rufus were having more and more trouble keeping up.

Then Sam and Jone were stopped, sitting their horses in the middle of the trail. Not fighting. Not saying anything. Just giving Ethan a chance to catch up. Though Ethan wasn't sure if they'd done so intentionally. They hadn't looked around for him in some time, and didn't seem to be paying him any mind at all.

As Ethan rode up and stopped beside them, he saw they had reached the intersection. It was marked with a wooden sign. Burned into the wood he read: "Sawtooth Camp: 3.7 mi." And an arrow pointing left. "Avery Trailhead: 11.1 mi." And an arrow pointing right.

They all three stared at the sign for a moment in silence.

Ethan's arms more than ached from holding his dog in place on the saddle—they fairly screamed. And his back had grown tight and sore from leaning forward to do so.

And it wasn't even time to stop for lunch.

"Which way do we go?" Ethan asked.

Jone snorted. "That would be the question, yeah," she said.

"You hear any of what we were saying?" Sam asked. "When we were trying to decide?"

"I did," Ethan said.

"We have a basic difference of opinion," Jone said.

You have a lot of them, Ethan thought. But he didn't say it. Marcus had been right. They were wearing down, all of them. Getting tired and sore and frustrated and discouraged. The battles would likely escalate from here. And Ethan would have to figure out how to be the peacemaker.

"The problem," Sam said, "is that everything is guesswork. He could've slipped off the trail a mile from home. He could've gone in miles farther than usual and gotten lost. We just have no way of knowing. We're just guessing. A man's life is at stake, and all we can do is guess."

"If he's even out here," Ethan replied.

They both turned their heads to look at him, but Ethan refused to look back. But he could feel the weight of their stares.

"Yeah, well, that's guesswork, too," Jone said. "But we're out here, so we're committed. We knew the risk going in. But we're doing it. So we better act as if we're sure he's here. Even if that sureness tends to flag some on the bad days."

They sat their mounts in silence for a moment or two. Ethan would have given anything to let go of the dog and straighten up. But he knew if he did, Rufus would hit the ground immediately.

"What time is it?" he asked.

Sam peered at his watch closely, as if his vision weren't too good.

Great, Ethan thought. *That's encouraging for the lead member of a search party.*

"Ten twenty," Sam said.

"Can we stop right here and have lunch early? Give ourselves some time to think?"

For a few beats, nothing but silence. Ethan was beginning to assume he'd proposed a laughable plan.

"I think that's a great idea," Jone said.

She dismounted, led the chestnut around closer to Dora, hooked one arm through the reins, and reached her hands out to accept the dog from Ethan.

Ethan handed him over, and straightened his arms and back, all of which screamed in pain at the sudden change in position.

"Ow," Ethan said.

—

"I keep thinking about those outcroppings of rock," Ethan said to no one in particular.

They were sitting cross-legged in the rocky dirt, eating mountains of pasta with a creamy cheese sauce. Rehydrated. But it was good. It was the best thing Ethan had eaten since he'd left the last bits of Joan's nonrehydrated chicken stew behind.

Rufus lay in the dirt next to them, eating kibble from a collapsible bowl.

"What outcroppings of rock?" Sam asked.

"The ones I was checking as we came up that steep section of trail this morning. The places where somebody could slip off the trail and not fall all the way down into the valley. Because there's something sticking out to break their fall."

"What about them?" Sam asked.

Jone was staring into her cup of food as she shoveled it into her mouth, seeming lost in thought.

"I keep thinking about that first steep trail we came up. The one with the drop-off on the right. I said it was snowy when he started his run that day. And that he might've slipped off that trail. You said if he did, he would've fallen all the way down into the valley. Five hundred feet at least. So no way he could survive that fall. But are you sure there's no place anywhere along that trail with those little shelves of rock to break his fall? Not even one?"

Sam chewed in silence for a moment.

"Can't say for a fact there's not even one. No. But if I'm remembering right, it's more of a sheer cliff than the one you were just checking. What do you think, Jone?"

She seemed to jump at the mention of her name. She'd clearly been far away.

"About what?"

"Ethan's thinking we should've been looking over the edge on that first piece of steep trail. But I'm thinking that's pretty sheer. Not too many places that could break a fall. At least, as I recall it. But I won't lie and pretend I ever looked at it from the valley with an eye for such a thing."

"Me neither," she said, still chewing. "But even if he did slip off the trail early on . . . that's where the rangers and the search team would've been most likely to find him. Either way. Whether a shelf broke his fall or whether he went all the way to the valley. They must've looked there."

"Unless they more or less looked right at him but he blended in," Sam said. "You know. Some people know to wear bright colors on the trail. Some don't think of it. Any idea what your dad was wearing that day, son?"

"Little late in the game to be asking him that," Jone said. "Don't you think? You know the ranger must've asked him that first thing."

It sounded like an invitation to another argument, the way she said it. A little dig at Sam. So Ethan jumped in fast, hoping to prevent another problem.

"Let me try to remember. Did he?" His conversation with Ranger Dave seemed like such ancient history. Like something that had happened months before. "I think he did. I must've said I was asleep when he left, and I didn't see him go. But all his running clothes are pretty much the same. He wears shorts and a T-shirt, and a fleece that he takes off and ties around his waist once he's warmed up. And they're all gray. You know. That sort of light heather gray."

Sam and Jone both groaned, and at almost exactly the same moment.

"Great," Sam said. "He went out into the mountains disguised as shale. You tell the ranger he was wearing rock gray?"

"I think I must have," Ethan said. "Because that groan sounded familiar."

"Such an experienced outdoorsman," Sam said. "You'd think he'd know better."

Ethan shook his head. "There are things he'll wear and things he won't. I don't know how to explain my dad any better than that. And he never goes out like something could happen. He never prepares for the worst. It's like he figures he can do anything. That he's immune from everything. Except he does take bear spray. I guess because it's life or death."

"So is all the rest of this," Sam said.

They ate in silence for a time.

Then Ethan said, "By the time he got to that steep trail we just climbed, the snow would've melted. It would've been at least late morning by then. And you remember it warmed up fast that day. That's the day the weather changed and it got hot."

"Meaning?" Sam asked.

Jone had gone away again. Figuratively speaking.

"I just think he was more likely to slip off the snowy trail."

"Wet rock with snowmelt running off it isn't much better in the traction department."

"But we looked over the edge of the second drop-off. We didn't look over the edge of the first."

No one chose to comment. In fact, most of the rest of their lunch break passed in stony silence.

"We still haven't figured out what to do next," Sam said after a time.

"I say we let Ethan decide," Jone said.

"Ethan?" Sam asked.

"Me?" Ethan chimed in.

"Yeah. Why not you? It's your trip. It's your father."

"But I know this place less than anybody."

"Not sure that matters," Jone said, setting her empty cup on a rock. "You can know this place like the back of your hand, but that won't tell you where the man got lost or hurt inside it. That's just guesswork. You're the one has to live with it most if we guess wrong. So I figure you ought to have your say."

Ethan ate the last of his pasta in silence.

He felt the weight of the decision but, surprisingly, did not feel overwhelmed by it. There was no right or wrong choice. No, that wasn't quite true. If his father was out here, there was a trail he'd taken and a trail he hadn't. But there was no way to know one from the other. Ethan accepted that—really let it sink in, all the way down to his gut. Guesswork was all they had. Ethan simply needed to choose. And if he chose wrong, he needed to live with it. Like Jone said. And he would. Because it had been his best effort. He was out here long after the professionals had given up. He was doing all that could be done. He had an approximately fifty-fifty chance of choosing wrong, but there would be no carelessness or negligence involved. Just the luck of the draw.

It's not like somebody else was smarter, or had more experience, and could do better. Lots of people had more experience. Sam and Jone, for example. The rangers and the search pilots. But they weren't doing any better.

"I say we turn right," Ethan said. "Take the trail that leads back home. I want to ride that first valley, right up against the edge. Right where he'd land if he slipped off that trail. Maybe they only searched that by plane, and maybe he didn't stand out from the rocks he landed on. And we can look up at the rock face from there and see if there's any place that could've broken his fall. And if there is, we can ride up onto the trail again and look down from above."

Ethan stopped, breathed. There. It was done. Right or wrong, it was done. He'd made the decision.

"Fair enough," Jone said, clearly pleased that he'd agreed with her thinking.

Sam said nothing. Not as they cleaned up from lunch, not as they mounted up and headed on.

So apparently Sam was not pleased.

—

Halfway back down the steep trail, winding downhill to the other side of the valley, Jone asked him a question.

"Anything special you factored into that decision?"

"Yeah," Ethan said. "One thing. If my dad says he does twenty miles, I figure the truth is he probably does less. That's just the kind of guy he is, you know? Based on what I know about him. And I guess I know him pretty well. After seventeen years."

Sam was close enough to hear them. But still he said nothing.

—

What might have been two painful hours later, they rode over a rocky pass that made Ethan's heart pound and his forehead sweat. But he convinced himself that it was not the same one. Still, he carefully chose not to look over his shoulder into the valley behind them, which would have been the best way to identify the location.

Ethan heard a sharp rapping sound, and looked up to see that Sam had just ridden over a familiar-looking shotgun lying on the trail. One of the bay's hooves must have knocked into it. Ethan could see it skitter a few inches along the trail.

Ethan's heart ratcheted up to what always felt like near-death speed. How hard could a heart beat before it exploded, anyway?

Rebar managed to miss the shotgun with all four hooves.

Jone stopped her chestnut right in front of it.

Sam rode on without noticing.

"This look familiar to you?" she asked Ethan.

She swung down off her horse and picked it up by its stock, holding it up high for Ethan to see. Ethan closed his eyes so he wouldn't see it. And so his heart wouldn't kill him.

"Yes, ma'am," he said. "I mean Jone. It's my father's."

Ethan wondered if she could hear the tremble in his voice. The shortness of breath.

"He takes it with him when he's running?"

"No. He takes bear spray. I brought it up here."

"You came up here with a shotgun?"

"Right."

"Why?"

"To find my dad. Oh. You meant why the shotgun. I thought it would protect me against bears."

"How'd that work out?"

"Not so well, actually."

"Yeah. Having a gun you don't know how to use tends to cause more problems than it solves. But it's worth something, so we'll take it home, anyway."

She swung up into the saddle and braced the weapon across her thighs. They rode on. It was a long, shaky ride down off that pass for Ethan.

It took them several minutes to catch up to Sam, who didn't seem to notice that he'd left them behind. Either that or he didn't care.

—

They rode through the afternoon, and Sam said nothing. And Jone said nothing. Ethan figured he knew why Jone stayed quiet. She simply had nothing to add to Sam's silent tantrum. Ethan said nothing because Sam was riding too far ahead, and so Ethan couldn't ask him why he was acting this way. And also because, even if he'd been closer, he likely wouldn't have known how to start.

So Ethan hunkered over his dog and tried to keep him from slipping off the front of the saddle, even though his arms were so sore and trembly he was tempted to cry.

The sky covered over with dense, white, scudding cumulus clouds, racing above and ahead of the team on a rising wind.

In time Ethan saw, in the distance, the high trail they'd ridden their first day out. The one they had vowed to recheck. It stretched Ethan's brain uncomfortably to think it had only been yesterday morning, so he stopped thinking about that. It was too hard to understand. The sheer face of the mountain looked a long way off across the newly green valley. Maybe farther than they could ride with the daylight they had left. Maybe only farther than Ethan wished they would.

They came upon a winding stream, wide, and with a steep bed. It looked about as deep as Dora's knees, yet Ethan could see the sparkle of rocks on its bottom. They shone bright and colorfully varied in a ray of sun that peeked out between a keyhole of two clouds and then disappeared again.

Ethan felt cold in the stiff wind.

They rode their horses and mules across without a word spoken to each other. Dora's hooves splashed occasional drops of water onto Ethan's jeans, but his shoes stayed dry, and he was thankful for that.

Their path across the valley was less an organized trail and more just riding across a valley, wherever you chose to ride. So Ethan put his heels to his mule and rode up beside Jone, and looked up at her face towering above him on her tall mount.

"Was that an extra-big creek we just crossed?" he asked her.

"That was the Blythe River."

"You're kidding," he said.

But part of him must have considered the possibility. Because he'd asked.

"Everything changes fast in the wilderness," she said. "Sometimes in just a matter of hours. It was all swollen with snowmelt and rain and hail that morning." Jone didn't say "yesterday morning," leaving Ethan to wonder if she couldn't believe the compression of time, either. "Now most of the snow has melted. Sure, there's more in the very highest elevations. But a whole bunch of it melted at once. Now the runoff has slowed way down."

Ethan found himself deeply comforted by the fact that someone was talking to him, for the first time in hours. He sincerely wanted her to keep talking.

"Remember when we rode up that trail?" she asked, pointing to the line snaking up the mountain before them. "Remember it had all these little waterfalls? Falling on us, falling over the trail and into the valley. Remember that? Now look at it. Nothing coming down."

They both looked at it for a moment—over and ahead of their mounts' ears—without speaking.

"Damn," Jone said. "Was that really just yesterday? Feels like a week ago."

"That's what I was just thinking!" he said, excited to hear something familiar come from the inside of someone else's head.

They rode in silence for a few steps. Ethan felt something nagging at his brain. Something unfortunate and dark.

"So if someone is stuck out here, that's bad, right? Less water is bad."

"Depends," she said. "It just all depends, hon. If someone was lost out here, it wouldn't be hard to find water. I mean, look at us. We've found it everywhere we've gone. Lakes, the river. The river snakes all the way through this place, the whole length of it. And all these little tributaries and creeks leading into it. But if someone was injured out here. You know . . . not moving around . . . Well, I know what you're thinking, Ethan, and I'm not going to lie to you. Time's running out for your dad."

"I know," Ethan said. "I'm really getting it, I think, that we're going home tomorrow without him. I mean, we're going to look in the valley underneath that trail. And ride up and look over the edge in case there's any place partway down. But then what? We're back close to home, and what's the point of riding out again? Where can we ride that we didn't already? What are we supposed to see that we haven't already seen? I mean, I know there's more wilderness. Lots more. But not that he could have gotten to in one day of running, and we'd have no idea which way to look . . ."

"We tried." Jone's voice sounded deeper than usual. Sad and a little consoling. "We said we'd try, right?"

"I guess," he said.

But still it felt like a hard pill to swallow. To turn around and go home and not know any more about the welfare of his dad than they'd known at the start.

"That's not a full day's ride tomorrow," she said. "Maybe a morning's work at best. Or at worst, I guess I should say. Even if we ride all along the base of the cliff and then go slow back up the trail so's you can look over. It's still only a handful of hours."

"So we'll be home early," he said, which sounded like a tragic thing to be.

"Or we can knock off a little early today," she said.

"Oh my God I would love that!" Ethan blurted out without thinking. "It is so hard to hold this dog onto the saddle with me. Every muscle in my body is killing me. My arms are killing me. My back is killing me."

She reined her horse to a halt.

"Sam!" she called out sharply, cupping one hand around her mouth.

Her voice was loud, and Sam wasn't far ahead. Ethan felt Sam must have heard her. But he and the bay and Rebar kept going as if he hadn't.

"No, wait," Ethan said. "No. I take back what I said. We can't stop now. If my dad is out here . . ."

"Honey. It doesn't matter. By the time we get there it'll be too dark to search."

"But if we keep going, we'll be there earlier tomorrow morning."

"Ethan," she said. And there was a deep gravity to the one-word sentence. Ethan winced in preparation for what would come next. "I think it's time we can stop acting like this is life or death. I'm sorry to have to say it. But I think you can take care of your own needs now and consider that we're more recovery than rescue at this point."

Ethan said nothing. He just sat his mule and felt the last thread of his hopes lift out of him.

Jone laid the reins down on the chestnut's neck and made a megaphone with both of her hands. "Sam Riley, you stubborn, pig-headed old bastard!" Her horse jumped slightly at the tone and volume. "We got a decision to make! So you get your ass back here and talk to us whether you're talking to us or not!"

A pause. Then Sam's bay stopped. Rebar took a step or two and then stopped behind them. But Sam didn't turn them around, or even look over his shoulder. Horse, man, and bad-tempered mule just stood their ground, facing off toward the mountains.

"What's wrong with him?" Ethan asked Jone quietly.

"He's a man," Jone said. "That answer your question?"

A moment later Sam's rein hand came up, and he turned his bay around and rode back to them, stopping a few steps too far away. His face looked blank and expressionless. If he was angry, Ethan thought, he had a strange way of showing it.

"It's like this," Jone said. "It's going to take us maybe an hour to ride to the edge of the valley and another hour to ride all along it. If we do that tonight, we'll have to camp there, with no water. Because it'll be too late to go up that trail again and have enough light to look proper. Ethan's tired, and I think we all are, so I propose we stay put right where we are. Right here near the river. What we got to do tomorrow we can do in a morning, easy. I think we need to knock off for the day."

Sam sat in silence for a minute or so. Ethan actually wondered if the older man had heard all that. He must have. But Ethan saw no sign that he had.

Sam swung down off his big bay.

"Wait," Jone said to Ethan. "Let me get down first, and I'll take the dog from you."

As he handed Rufus down to Jone, Ethan couldn't help letting out a telling expression of pain. A kind of muffled grunt.

"Holy crap, that hurts," he said, in hopes of explaining the strange noise.

"Need help getting down?"

"I don't think so. Let me just stretch a minute. It's down, you know? Gravity ought to get me there."

Meanwhile Sam was unsaddling his horse and taking the packs off his mule.

Ethan stood in the stirrups, kicked his leg out of the right-hand one, and lifted his right leg. It didn't lift far. Not nearly far enough to clear Dora's back.

"Here," Jone said, and stepped in. "I realize this is mighty undignified, but just bear with me."

She came up on Dora's left side, wrapped an arm around Ethan's waist, and simply pulled him off the saddle. His right leg, and then his foot, slid over the saddle seat, and both feet landed on the ground.

"Ow!" he said.

"Sorry. I wasn't aiming to hurt you."

"It wasn't that. It wasn't your fault. There's no move I can make right now that doesn't have me saying 'ow.'"

They stood a moment, smiling small commiserating smiles at each other.

When they looked up, Sam was walking away.

"Where's he going?" Ethan asked, though he knew Jone could know no more about the subject than he did.

"No idea. Maybe he has to relieve himself."

"Oh. Right."

"I know you're tired," she said. "But I'm going to walk the couple hundred yards back to the river and fill up that big water sack. The one that filters water by gravity."

"Oh. Is that what that hanging bag was? I wondered."

"Might do you good to walk with me. Keep from getting too stiff."

Ethan took a few steps with her, then looked around for his dog.

"I'm worried he'll try to walk with us."

"If he does, you can stay back with him if you want."

They took two more steps. Rufus sat down to watch them.

"Guess I was worried about nothing," Ethan said.

—

"I don't know how long he's been gone exactly," Ethan said. "But longer than it would take to do what you said."

Jone only grunted.

They were lying side by side on sleeping bags in the grass, watching the clouds slide through. Resting up for the work of setting up tents and cooking dinner. Hoping Sam would come back and help. At least, Ethan was hoping that.

"I'd ask what was wrong with him," Ethan said. "But I figure I already did. And you told me."

"I'd like to withdraw my answer," she said, "and apologize for it to boot. You'll be a man yourself in a year or so, and I shouldn't make blanket statements. All I can say is, you'll have a choice about what kind of a man you want to be. Don't be like that one. At least, not like that one's being right now. Aw, hell, I already know you won't. I can tell."

Ethan mulled that over in silence for a moment.

"I'm not sure *exactly* what it is I'm supposed to avoid."

"One word, kid. Pride. Don't get all hung up in false pride. Don't always have to be the leader. Don't always have to be right. Don't get your feelings hurt over every little thing and take it out on somebody else. Everybody makes mistakes, and you get to be part of everybody." She rolled over onto one elbow. Looked down at Ethan's face. "You okay? You don't look so good."

"I don't think I'm sick, if that's what you mean. I've just never been this tired and sore in my life. It almost feels like being sick. Like I feel cold, and a little shaky, and almost sick to my stomach, but not quite. But it feels like it's because my muscles are so sore."

"Lactic acid," she said, and dropped over onto her back again.

"Oh," he said.

"Your muscles are releasing lots of lactic acid. You should push a ton of fluids tonight. All night, till you go to bed. You'll have to wake up and pee, but you could do worse. It's better than being in so much pain you can't sleep in the first place. I'll get you some water and some ibuprofen. That'll help at least a little bit."

"Wait. No. Aren't you just as tired?"

"No," she said. "I'm tired. But I'm not that bad. I'm old, but I'm tough. This isn't all that far off the curve of what I do on an average day."

And with that, she got up and wandered off.

Ethan shivered and breathed, and watched the clouds roll by. And wished there were some way out of his own skin. It was a purely miserable place to be.

A few minutes later she returned, and helped him sit up. She handed him a tall plastic cup of filtered water, and four white tablets, which Ethan swallowed all at once.

She wrapped a stiff blanket around his shoulders, and he pulled it more tightly to himself.

"Thanks," he said as she sat cross-legged on her sleeping bag. "Hey! Rufus! Don't chew on that sock." Then, to Jone, "He's chewing on the sock."

"One of yours or one of Sam's?"

"Mine."

"Just as well it's not Sam's, based on his mood. I'm sure it's no coincidence that Sam put yours on the front paws. Hey!" she said sharply to the dog. She reached over and bumped his head with her hand, and he stopped worrying the edge of the sock. "When you get into the tent tonight and out of the dirt, take all that off him. Bandages and everything. He wants to lick those sore places. Let him. Tomorrow before we head out we'll get him set up again."

"Oh," Ethan said. "I just remembered. I was going to wash out a pair of socks tonight." He stared in the direction of the river for a time. "Command decision. I'm wearing dirty socks tomorrow. I just can't make myself do it."

"Give them to me," Jone said.

"No. I draw the line at you washing out my dirty socks. You've done enough."

"If I'm down there doing something else, and it's convenient, I'll do it. If not . . ."

Then they didn't speak for a time. Maybe fifteen minutes or more. Ethan was too exhausted to speak.

And Sam still had not come back.

"I don't really know Sam all that well," he said at last. "I like him, so I hate to say what I'm about to say. But I guess I can kind of see why you keep him at arm's length. Please don't tell him I said that. He'd be hurt."

"I won't. Aw, hell. What can I say about me and Sam? My husband's been gone a damn long time, kid. Over ten years. Part of me wouldn't mind a little company. And it's not like there's much of anybody else around. If Sam'd only come at me some better way all this time, you know? Not so . . ."

But then she didn't seem to know how to finish.

"Like the kind of man you don't want me to be?"

"Right. But I know you won't be."

"What about your husband? Was he like that?"

"Oh, no. He was different. He didn't waste his time with crap like that. He had living to do. He knew who he was and he didn't have anything to prove to anybody. He had no problem saying he made a mistake, or he didn't know. That's a sign of confidence in a person. People think it's the other way around. But it's only people who don't have their acts together who work so hard to make you think they do."

"I guess I see what you mean," Ethan said. Then, a few scudding clouds later, "Those ibuprofen are starting to help. Thanks."

"I'll go get started on some dinner. Sam can come back and eat it, or his helping can sit there and get cold. I don't see it as any of my business. And frankly, I don't rightly care."

And not caring proved to be a good thing, too. Because dinner came and went. The sky faded to night. And Sam did not come back.

—

It was dark when Sam unzipped the tent flap and ducked in. Ethan would have guessed it was around ten o'clock, but he didn't know for sure. But he was not asleep. He'd been lying awake watching the moon rise to directly overhead—where he could see it through the mesh top of the tent—and listening to Rufus lick his paws.

Sam stripped down to his boxers and climbed into his sleeping bag without comment.

A few minutes went by. Maybe three. Maybe ten.

"What the hell are you doing?" Ethan asked Sam, without realizing he was about to speak.

Sam sat up straight, sleeping bag and all.

"What am I doing? What am *I* doing? What are *you* doing? Yelling at the person who brought you out here just to be a nice guy?"

Ethan hadn't yelled. But he couldn't get a word in edgewise to point it out.

"Hell, I don't need this, Ethan. I got enough problems without you getting on my case. I could ride right out of here. Right now. By headlamp. And you and that . . . you two can just finish this little project by yourself."

Then Sam seemed to run out of steam.

"I just don't get what you're so upset about," Ethan said quietly.

"Because. I'm. *Blowing it!*" Sam shouted. "Everything I try to do to impress her just backfires on me."

"But you keep trying the same things."

"What do you mean?" Sam's voice quieted. As if he was interested now. Because maybe Ethan knew something. Saw something Sam didn't see.

Hell, Ethan thought. *Everybody sees something Sam doesn't see.* Of course, he didn't say so.

"You keep trying to impress her the same way. First you tell everybody to talk you up to her. Then you get all upset because there's another man along on the trip. Like you're a wild stallion or something and you have to drive all the other males away. Then you get even more upset because you had a different idea than she did about which way we should turn and I chose hers. I didn't choose it to side with her. I chose it because I'm trying to find my dad. We're out here to find my dad. Remember? It's really not so much a dating thing, you know?"

Ethan waited for Sam to blow. Maybe stomp out of the tent and ride home. Instead the older man just sighed deeply.

"It was both for me. Okay? I don't think you need to begrudge me that."

"I don't," Ethan said. "I mean, mostly I don't."

Ethan breathed more deeply, happy that the explosive part of the conversation seemed to have passed on its own.

"But it doesn't matter now," Sam said, "because it's over. I lost. I made an ass of myself. I finally got my big chance and I blew it. I don't know any other ways to impress her. I don't know what the hell she wants."

"I do," Ethan said. A brief, reverberating silence. "I know what impresses her."

"How? *How* do you know?"

"She told me."

"You were talking about me?"

"We were talking about her late husband, actually," Ethan said. Because it was true enough. And more diplomatic. "She said he knew who he was. He had nothing to prove to anybody. If he made a mistake, he admitted it. If he didn't know, he admitted it."

"That doesn't help, buddy. Because that's not me."

"She said something else. She said only people who don't have their act together work so hard to make you think they do."

"Yeah. Well. It's too late. I did exactly that, and she hates me."

"I don't know about that," Ethan said. "She told me her husband's been gone for a long time and part of her wouldn't mind the company. You just keep coming at her the wrong way. She said if you'd come at her differently—"

"Wait. She said that?"

"She did."

"You wouldn't tell me she said that if she didn't. Right, buddy? Because that would be downright cruel."

"She said it, Sam."

"So what do I do?"

"I can only tell you what I would do. I'd go over to her tent and see if she was awake, and if she was, I'd tell her I was sorry. That I'd been acting like an idiot. You know. The truth. Tell her why as best you can. Tell her you can do better."

Sam sat frozen like a statue in the moonlight for what struck Ethan as a strange and unlikely length of time. Ethan waited to see when he would break, and in which direction.

"Okay, thanks," Sam said.

He unzipped his way out of the tent, zipped it back up, and disappeared.

Ethan lay still a moment, wondering if Sam was really going over there in just his boxer shorts. A moment later the tent flap unzipped again.

"Guess some clothes would help," Sam said.

"Yeah," Ethan said. "I didn't mean you should come at her *that* differently."

It felt good to joke. For a change.

—

Ethan woke in the middle of the night, or at least what felt like the middle of the night. He needed to get up and pee, just as Jone had predicted.

Sam was still gone.

He left Rufus inside the tent, so the dog wouldn't get dirt on his raw paw pads. And Rufus didn't seem inclined to argue about coming along. So he must have been one tired, sore dog.

Ethan stepped out into the night and stretched his ruined muscles.

The moon had gone down behind the mountains, so he knew he had slept for a long time. And the stars were out in an absolute riot. Ethan had never seen anything like it. It felt like being inside the dome of a planetarium during one of those projected star shows. Except for one thing: this was real.

Ethan craned his neck back, sure he could see the eroded-looking, slightly more colorful band formed by the edge of the Milky Way.

He still needed to pee, but somehow the stars seemed more important.

Besides, it was probably his last chance to see them this way.

He heard a rustling, and whipped around. Immediately thinking, *Bear.*

It was Sam, letting himself out of Jone's tent and zipping it up again.

"Ethan?" Sam whispered.

He walked over and stood shoulder to shoulder with Ethan, under the stars, and craned his neck back. As if he couldn't imagine what Ethan saw above him and found so fascinating. As if there could be more than one answer to what was up there. In his peripheral vision, Ethan could see the dark silhouettes of the horses and mules huddled together in the dark.

"What time is it?" Ethan asked.

"'Bout two thirty."

"That's a long time to be in Jone's tent."

"It's not what you're thinking."

"I wasn't thinking anything."

"We just talked."

A moment of silence, then Sam threw his arms around Ethan's shoulders and hugged him sideways.

Ethan wanted to say "ow" but he didn't. He just laughed.

"What was that for?" he asked Sam.

"Because . . . *we talked.* For like *four hours.*"

"That's good."

"Good? *Good?* That's a freaking miracle, Ethan. And I owe it all to you. You have a real way with people, you know that?"

Ethan laughed again.

"I *so* do not have a way with people."

"You do. You just don't see it yet. You have a talent for getting along."

"I have no talents. I'm the least talented person I know. You and Jone have talents. You can ride and shoot and live in the wilderness. I have nothing like that."

"Riding and shooting are okay," Sam said. "They have their uses. But it's a limited application. You know what I mean? But knowing how to get along with people . . . or, you know, helping other people get along better . . . hell, you give me the choice, I'd take people skills over riding and shooting any day."

Ethan briefly wondered if Jone was still awake, and if she could hear them. Also if that had been a shooting star he'd seen, faintly, at the corner of his field of vision.

"All I said was to be honest with her. That seems pretty basic."

"Maybe to you. But do you really think everybody in the world's walking around getting it that they'll impress people more by being honest about their own failings? Well, I'll tell you. They're not. Trust me. They're not. This's not as popular a theory as you might imagine."

Ethan looked away from the stars for the first time. Looked over at his friend Sam's face. Then he slung an arm over the older man's shoulders. Even though it hurt.

"I'm glad if I helped," he said.

"That would be putting it mildly. So what are you doing out here looking at the stars?"

"Oh. Right. I came out to pee. But I haven't gotten around to that yet. I guess I just felt like this was my last chance. The stars, I mean. Not the peeing. I'm going back to Manhattan pretty soon here. Let's face it. We're wrapping up our search soon enough. And then the next step is flying home to my mom. We don't have stars like this in New York. I figured I should enjoy the show while I can."

"Well. I'm going to sleep. Or I'm going to try, anyway. I might be too excited to sleep."

Sam patted Ethan's hand where it sat on his shoulder. Then he ducked out from under Ethan's arm and back into the tent. It hurt when the arm came back down to Ethan's side. Everything hurt.

Well. Almost everything. All the outside parts of him. On the inside, things felt slightly better.

Chapter Fourteen: Designer Fleece

Six days after his father disappeared

Ethan woke up late. At least, late by the standards of a wilderness search team. The sky was fully light, the sun just ready to peek over the mountains, to light up the trail they were about to search. Or, rather, search again.

Jone was making coffee on the camp stove, and Ethan could smell it. He'd had coffee a few times in his life, but had never depended on it or craved it. Until that morning. Sam was stuffing two of the sleeping bags into their stuff sacks, whistling. And humming. Intermittently.

Rufus was lying half on his side in the dirt, paws unbandaged, watching. Smiling. Or so it seemed to Ethan.

Ethan ran his fingers through his hair in lieu of a comb. It hurt to raise his arms, but he did it anyway. He sidled over to Jone and the coffee. He squatted down near her side, which was no easy task with just about every muscle in his body locked up like steel.

"Wow, I know I ask this a lot," he said quietly near her ear, "but what the hell is wrong with Sam?" But this time he said it in a wry, joking way, as if it were abnormal for anyone to be so outwardly happy at a time like this.

She burst out laughing. Sam turned around and looked at her, smiled, then went back to his work.

"You're a funny kid," Jone said. "You know that?"

"Not really. I'm funny?"

"When you're not worried or scared, you are. So I guess that's why it took me some time to notice."

"Oh. Thanks. I guess that's two things, then."

"Two things?"

"Last night Sam told me I had people skills. That I'm good at getting along with people and helping other people get along with each other."

"Yeah," Jone said. "I can see that. Coffee?"

"Oh, God yes."

She poured him some in a light metal mug with foldaway handles. He sipped the coffee. It tasted like salvation.

"So last night . . . ," Ethan said. He noticed a quick pause in which Jone's hands stopped moving. He talked through it. ". . . I was outside looking at the stars. And I was thinking it's nice that I learned something good about myself. Because when I go home with that . . . with that new thinking about being good at something . . . well . . . maybe it'll make it a tiny bit easier that I don't go home with anything else. I think you know what I mean. So that's why I was happy to add funny."

Jone smiled, a small and lightly sad thing.

"Let me give you another big one for your list," she said. "Number three. Brave."

A laugh burst out of Ethan. It sprayed through his lips and sounded a little like a donkey braying.

"Brave? Is that some kind of joke?"

"Not at all," she said, and then carefully sipped at her hot coffee.

"See if this sounds familiar." He rose to his feet, using his hands for leverage, and purposely not saying "ow." He definitely thought it, though. "'Shoot the bear!'" he squeaked, in a parody of his panic-driven voice. "'Shoot the bear!'" He danced around slightly, waving his sore arms, careful not to spill his precious coffee. "'If it moves, shoot it!' And then you have to put a hand on my shoulder and point out that it's on the other side of the lake drinking water and paying no attention to us."

Jone chuckled at his self-imitation. "See? Funny kid."

"Okay. I'll take funny. But brave?"

"Listen," she said, and leveled him with a gaze that looked deadly serious. "How hard was it to come out here, nervous as you are, and after a close encounter with a grizzly?"

Ethan swallowed hard. Paused before answering.

"Very," he said quietly.

"And that's called brave."

Ethan said nothing. There was nothing he could say. She was right. And it was not in his nature to address that deep a compliment head-on.

He sat down beside her again, cross-legged in the dirt, and they drank coffee together and watched Sam feed and saddle up the horses. Jone leaned over in Ethan's direction and handed him a clean pair of his own socks.

"Not sure I did you a favor," she said. "Because they're still just a tiny bit damp."

"You're amazing. It's a huge favor. Huge. I hate wearing dirty socks. Hate it. Thank you."

"No worries."

"What *is* that thing he's whistling?" Ethan asked, a note of joking derision in his voice. As if there was such a thing as too cheerful early in the morning, after sleeping on the hard ground all night.

"Not sure," she said. "Might be something from an old Disney film."

"Ah," Ethan said. "*That* explains why I keep expecting a cartoon bluebird to land on his shoulder."

—

"Look at his paws and tell me what you think," he said to Jone.

She came over and lifted Rufus's paws one by one, examining the sore pads.

"I don't think they need to be bandaged," she said. "They're dry. Almost the very first phase of scabbing over. But I don't think he should be walking on them, either. Half a mile or less and I guarantee you they'll be bleeding again."

"Oh," Ethan said. It was impossible to keep the disappointment out of his voice.

"What's the problem?" Sam asked, appearing suddenly behind them.

Jone answered for him.

"Kid's arms and back are sore from holding the dog on the saddle with him."

"Oh," Sam said. "Why didn't you say so?"

He wrapped the dog up in his big arms and lifted him off the ground. He carried Rufus over to the stock, who were standing ready to go, and plopped the dog down on Rebar's packs. Rebar turned his head around and bared his teeth as if to bite. Sam, or the dog; Ethan wasn't sure which. Sam cuffed him on the muzzle, and he straightened his neck and looked ahead again.

Sam rummaged around in one of the packs and found the makeshift rope harness he'd used to get Rufus safely across the river. He tied it onto the dog and then used its length of rope to snug it down to the packs on both sides, so Rufus was literally strapped down with the rest of Rebar's load.

"Got to keep that ornery head forward, is the only thing," Sam said. "But I'll deal with it. Well? I'm ready to ride when you two are."

—

The edge of the valley—just where it touched the base of the cliff—was a hard place to ride. It was rocky, a sea of scattered boulders that Ethan could only guess had come down from the side of the mountain. Maybe yesterday. Maybe before any of their grandparents were born. Some were the size of a suitcase, others the size of a car.

Sam took the job of swinging down from his horse and walking over and around the rocks to check out the places that couldn't be accessed on horseback. Sam seemed to have energy coming out of his ears.

At first he handed Rebar's rope to Jone so she could keep the mule's head forward, away from the dog. Soon it became clear that Rebar had forgotten the dog was even up there. But still Jone held the rope, just in case.

It was a slower job than any of them had anticipated.

By the time they'd covered three-quarters of the fall zone and reached a trail intersection, the sun was high overhead and Ethan was hungry for lunch. But he didn't want to stop. He wanted to finish.

"Is this another one of those tricky intersections?" he asked. "Like a judgment call we'll end up arguing about?"

"Maybe," Sam said. "But we're not going to argue. We're just going to decide. This is really more of a use trail. Unofficial, you know? But we can ride it. It's wide enough, and it's safe. It switchbacks up the side of this mountain and joins the high trail about a quarter of the way along."

Ethan craned his neck and looked up.

"This is the first time I've seen anything that looks like it could break a person's fall," Ethan said.

Sam raised his binoculars. That seemed odd to Ethan. It was right there, plain to see. Was there really that much difference between seventeen-year-old eyes and fifty-something-year-old ones? There must be, he figured.

"I don't know," Sam said. "Pretty narrow. A person could slip off the trail and shoot right past that skinny little ledge and into the valley."

Jone raised her binoculars, as if to offer a second opinion.

"Depends on how you fell, I think," she said. "If you put your outside foot down on some snow and ice, thinking it was trail, you might drop straight down onto that little jut."

"And it's long," Ethan said.

"Yeah, I'll give it that," Sam said. "It's long. You could go about a tenth of a mile, all the while keeping that little shelf underneath you. Still not sure a person could hit it, though."

"What's the downside to going up this use trail?" Ethan asked.

"We miss searching the last bit of the base of the cliff."

"Can't we get it on the way down?"

"Yeah. But then we miss looking over the edge of the last little piece of the high trail. We could always circle back and do both if you don't mind it taking most of all day."

"Can I borrow your binoculars?"

He rode his mule over to Sam, who reached them out for Ethan to take. Ethan used his left leg to nudge Dora sideways, closer, so he could reach them. He was getting good at that. Too bad that, after that morning, he wouldn't need the skill again as long as he lived.

Ethan took the binoculars and searched along the sheer rock face on the other side of the use trail.

"It looks pretty straight up and down farther on. I say we go up. Look down on that shelf. Then we can come back the way we went up. Search the rest of the edge of the valley."

"Done," Sam said.

He put his heels to his bay horse, and steered him up the use trail toward higher ground. And the horse surged forward. But he never really gained much traction. There was a problem hampering his forward motion. It was an anchor named Rebar.

"Move, you damn mule," Sam spat over his shoulder.

Rebar didn't budge.

"What's wrong with him?" Ethan asked, sitting his mule behind Rebar, waiting to follow them up the mountain. If they ever moved.

"He wants to go home. We were almost back to the trailhead. Only a couple miles. He thought we were going home. He doesn't want to climb that mountain. He doesn't want to turn around." Then, to the mule, Sam bellowed, "Move, damn you!" and gave a sharp yank on the rope.

Rebar moved. The problem was, he moved backward.

"Get out of his way, son!" Sam shouted at Ethan. "Don't let him back into you. He'll kick if he backs into you."

Ethan didn't know how to make a mule back up, so he reined Dora around in a circle. Off into some high weeds. Rebar continued to twist backward and pull on Sam's horse, so Ethan kept moving out of the way.

Dora was upset now, because Rebar was upset. She held her head high, her eyes wide. And her hooves danced, rather than plodding. That scared Ethan.

She began twisting around in circles even though Ethan was now trying to rein her into a stop.

"Don't pull back on the reins," Sam shouted to him. "That's how you back her."

Oh, that's *how you back her,* he thought. He loosened the reins, and she surged forward into the path of Rebar, who was still in reverse, and Ethan had to steer her off into the weeds again.

Sam dismounted, walked around toward the back of his mule—carefully staying out of range of those dangerous hooves—and smacked Rebar hard with the flat of his hand. Ethan could hear the crack of it.

Rebar moved forward.

Sam shook his right hand in the air, making it clear that the slap had stung him as much as the mule. Then he got back on his horse, fast.

"Should've brought along a piece of what he was named for," Sam said, and kicked his horse forward. "I'm kidding," he added. "I wouldn't hit him anything worse than I just did."

Sam kicked his bay, and this time the train moved again.

All except Ethan and Dora. Dora was still going around in twists and circles, and her right rear hoof seemed to be anchored down somehow. Ethan could feel her try to lift it, but she didn't seem able to lift it very high.

"She caught on something?" Sam yelled back.

Ethan could tell Sam wanted to keep moving up the hill before Rebar stalled again.

"Seems like she is," Ethan shouted back.

"You may have to get down and sort it out."

Ethan spoke quietly to his mule. "Okay, ho," he said. "Ho." He waited for a beat or two, and the mule seemed to settle. But not until Sam and Jone stopped moving the rest of the stock up the mountain and waited. Dora clearly didn't like the feeling of being left behind.

"Ho," Ethan said one more time.

Then he swung down. It hurt a lot, and it was clumsy. He kicked poor Dora behind the saddle again. But this time she laid her long ears back and not much more.

Ethan dropped to the ground in the tall weeds.

He walked around the front of the mule, just to be safe, and examined her right rear hoof. It wasn't stuck, exactly. It wasn't anchored down to anything, as he had thought. She had just managed to get something wrapped around it, and the weeds were preventing her from shaking it off, and she didn't like the feeling. Ethan couldn't quite see what it was, but it looked like some kind of filthy fabric.

"Ho, girl," Ethan said. "Let me see what you've got there."

With that, the mule seemed to understand that Ethan was going to help her. She stopped dancing and kicking and stood still.

Ethan carefully reached down and grabbed the edge of the fabric. It was fleece, he realized. As soon as he got his hand on it he knew it was fleece. He could feel it. He couldn't tell a color—it was too dirty for that. But it had sleeves, one of which Dora had ripped trying to extricate herself.

It was a fleece zip-up jacket like the kind just about everybody wore to go into the outdoors.

Ethan pulled it hard. It wasn't wrapped around the mule's hoof. It was stuck on the burs or thorns of some of the vegetation behind her hoof, so it hadn't given enough when Dora had tried to kick forward.

One more good pull, and it came free in Ethan's hand.

Dora dropped her head and sighed deeply.

Ethan held the fleece in his hands and examined it. It hadn't been out in the elements for months, or years. It was fairly recently dropped. But it had been through at least that most recent rain. It was stiff from having gotten wet and then dried in its flattened position. It was more brown with mud than any other color Ethan could identify.

He turned it around so the hood was on top and tried to tell the inside from the outside. The inside was fairly clean. And gray. Light heather gray.

Then Ethan found the tag.

The tag was surprisingly white and easy to read.

It said, "Gilligan's Ltd., New York."

Ethan just froze, looking at it, for a long time. Literally froze, from the feel of it. His belly felt icy inside, and it buzzed.

He couldn't have said how long he crouched there, staring at the fleece jacket. But soon he saw the shadow of Jone and her horse fall over him.

"What'd you find there, son?" she asked him.

"It's my father's trail fleece," he said.

"You sure? They all look a lot alike. Everybody wears the same two or three brands up here."

"Sure. I bet. Are any of them Gilligan's Limited?"

"I never even heard of that brand."

"Right. I didn't figure you would have. That's because it's a sporting goods store four blocks from our apartment in Manhattan."

A flicker of silence. Then Jone cupped her hands and called up to Sam on the trail above them.

"Come on back down here, Sam," she said. "I believe we have ourselves a development."

—

"He's here," Ethan said. "He's out here. Just like I thought."

They stood, dismounted, in a circle around Ethan's find. Rufus whimpered to get down but Ethan ignored him.

"I knew he was here," Ethan added. "I just knew it."

"Just to play devil's advocate," Jone said, "just so we don't get ahead of ourselves . . . let's go over what this does and does not prove. He was here. Yes. We've established that. But we knew he came up here all the time."

Sam chimed in.

"You told us he used to take off the fleece when he was warmed up, right? So if he was running that high trail above us, about this far up he'd be warmed up. You said he'd tie it around his waist. Didn't you say that?"

"Either that or stick it under one of the straps of his hydration pack," Ethan said.

"So it could've sailed out," Jone said. "And maybe he didn't know it, or maybe he knew but didn't care enough to go down after it."

"Or maybe it came loose when he fell," Ethan said, creating another brief space of silence.

"Here's a really important question," Sam said. "So think hard on this one, Ethan. Don't answer off the top of your head. How sure are you that he had it with him on the day in question?"

Ethan felt his forehead furrow.

"I was asleep when he left that morning."

"Okay, we'll go at this another way. How sure are you that he didn't lose it on an earlier run? When was he last up here before the day he disappeared?"

"I think it was three days earlier," Ethan said.

"Were you awake when he left?" Sam asked.

"No."

"Were you there when he came back?"

"Yeah. I was."

"This is big now. So try to get this right. Did he come home with the jacket?"

Ethan squeezed his eyes closed and tried to re-create the moment.

"I was sitting on the couch. Reading. He came in." A pause. Ethan knew. But he had to be sure. Surer than sure somehow. "He had the jacket tied around his waist. I know he did. He took it off, right in front of me, and looked at it to see if it was sweaty. And he sniffed it. And then he took it out into the garage and started a load of wash."

"He's here," Jone said.

"Starting to look that way," Sam said. "I guess there's a tiny chance he could have come out here that last day, run, lost the jacket, then gone elsewhere. But now the odds are way against him being any place else."

"Think it's enough to get the search reopened?" Jone asked.

"I do," Sam said. "But I don't think that's the way to go right now. Because of time. It'd take us almost two hours to ride home. God only knows how long it would take them to mount a search on no notice. If we think he's right around here someplace, our best bet is to damn well find him. Sooner being better than later."

"You could call them on your sat phone," Jone said.

"Oh!" Sam said, sounding pleased. "Right. I knew there was a reason I brought that thing."

He moved off toward Rebar, probably to fetch it.

"What's a sat phone?" Ethan asked Jone while Sam was gone.

"Works off a satellite. Like the kind they use up on Mount Everest."

"Oh. Right. My dad climbed Everest. When he was younger. Did I tell you that?"

Ethan's mood had transformed strangely, but into what, he couldn't say. He felt excited and full of dread at almost exactly the same time.

"No. You didn't. I'd have remembered that. He must've been quite the athlete."

"Yeah. He was. Is."

"Sorry," Jone said.

"It just seems weird that he could get to the top of Mount Everest and back in one piece, and then slip off a trail a couple of miles from where we're staying. On a routine run."

"Happens more than you think. People let their guard down, and it's the routine ones that get them every time."

Ethan looked up to see Sam return, shaking his head.

"Bad news. Something wrong with it. It won't get a signal."

"So do we ride back?" Jone asked.

"I think we need to go over this area with a fine-tooth comb first," Sam said. "The chances of finding him alive are damn slim. Sorry, Ethan, but I figure you already know it's true. But let's say he's around here somewhere, alive. You just know he won't be alive much longer. I'm not sure we can afford to get a fair bead on his location and then ride away and send help in five or six hours."

"But if we find him alive," Jone said, "he'll still have to lie there while you go get help."

"But we have water," Sam said. "And food. And first aid. And if we know for a fact where he is, they'll send a medevac helicopter right away, on an emergency basis."

They all three looked at each other. Nodded.

Then they mounted their horses and headed up to the high trail.

On the ride up, Ethan's mind twirled around and through the ins and outs and illusions of that strange sensation of knowing. Long before they'd ever come up here, he'd told Sam that his father was in this wilderness. That Ethan knew it. That he wasn't wrong. But now his father was up here, and Ethan wasn't wrong. And that was a strangely, entirely different situation. It was real in a way he'd somehow not anticipated.

"What's the deal with that store?" Jone asked, startling him. She was bringing up the rear on the chestnut. "That Gilligan place? I only ask because most sporting goods stores have a name you've heard of. Or at least they sell fleece jackets with names you've heard of. So I wondered what kind of store that is."

"Snooty," Ethan said.

"Hmm. That's what I was picturing. But if it's just for running, why not buy a good old West Boundary fleece like everybody else?"

"You'd have to know my dad," he said.

"But they both keep you warm, right? I mean, who needs prestige out on the trail? What could possibly be the difference between the two jackets?"

"About two hundred dollars," Ethan said. He rode in silence for a moment. Then he added, "I'm only joking because I'm scared."

"I know," she said.

They fell silent again, and Ethan went back to reflecting on the strange shock of having been so concretely not wrong.

—

Ethan lay on his belly on the trail, most of his upper body extending terrifyingly over the edge. Sam had hold of his feet for good measure. But it was still a sickeningly shaky feeling. Ethan had to concentrate on his bladder control just to be sure everything held.

"I can't see a damn thing," he said. "I mean, I can see an edge of the shelf. But there's nobody on it. But then I feel like there's another part of the shelf in closer to the mountain. And I feel like I can't see that. Part of it I can. But right underneath me here there's this part of the rock that bulges out. Maybe the bulge goes all the way down to the shelf and there's no space underneath it to see. But I can't tell from here. I just don't know how to get a good look down there."

He waited, hoping Sam would pull him back onto the trail. Or offer some simple solution Ethan hadn't known enough to consider.

Then a memory hit Ethan's brain, and it turned his whole body to ice. Before they left, Ethan had asked Sam why more people were better for a search party. What could an extra person do? Sam had said they could hold the rope if somebody had to go over a cliff.

"Pull me back!" Ethan called.

It hurt to be dragged over the sharp little stones at the edge of the trail. But it was worth it not to have five or six hundred feet of empty space between the valley and his chest. The last thing Ethan wanted was to prove to himself whether that skinny ledge was enough to break a person's fall.

He pulled up into a cross-legged sit, and the three team members looked at each other. The more time went by with no one saying anything, the more Ethan knew what was waiting to be said.

"We can do this two ways," Sam said. "We can ride home and tell the ranger we found Noah's fleece right under this shelf. Ask him to re-search the area." He looked right into Ethan's face. "Or you can go down there."

"Me," Ethan couldn't help noting.

"I think you know why I say you. You're the lightest member of the party by quite some, and the youngest by an even bigger margin. Look, I don't blame you if you don't want to do it. You've done a lot, especially for a man you claim to hate. Option number one is pretty responsible. No one is going to hold that against you."

"How safe is it to go down?"

"Pretty damn safe. I brought a couple of harnesses, and the rope is good. My carabiners lock, and they're in good shape. I'll wrap the rope twice around my saddle horn and hold the end. Biggest danger is if you spin around and hit your head on the rocks. Going all the way to the valley is not a danger. I'm not about to let that happen."

Ethan just sat a moment. He didn't speak, and he almost couldn't have quantified what he was thinking.

"We can go get the pros," Jone said. "You decide."

"But Sam said if he's alive, even a couple of hours could make a difference."

No one answered. No one needed to. It had already been said. Nobody wanted to repeat it, apparently. Nobody wanted to put pressure on Ethan's big decision.

"I can almost picture being lowered down there on a rope," Ethan said. "Almost. What I can't picture is that moment when you first go over the edge. And you have to let go."

"We're here to help you with it if you want to try," Jone said. "That's all we can really say."

Another blank moment, absent of communication. It flitted through Ethan's mind that he had no right to stall, under the circumstances. If he were lying injured down there, he would take exception to long, drawn-out decisions.

Jone spoke again, suddenly. "Aw, hell, I'll go," she said, mostly to Sam. "If you can handle my weight."

"Between me and this big horse, twice over if I had to."

"No," Ethan said. "No, that's not right. He's my father. I'm the one who wanted to come up here. I'll go."

He rose to his feet, aware that he was already shaking. Badly, as if he might shake himself apart. He couldn't help wondering what the trembling would become when he was dangling on a rope five hundred feet over the boulders below.

—

"Okay, I'm going to let go of your hands," Jone said. "And you let go of me. But nothing's going to happen. The rope is tight. You won't move.

Only thing is, you might feel yourself tipping over backwards some. See if you can keep your feet braced against the rock."

Ethan tried to say "okay." He failed.

But, oddly, the shaking had stopped. Maybe he was beyond that level of fear now. Maybe he just couldn't afford to feel.

"One," Jone said. "Two. Three."

Jone let go. Ethan did not.

"Okay, let's try this another way. I'm going to take one of your hands and move it from my arm to the edge of the cliff. Okay?"

He might have nodded slightly. He tried.

She moved his right hand, and he grasped desperately at the rock edge of the cliff, just above his head. It held, but felt less secure than Jone's sleeve.

Ethan thought about the time earlier that morning when Jone had called him brave. Not because he wasn't afraid, but because he was afraid but he was doing it anyway. He hadn't meant to think about that. He hadn't really tried. It just popped into his head.

He moved his own left hand. Let go of her sleeve. As he did, he proved to himself that something she had told him was true. The rope was taut. And solid. He was not in danger of falling.

"Lower me down," he said.

"Sam!" Jone called. "Take him down!"

Then Ethan was moving, but slowly. He kept the toes of his athletic shoes braced against the rock and more or less walked down. Or so it felt.

He didn't look around. He just kept looking up at Jone, who gave him a thumbs-up.

"You're doing great," she said.

"I don't know about that," he said, happy to have his voice back. "But I'm doing it."

"You're almost down. You're going to be able to put your feet down in . . . three . . . two . . . one. Okay, if you take your feet off the wall now, you can stand up."

Ethan felt around gingerly with one foot only. Jone was right. It was solid. It was horizontal. It was there.

He looked around to be sure he wasn't about to step down too close to the edge, and in doing so got a glimpse all the way down into the valley.

"Oh, crap," he said, his head spinning dangerously.

He squeezed his eyes closed until the feeling passed. Then he stepped down with his other foot and straightened up.

"Leave the harness on," Sam called. "It's safer."

"Roger that," he called back up. Then, more to himself, "Like I needed convincing."

"What do you see?" Sam bellowed.

"There's a space under that bulgy rock. It's not much, but it's a space. But I have to crawl along it to really see what's under there."

"Let me know if you need me to play out more rope."

Ethan moved two steps toward the rock face and ducked down. Nothing underneath. He eased forward onto his hands and knees and crawled along. He literally needed to duck his head down just inches from the dirt to see underneath the overhanging rock. Nothing.

He moved along it to the left, crouching, ducking, looking.

And then . . .

In a strange moment, one Ethan would go over literally hundreds of times in his head, Ethan saw a human figure lying on its back under the rock. A man. A man Ethan felt quite sure was not his father.

Still, he felt the discovery like a near-fatal jolt of electricity.

The figure in the tiny crawl space was thinner than his father. Thinner than even six days out here alone, without food, could possibly explain in Ethan's head. His closed eyes were too sunken. His tangled hair was no color at all. His short beard—less than a full growth but much more than a five o'clock shadow—was no color at all. His skin was no color at all. Ethan literally could not see where the man's dirty gray skin ended and his dirty gray shorts and T-shirt began.

And yes, in a distant way Ethan registered the gray shorts and T-shirt. Yet still he could not click his father's image into anything he saw before him in that moment.

He ran his eyes down the man's long body.

Both of his legs appeared to be attached at an incorrect angle. His right knee was swollen to two or three times a normal size. But there was no blood. Just a disconnected appearance to the leg below the knee. His left leg had something plunged into it. Some whitish, long object, like a white stick that looked as though it had been stabbed into the flesh halfway up his thigh. And on that leg there was blood. A lot of blood. But it was old, and dried, and even that blood seemed to have too little color. A faint, dusty reddish-brown.

Ethan crawled two steps closer, partly drawn to look, partly having to force himself to approach. He stifled a reflexive gag as he saw a flurry of tiny movement—a light swarming of ants—on the open leg wound around the impaled object.

He heard Sam call down to him.

"Hey. You okay down there? What d'you see?"

Ethan didn't answer. He looked more closely at the long object shoved into the man's leg. Part of him must have known by that time that the man was his father. But another part of him simply had not caught up with it. Had not allowed it to click into place.

It was a bone.

Ethan scrambled back a step at the shock of seeing such a thing. The guy didn't have something sticking *into* his leg. He had something sticking *out* of it. It was his femur.

Ethan backed up a few more steps.

His eyes moved down the savagely, illogically bent leg. It hurt just to see a leg forced into such an unnatural angle.

At the bottom of the leg was Ethan's first look at a blast of color. In fact, he was surprised the bright red hadn't caught his eye sooner.

His father's running shoes.

"Oh my God," Ethan said quietly.

He scrambled back another few steps and climbed to his feet.

He looked up to see both Sam and Jone peering at him over the edge.

"You okay down there, Ethan?" Jone asked.

"Did you find anything?" Sam added. "What do you see?"

Ethan opened his mouth. Only the tiniest squeak slipped out.

"Did you say something?" Sam called down.

"Yeah," Ethan said. But maybe not loudly enough.

"What did you find?"

"He's here," Ethan said. With a little better volume.

"Is he alive?" Jone asked.

"Oh. I don't know. I didn't think to check."

Part of Ethan stood outside himself in that moment, critiquing the ridiculousness of the statement. And of the truth behind it. It was true. Inexplicably true. He hadn't thought to check.

But it was shock. It was just that simple. Ethan was in full-on shock.

"I'll go see," he said.

He took two steps in toward the spot that held his father. Then he fell to his knees. And did not move.

"What're you doing, hon?" Jone asked. "You okay?"

"I . . ."

"You need help down there?"

"I don't want to know," Ethan called back. "I'm afraid to find out."

A long moment passed. Nobody called to him, asked any questions. Nobody gave him any advice. Because it was no longer that easy. Sure, anybody could call down and tell him to check the pulse at the wrist or the carotid artery. Or hold a hand in front of his father's nose to check for breathing. That wasn't hard. But to be this man's son . . . to hang in that moment, where the father's dead and alive possibilities existed almost simultaneously, and to have to snap that answer into place. Forever. Whichever way it fell, it was pretty damned permanent, and Ethan knew that all too well.

Which of them was about to advise Ethan how not to be too afraid to move?

"I'll come down," Jone said. "I'll do it with you."

"No," Ethan called. And he held one hand up high—a stop sign for her. "No, if the answer is no, you don't need to do that. I'll find out."

He swallowed hard.

At first he told his knees to crawl and they didn't. Like Rebar refusing to turn onto the trail that led up the mountain, away from home. But a deeper, more solid part of Ethan knew this wouldn't cut it. He didn't have the luxury of breaking inside. Not now. He was on a narrow ledge in the middle of a wilderness, not really accessible from any direction. It was simply no place to get stuck.

"Dad," he said. "I don't know if you can hear me. But I'm going to come in there and take hold of your wrist."

Ethan crawled forward.

The hand he reached for seemed wholly unfamiliar. Ancient, paper-skinned, and gray. But Ethan saw something else he missed the first time around. His father's watch. It was caked in dirt, the crystal shattered. It said eight ten, which meant it was broken. Stopped. But it was still the twin of the good, expensive watch he'd given Ethan for his sixteenth birthday. The one that was now gone. Run off into the night with a man and a knife.

See? Ethan thought, in a weirdly disconnected moment. *You didn't take good enough care of yours, either.*

Ethan wrapped his hand around the bony wrist. As he did, he felt a jolt of fear and negative anticipation. Just the touch of his father's skin would tell him a lot. It might be stiff and cold.

It was not stiff. The skin felt cooler than Ethan might have liked. But not cold.

He watched his father's face—still not wholly recognizing it—for any reaction to being touched. There was none.

For what felt like long, torturous minutes—but was probably less than ten seconds—Ethan felt for a pulse. When he felt nothing, he tried to convince himself he was looking in the wrong place. On the fourth spot he tried, something. But it was something so small. So small it might have been nothing. It might only have been imagination. Wishful thinking. It might not have existed at all.

He held his fingers still, and concentrated all his will on feeling it again. But too much time went by. It couldn't be that long between heartbeats. Could it?

And then there it was again. Something tiny.

Ethan was feeling a pulse that was so weak, so slow, that he could barely register it as having happened. Barely believe it was real.

But that meant he was feeling a pulse.

He leaped to his feet, hitting his head hard on the rock overhang.

He scrambled out into the sunlight.

"I think he's alive!" he called up to Sam and Jone. His voice sounded excited and big. And as though it belonged to someone else entirely. Someone less shocked. "It's just the tiniest pulse you can possibly imagine. But I felt it. I swear I felt it."

"I'll ride for help!" Sam called back, followed by a big whooping sound. Like something you'd hear in the roundup scene of a cowboy movie.

"Don't go yet!" he heard Jone yell at Sam. "First we're going to load me up with food and water. And I'm going down to wait with Ethan and his dad."

In the time between her announcement and her arrival, Ethan sat down hard in the dirt, cross-legged, and stared at the barely familiar man under the rock overhang. And, for the first time, he allowed himself to believe, to know, to absorb, that they had found him. Against all odds, they had found him.

Even more amazingly, they had found him before it was too late.

—

"Know what I was just thinking?" Ethan asked her.

He watched Jone squeeze water onto yet another clean spare bandana, and brush the liquid over his father's lips.

"Can't imagine," she said. "I figure you must be thinking a million things at once."

"Kind of," he said. "But mostly I'm thinking back on two mornings ago. When we rode up that trail. Right over his head. Maybe he wasn't unconscious yet. Maybe he heard us calling for him. I'll bet he was in better shape two mornings ago. Wish we'd found him then."

"We didn't know," she said, without any further editorializing. Not even by way of her tone.

"I guess. It still feels weird to think of riding by right over his head. We were barely two hours out."

"Life is a funny thing. I think we need to get him out of this tight little spot. Because I need to tip his head forward. So I can get a little more moisture into his mouth without choking him."

"They say you're not supposed to move a person after an accident. He could have spine damage."

"First of all, it's pretty clear he landed on his feet." She nodded down toward Noah's shockingly damaged legs. The shock of those injuries had not worn off for Ethan. He simply had been trying not to look.

"Second, he's so close to the line here, I think water trumps everything. I'd rather he end up in a wheelchair than what could happen if he goes a couple more hours without water. Survival would be priority one."

"I guess that's true," Ethan said.

"Third, it's clear he's already moved himself."

"Why do you say that?"

"He couldn't have fallen under that rock overhang. It's a physical impossibility. You fall straight. There's no such thing as a curveball fall. He must have pulled himself back under here."

"That seems strange," Ethan said. "You'd think he'd want to stay out where he could be seen. I wonder why he did that."

Jone wrapped her strong arms under Noah's armpits and gently slid his upper body out into the light. In full sunlight, Ethan did look at that face and recognize his father. But at the same time the changes to his condition seemed even more shocking. Even more impossible to accept. Even to comprehend.

It seemed unimaginable that a living person could look so entirely dead.

"I've just been wondering that myself," Jone said. She sat down close to Noah and carefully lifted his head onto her lap. Then she soaked the bandana again, a little more liberally this time, and gently opened Noah's mouth, swabbing it with moisture.

"Think that'll be enough water?" Ethan asked.

"If I keep doing it until the medevac team gets here, it'll be something. Not much, because I want to be careful not to choke him. But better than nothing."

"Here's what I hope," Ethan said. "About why he dragged himself under there. I hope I get to ask him."

"Yeah. That makes two of us, son. Could've been to get out of the sun. When it was hot, he might've done that to help himself stay hydrated. Or there could've been a waterfall coming down right on him. Or maybe the hail hurt like a son of a bitch when it hit those legs. Any of which make sense. But it's hard to see prioritizing anything over rescue. I would think he'd at least try to get back out later. Maybe he thought he could, wanted to, but maybe he just couldn't do it. I'm going over and over it in my head, but I just don't know, Ethan. All I know is this: All this time we been riding out here I thought if we found him I'd be ticked as hell at Dave and the other rangers for not doing their job.

But now that I see where he was hiding, I've got to say I truly get why they didn't find him. What I want to know now is how in hell *we did.*"

—

"How long has it been?" Ethan asked Jone.

The sun felt baking, radiating heat through his shirt and under the bandana covering the back of his neck. But he didn't ask because of his own discomfort. He asked because he was worried about his dad.

"'Bout thirty-five minutes," she said.

"Oh. And you said it would take two hours for Sam to ride out?"

"We said it would take the team about that long to get home. You know. At a walk. I have a suspicion they're going at a better clip than that. We'll see how much time Sam can shave."

"You want me to do that?"

Ethan indicated the work she was doing with the water bottle and the bandana. Swabbing tiny bits of moisture into Noah's mouth without dripping, because he was in no shape to swallow. She also had taken to leaning over Noah to throw her shadow on him. Keep him out of the direct sun.

She didn't answer right away.

So he added, "He's my dad. After all."

"No, I don't want to have to move his head again. But you can sit over here by me so the rest of him is in the shade. We want more water going in and less sweating out."

Ethan tried to pull to his feet, but he'd stiffened considerably in the thirty-five minutes of sitting on the rocky ground. He tried to stifle an expression of pain, but a puff of air and noise escaped.

He sat down carefully where the shade would help his father.

"Pretty stiff and sore, huh?"

"More than I've ever been in my entire life. I swear. I have never hurt this much. And you know what's weird? I didn't think about it until just now, but the whole time I was getting into that harness and going down the side on a rope and crawling around on my knees looking for him, I didn't think about it. I didn't even notice."

"Adrenaline," she said.

"Oh. That makes sense. Well, it's wearing off now. And I—"

"Look at that," Jone interjected. "Did you see that?"

"No. See what?"

"His mouth moved. Just the tiniest bit, but it wasn't my imagination. I put that wet bandana in there, and he made this tiny move, like to suck the water out of it."

"Is that good?"

"Everything is good at this point, son. Everything that living people do is something we like to see. I'd give him more, but I'm not sure if he'd swallow it. I don't want to be getting water down into his lungs. Let me give him a tiny bit more and see."

Jone soaked the bandana again and then squeezed it gently into Noah's open mouth. Ethan watched his Adam's apple, hoping to see it bob. At first, nothing. Then he saw it twitch.

"He swallowed!" Ethan shouted.

"Well, anyway, he tried. If he gets better at it, I'll give him more."

"And that's good, right? Because only living people try."

—

Ethan was wrestling with himself about whether he should ask her for the time again, when she seemed to read his mind.

"An hour fifteen," she said.

"Oh," Ethan said. "It feels like about a year."

"We should be doing a better job helping the time go by."

"How do we do that?"

"Well, we don't exactly have cable TV or an Xbox up here," Jone said. "But we can talk."

"Okay," Ethan said. "Tell me about last night."

Her head jerked up and she eyed Ethan suspiciously.

"What about it?"

"I don't know. Sam seemed so happy. I just wondered if you were, too."

"What did he tell you?"

"Not much. Just that you two talked for hours."

"Oh. Good," she said, visibly letting her guard down. "For a minute there I thought you meant he was telling tales."

Then more silence fell.

"Well, that didn't help much time go by," Ethan said.

"Tell me about you and your father. Why do you hate him?"

"I don't know if I want to get into that right now," Ethan said. "What if he can hear?"

"Doesn't seem likely," she said.

"They say people in comas can hear. When you read to them."

"They say people in a coma like to be read to. I never heard anybody say they're catching every word. But anyway, it's up to you." Then, after a brief pause, "You trying to tell me whatever he did to make you hate him is something he doesn't even know about yet?"

"He was there. Just because we didn't talk about it doesn't mean he doesn't know."

"But you haven't told him right to his face how you felt about it."

"No."

"Maybe it's time."

That sat in the air for several long minutes before Ethan decided to speak. Or maybe he didn't even decide. Maybe he just spoke.

"He cheated on my mom a lot," he said, vaguely surprised that he was doing this thing. "I kind of knew . . . but at the same time I didn't know. I saw things. Like I saw him talking to younger women and getting their phone numbers and stuff. So then when I actually knew,

I thought, *Hey, you knew this already.* But only after the fact. Looking back. I'm not sure if that makes sense."

"It does," she said quietly.

"I got that same weird feeling when I found him up here. You know. An hour and fifteen minutes ago, you said. Seems longer. The whole time he was missing I kept saying, 'I know he's up there.' And the whole time we were up here looking I kept saying, 'I know he's up here.' And I swear I meant it. With every cell in my body I meant it. Even though I said the opposite once, and maybe thought it more than once. But it's like I knew, but then I second-guessed what I knew. But I still knew it. And then I bent down and stuck my head under that rock overhang. And he was up here. And I was totally shocked.

"Anyway. I'm getting off track. There was this girl. Jennifer, was her name." Ethan could feel an inward wince as he spoke the dreaded J word. Like something pinching him with too much pressure. Like the name was a weapon with a sharp edge and a point. He had been careful not to say her name out loud since . . . well, just "since." He preferred to leave the sentence at that. He even tried not to say that name in his head, but instead leave a blank space where it used to live. "She was his assistant. She was twenty-four. Way too old for me. Way too young for him. Although, I don't know. Looking back, I think twenty-four fits with forty-one better than it fits with seventeen. Especially when the seventeen-year-old is the boy."

Then Ethan felt his will to tell the story fade. So he let a silence fall.

"You loved her," Jone said. It wasn't a question.

"You're good at this."

"It comes through when you talk about her."

"Yeah," Ethan said. "That was part of the problem. I don't have what you might call a poker face. So everybody knew. It was humiliating. And my dad took every opportunity to tease me about it. I mean, he never acknowledged it straight-out, but I could tell he thought it was funny."

Another stall. This time Jone didn't fill the gap.

"My mom and I were going on a trip to Peru, only there was this mix-up between e-tickets and paper tickets. We'd always used e-tickets, as long as we could remember. I think we both thought paper tickets were completely a thing of the past. But it was something about the fact that it was a Peruvian airline. Anyway, we missed the flight. Came home. Let ourselves into the apartment . . ."

Ethan stopped. Wished he hadn't started with this. He didn't want to say the next thing. In fact, he refused to.

"Don't tell me," Jone said. "Let me guess."

"Yeah," Ethan said. A few deep breaths. "I think that would have been enough to hate him for. But it wasn't the worst part. It was the look in his eyes. *She* looked away. She scrambled to get more clothes on and get herself together. My dad just looked right into my eyes. Not at my mom—she'd run out of the room anyway. He was just looking right at me. And it was so awful, what I saw there in his eyes. It was so bad that I just ran out. Out into the street in Manhattan in the middle of the night. And I got in trouble doing it, too. I almost got myself killed. I kept thinking of that look in his eyes, but I couldn't wrap words around it. Even in my head. I could still see it, and I could still feel what it made me feel. But I couldn't describe it. But now that I'm looking back on it—which I hate like hell to do, by the way—it seems easy to say what it was. He was proud. He was looking into my eyes with this fierce pride. Like he was telling me, 'Look what I can do that you can't. Look what I can get that you couldn't. Look who's the man here.'"

Jone waited briefly, to see if Ethan cared to go on. He didn't.

"Sounds like he has a real problem with women. And with his own self-worth."

"Oh, his self-worth is fine. He thinks he's worth more than everybody else."

"No he doesn't."

"Trust me. I know him."

Ethan looked down at the gray figure of his nearly dead father and felt vaguely guilty. As if he were kicking a man when he was down. So down.

"No. That's not how it works. People with really good self-worth think they're the same size as everybody else, and they never make anybody else feel small. Any time somebody tries to act like they're more than you are, deep down they're afraid they're less. Otherwise they'd have nothing to prove."

Ethan looked at his father again, then past those ravaged legs and into the cave-like space in which he'd been hidden for so many days. The sun had shifted, lighting up more of the space, and Ethan saw five energy bar wrappers scattered in the dirt. Along with his father's hydration bladder in its pack. He felt an overpowering urge to reach in there and pick up the wrappers. Tidy the area. It was a strange, out-of-place urge that Ethan could only imagine sprang from a deep desire to move past this conversation.

He stayed put. Stayed in.

"I believe you," he said. "But I still hate him when I replay that moment."

"It's a true thing, what I just told you, but it's not the kind of thing that changes everything when you first hear it. It might be the kind of thing that can help you put your hate aside over the years. I'm not suggesting you need to welcome him back into your life with open arms as the years go by. Some people just plain aren't worth it. Whether this one is or isn't, that's for you to judge. I'm just advising you to let go of the hate in yourself, because you're the one swallowing that poison every day, not him."

Ethan didn't answer, because he didn't know how. Because it wasn't years down the road. It was only now.

"Next tell me what you love about him," Jone said.

Ethan laughed. It felt strange and out of place.

"That's a little trickier."

"Don't tell me you don't, though. Because here we are."

Ethan made up his mind to try. But it felt as though everything he reached for had changed.

"It's hard," he said. "When I was little, he was kind of a hero figure. He was all brave and strong, and going on these huge adventures, and doing all these nice father things for me. I would've told you he was the best dad in the world. I know I would have. But now I look back and everything looks different. Like the Everest thing. When he was twenty-four he made it to the top of Mount Everest. There's this huge blown-up picture of him in our living room. Well, there *was*. My mom took it down. Since we found them on the couch right underneath it and all. He'd taken his oxygen mask and his goggles off so you could see it was him. He had one of those suits on that make you look like you're in outer space. And he had all this ice in his beard. He had a beard back then. And his skin was all red. My mom would always look at that picture with me and tell me my dad was this really brave guy. This heroic guy. Now I look back and all I can think about is how I was born while he was gone, and he missed it. He'd been planning the thing for a year, and he wouldn't reschedule. He left my mom seven months pregnant to go on this expedition. I think at the time the odds were something like one in seven of dying on Everest. Out of all the people who moved up from base camp, for every six who summited, one died. It changes from year to year. But he left my mom home alone to have me and maybe even raise me. Some hero.

"And all the great dad stuff he did. Taking me to the zoo and the circus. And getting girls' phone numbers all the way. It was a great way to use a cute little kid. It was like the equivalent of having a puppy. Great icebreaker, you know? To start a conversation. Especially with those pretty young women who get misty-eyed and in a hurry to have kids every time they see a toddler."

Ethan stopped. He felt drained. Tapped out. Like there was nothing much left in him to say.

"But you loved him," she said. "And you still do."

"Well. That's the problem with some dads, I guess. You love them when you're too little to know they don't deserve it. And then when you grow up and know better, the love doesn't just go away."

"No," she said. "It doesn't. What about your mom?"

"What about her?"

"Do you get the support you need from her?"

"Not really. She's a pretty nice person. But she's into that extreme sports thing, too. She kind of . . . she values being tough. So her idea of giving me what I need is kicking me out of the nest and telling me I'll feel better when I'm flying."

Ethan looked over his shoulder, down into the valley. It made him a little dizzy, but he kept looking. Kept trying to be somewhere else.

"The river looks like silver," he said.

"Yeah. It's real pretty when the sun hits it just right like that."

"Can you imagine slipping off that trail and seeing all the way down into that valley like that? And thinking you were about to fall all the way down?"

"I'd rather not imagine it," she said. "He's actually swallowing water now. It's a weak effort, but it's keeping it out of his lungs. I might even squirt a little water right in his mouth and see if he can take it."

Ethan watched her place the sip tube of the filter bottle between Noah's lips, which she gently closed around it. She gave the bottle a tiny squeeze, and Noah's jaw moved slightly, as if to try to react. And he swallowed. Ethan could see his Adam's apple jump.

"That's a real good sign," she said.

They watched him drink in silence for a few moments. One tiny, weak swallow at a time.

"I feel weird now," Ethan said.

"Weird how?"

"Like I told you too much about myself. I mean, stuff that was too personal. That was too hard to say."

"Okay," Jone said. "I'll match you hard for hard. This thing I been doing. Wetting his mouth with water from a cloth. That's a bad flashback situation for me. Because that's something I had to do for my husband when he was dying."

"Oh. I'm sorry. How did he die?"

"He had cancer. In his throat. Well, he had it lots of places by then. But he could hardly swallow. He was on hospice and he was at home. He insisted on being home. No heroic measures, you know? He wouldn't put up with lying in a hospital on IV fluids. He was miserable and he was ready to go. I was just trying to keep him comfortable at the end. It was hard for him when his mouth got too dry. He hated the feeling. So I had this stuff the hospice lady gave me, in a tube, that I could swab around in his mouth to keep it moist. But also he liked to be able to suck on a wet cloth. Just enough so he didn't feel parched. Not so much that he had to swallow. That's why I trusted myself to put some moisture into your dad's mouth while he was unconscious. I know how to do it without getting anything down his throat. I have a lot of experience."

Ethan waited to see if there was more. Apparently not.

"I'm sorry. I don't know what else to say besides I'm sorry."

"Nothing *to* say. Just stuff that is. Or was. No matter how we wanted it to be."

A long silence. Minutes long. Maybe five or ten minutes. Or even twenty. Ethan wanted to ask her what time it was. Or to move around enough to be able to see her wristwatch. But instead he just sat.

Then he decided to jump up quickly and take care of those wrappers. It didn't quite pan out. He'd stiffened up a lot in the sitting. But in time he did make it—painfully—to his feet.

Jone watched him without comment for a time.

As he reached in and gathered up the last of the wrappers she said, "Interesting time for housekeeping. Or cave-keeping in this case."

"They were just bothering me," Ethan said. "I can't really explain why."

"I'm all for not littering the wilderness," she said.

Ethan stuffed the wrappers into his pocket. Pulled the hydration pack out, as if they'd want it later for something.

Then he had no choice but to sit with Jone and his barely alive father again.

"There's still water in this bladder," Ethan said.

"I'm sure he had opportunities to refill it with snowmelt and hail. That's why he's alive."

"Why didn't he drink what he had, then?"

"Hard to drink after you've passed out."

A long silence. Jone filled it.

"He's a handsome man, your dad," she said.

"Yeah. Maybe too much so. But I don't know how you see that. I mean, looking at him now."

"Actually, I was basing that on a time I saw him in town."

"Oh."

Ethan looked over his shoulder at the silver river again. The sun was hitting it in a slightly different spot. Now it was an S-shaped bend that shone and reflected light like a newly minted dime.

"Was your husband a handsome man?"

"Not really. Not so's people would stare at him wherever he went or anything. I liked to look at him."

"I'm sorry for your loss."

"Thank you," she said. "I'm sorry for yours."

"But my dad's not dead."

"That's not the loss I meant. I was talking about the one where you found out the dad you loved so much wasn't really worth all that love you'd invested."

"Oh," Ethan said. "That one. Yeah. Thanks."

Then he didn't say more. Partly because he didn't know what more to say. Partly because he didn't want to cry. Not in front of Jone. Not in front of his father. Even though his father was likely unconscious, and his eyes were closed. Still, Ethan didn't want to take a chance of giving Noah the satisfaction.

"Tell you something else about me," she said. "A little secret. I'm not seventy. I'm only sixty-seven. Nine years older than Sam. I just like the look on people's faces when they see what good shape I'm in and how much I can do, and then when they hear I'm seventy. It's only a mild exaggeration, and it's only a lie if I'm not doing all the same stuff in three years. But I will be."

"Oh," Ethan said. Because he didn't know what else to say.

"Now that I made that little confession, you got anything you want to tell me?"

"Like what?"

"Like about *your* age?"

"No," Ethan said, half laughing. "I really am seventeen. I'll show you my damn birth certificate if you like."

"Dang. I really thought . . ." But then she trailed off. As if she had lost the thread of the conversation in midsentence. "It's here," she said.

"What's here?"

She pointed. Out toward home, and up.

Ethan followed her finger, but saw nothing. Just brilliant blue sky. But a second later a movement caught his eye. A tiny object that could have been a close insect or a far-off plane.

"Wow, you've got good eyes," he said.

"Actually, I heard it."

"Oh. I thought that was just something the wind was doing. Is it help?"

"Yeah," she said. "It's the copter. We all get to go home."

At that exact moment Ethan felt the tears let go. And almost more. He almost could have lost his bladder control in that moment if he hadn't been careful, which seemed odd, because it was not a moment of fear. It was the sudden lifting of it. Relief from the pressure of a fright that Ethan didn't realize had been crushing him so completely.

Maybe only at the moment it lifted was he able to feel the full weight and depth of it, and it startled him.

And maybe something about the word *home*.

In any case, he won the battle with the bladder and lost the one with the tears.

—

The medevac helicopter was red and white, unless it was yellow. Ethan would go back over details like that almost obsessively in the days that followed, usually when he wished he could sleep. And would continually be surprised by how the emotion of the moment muddied everything. Except the emotion of the moment.

The copter hovered above them, higher than Ethan would have guessed. Or wished. Maybe to keep its rotor blades as far away from the sheer rock face as possible.

It was loud. So loud that if Jone was saying anything to him, he wasn't hearing it. And it brought its own little windstorm, one that flattened them down from above. It blew the spare bandana Jone had loaned him out from under his baseball cap and blew it down to the valley floor, where it would be lost forever. Unless some city kid was riding a mule who got her hoof stuck in it. A disjointed thought, but one that reminded Ethan that the strange encounter with the fleece jacket was not something that happened every day.

Then two men in jumpsuits and helmets were coming down to them, both at the same time, both clipped to the same cable, and with nylon bags and something that looked like a kid's toboggan. Ethan had to look up into the sun to see them, and by the time their boots touched down, almost all he could see was spots in front of his eyes.

They unclipped from the cable, and the metal disk at the now-free end of it rose and slid away from the mountain at the same time, and then the noise of the blades grew fainter, and Ethan could hear himself think. But he was so shocked. And his insides felt the way insides feel when you've been crying for hours, when you've cried all the tears you can find to cry. Even though he'd barely scratched the surface. And he didn't know what he thought, even though he could have heard his thoughts if they'd existed.

Jone talked to the men for a few seconds, and then she came to Ethan and took him by both hands and turned him around so his back was facing his father.

"What are we doing?" he asked her.

"We're going to come sit over here and let them work."

"Why did the helicopter go away?"

"It's just circling until they call it back."

"Oh."

A silence, during which Ethan felt overwhelmed by the parts of the experience he couldn't understand, and the questions he couldn't put into words. And she was still holding both his hands. As if to forcibly keep him from turning around.

He tried to look over his shoulder, but she pulled hard on his hand and brought him back to face her again.

"Don't," she said. "The guys asked me to take you over here and talk you into not looking. They said it's one of those things. Once you see it, they figure you'll never be able to unsee it again. And you might wish you could. They have to stabilize both his legs in splints. Inflatable splints. It's not a pretty thing to watch. You were having trouble looking at his legs even when nobody was moving them."

"I didn't tell you that," he said. "Did I?"

"You didn't have to."

That was the moment Ethan heard the noise. The sound. That part of the experience Ethan would always remember very clearly, no matter how much time went by. It was a sound that could have come from an animal. Except the only animals up here on the ledge were human. It wasn't so much a purposeful, outward cry of pain as something that just couldn't be suppressed. It was guttural. Vocal rather than verbal. It was the size of the world, Ethan thought, if not bigger.

It raced through his gut like a hot knife, leaving him feeling as though he'd been sliced open.

Jone reached out and grabbed his head, one rough hand over each of his ears. Even though it was too late. She just did it anyway.

Then she pulled his head close to her and pressed his forehead against her shoulder and held it tightly. Ethan didn't cry anymore, because he didn't remember how. He couldn't find tears. He couldn't find anything he'd ever used in the past. Except shaking.

The sound had made him feel as though someone had scraped out the inside of his gut. It would take time, he knew, to get over a thing like that.

There may have been another sound, a second one, but it was more muffled, and his ears were more covered, and it could have been something else entirely. But probably not.

A few moments passed in silence, except for the sound of the distant helicopter blades.

Her hands disappeared from his ears.

"Okay, you can look now," she said.

Ethan turned to see the men waving the helicopter back. His father was on the sled-like litter, only his face bare and showing. His wrists were strapped together over his chest, and the rest of him was wrapped in a nylon sheath and strapped down in three places.

The copter came back and took away Ethan's ability to hear again. Then it took away his father. It lowered the cable with the disc on the end, and the men attached it to a harness on the litter, and then they stood up and away, and signaled again.

The helicopter flew away. It flew away with Ethan's father still dangling below it. It didn't even take the time to bring him on board first.

Just as Ethan was wondering if Noah would have to dangle there all the way to the hospital, he noticed the cable getting shorter. The litter was dangling closer to the belly of the craft.

Then they disappeared behind a mountain, and it was over.

Ethan blinked and looked around. One of the men smiled at him. He came over and clapped a hand down on Ethan's shoulder.

"Don't worry," he said. "They'll come back for us."

"Good to hear," he said, sounding more relaxed and normal than he felt.

"They're going to set down right where the pavement ends. There's an ambulance waiting for your dad. Then they'll come back and pick us up."

Ethan briefly pictured dangling from the end of that cable. Then he pushed the image away again.

—

Ethan watched Jone and one of the rescuers as they were winched up to the helicopter at the end of the cable, both of their harnesses hooked together at their chests. It looked terrifying. More so than Ethan could even allow himself to process.

The same man who had clapped him on the shoulder and reassured him helped Ethan into his harness. It was not a harness like the one Sam had loaned him. It was enormous and weighty in comparison. It came up all the way to his chest. It had two huge, heavy rings that came together almost at his chin.

The copter was hovering directly overhead, so it wasn't easy to talk.

"You afraid of heights?" the man asked, loudly, into Ethan's ear.

"Yes, sir," Ethan shouted. "Little bit."

"Don't look down. Don't look around. Just look right here."

The man pointed to a round patch on his nylon jumpsuit. It was embroidered with a mountain range, and letters that must have added up to a particular rescue team. That was another one of those details that didn't stay clear in Ethan's head.

Especially since he didn't follow the man's directions.

Deafened by the noise, battered by the wind, Ethan squinted his eyes and watched the man grab the disc end of the descending cable, slip its huge, heavy-looking hook through all four of the rings on their two harnesses, and lock it into place.

Ethan felt his feet lift off the ground.

He did what he was told not to do. He looked down. And around.

Not because he was afraid, although he was.

Because he wanted to see the Blythe River Wilderness one last time. Because, exhausted though he was, much as he longed for a hot bath and a warm bed, part of him didn't want Blythe River to go away. It was dizzying to look, but somehow, in that moment, dizzying didn't seem like such a bad way to go.

What felt like only a second or two later a gloved hand reached out and grabbed the cable, and pulled. Then Ethan was inside the helicopter, with his feet on something horizontal and solid.

He felt himself being strapped into a padded seat, with belts secured across his waist and vertically over both shoulders. But he didn't know who buckled him in, because he was still looking out the window. Staring at the snowcapped peaks, and that amazing wet snake of a river. Which was less silver now and more gold.

His stomach dropped as the copter peeled away, tilting and turning toward civilization. Toward home.

Jone patted his knee.

"We did it!" she shouted into his ear. To be heard over the *thwap* of the copter blades.

A pause, during which Ethan only smiled. Or thought he smiled.

"*Yeah* we did!" he said.

Then he looked out the window and watched the wilderness disappear.

Ethan didn't know he was crying again until he felt the taps of teardrops hitting his own arms and lap. Flowing with surprising gusto. Freely.

Ethan wondered if it was the first time any of his emotions had ever felt free.

—

Ethan stepped down out of the copter and onto the tarmac of the road between his house and Sam's. A bit dreamily. And dizzily. As if this might or might not be reality.

The copter's motor had shut down, and the blades had stopped spinning. And the silence felt absolutely stunning.

Sam was waiting in his jacked-up 4x4 pickup, and he had Rufus in the back.

Ethan wanted to say thank you to his personal rescuer. The one who had comforted him. Winched up on the same cable at the same time. He turned and walked back to the man, but no words came out. So instead he just threw his arms wide and gave the guy a hug. And received one in return.

Then he walked stiffly to Sam's truck.

"You all ready to go to the hospital?" Sam asked.

Ethan climbed, with much difficulty, into the truck bed with Rufus, without speaking. Jone took the shotgun seat Ethan had purposely left for her.

Sam made a U-turn in the road and headed toward town.

The truck had rolled not ten feet down the road when Ethan found his voice again.

"No," he said out loud, to no one. Well, no one except Rufus, who was leaning over his lap and licking his face with exaggerated enthusiasm. As if he'd been sure he'd never see Ethan again.

Ethan knocked on the truck's back window.

Sam pulled over and opened the window's sliding middle section. "Yeah?"

"No," Ethan said. "I can't do this."

"Do what?" Jone asked. Soothingly, Ethan thought. "What can't you do after everything you just did?"

"I can't do this next part. Not without rest. I'm just so exhausted. You have no idea how exhausted I am. I can't even describe it. It's like being in this unbearable pain. And not just physically, either. My brain is exhausted. My gut is exhausted. My heart can't go another step, I swear. What we just did, that was easy compared to this next part. The part where I go to the hospital and the doctors are all touched by how we rescued him, and they figure we're about to have this wonderful, emotional reunion. And they say something like 'Your dad is awake now. You can go in and see him.' And I have to say, 'I don't want to see him. I hate him.' I can't do that part without at least a good night's sleep."

A long silence.

Then Sam popped the truck back into gear and made another U-turn in the narrow road. Ethan sighed deeply and let a part of himself relax. A part that had been needing relaxation for a very long time.

Longer even than Ethan had known this place.

Ethan said a little prayer that his dad would make it through the night. That Ethan wasn't giving up his last chance to see him. Which felt odd, because he tended not to pray. And because he tended not to cherish moments with his father. Still. He wouldn't want to miss the last one.

—

"You going to be okay here in the house all by yourself?" Jone asked him.

Ethan looked up at her, squinting. As if she'd wakened him. As if she were a bright light and he were a hangover.

"I'm not alone," he said. "Rufus is here."

"Right. Sorry. You got something to eat?"

"I still have one helping of that good chicken stew. It's been in the fridge. It should still be okay. Right? I hope so. I've been thinking about it for a long time."

Jone counted days out loud, and on her fingers.

"Yeah. Five days or so. Should be okay. Sure you don't need anything?"

"A hot bath and lots of sleep," he said.

She nodded once and made her way to the door.

"Jone," he said. Before she could get away.

"Yes?"

"Thank you."

"I was happy to be part of the thing."

"Tell Sam I appreciate it. All of it. Even putting me back here at home and telling the hospital we're not coming till morning. I'll tell him myself tomorrow. But tell him I appreciate him anyway. Okay?"

"He knows. But yeah. I will."

Then she let herself out.

Ethan savored the silence for a few minutes before rising stiffly and heating up his dinner.

Even a couple of days later Ethan would be unable to remember what he was thinking that evening. He would think he'd forgotten. But there was nothing to forget. He wasn't thinking. Thoughts would have required a minimal level of energy that Ethan did not have to give.

Chapter Fifteen: Legs

One day after his father was found

Ethan felt himself blasted out of sleep by a sharp rapping on the door. He opened his eyes.

Just for a split second he entertained the thought—well, not even a thought exactly, but a sudden wash of possibility—that the whole rescue adventure might have been a vividly detailed dream. After all, here he was in bed. As usual.

He tried to sit up. And failed.

Every muscle in his body felt rigidly locked into place. Ethan could swear even the muscles in his forehead and ears hurt. But that might have been sunburn. Or sheer sleepy imagination.

"Just a minute!" he called. It hurt even to yell out words.

In tiny movements continually punctuated by the word "ow," Ethan pulled on a clean pair of underwear and jeans, and a sweater, and limped his way stiffly to the door. Except he was limping on both sides. Which might not have qualified as limping at all. It might just have been . . . ruined. And pathetic.

He opened the door.

Jone stood on his welcome mat, a small brown paper bag in one hand, a larger paper grocery sack in the other. Her expansive white hair was clean and freshly braided, and she wore a long denim dress embroidered with flowers. Her face looked lighter and airier than he was used to seeing it. Ethan squinted at her, then past her into the light. Sam was waiting in the driver's seat of his pickup.

"I wake you up?" she asked him. She sounded rested. And more than a little cheerful. It was more cheerfulness than Ethan knew how to process.

"Yeah. But it's okay. What time is it?"

"Nearly nine."

"Oh. Wow. I slept a long time."

"Feel any better?"

"I had nowhere to go but up."

"Here's the stuff of yours you left in Dora's saddle bags," she said, handing him the paper grocery sack.

"Oh. Thanks."

"Sam says to tell you he forgot your dad's shotgun, but he's still got it. He'll get it to you next time he sees you. Your toothbrush is in there. You can brush your teeth now. And then we can go."

"I need to grab something to eat."

Jone held the smaller paper bag out and up, between them.

"I brought you a scrambled egg burrito. With black beans and salsa. It's big. Made specially for day-after the-wilderness appetites. And I wrapped it in foil, so it's still pretty warm."

"Oh my God, that sounds incredible. Okay, let me just put on some shoes and let the dog out to pee, and then I'm ready to go."

—

Just as they passed Sam's house, Ethan shouted, "Wait!"

Sam slammed on the brakes and skidded to a stop in the road.

Ethan had been stuck between the two of them on the bench seat. Probably because it was less embarrassing to have Ethan ride the gearshift.

"I'll be right back," Ethan said. Then, to Jone, "Will you hold this, please?"

It was hard to let go of the enormous burrito. It felt like a treasure he'd die without. But he handed it to her, and she stepped out to let him by.

Ethan eased his sore muscles down Sam's driveway and carefully ducked through the boards of the fence. He limped his way along until he reached the fenced paddock that held all of Sam's stock—the horses and mules.

"Dora!" he called, cupping his hands around his mouth. Even raising his arms that high felt shockingly painful.

Her head came up. She made a rumbly sound in her throat, and moved to the fence to meet him, all of which Ethan found almost more wonderful and more emotional than he could bear. His gut hadn't had enough rest. Maybe there was no such thing as enough. He still felt scraped out and sore inside, unable to hold much weight without collapsing.

He wrapped his arms around the mule's hairy head. She had a wonderful, horsey smell. Earthy and rich. It reminded him of being out riding the wilderness trails, though he hadn't consciously registered the smell before that moment.

"Thank you for everything," he said. He felt almost as though he could cry, but his eyes remained dry. Probably fresh out of moisture. "Especially for getting your foot caught in that fleece. And I'm sorry I kept kicking you up at the lake when I saw those bears. And I'm sorry my legs got tired and I kicked you every time I got on or off. I wasn't a very good rider. But you were a very good mule. Thanks."

He kissed the long, bony front of her face.

Then he made his way back to the truck and the burrito, looking once over his shoulder. Dora stood at the fence watching him go. As though she cared about Ethan, and where he went.

Jone climbed out to let Ethan back into the middle.

"Okay," he said. "I'm ready. Let's get this next part over with."

He sat back in the narrow space and took a huge bite of the still slightly warm burrito. The salsa was mild, and there was a lot of it, and the cheddar cheese was melty, and the flavor combinations were perfect. Just perfect. But there was an added factor that sharpened Ethan's enjoyment of it. It was that ravenous hunger that comes of using your body to the brink of utter exhaustion, and then surviving to enjoy that moment when it scrambles to resupply and repair.

He sighed deeply. Chewed slowly. Almost not wanting the bite of food to end in being swallowed.

"Wow, is this good," he said.

"Isn't it?" Sam said.

"Oh, you got one, too?"

"Yup. I'm lucky. The woman can cook on top of everything else."

There was something in the statement, but Ethan couldn't quite pin it down. Something akin to the cheeriness in Sam's whistling and singing the previous morning. It lived in the whole truck cab, he realized. On either side of him. Not in Sam and Sam alone.

He looked up from his breakfast to Sam. Then to Jone. Then to Sam. Then back to Jone.

"Oh, just eat your burrito," Jone said.

—

"I can take you in to see him now," the doctor said. "Or I can tell you what we've learned about his condition first."

The doctor was dark skinned, with short hair and a lilting accent that Ethan found oddly comforting. His face wore a light trace of smile that never seemed to fade.

The four of them stood near the long desk of a nurses' station on the hospital's second floor.

"Is he awake?" Ethan asked.

"Yes and no. He's not unconscious, but he's very groggy. He's on a lot of powerful painkillers. He slips in and out."

"Tell me about his condition first."

"All right," the doctor said. "He's stable. We've upgraded him to stable. No guarantees, but we all feel positive about his situation. We have him hydrated, and his blood pressure is within a fairly normal range now. I'm sure it will come as no surprise to you when I tell you he was very close to death when he was brought in. I think we all feel hopeful that if he made it through the last few hours, he can make it through the rest of his recovery. That's the good news. His legs of course are another matter."

"Right," Ethan said. "His legs."

"We may as well get that bad news over with, yes. The right patella is shattered. There's no saving it. He's lucky we live in an era of good prosthetic joints. We haven't done that surgery yet, of course. We want him as strong as possible first."

"The left one will be easier," Ethan said. "Right? Because it's just a break in a long bone?"

The doctor's face lost what Ethan had thought was a perpetual smile, and his forehead was no longer without lines or creases.

"No, the open fracture is the greater problem, I'm afraid. He spent six or seven days outdoors, uncovered, with a wound that went all the way down to the bone. Down through the bone, in fact."

"You're worried about infection," Ethan said. It wasn't a question.

"We have infection already. We're worried we won't be able to get on top of it. He's on intravenous antibiotics, but he's weak and depleted, and the infection has a strong foothold. Last night he underwent an initial surgery to remove as much of the infected tissue as possible. Much of what was removed was muscle tissue, so he may not regain full use of that leg, even if he's lucky and we can save it."

"Oh," Ethan said. Realizing for the first time the gravity of the sum of the doctor's words. "And if not?" he asked. Part of him knew. It went without saying. Everybody knows the opposite of being saved. But

Ethan was deeply tired, and he didn't have access to all parts of himself. Especially on short notice.

"Then we may have to amputate his left leg a few inches below the hip joint."

"Oh," Ethan said again.

In the silence that followed, Ethan noted that he was blinking too much.

"But let's not get ahead of ourselves," the doctor said. "You should come in and see him. I'm sure it will help him to know that you're here." He glanced up at Sam and Jone. "Maybe just kin for now. You understand, I hope."

Just before they stepped away from the nurses' station, Ethan was struck with a sudden thought. More than struck, really. Leveled. He looked away from the doctor and looked to Jone and Sam, one after the other and in that order.

"I didn't call my mother," he said. "I can't believe I forgot to call my mother."

"If you want," Jone said, "leave us with her number and we'll call her. We'll tell her what happened and say you'll call later, when you can."

"Yeah," Ethan said. "Good. Okay. I can't believe I forgot that."

"You were pretty tired," Sam said.

"I think I still am," Ethan told him. "Anybody have something I can write with? And on?"

—

Ethan followed the doctor down the hall toward his father's room, still favoring . . . well, everything. Wishing he could move without pain. Wishing he could keep up.

"I'll walk more slowly," the doctor said. "I can see you've not yet recovered from your experience. I heard about what you did. Everybody is talking about it. Everybody knows this is the man every person gave up on finding except his son. That was quite a remarkable thing you accomplished."

"We had some luck," Ethan said, vividly reliving the sensation of sitting on Dora's saddle as she tried to kick her hind leg out of the fleece jacket.

"I think the point here," the doctor said, "is that you stayed out there long enough for luck to find you."

—

Ethan stared at his father's face, thinking Noah looked better. His color was better. His skin had lost that papery gray look. But the wildly tangled hair and rough beard made him look like a man you'd see sleeping in a doorway in Manhattan, which Ethan found disorienting. And disconcerting.

He had a sheet pulled up to his armpits, so Ethan did not have to see his legs.

"I'll just leave you alone with him," the doctor said. "I'd keep it to a few minutes this first time." He hesitated. Turned away. Turned back. "And another matter that feels a little sensitive," the doctor said. "Maybe this is a bad time to say it to you, and maybe any time would be. But someone will have to bring it up. Your father was brought in with no wallet and no identification of any kind. We'll need his insurance card."

"Right," Ethan said.

He had no idea where his father's wallet was hidden, but he pushed the problem aside again because he didn't feel ready or able to deal with it.

"Take a few minutes," the doctor said.

Then he slipped out of the room.

Ethan walked around the foot of his father's hospital bed and sat in a white plastic chair. He stared at his dad's face. It looked placid. As though the man didn't have a care in the world.

Morphine will do that for you, Ethan figured. He found himself almost wishing he had some, too.

As he sat staring, he thought about what Jone had said. The true thing that might help him let go of his hatred. Over time. How his father pretended to be better than everybody else because he was afraid he wasn't as good.

It didn't help.

"Not enough time," he said out loud. Then, without realizing the words were about to rise up through his gut and burst out, Ethan said, "I still don't forgive you, you son of a bitch." His voice sounded solid and sure.

The words vibrated in the air for a few beats.

Then his father's lips moved.

"I can hear you," Noah said. Or barely said. His voice was a hoarse whisper, barely strong enough to come out into the world and be heard.

"Good," Ethan said.

—

A few minutes later, just before letting himself out of the room, Ethan said, "Dad. I need to know where you hid your wallet. I have to give the hospital your insurance card."

Nothing. Apparently Noah had slipped down into the deep land of morphine again.

"That figures," Ethan said out loud. "There when I don't need you to be. Not there when I do. Just what I've learned to expect."

—

"Hey, Mom," Ethan said.

He held the phone pressed between his ear and shoulder. He was tossing his father's closet, looking for the wallet.

"Thank God you called," she said. "I mean, it was great news. And at least they called. Until they called . . . you don't know how close I was to getting on a plane and coming out there. But another half a day . . . But then they called."

"But what about Grandma?"

A silence, which told Ethan as much as the sentence that followed.

"Your grandma passed away."

"When? Just while we were gone?"

"Yeah," she said. "Yesterday."

"Oh. That's too bad. Are you okay?"

"Yes and no. Are you?"

"Um. I think I'll process it later."

"Got it."

"What about Grampa?"

"I found a care facility for him."

"That's good."

A long silence. Painfully long.

"I'm glad I got to see her again," Ethan said.

"Me, too, sweetie. And I'm thrilled that you're back and safe. And that you found your dad. But not hearing it from you . . . hearing from a stranger that you were both okay. It was almost . . . well, it was almost hard to believe."

"I know," he said. "I'm still having a little bit of trouble with it myself. But look. Mom. *I'm* fine, except I'm exhausted and saddle sore and every muscle in my body hurts. But I don't know if I'd say Dad is fine."

"Your friend told me a little about his situation. He said Noah's been conscious and he's been upgraded to stable."

"It's his legs."

"I know, honey. But they'll heal."

Ethan pulled his head out of the closet and eased onto the hardwood floor. Braced his sore back up against the wall.

"He might lose the left one," he said.

A long, reverberating silence. Or at least it seemed to reverberate.

"Oh," she said.

"I know," Ethan added. "If it was anybody else . . ."

"Right. But your father is so athletic."

"And so vain."

"This is going to be hard on him."

"I know," Ethan said.

"Well, you know what, Ethan? I just really think that's not your problem. He's a grown man, and he always knew the risks of this extreme sports addiction of his. He's just going to have to buck up and deal with it."

Another strained silence. She broke it.

"So how on earth did you—"

"Long story," Ethan said. "Very long. And I promise I'll tell it to you. Maybe when I see you in person again. I promise I'll tell you every single detail. It was quite the adventure. But right now I have a problem. You know how you made him hide his wallet every time he went out? So I couldn't use his credit card to fly home?"

"Oh," she said. "We didn't know you knew that."

"Well, I did. But I don't know where his hiding place is. Which means I don't have his insurance card. And neither does the hospital. Did he tell you where he was hiding it?"

"No. I'm sorry. He didn't."

"Oh," Ethan said. It was impossible to mask his disappointment, even over the course of that one tiny word.

"Don't take it on. Let me deal with it. I'll call his insurance company and get them to communicate directly with the hospital."

"That would be good," he said.

"So . . . you looking forward to coming home?"

"Yes and no. Don't take that the wrong way. I'm definitely looking forward to seeing you again. But this place . . . I don't hate it like I used to. No fair saying 'I told you so.'"

"I wouldn't stoop so low. I know you're exhausted and busy, Ethan, and if you need to go I understand."

"Thanks. I'm thinking nap."

She didn't say anything for several beats, and Ethan couldn't imagine why. A nap hadn't seemed like a controversial plan.

"I know one place you should look," she said. "Have you looked in his truck at all?"

"No. Just the house."

"Go out to the truck. Put your hand under the driver's seat and then lift up the back of the carpet mat and see if there's anything under there."

"That's pretty specific. What made you think of that?"

Enough of a pause that Ethan knew she'd rather not say. But she said it all the same.

"Right before we moved into the city I had our car detailed so we could sell it. The detailer found an envelope there. Underneath the edge of the mat under the front seat."

"I hate to even ask what was in it."

Ethan imagined scraps of paper with women's names and phone numbers.

"A key," she said.

"To what?"

"I never found out."

"What did he say about it?"

"That it must have been there when we bought the car."

"You didn't buy that car used. Did you?"

"No," she said.

Ethan decided he didn't want to push the matter further. Especially not at his poor mother's expense. Jennifer hadn't been Noah's first secret. That was not much of a surprise.

"You want to hold on while I look?" he asked.

"Sure."

Ethan set the phone down and eased painfully to his feet. He walked to the door and stepped out into the front yard, Rufus wagging and dancing behind. He looked around once for bears—never hurts to be smart, especially since the trash cans lived on the side of the house near his dad's broken-down truck.

He eased his way around the house and reached for the driver's side door handle, wondering what he would do if it was locked. He didn't know where his father had been keeping the keys, either.

It wasn't locked.

He leaned in and ran his hand under the front of the seat—and felt it immediately. It was opened out and lying flat, one half of it hidden under the carpet mat, which extended just far enough under the seat to hide the bulge.

He pulled it out and looked inside. His father's smug face smiled at him from the New York State driver's license.

"So that *is* your hiding place, you son of a bitch," he told the picture. "And that *was* your key. To what? I guess we'll never know now."

He slammed the door and called Rufus to come back inside with him.

Halfway to the door he said, out loud and to no one, "Never mind. I don't even want to know."

He closed them both safely back into the house and carried the wallet into his father's bedroom. Picked up the phone again.

"Thanks for the tip," he said. "I've got it. I need to call the hospital now. Oh. Wait. Mom?"

"Yes?"

"Will you hold off on the . . . I don't know. Funeral? Or memorial? For Grandma? I don't want to miss it. Or do you have to do a funeral right away?"

"It'll be a memorial. And it'll hold just fine."

"Thanks."

They said quick good-byes and ended the call, and Ethan noticed a feeling as he did so. A good feeling. Not that everything was good—far from it. But he was handling things. It felt very . . . adult.

For the first time in a long time, Ethan felt as though his own life was in fairly good order, and more or less under his control.

Chapter Sixteen: Out of Control

Two days after his father was found

For the second day in a row, a knock propelled Ethan out of sleep. Out of a dream. He couldn't grasp the dream, or recall any images from it, but he could still hear the echo of helicopter blades in his head.

And he was pretty sure he had seen his grandmother in there somewhere.

"Just a minute!" he called.

He stumbled into his clothes and walked stiffly to the door, rubbing his eyes and wondering if it was possible to feel even more sore on the second day after a big adventure.

He threw the door wide, wincing into the light.

On his doorstep stood Marcus.

"Oh," he said. "Marcus. Hey."

"Wanted to come say good-bye," Marcus said.

"Which one of us is going somewhere?"

It was a sleepy question, but a reasonable one. Because Marcus might have assumed that Ethan was flying home to New York.

"Me," he said. "I'm going back to L.A. This mountain man thing just isn't working out. One of those things that looks better on paper, you know?"

"I do," Ethan said.

But he didn't. At least, not from any personal experience. For him it had looked terrible on paper and panned out better than expected.

"Anyway. I wanted to say how happy I am that you guys found your dad. Could've knocked me over with a feather, but I'm really happy for you. And also I wanted to tell you . . . you're a very good peacemaker."

"I so am not!"

"No, you are. You just don't know it yet. I was in town last night having a beer at the tavern. Well, okay, three beers. And guess who was there having a couple of steak dinners?"

"No idea," Ethan said. Probably because he was still too half asleep to realize he knew a limited number of people in the area.

"Oh, come on," Marcus said.

"No, really. I just woke up."

"Sam and Jone."

"Really," Ethan said. It was not a question. More of an exclamation.

"When I said you'd have to be the peacemaker I meant I was hoping you could keep them from killing each other. I wasn't setting my sights quite this high. I didn't think anybody could get them together."

"I don't know that it was me so much."

"They sure weren't headed that direction on their own. Come on. What happened?"

Ethan sighed and tried to remember. It seemed so long ago. So much longer than a small handful of days—days that could be counted on one hand, with a finger or two left over.

"Let's see. *So much* happened. Sam was being an ass, and he sort of knew it, but I guess he didn't know how to stop. And he knew he was blowing it with her, and the more he knew he was blowing it with her, the assier he got. I might have given him some advice on how to turn it around again. But if it worked, it's the only time in my life I ever made peace. It never worked at my house."

"Everybody has to have a first time."

Marcus held out one hand and brought the outside edge of it—slowly and ceremoniously—down onto one of Ethan's shoulders, then the other.

"I dub thee . . . Peacemaker-in-Training. Go forth and practice. Have a good life, kid."

Then he walked back to the road, and he was gone.

—

Jone appeared on his doorstep fifteen minutes later.

"Where's Sam?" Ethan asked.

"One of his horses is colicky."

"What's colicky?"

"Colic. It's a digestive thing horses get."

"Oh. One of the ones who was out with us?"

"No. No connection with the trip. One of the yearlings. I told him to stay home and wait for the vet. Doesn't take two of us to drive you to the hospital."

"Well, I appreciate it," Ethan said. "And I'm ready."

They walked together to her big Land Rover SUV, a vehicle Ethan hadn't seen before.

"Did you know Marcus is moving back to L.A.?" he asked her.

"Yeah. He said good-bye when he saw us at the tavern last night. I'm guessing he told you about that."

"He mentioned it."

"Don't go making it out to be a bigger thing than it is," she said. Her old, stern Jone voice was back, and she pointed at Ethan's nose with a formidable index finger. "It was a steak dinner. Just steaks. Nothing more."

"Just steaks? No salad? No baked potatoes?"

She cuffed him lightly on the back of the head, and Ethan stifled a smile.

"You know what I mean, wiseass. Just don't get carried away with where this is going."

"I didn't say a word," Ethan said. Then his smile faded, and he remembered what he'd been pushing away. "My grandmother died," he said.

"Oh. I'm sorry. How're you doing with that?"

"Hasn't really hit me yet," he said.

—

"Thank goodness you're here," the doctor said. He had hurried down the hall in answer to a page. The nurse had paged him the moment she saw Ethan approaching. "We need you to have a talk with your father. He's wide awake now, and being very unwise."

Hardly surprising, Ethan thought. *And probably nothing I can fix.*

But all Ethan said was "About . . ."

"We told him this morning that we will need to amputate that left leg. The infection is spreading, including upward toward his hip. If we wait even another day or two, we might not be able to leave him any stump at all. And a stump is very useful to a person using a prosthetic limb. If we wait much longer than that he will lose his life. But he refuses. He refused to consent to the surgery. He says he'd rather die than lose his leg. It's quite heartbreaking for all of us, and for you, too, I'm sure. So much effort to save his life. I can't believe he would then turn around and throw it all away again. People live good lives after an amputation. Active lives. It takes courage at first, but people do it all the time. But I couldn't make him listen to reason."

"I don't know if I can make any difference," Ethan said. "But I'll talk to him."

As he walked down the hall to his father's room he remembered Marcus knighting him earlier that morning. Dubbing him Peacemaker.

He hoped his new official title would be of use to him now.

—

Noah was wide awake, as advertised. And scowling. He looked at Ethan as though a look could form a brick wall, keeping everything undesirable outside.

Apparently Ethan was undesirable.

"I see," Noah said.

But it was impossible for Ethan to know what his father saw.

"What do you see?"

"They're breaking out the big guns. Into the ring comes Ethan Underwood, standing five foot two and weighing in at a whopping one hundred twelve pounds. To do the dirty work the doctors can't manage on their own." Then he winced deeply. "They need to up my painkillers, Ethan. You need to tell them that. I'm still in agony here. I need more morphine. Or whatever the hell this is in the nice little drip tube."

"So," Ethan said, taking a seat by his father's bed, "you're back to your old self again."

Ethan had been nursing a hope that his father had been humbled by the near-fatal experience.

"I'm serious, Ethan. Go get the nurse and tell her."

"You have a call button for the nurse," he said. "But please. Not yet. Not until we've talked. Once she ups that dosage, you'll wink out on me. I need you awake while we have this talk."

"I'm in pain here."

"Then we'd better get this done," Ethan said.

His father narrowed his eyes and looked right into Ethan's face. "You've changed," he said. "You seem different."

"Thank you."

"It wasn't a compliment. I don't like the new you."

"Well, it's a good thing I did it for me, then. Not for you. So the doctor tells me you'd rather voluntarily die than lose one leg. Do you have any idea what a slap in the face that is for me?"

"You? This has nothing to do with you."

"The hell it doesn't. Do you really not have any idea what I went through to find you out there and get you back to civilization? Do you know how scary it was? And how sore I am? And not because we have such a loving relationship and get along so great. But I did it because I wanted you to have your life at least. And then, after all that, you say you don't want it. Unless it can be just the way you want it to be. You're acting like a child."

Ethan paused, almost as if to take a breath. But really he was making a space to allow some reaction.

"What the . . . ," Ethan's father began. Then he paused as if editing out a stronger obscenity. ". . . hell are you talking about, Ethan? I have no idea what you're talking about."

"You don't know? You don't know how you got here?"

"Medevac helicopter. A rescue team brought me in."

"Because we called them."

"Who's we?"

"Our neighbors, Jone and Sam. We went out into the wilderness on Sam's horses and pack mules. The rangers and search and rescue looked for you for two days and then called off the search, because the more they found out what a swell guy you are, the more they figured you just took off and left me. You would have stayed out there to die, but we put together our own search team. And we found you. And Sam rode home and called it in."

A long pause. Noah's eyes pressed closed.

"I think you're delusional," he said. "I think you're on too many drugs, and I'm on not enough."

Ethan sighed. He stood up, leaned over his father's bed, and pressed the call button for a nurse. Then he sat back down.

A moment later the door popped open and a middle-aged nurse with a pleasant face stuck her head in.

"Problem?"

"I'm sorry in advance," Ethan said, "because this is not a medical emergency. But please tell my dad who found him in the wilderness. It'll help with this important talk we're trying to have."

The nurse looked at Noah, who looked back, but a little sheepishly. As if he already knew it was true, and didn't want to hear it confirmed.

"You don't know yet?" she asked. "I was sure they told you. Your son found you. Everybody else had given up. He joined up with the man who does the pack trips and another neighbor, and they just kept looking until they found you."

"Thank you," Ethan said to her.

The door swung closed again.

Noah squeezed his eyes shut.

"Oh," he said, quietly, as if to himself, but he drew the word out long. "That explains something. I thought I had this really vivid dream that you were sitting with me on that ledge talking about what a terrible father I'd always been."

"Not a dream," Ethan said. "Real."

"That makes no sense. How the hell did you get on the ledge?"

"With a climbing harness and a rope."

"You?"

That marked the edge for Ethan. The dropping-off point. His voice came up. He lost his temper, which was something he rarely did. Maybe it was something he'd never done. In the confusion of the moment, he couldn't remember. He just knew it felt unfamiliar.

"Yes! *Me*, Dad! I did that! So it's damn well time for you to stop treating me like I couldn't. Because I did. And you can't change that. No amount of put-downs will ever change what I did. You're just going to have to drop the 'Ethan can't do shit' routine and the 'Ethan is so hopeless and funny' routine and treat me with a little more respect."

Then he waited. Nothing. So he raged on.

"It doesn't 'make no sense' that I was on that ledge with you. It makes perfect sense. You're just not thinking clearly. Which I don't blame you for under the circumstances. It's pretty much the only thing I *don't* blame you for. If I hadn't gone down onto that ledge, there's no way I could have found you. You couldn't be seen from the trail above.

You couldn't be seen from the valley below. You pulled yourself under a rock overhang, like you were trying to be invisible to the search teams. Jone and I had so much trouble figuring out why you would do that."

Silence. A long one. Ethan wondered if his dad might have slipped into a drugged unconsciousness again.

But in time Noah spoke.

"Because I didn't want to lose my leg."

"Everything's a joke to you," Ethan said.

"It's not a joke, Ethan. I'm trying to tell you a true thing here. It got warm, and the snow was melting, and it was like rain. Like being under a waterfall. Except it was coming off the trail, so it was bringing down dirt and little stones. And I had this open wound right down to the bone. I knew it might be awhile until anyone found me. I didn't want it to get infected. I didn't want to lose the leg."

"But the searchers couldn't find you under there. So you would have died."

"That would have been better than losing the leg," he said.

"Oh my God," Ethan said. "You're pathetic." He didn't raise his voice. He didn't need to.

"Now, listen—" Noah began.

He didn't get the chance to finish. Ethan saw to that.

"No, *you* listen, Dad. You think I don't know why you feel so strongly about this? Of course I know. Because you think it'll be harder to date girls with only one leg. That you won't have this perfect body anymore. And they won't find you attractive. And that is totally pathetic. There's more to life than getting younger women into bed, and if you don't know that, you're just going to have to find out. Figure it out, Dad. There's so much to the world, and if you don't know what, find out. You're forty-one years old. You have half a life left. By the time you're eighty-two you'll have to find something else worth living for besides twenty-four-year-olds anyway. Figure it out a little early. Don't you dare insult the people who worked so hard to get you that second forty-one years by saying it's not worth anything if you can't sleep around. You think that's being a man? Well, I don't. I think you're acting like a spoiled child. You'll get a prosthetic leg and a new right knee, and you'll learn to walk on them, and life'll go on. Remember that movie you made me sit through about the guy who summited Mount Everest with two prosthetic feet? Look at the people in the Paralympics. You want to still be an extreme athlete? Then be an extreme athlete. You still can. You just have to buck up and show some courage. I'm not saying this should be easy for you. Of course it's not. But it's what's in front of you. So deal with it, you know, Dad? Deal with it."

Silence.

There was no way to read the silence, and Ethan only knew his father's reaction was not at all what he had expected. Noah's face looked drained. Almost calm.

"Could you just leave me alone with this?" Noah said after a time.

Ethan sighed. Stood.

"And tell the nurse I need more pain relief," Noah added.

Ethan hit the swinging door hard with the heel of his hand and burst out into the hall. He hobbled back down to the nurses' station.

Jone looked up at him, her eyes full of questions, but Ethan only shook his head.

"I messed it up," he said when he was close enough to be heard. "I lost my temper. Probably only made things worse. But I don't think anybody was going to get through to him anyway. Trying to change my dad's mind about anything always was a big waste of time."

—

"They didn't even tell him I was the one who found him," he said to Jone.

They were sitting in hard plastic bench seats in the waiting room. Waiting. But Ethan didn't know for what.

"Yeah, they did," Jone said. "I was standing right there when they told him."

"You were here last night?"

"Yeah. Sam and I both were. But he was groggy and on a lot of drugs. He probably just doesn't remember."

"Yeah, maybe," he said. "I'm hungry."

It was barely ten a.m.

"You didn't have breakfast?" she asked.

"I forgot to. Did you have breakfast?"

"Yeah. But that was before five. I could have a little something. You want to see what the cafeteria has going on?"

—

"He might change his mind," Jone said. She indicated Ethan's plate of scrambled eggs and bacon. "How is that, anyway?"

"For hospital cafeteria food, not too bad. I don't know, Jone. It's my dad. He's not a 'see the light' kind of guy."

"But in a couple of days he'll be staring death right in the face. That changes a person if anything ever will."

"He just spent almost a week staring death in the face. And he stayed under that rock overhang to try to keep that leg wound cleaner. Even though it made it impossible to be found."

"That doesn't make a damn bit of sense. Because they could have saved the leg if he'd been found sooner."

"Welcome to my dad."

They ate in silence for a few minutes. Ethan looked out the window and watched occasional cars flash by on the long, flat county highway. They were a good thirty miles south of Avery, and the land was not mountainous. And that struck Ethan as a shame. Even a loss.

"Don't you think it's strange," he asked, "that we haven't heard a word from Ranger Dave?"

"There might be a legal component to that."

"Not following."

"I don't know if a person could sue over a thing like this. Probably not successfully, because the first rule of any national park or wilderness is that you're responsible for your own safety. But people can try, and I'm sure they do. If Dave comes to you and apologizes, it might be like admitting fault. In a strictly legal sense."

"Well, that's too bad. Because all I would say is that I don't blame him. You know. Knowing what we know now."

They fell silent again.

After a time Ethan spoke suddenly, almost without realizing he was about to.

"If my dad doesn't change his mind, I'll just fly home. Leave him here. If he has the amputation, I'll stay and help him out. He'll need help getting home and getting all his stuff together. And then he'll have to fly somewhere. Back to New York. Or maybe . . . he has family in Chicago. But until he gets settled in and has somebody else looking after him, I'll stay and help him. But if he just keeps being the way he's being now . . . I mean, what the hell am I even doing here, Jone? He can die just fine without my help."

He picked at his food for a moment or two in silence. His appetite seemed to have dropped off the edge of a cliff, and the food no longer tasted like anything. But he knew he should finish it, if only to help himself with the long and difficult day ahead.

"I didn't mean that the way it sounded," he said. "I meant if he chooses to die I can't bear to stay and watch and not be able to do a damn thing."

"I knew what you meant," she said quietly.

"I can't believe we went through all that," he said, "and now it's just for nothing."

"Hey!" Jone said. It was a sharp tone. Almost a bark. A man and woman at the next table jumped slightly. "Don't ever say that to me again. It was not nothing. You did an incredible thing for your father. And *you* always have that. It's part of who you are now. You stepped up to it, and now you're up on a higher level than you were before. You gave the man a gift. The fact that he doesn't know how to value it doesn't mean it wasn't a great gift. It just means he has lousy taste in presents."

—

When they arrived back at the nurses' station, the doctor was there, leaning on the counter and smiling broadly. It looked out of place to Ethan. Discordant. Like those "What's wrong with this picture?" games Ethan used to like as a child. Finding one thing in the picture that didn't fit with everything else.

When he saw Ethan, his smile grew wider.

"You are a worker of miracles!" the doctor called out.

Ethan stopped and looked over his shoulder, seriously considering that the doctor might be speaking to someone behind him.

"Me?"

"Yes indeed, you."

"I told you. That was more luck than anything."

"That's not what I meant. I'm talking about your second miracle. I don't know what you said to your father, but thank you. He just now signed the consent form to undergo amputation surgery."

"Well, I'll be damned," Ethan said.

—

"Dad?" Ethan asked.

He stood with just his head poking through the door into his father's room.

"Don't," Noah said. "Just don't."

"I was just going to say it's great that you—"

"Right. That. Don't."

Ethan hung in the doorway a moment longer, not quite sure what to do or say next.

"You really want me to just go home and leave you alone?"

A long silence.

"No," Noah said. "No, come in. Just . . . let's not talk about *that.* Okay?"

"Okay," Ethan said.

He pushed his way into the room and sat in the plastic chair beside his father's bed.

"You eat?" Noah asked.

"Yeah. Just now. In the cafeteria."

"Yuck. Hospital food is always terrible."

"This wasn't bad. It wasn't great, but it wasn't bad."

"What'd you have?"

"Scrambled eggs and bacon."

"Okay."

A painfully long and awkward silence. Ethan thought he could feel it grind on both of them.

Then Noah said, "We don't really have anything to talk about, do we?"

"Not really, I guess."

"We never really did have anything to talk about."

Ethan wanted to argue. But he had no facts on his side. So he said nothing.

"I was a great dad for a baby. And a toddler. I was a great hero figure. You know, for somebody who's too small to look too close or ask too many questions. But then you grew up and started talking. And you were smart. And I never really knew what to say to you after that."

"I didn't need sparkling conversation, Dad. Just the truth would have been fine."

"I never much liked the truth. I always figured I could improve on it."

A pause, which Ethan didn't fill. Couldn't fill. How do you counter a statement like that?

"Speaking of the truth," Noah said, "what I told you about pulling myself under that rock wasn't entirely true. I made it sound like I wasn't afraid of dying. But I was. I wanted to be found. Truth is I went under there for the reason I said I did, but then I couldn't get back out. I could move about an inch at a time backward—the direction my head was facing—without it hurting so much that I passed out. But then I got stuck. I couldn't go sideways or in the direction my feet were pointing. It hurt too much. I tried it when I heard the plane overhead. But I passed out from the pain, and when I came to again it was gone."

"Oh," Ethan said. "That makes more sense. Can I ask you one other question? If it has nothing to do with legs?"

"I guess."

"Why did you take five hundred dollars in cash out of the bank the day before the accident?"

"Oh. That. That was for you. I was going to give it to you and tell you to have a different kind of adventure. The kind where you find your own way home to New York. I was going to let you fly back alone and stay on your own there."

Ethan thought back to the day before his father disappeared. At the time, he realized, that would have seemed like quite the adventure. It would have made his heart pound to think about crossing the United States alone. Now it sounded like nothing. Compared to riding the edge of a cliff over a two-thousand-foot drop-off? Or staring into the bared teeth of a peeved grizzly sow? Just buying a plane ticket and hailing a cab sounded easy.

"Why?" Ethan asked. "Why would you do that? You were so dead set on keeping me here. At least until I had somewhere better to go."

"I told myself it was to make you happy. And I'm sure that's what I would've told you. And it was true, of course. That was a big part of it. But also I wasn't too keen on being stuck in that tiny place together all summer."

"Oh," Ethan said. "Me neither."

"I mean, I wanted us to have the time together. I did and I didn't. I wanted us to work again. To get along. But it wasn't panning out that way. How did you even find out about that cash withdrawal thing?"

"The rangers were doing some digging, because they weren't sure you were up there in the wilderness at all. It was a big part of why they called off the search. People take cash out of the bank to make a getaway. Not to go running in the mountains."

"Just my luck," Noah said.

Then they ran out of things to say again.

Before they could solve the problem, a male nurse or orderly came in and announced that it was time to prep Noah for surgery.

Ethan took his father's hand before leaving. Squeezed it tightly.

Ethan searched his memory but couldn't remember an example of physical contact between them. At least, not since Ethan was old enough to talk. Maybe there had been something. Sometime. But nothing came to mind.

Noah squeezed back.

"I don't know who I'm going to be when this is over," Noah said, avoiding Ethan's eyes.

"You'll still be you."

"I don't really know who that is, though."

"Right," Ethan said. "I guess now you get to find out."

—

"The surgery went well," the doctor said. "We did everything. Both legs. That's why it took so long. We replaced the right knee with a prosthetic joint, and now it's just a matter of a lot of time to heal. Of course, he'll be in a wheelchair at first. But in time he should be learning to walk again. He's a fortunate man."

Except in his own head, Ethan thought. He didn't say so.

"Can I go in and see him?"

"Not yet. He's in recovery. Then he'll go back to his room, but I doubt he'll be conscious. I'm afraid visiting hours will be over by the time he's awake and ready to see you. It might be late in the evening.

Perhaps it would be best to go home and get some rest and come back in the morning."

Ethan looked up into the doctor's face, then over at Jone. Then back at the doctor.

"Can't I stay with him?"

Jone said, "It might be best for everyone just to get some rest, like the doctor said."

"Couldn't I stay here tonight? Jone, you could just go home without me and come back tomorrow."

Jone raised one eyebrow but asked no questions. Well, no questions of Ethan. She asked the doctor, "Is it against policy?"

"No, we sometimes allow it. Usually parents of young children like to stay. Because they're afraid their child will wake up in the night and be all in a panic."

"Yes," Ethan said. "Exactly. That's exactly why I want to stay."

The doctor scratched his stubbly cheek for a moment. "All right," he said. "I'll have an orderly bring a cot into his room."

—

The moon was waning but still bright, and it shone through the window and lit up his father's face. Ethan noticed this while he was not sleeping. In fact, he found himself staring at his dad. His mind ran over details of his wilderness days, including imaginings of what the ordeal must have been like from his father's point of view.

Noah's eyes flickered open.

"Dad," Ethan said. "You doing okay?"

"Oh, you're here," Noah said.

His voice sounded soft and, well . . . there was really only one way to say it. Loaded. Almost like a drunken man, though Ethan knew it was the IV drugs.

"Yeah, I stayed."

"Is it over?"

"Yeah."

"They did it?"

"Yeah. They replaced your right knee, too."

Noah tried to lift his head, and at the same time he raised the stump of his left leg. His body was under a sheet and a light blanket, but Ethan could see the outline of what was left of the leg—and what was gone. He could see clearly where it ended. It was more of a shock than he'd expected, even though earlier he'd gotten used to seeing the blanket sag in the space a leg had so recently occupied. Still, it was different to see it move.

"Dad, don't do that. You just got out of surgery a few hours ago. You'll hurt it."

"Oh."

"Doesn't that hurt?"

"Yeah."

"Just be still if you can."

No reply. For a very long time. Ethan looked over to see if his father was asleep again. But Noah seemed to be looking at the moon.

"Why did you stay here?" he asked Ethan.

"I thought you might wake up and be scared. And . . . you know. Upset."

"I need more of this pain stuff. Get the nurse for me, okay?"

"You have a pump."

"A what?"

"A pain pump. You just press this button on the IV tube."

Ethan sat up on his cot and leaned over. He took his father's hand and placed it on the button.

"Oh," Noah said. Then, a few seconds later, "Oh. That's better already. Good. Did I have a button before?"

"I don't know," Ethan said.

They both lay still and quiet for a long time. Ten minutes or more. Ethan assumed his father would drift back to the underneath side of consciousness. Even though his eyes were open.

"The moon," Noah said. His voice sounded even more filmy and insignificant. And even more stoned.

"What about it, Dad?"

"I watched it. Every night. And every night I wondered if it was the last time I'd see it. But there it is."

"I'm glad you're here to see it."

"I didn't want to die."

"I know."

"I was so scared."

"I know that, too. But you're okay now."

"You're right. I'm pathetic."

"I . . . shouldn't have said that."

"No, you should. Have. It's true. That's why I had the . . . you know. What do you call it again?"

"The surgery?"

"Right. Because when little five-foot-two Ethan is looking down on me I know it's time to stand up taller. You know? And be braver. And . . . what was I saying?"

Ethan felt his own reaction to the dig at his height, felt it as an actual physical sensation, a palpable irritation in his body. He tried to push it down again. Let it go by. But he'd been letting it go by his whole life. This time it didn't push down. It pushed back.

"You just can't resist putting me down about my size, can you?"

"No, no, no," Noah said. "No. I didn't mean it like that at all. I'm not saying things right. It just made you so much more like your mom. It was like I wasn't even part of making you at all. Like I wasn't even in there anywhere. The two of you were like this perfect match, like you rejected my DNA or something. I resented that. It made me feel left out. And you were always so smart. You didn't really know how smart you were. It seemed like a mean joke from . . . I don't know, nature or whatever that you ended up looking like a younger kid than you are. Because you're so smart, you're like five years ahead of your age. Seven years. Hell, you were smarter than me and that's a lot of years. That's why I teased you about it."

He didn't go on to say what "it" was, but Ethan got the general drift of the point.

"You were smarter," Noah continued, "but I was taller."

Ethan thought his dad was doing an awful lot of talking for a man who should be drifting back out of consciousness. But Noah seemed wound up about something, and unable to let it go. So Ethan just waited and let his father speak.

"And I was better looking, and I thought I was braver. But then you yelled all that stuff at me this morning, and then I knew I wasn't. Braver. Than you. I mean, than anybody."

"Dad, maybe just lie still and see if you can get some sleep. This stuff doesn't matter."

"It does," Noah said. "It matters. That's why I had to have the operation. Because I had to be brave. Otherwise you'd be braver and I'd be losing again."

"It's not a competition, Dad."

"Everything's a competition," Noah said.

Ethan sat up in his cot. Pushed the covers off himself.

"I don't want to do this anymore. I can't sleep. I'm going to go out and see if there's a soda machine or something. Try to get back to sleep, Dad."

He let himself out of the room.

As the door closed with a little whoosh sound behind him, Ethan took a deep breath and shook his head and shoulders slightly, as if he could physically knock away the troubling thoughts that surrounded him.

He eased his sore legs down the hall to the nurses' station. He expected it to be empty, but there was a night nurse. Of course. Ethan should have known there would be a night nurse.

She had jet-black hair and eyes that were almost black, and a round face. And she smiled at him. And he realized how badly he'd needed that smile. From just about anyone.

"Can't sleep?" she asked him.

"No, ma'am."

"Is your father asleep?"

"Not exactly. He was just talking my ear off."

"Is he okay?"

"No."

The nurse rose immediately, as if to go to him.

"No, I'm sorry," Ethan said quickly. "He's okay. Physically he's okay. He's just . . . he's such a sad man."

He'd almost been tempted to add the word "little." Such a sad *little* man. But he kept that part of the thought on the inside of his head, away from others.

She smiled at him again, but more pityingly this time.

"It's hard, isn't it? When you find out your parents aren't what you thought they were?"

"Yeah, that happens all the time with my dad. I still can't pin down what I think he is. But right now I'd settle for a soda machine. Leave the big questions for morning."

She laughed. A light, lilting thing. Like something the wind could toss around. Then she pointed Ethan down the hall.

He bought a soda, then carried it past the nurse on the way back to his father's room.

"Going back in," she said, clearly understanding all the subtext of such an act.

"I am," he said. "It's a hard time in his life. And . . . you know. He's still my dad."

Chapter Seventeen: Smart

Three days after his father was found

Morning light blasted through the hospital room window, and Ethan opened his eyes. He squinted and winced, took a moment to adjust, then looked over to see how his father was doing.

Noah was sitting more or less upright, his eyes wide open. He'd apparently used the bed controls to adjust into more of a sitting position. He was staring at the spot on the bed where his left leg should have been.

He seemed absorbed in what he was thinking, so Ethan was surprised when his father spoke to him—surprised that Noah had even noticed Ethan was awake.

"You slept in," Noah said.

"I was awake a long time in the night."

"Oh." Still his father never took his eyes off the empty spot on his hospital bed. "I slept like the dead."

"Actually . . . ," Ethan said. Then he wasn't sure whether he should finish.

"What?"

"We had a long conversation. Well. Longish. For us, anyway."

"What did I say?"

"You really don't remember?"

"No. I thought I was asleep all night. What did I say?"

"Oh. Nothing much."

"You said it was a longish conversation."

"You talked about the moon. You were staring at the moon, and you said you'd been staring at it every night out there in the wilderness and wondering if it would be the last time you'd ever see it."

No reply.

"And you said I was really smart."

"Well, you are."

"Thanks," Ethan said.

Then he decided there was no point in pushing the issue any further.

"Think I'll get used to this?" Noah asked, still staring at the missing leg.

"Yes. I'm sure you will."

"How can you be so sure?"

"Because people get used to things. We just do. What other choice do we have? We always say we'll never get used to change, but then the change happens and we do."

"See?" Noah said. "Smart."

—

Sam was waiting for Ethan down by the nurses' station, smiling. More or less at nobody and nothing. Just smiling.

"How's the yearling?" Ethan asked him.

"Oh, she's okay now."

"Where's Jone?"

"She hadn't been to see her family since before our pack trip. I told her I could take care of things here at home. So she's over on the reservation on the other side of the foothills today. Seeing her kids and grandkids and great-grandkids."

Because Sam couldn't seem to wipe the goofy grin off his face, Ethan asked, "She been seeing anybody else lately?"

Sam grinned more widely, and they turned and walked down the hall together, toward the elevator.

"I have no idea what you're talking about," he said.

But just at that moment he broke into the funniest little dance. Only two or three steps, but it made Ethan laugh out loud. Then Sam stopped dancing and placed a finger to his lips in a shushing signal.

"I didn't say a word," Ethan said.

"So, on a more serious note," Sam said, "how do you feel about reporters?"

"What about them?"

"You okay with them?"

"What kind of reporters?"

"Like newspaper reporters. Although this might be a good time to figure out how you feel about other kinds of reporters, too."

"I must be missing something, Sam. I pretty much just woke up."

"There's a newspaper reporter down in the lobby. He's hoping to get a word with you."

Ethan stopped walking. It took Sam a step or two to notice.

"Why?" he asked Sam, when Sam had noticed.

"Because it's news. It's not such a small thing, what just happened. It's a human interest story. Man goes out into the wilderness and almost dies and everybody gives up on finding him except his teenage son, who actually does. You didn't think people would want to hear about that?"

"I don't know," Ethan said. "I guess I hadn't thought about it. I've had a lot on my mind."

They began walking toward the elevator again. Slowly.

"I didn't promise him you'd have anything to say to him," Sam said. "Only that I'd ask."

"Oh, you talked to him?"

"A little bit. Yeah. I hope you don't mind. I thought a story like that'd be good for Friendly Sam's Pack Service."

"Oh," Ethan said. "Right. Well, that's fine. You have a right to get a little publicity off this. I hope it helps."

They stopped at the elevator, and Sam pushed the "Down" button.

"I'm glad you're not mad," Sam said.

Silence. They stared at the readout of floors. Floor number four was lighted up. But nothing seemed to move.

"So, are you going to talk to that reporter?" Sam asked.

"I can't decide. I don't really like the idea. I don't want this being all about me. And I don't think it's something I meant for everybody to know about. I feel like it's more of a situation you talk about with your own family. And another thing. I have this idea that the great human interest story about the son who won't give up on his dad revolves around the idea that dad and son adore each other. I think the whole thing sort of falls down without that."

The elevator's lighted floor display began to move. Toward them. Ethan felt more relieved than he could consciously justify.

"Well, it's up to you," Sam said.

Ding. The elevator doors slid open and his father's doctor stepped out. Smiling, as always.

"How is the patient this morning?" he asked Ethan.

"Seems okay," Ethan said.

Then Ethan and Sam stepped onto the elevator together.

The doctor reached out and held one of the doors to keep them both from closing.

"One question, Ethan, if you don't mind. Does your father take a lot of prescription pain medication as a matter of course?"

Ethan blinked under the fluorescent lights and considered the question. And felt as though he didn't have enough time to consider it. What with the elevator doors being held pending his answer.

"I don't know. I don't think so. I mean . . . not that I know of. Why?"

"It's just that we're giving him quite a lot of pain medication. As much as I dare prescribe. It should be enough for a much larger man.

But he never seems to feel it's enough. I just thought maybe it was a tolerance issue. That maybe he takes medication regularly and has built up a high tolerance."

"Or maybe just a low pain threshold," Ethan said.

"Yes, yes. Maybe so."

The doctor let go of the doors and walked off down the hall with a wave and a nod.

"One other thing about the reporter," Sam said as the elevator headed down. "He asked a lot about whether we think the park service was at fault."

"What did you say?"

"Just that your dad was pretty well hidden."

"Yeah. Hmm. Maybe I should talk to him a little bit. You know. Just to let Ranger Dave off the hook."

—

"You're Ethan?" the reporter asked.

The man jumped to his feet. As though to be Ethan was to hold a position of respect. As if Ethan were royalty, or a judge, and the world had to jump to its feet every time he entered a room.

The reporter had a sharply receding hairline, but he looked too young to have lost so much hair. Early thirties, maybe. What hair he had was bushy and wild. He wore nice dress pants and a white shirt with a tie, but no jacket. The clothes and the hair seemed mismatched.

"I'm Ethan, yeah. But I'm not sure how thrilled I am with a news story about Ethan. I mean, I know it's a story, what happened. I was thinking it was more like a story for the next family Thanksgiving. Not for the front page of anything."

"Don't take this the wrong way, but the story's going to be in the newspaper one way or the other. It's a newsworthy thing that happened around here. It's really more a question of whether you want any of your own words in the article."

"Oh," Ethan said. "Hmm. I'm not sure."

"Maybe I could ask you a few questions. You don't have to answer any you don't want."

"Okay."

"What made you go out into the wilderness to look for your dad? No, wait . . . let me rephrase that. I know why you wanted to find him. I guess what I'm trying to ask is . . . what made you think you *could* find him?"

"I didn't."

"You didn't . . . what?"

"Think I could find him. None of us did."

"Then why go out there?"

"So I would always know I tried," he said. *And to be brave for a change,* he didn't say.

The reporter scribbled notes on his pad. For longer than Ethan would have liked. While the man wrote, Ethan glanced around at Sam, who was standing over by the gift shop. Sam smiled reassuringly.

"Do you blame the park service and search and rescue for not finding him?"

"No," Ethan said. "I was disappointed when they called off the search. Who wouldn't be? But I know exactly why they did what they did. And once we found him, we totally understood why the searchers didn't. He was really hidden well. It would have been almost impossible to find him."

"Then how did you?"

"Yeah, good question," Ethan said. "We asked ourselves that a lot. And we asked each other. It was a weird stroke of luck. One of the mules started acting up and drove my mule off into the weeds, and she got her hoof caught on my dad's fleece jacket. It was one of those things you couldn't repeat in a million years no matter how hard you tried. And then that was like an arrow pointing to where he went off the trail."

"But you didn't call the searchers and ask them to go out on that ledge."

"No. You can't get cell reception up there. And Sam's sat phone wouldn't get a signal. We were a couple hours from a phone. We didn't figure we had that kind of time."

"How did you feel when you saw your dad again?"

Ethan instinctively took a step backward.

"No," he said. "This is the part I don't want. I don't want to tell a bunch of strangers how I feel. It won't be what they're expecting anyway. I have to go."

Ethan signaled to Sam and then headed for the parking lot. At a good clip, considering his legs still felt welded on and mostly immobile.

He purposely didn't look back to see how the reporter felt about his abrupt departure.

Chapter Eighteen: I Give Up

Eleven days after his father was found

"Thanks for bringing us home," Ethan said, more or less to both Jone and Sam at the same time.

His father had no comment. On anything. He just stared out the window of Jone's SUV as the A-frame came into view. He hadn't said a word since checking out of the hospital.

"Of course," Jone said.

"We're not about to leave you on your own with a thing like this," Sam added.

"It's just that . . . you've both put so much time into this," Ethan said. "I'll bet you never guessed what you were getting yourself into when this thing started."

"We've come this far together," Sam said. "Might as well finish the job right."

Jone swung the SUV into the A-frame's driveway and pulled up close to the front door.

"Sam, go get the wheelchair from the back," she said. "Okay?" She met Ethan's eyes in the rearview mirror. "When are you and your dad headed back to New York again, Ethan?"

"Monday. We think. But my mom got refundable tickets. Because he has one more medical appointment before then. On Friday. And the doctor has to clear him to make the trip."

Ethan glanced over at his father, to see how Noah felt about being discussed as if he weren't in the vehicle at all. Ethan wasn't doing it on purpose. But Noah seemed distant, and would not engage, and Ethan had no idea how to solve that.

"What time should I pick you two up on Friday?" Jone asked.

"No, you've done enough, Jone. I'll call a cab."

"Out here? It'll cost a fortune."

"You've already done so much."

"Oh, hush. What time?"

"We have to be there at eleven."

Then there was no more time to talk, because Sam had the door beside Noah open and the wheelchair in position with the brakes on. And it was time for the difficult—and, at least to Ethan, nerve-racking—task of getting Noah from the car into the chair.

Jone took one of Noah's arms and Sam took the other, and they got him turned around with his back to the open door. Which was a little scary in itself. Ethan hoped his dad knew enough not to move or lean back. But it was impossible to know, because Noah still wasn't talking.

They did the big transfer, and it was fast. Sam and Jone did the heavy lifting. Ethan just steadied his father's right leg.

Then it was over, and all they heard from Noah was a pained grunt.

"I can take it from here," Ethan said when they had helped him get the wheelchair up the front steps.

"You're sure, now?" Jone asked.

"Yeah. I think so. I mean, I can wheel him into the house. That's nothing. I might need help getting him into bed tonight."

"You should let us come in," Sam said, "and get him into bed right now. I think he'll be more comfortable there."

"No," Noah said.

It was flat, and loud. And sudden. It created its own curtain of silence. Ethan was the one to break through it.

"Why don't you want to be in bed, Dad?"

"I'm sick of lying in bed. Besides. I might have to go to the bathroom."

"We have a bedpan."

"Right. That's exactly why. That's just what I don't want. I don't want you bringing me a bedpan and emptying it for me. Cleaning up after me like I'm a baby who doesn't know how to use the potty yet. I've been housebroken for forty years, thank you very much."

Ethan looked into his father's face, but couldn't engage his eyes. Noah saw to it that he couldn't. Ethan looked up at Sam and Jone instead.

Sam shrugged slightly. Jone kept her reactions to herself.

"That doesn't quite work, Dad. I mean, I can wheel you into the bathroom, or you can wheel yourself in. But I'm not sure how you're supposed to get from the wheelchair to . . . you know."

"Can we discuss this in private, Ethan? You know. The two of us?"

"We'll drop in once or twice later today," Jone said. "See how you're doing."

"Thanks. We've got a ton of groceries. Thanks to you guys."

Ethan watched them pile into the vehicle and turn it around, and drive off down the driveway to the road, kicking up a cloud of dust behind them.

He looked down at his father, who pointedly did not look back. It was just the two of them now.

"If I can wheel myself into the bathroom," Noah said, "at least I can dump my own bedpan."

"Okay," Ethan said. "We can give that a try, anyway. If you're sure it's what you want."

"Quite sure," Noah said.

Ethan undid the brake on the chair and wheeled his dad into the house. Rufus reared and danced to see Noah, or to see that Ethan was home, or both.

Ethan realized the moment had arrived, the one he and his father had both been dreading. The one Noah had been willing to withdraw five hundred dollars in cash from the bank to solve. They were stuck in this tiny house together. There was absolutely no way out.

But Noah wheeled himself into his bedroom, swinging the door mostly closed behind his wheelchair, and Ethan barely saw him after that.

—

A good two hours later Ethan heard a big sound from his father's bedroom. It sounded like a huge, explosive expression of pain.

He ran in to see his father positioning himself on his back on the bed.

Noah looked up into Ethan's face with exaggerated pride.

"See? I can get from the wheelchair to the bed and back again. By myself. So tell your friends they're no longer needed."

"They'll still be stopping by."

"Whatever. You can keep them out there with you."

Ethan shook his head. More of a comment on his father's behavior than he should have let show. Than he would have let show if he'd been thinking better. He turned to leave.

"Ethan. Wait. I need more of those painkillers."

Ethan looked at his cheap watch. As always, the gesture was punctuated by a pang of loss and old, stale fear.

"You're not due again for another two and a half hours."

"But I need them now."

"But the doctor was very specific. This is a scary-high dosage he has you on. He told me to hold on to the pills and be careful how I dispensed them."

A silence. Ethan could feel his father's mood crackle. In the past, it would have frightened him. Now all he had to do was walk away if things got too bad. And even if he didn't walk away, well . . . he just wasn't afraid of the man anymore. Things between Ethan and his father weren't anything like they had ever been. Ethan wasn't quite sure what they were. Just that they were new.

"You're dispensing my medication now?"

"Yes. I am."

"Because this wasn't demoralizing and emasculating enough for me?"

"Because the doctor suspects you've been taking a lot of painkillers for a long time. And that you might take a harmful dose . . . maybe even a fatal one . . . you know . . . because of having such a high tolerance."

Another silence. Ethan glanced at his father, who pointedly did not glance back.

"Are you asking me if that's true?" Noah said after a time.

"Sure," Ethan said. "Why not?"

"Nobody my age does what I do—what I *did*, I mean—without painkillers."

"I'm not sure that's right," Ethan said. "But either way, you've got yourself in a bind where no safe amount is enough. There's not much I can do about that. Why did you take so many pills? You weren't already injured, were you?"

"Depends on what you call injured. I had shin splints and a pulled hamstring. And anything over twelve miles, my knees would swell up."

"I can think of a way to solve that. Only run eleven miles."

"Not how I solve things," Noah said. "But I sure solved it now, didn't I? Because I'm fresh out of knees."

"Give me a yell if you need anything," Ethan said, pulling the door closed behind himself.

"I need another of those pills," Noah yelled through the door.

"Two and a half hours," Ethan called back.

—

Ethan wasn't sure how much time had elapsed between that unpleasant exchange and the knock on the A-frame's door. Maybe an hour. Maybe less.

He assumed it was Sam, or Jone. Or both. So he moved to open the door with a lightness in his heart and gut. Because seeing them would be just what he needed. Their calm, helpful energy would erase the bad taste left over from dealing with his dad. Or so Ethan hoped.

He threw the door wide.

Standing on his stoop was Ranger Dave.

The ranger had his hat in his hands, in more ways than one. He literally held his wide-brimmed ranger hat in front of his belly. But he also carried his head slightly down, his eyes averted, like a man forced into a conciliatory, hat-in-hands gesture.

"Oh," Ethan said. "It's you."

"If I shouldn't be here, I'll go. I mean . . . I shouldn't be here. In an official sense I probably shouldn't be. I guess I came here more as me and less as a ranger. But if you don't want me here, I'll turn and walk away right now. It's not my intention to intrude."

"No, it's okay. You want to come in?"

"This won't take that long. I just wanted to apologize. Unofficially."

"I understand why things happened the way they did," Ethan said.

"It was very generous of you, the way you said in the paper that you didn't blame us. I wanted to thank you for that. Unofficially."

"No problem."

"It's a hard thing to deal with. For us, I mean. For me. Having been so wrong."

Ethan didn't answer. Because he had no idea what he could say to alleviate that feeling. Or even if it was his job to do so.

"You sure you don't want to come in?"

"No. I'm almost done here. I just want to say I'm glad your father is okay. And, yeah, he was hidden. He would have been really hard to find.

Even if we had stayed out there, I'm not sure if we ever would have found him, given where it turned out he was. But I see now we should have kept trying. I think what I feel worst about is how I misjudged him."

"Misjudged him?"

"Yes. I think you know what I mean."

"I'm not sure I do," Ethan said.

Behind Ranger Dave, Ethan saw the tiny dot of Sam's pickup moving up the road in his direction. It made his gut feel lighter and less pinched.

"I thought he was this rotten guy who just took off on you. I guess I formed a mental picture of him based on a few facts we uncovered. I'm sorry for thinking your dad was a rotten guy."

"My dad *is* a rotten guy," Ethan said.

That sat clumsily in the air for a time, stopping the conversation.

Ethan glanced over his shoulder into the house. He wasn't even sure why. Had there been a small sound? Maybe.

His father was there, in his wheelchair, not three steps behind where Ethan stood—off to one side, where the open door had blocked the ranger's view of him. Close enough to hear everything. Ethan didn't know how long he'd been back there. But in another way, by the look on Noah's face, he knew.

Sam's truck turned into the A-frame's driveway, and Ethan was pleased to see that it was both of them coming to check in. Both Sam and Jone.

Ranger Dave glanced over his shoulder at the truck, then set his hat back on his head. He nodded a quick good-bye to Ethan and hurried to his big white SUV.

Ethan looked around at his dad again.

"Sorry," he said. "But . . . this is Sam and Jone, so if you really don't want to see them . . ."

Noah wheeled his chair backward, turned it fairly skillfully, and disappeared back into his bedroom. Without comment.

—

The next word Ethan heard from his father came more than ten hours later. It woke Ethan from a filmy and confused sleep.

"Ethan?"

Ethan sat up in bed. The moon was just a light crescent through his window, and he waited for his eyes to adjust to the dimness.

"I'll be right there, Dad."

Rubbing his eyes, hopping slightly on the cold floorboards, Ethan made his way to his father's bedroom, Rufus trotting faithfully behind.

As he opened his father's bedroom door, he half expected to find Noah on the floor, or in some other disastrous position or situation. But his dad was only sitting up in bed. Noah had turned on the soft light of a bedside lamp. His face looked much more conciliatory than Ethan remembered having seen it. Maybe even ashamed or afraid.

"I give up," Noah said. "I need the bedpan."

A thin layer of the ice around Ethan's heart melted. Because his dad looked and sounded so helpless. And because it was so rare for Noah to drop his big-man act.

"Sure," Ethan said. "Good decision."

He padded away to fetch it from the one small bathroom.

"Thanks," Noah said, as Ethan carried it back into the room. "It just hurts too much when I try to move around."

"I never suggested you try to move around."

"I know," his dad said. "I get it. I know whose idea that was."

"I'll just leave you alone with this for a minute. And, look. I'm sorry for what I said today."

Ethan watched his father's face for any sign of emotion. But Noah had a flawless poker face. Always had.

"To the ranger, you mean."

"Right."

"No, you're not. You're not sorry." He didn't seem angry. Ethan waited for a flare of anger. But it seemed there was nothing there. "You're sorry I heard it."

"Yes. I'm sorry you heard it."

"But you're not sorry you said it. And you don't have to be. It's not required. If you'd made a statement that was malicious or . . . well, let's face it, false . . . then it would be appropriate to apologize. But if it's only the damn truth . . ."

"I'm just going to leave you alone to—"

"Wait. Before you go."

Ethan waited. But nothing seemed to happen.

"What is it, Dad?"

"I'm sorry."

"For what, exactly?"

"All of it. Everything. Specifically . . . you know. I don't want to say her name, but you know where I'm going with this. But all the other stuff, too. Including the stuff you don't know about."

"Let's just leave it that way, okay? I don't need to know."

"Yeah, okay."

Ethan turned to leave again.

"Wait," his father said. "Also thank you. You know. For the fact that I'm still here to say thank you."

Ethan stared at his dad for a long time. Probably too long. Part of him was wanting to believe what had just happened. Another part was waiting for a catch. But there didn't seem to be one. The apology seemed sincere.

"You're welcome," he said. He probably should have said more. But that was all he could manage.

"Boy, this whole thing sure didn't turn out the way I pictured it."

"What whole thing?"

"My life. My adventures. The whole extreme sports thing. I figured I'd do it for another two years, or ten years. Or maybe twenty. And then one day I'd slip off a trail and that would be that. I remember when I was falling. Just in that split second. I thought, well, I was hoping for later, but I knew this was how it would turn out. And then I was lying there for days wondering why that wasn't the end. Why things didn't work out the way I planned."

"Life never turns out the way anybody plans," Ethan said. "It almost doesn't pay to plan."

"See, it's depressing that you know that and I don't."

"I'll just get that bedpan in the morning."

Ethan let himself out, leaving the door open in case his father needed anything else in the night, and made his way back to his own room.

"You didn't say anything," Noah called just as Ethan was tucking back under the covers.

"About what?" Ethan called back.

"I said I was sorry. And you didn't say anything."

Ah, Ethan thought. *Here's the moment.*

It's hard, he realized, when someone asks you straight-out for forgiveness. *Truthfully,* he thought, *it's not a fair request. It's not fair to repeatedly hurt someone and then pressure them to let you off the hook.*

And Ethan felt disinclined to lie.

"Thank you for being sorry," Ethan called. "It feels like progress. And I'm really happy that you're glad to be saved. That means a lot to me. Will that do for now?"

"I guess it'll have to," Noah called in reply.

Amazingly, Ethan got right back to sleep.

Chapter Nineteen: Just the Thing

Sixteen days after his father was found

They stood together at the airport curb in Casper, close to Jone's SUV, so no airport authority would think they were leaving the vehicle unattended.

Ethan's mother had notified the airline about his father's condition. All Ethan had to do was wait for two airline employees to come down with a wheelchair and help Noah to the gate. That and get a rolling cart or a skycap to help move poor tranquilized Rufus to the check-in desk in his plastic pet carrier.

"So you're going to be on the flight to Chicago with your dad?" Jone asked.

She had asked before. But there had been so much going on. So much packing, so many plans. So much to remember.

"Yeah. Yeah, my mom got me the same flight as my dad to O'Hare. And then she got me a connecting flight from O'Hare to New York."

"Good," Jone said. "Good."

She stood with one arm hooked through Sam's. None of them seemed able to look the others straight in the eye. It was hard, saying good-bye to them. Harder than Ethan had realized it would be.

"That way you two can take care of each other," Jone added.

Sam was still acting balky and silent.

"Yeah," Ethan said, unable to keep the emotion out of his voice. "You two take care of each other, too."

Jone smiled a tiny sad smile, and Sam blushed and continued to say nothing.

"I know people always say they'll stay in touch," Jone said, "and promise they'll visit. But you really will, right?"

"Try and stop me," Ethan said.

He looked over to see two uniformed airline employees inside the terminal, heading their way. Heading for the sliding glass doors. With the wheelchair.

"I'd miss Blythe River too much if I never saw it again," Ethan added.

"So come back for a camping trip," Sam said, apparently finally getting his voice unstuck. "Friendly Sam's Pack Service is always at your beck and call. No charge. For old times' sake. But just be sure to give me a month's notice or more. Ever since the AP picked up that story about your dad, I've got more business than I know what to do with."

"Good," Ethan said. "You deserve it."

He glanced nervously over his shoulder again.

"They're almost here," he said.

"It's fine," Jone said. "Just go. We'll talk."

Ethan rushed in and gave her a hug.

"You know I'm never going to forget you, right?" he asked into her snow-white hair. "And everything you did for me? And him?"

"Oh, hush. Stop acting like we'll never see you again."

"No, we will. I know."

Ethan let her go and grabbed hard on to Sam.

"I'm bad at this," Sam said. "I hate good-byes."

"It's not good-bye," Ethan said.

But it was time to help his father into the wheelchair and to their flight gate. And they'd brought a cart for the dog, too. So, much as Ethan hated to admit it, it was at least good-bye for now.

—

"See, there's Aunt Patty," Ethan said. "Right on the other side of security."

Ethan stood in the busy Chicago airport, one hand on his father's wheelchair, feeling the sensation of masses of people flowing around them like water. As if Ethan and his dad were an island in a fast-flowing river. Creating changes in the current. Even in the banks. Shaping the flow of everything simply by refusing to flow.

Ethan couldn't focus off the weirdness of the feeling. All these people. Being back in civilization.

"Can't believe I'm forty-one years old and I'm going to live with my damn sister," Noah said.

"Not for that long. Just till you're back on your feet."

"Feet? Plural?"

Ethan was growing tired of such comments from his dad, but he didn't say so. All he said was "You'll have a prosthetic leg soon. And it'll have a foot. Look. I'm going to see if I can get a TSA person or somebody to walk you through to her. Otherwise I'll have to go through the security line again. I don't want to miss my connecting flight."

"Yeah, whatever," Noah said. "That's fine. Don't miss your flight to New York."

Ethan walked over to the large man who sat at the entrance to a cordoned-off pedestrian lane leading out of the secure gate area.

"Is there someone who can push my dad's wheelchair through to that woman standing right there?" He pointed at Aunt Patty, who waved. Ethan waved back. "I have a connecting flight, and I don't want to miss it."

"Ethan!" he heard from behind. "Wait."

He turned to see his father wheeling himself along.

"I can go through myself."

"Okay, if you're sure, Dad."

"I'm sure."

"Tell Aunt Patty I'm sorry I didn't get to say hi."

Then they just stood a minute. Ethan looked down to see his dad looking up at his face. He couldn't shake the feeling that Noah was looking up to him in more than just the physical, logistical sense.

"This isn't the last time we ever see each other," Noah asked, "is it?"

"I don't think so. Not ever. Just . . . for a while. It's just one of those things that take time."

"Right," Noah said. "That's honest. Well. Thanks again for the next forty-one years. Hope there's at least a little of you in it."

Then he wheeled himself away.

Ethan watched, wondering if there was any part of him that was sorry to see his father go. But he never got a clear answer on that. Feelings are a funny thing, he realized. They're always more tangled and contradictory and complex than we want them to be. Than we care to admit.

—

"Oh my God," his mother said. "Look at you!"

She was standing in baggage claim, staring at Ethan for several seconds before rushing in to close the distance between them and give him a hug.

Before she could get there, Ethan looked down at himself to try to see what she'd seen. As though he might have spilled food on himself or something.

She hit him so suddenly and so hard that he let out a little involuntary "oof" as she embraced him.

"What *about* me?" he asked into her ear.

She stepped back and looked again.

"You just look so different. Look at you!"

Ethan laughed. "Can't really do that," he said. "You'll have to tell me."

"Your eyes are totally different. And your face has changed. I can't explain how, but I swear I'm not making it up. And you looked right at me. You used to look down at your feet. You looked right into my eyes."

"Oh," Ethan said. "Well . . . thanks."

"I expected you to be different. Some different, anyway. I mean, how could you not be? And part of it . . . I could just hear it in your voice. So I was prepared for you to seem . . . but not this much. It still surprised me."

At first Ethan didn't answer. He just walked with her to the baggage carousel. He could already see Rufus waiting in his carrier against the far wall. Apparently he'd been brought in separately, and first.

Ethan could feel himself smiling. Maybe only inwardly. Maybe it shone out from his face as well. Ethan had no way to know.

Not that it mattered anyway.

As the carousel beeped, and started moving, Ethan said, "Turns out you were right about Blythe River. It was just the thing for me."

"Hmm," she said. "That flies in the face of what I was about to say."

"Which was?"

"Not sure it matters now."

"Tell me anyway."

"I was going to say I pushed you too hard. I know I did."

Silence as the bags began to slide down and drop onto the carousel. Somebody else's bags.

"That's true," he said. "Maybe not that you pushed me too hard. Maybe more that you pushed me to be you and Dad. Instead of to be me. But it's okay."

"How can that be okay?"

"Because I figured it out for myself. And because I know you were trying to be a good mom."

She reached for his hand and gave it a squeeze.

"Here's a question," he said. "Think Dad was trying to be a good dad?"

"You know . . . I actually do. I don't think he tried to be the best husband he could be. But I think he tried to be the best dad he could. His best isn't very good most of the time. But that doesn't mean he wasn't trying."

Ethan saw the first of his bags drop, and prepared himself for the slow journey to the edge of the carousel.

"Maybe I'll give him a call, then," he said. As much to himself as to his mom. "See how he's settling in at Aunt Patty's."

Epilogue

Twenty months later

"She's been looking at you," Glen said. "Accept it or don't, but she keeps looking. She followed us over here."

They walked up the steps of the university library together, Ethan resisting the strong urge to look back.

"Yeah, that's what I've been hoping pretty much all semester, Glen. But with my luck she's probably looking at you."

"I'm not saying it's not weird," Glen said.

Ethan punched him on the arm. Fairly hard. Then he looked back to see if the girl had noticed. Glen was right—she was watching. Ethan didn't know her name, but she had curly hair and muscular calves and a pretty smile, and she was in his communications class. It was not the first time he had noticed her. Far from it.

She smiled at Ethan and he smiled back. Then he faced forward again.

"Smooth," Glen said.

"Oh, shut up, Glen."

"I'm going to do you a favor. We're going to find ourselves a nice seat in the library. And then I'm going to go off like I need to find the bathroom or something. And then she can sit down if she wants to.

See what a good friend I am? Aren't you glad we ended up at the same university?"

Ethan didn't admit it in that moment, but he was. Very glad.

—

"Is this seat taken?"

As he looked up into her eyes, Ethan could feel his face flush. He desperately wanted to think it didn't show. He knew it probably showed.

"It's not," he said, "no."

"Your friend isn't coming back?"

"If he does, he can sit somewhere else."

She examined Ethan's face for a moment, as if to decide whether he was joking.

"It's fine," Ethan said. "He won't be back for a while."

"I'm sorry. I just have to ask. Are you Ethan Underwood? *The* Ethan Underwood? The Blythe River guy?"

"I am. But I'm not sure why you say that like it's a notable thing to be."

"It is, though! It is! I read all about you in the paper. Last year. Or was it the year before?"

"Summer before last," he said.

She sat. They smiled at each other. Briefly. Then they both looked away.

"Amanda," she said.

"You're in my communications class, right?"

"Right. I thought I recognized your name from that article in the paper. But then I figured there could be more than one person with the same name."

She swept her curly hair back behind her shoulders, as if it were distracting her somehow. But Ethan sensed it was a bit of edginess. That it was merely something to do with her hands. It seemed unimaginable to Ethan, who saw himself as the only party who could possibly be nervous in a meeting such as this.

Meanwhile Ethan was not talking. So Amanda raced on.

"I saved that article, but then I couldn't figure out where I put it. And I tried to do an online search, but nothing I came up with had a picture of you or anything. So I figured I'd just ask."

"Why did you save it?"

"That's kind of hard to explain. Partly . . . I just have this thing about adventure. And that was such an amazing adventure story. I love true-life stories like that. I like to read about people lost in the wilderness. I like to watch movies about mountain climbers in trouble. Sounds terrible, but what I like about it is . . . you know . . . when it works out okay. When people overcome the odds. And survive. And also I have a thing about certain wilderness areas. I have kind of . . . well, I started to say a bucket list, but I guess I'm too young to have a bucket list. But there are about three wilderness areas that I've read all about, and that just have a hold on me for some reason. I've done a lot of hiking. But I've never been to the Trinity Alps in California, or Badlands National Park in South Dakota. And I've never been to the Blythe River Range. And I want to go there so bad I can almost taste it."

Ethan looked up to see Glen come around a corner and into view, stop, survey the scene at Ethan's table, and kindly disappear again.

"Well, if you want to go," Ethan said, "I'm really good friends with the guy who does pack trips up there."

"Friendly Sam!" she screeched, as if she'd known him all her life and couldn't wait to see him again.

Two young women at the next table shot Amanda a dirty look. One made a shushing noise.

"That's the guy!" Ethan said in an exaggerated whisper.

"Are you ever going back there?"

"Definitely."

"Hiking?"

"Maybe. Maybe partly. But Sam has these great horses and mules, and you can cover so much more ground that way. But I do hike. In fact, my mom and I hiked the Inca Trail to Machu Picchu over the holiday break."

"Over Christmas? Wasn't it freezing up there in the mountains?"

"No, it's—"

"Oh, God, that sounded so stupid. I'm really not that stupid, I swear I'm not. I just wasn't thinking. Peru. South of the equator. Winter here, summer there."

"Right," Ethan said.

"How was the Inca Trail hike? That's on my bucket list, too."

"I thought I was going to die. Especially going over those two high passes. But, you know what? By the time it was over I was so glad I'd done it."

"So when are you going back to Blythe River?"

"I don't know," Ethan said. "Maybe this summer. I'm sure Sam would be happy to have another rider along. No charge for the tour. He promised me a freebie. You'd just have to cover your airfare."

"You're inviting me to go to Blythe River with you?"

"Oh. I'm sorry. That probably sounded really bad. I wasn't trying to—"

"No, it's okay. It was nice."

"But we don't even know each other."

"But we could by then," she said.

A long, ringing silence. Ethan didn't break it. Because it felt so perfect. So right. He felt he could do it nothing but harm. It had nowhere higher to go.

"In the meantime," she said, "will you tell me about the place?"

"All about it."

"And your big adventure?"

"Everything there is to tell."

—

Glen caught up with him at the Starbucks a few hours later.

"I kept trying to get back to you in the library," he said, "but you just looked like you were having too much fun."

Ethan felt his slight smile grow. It had been with him most of the day, whether he thought about it or not.

"I do have to admit it was fun."

"Tell me you have a date with her."

"I can tell you better than that."

"What's better than that?"

"We're going away together over summer break."

"Get. Out. Not seriously."

"Seriously. She has this thing about Blythe River. And adventures. So we're taking a pack trip. I called Sam and booked a spot."

Ethan looked up at his friend and smiled more widely to see Glen's mouth drop open.

"How in hell did you . . . Ethan Underwood . . . of all people . . . get so lucky?"

"That's a really good question," Ethan said. "I was just sitting here wondering that same thing myself."

About the Author

Photo © 2014 Hunter Kilpatrick

Catherine Ryan Hyde is the author of thirty published and forthcoming books. Her bestselling 1999 novel *Pay It Forward*, adapted into a major Warner Bros. motion picture starring Kevin Spacey and Helen Hunt, made the American Library Association's Best Books for Young Adults list and was translated into more than two dozen languages for distribution in more than thirty countries. Her novels *Becoming Chloe* and *Jumpstart the World* were included on the ALA's Rainbow List; *Jumpstart the World* was also a finalist for two Lambda Literary Awards and won Rainbow Awards in two categories. More than fifty of her short stories have been published in many journals, including the *Antioch Review*, *Michigan Quarterly Review*, the *Virginia Quarterly Review*, *Ploughshares*, *Glimmer Train*, and the *Sun*, and in the anthologies *Santa Barbara Stories* and *California Shorts* and the bestselling anthology *Dog Is My Co-Pilot*. Her short fiction received honorable mention in the Raymond Carver Short

Story Contest, a second-place win for the Tobias Wolff Award, and nominations for *Best American Short Stories*, the O. Henry Award, and the Pushcart Prize. Three have also been cited in *Best American Short Stories.*

Ryan Hyde is also founder and former president of the Pay It Forward Foundation. As a professional public speaker, she has addressed the National Conference on Education, twice spoken at Cornell University, met with AmeriCorps members at the White House, and shared a dais with Bill Clinton.